# FIFTH AVENUE

**Fifth Avenue**

**A novel by**

**Christopher Smith**

# FIFTH AVENUE

For my father, Ross Smith, for always pushing and never giving up.

For my mother, Ann Smith, for her enthusiastic support.

And for Constance Hunting, who edited this book over the course of many years but who didn't live to see its publication. This is our book. I thank you and I miss you.

# FIFTH AVENUE

# FIFTH AVENUE

http://www.fifthavenuenovel.com

10 9 8 7 6 5 4 3 2 1

For their help with this book, the author is particularly grateful to Erich Kaiser and Sanford Phippen; to Roslyn Targ; to Ted Adams; to Deborah Rogers, Paul Ersing, Bari Khan and Faith Benedetti; to Kathlyn Tenga-Gonzalez; and to those men and women who introduced me to the real Fifth Avenue while I researched this book over a decade; and to friends old and new, all of whom either helped to shape this book or who offered support as it was written.

# FIFTH AVENUE

**BOOK ONE**

**FIRST WEEK**

**CHAPTER ONE**

July
New York City

The bombs, placed high above Fifth Avenue on the roof of The Redman International Building, would explode in five minutes.

Now, with its mirrored walls of glass reflecting Fifth Avenue's thick, late-morning traffic, the building itself seemed alive with movement.

On scaffolding at the building's middle, men and women were hanging the enormous red velvet ribbon that would soon cover sixteen of Redman International's seventy-nine stories. High above on the roof, a lighting crew was moving ten spotlights into position. And inside, fifty skilled decorators were turning the lobby into a festive ballroom.

Celina Redman, who was in charge of organizing the event, stood before the building with her arms folded. Streams of people were brushing past her on the sidewalk, some glancing up at the red ribbon, others stopping to glance in surprise at her. She tried to ignore them, tried to focus on her work and become one with the crowd, but it was difficult. Just that morning, her face and this building had been on the cover of every major paper in New York.

She admired the building before her.

Located on the corner of Fifth and 49th Street, the building was the product of thirty-one years of her father's life. Founded when George Redman was twenty-six, Redman International was among the world's leading conglomerates.   It included a commercial airline, office and condominium complexes, textile and steel mills and, soon, WestTex Incorporated--one of the country's largest shipping corporations.  With this building on Fifth Avenue, all that stood in George Redman's way was the future.  And by all appearances, it was as bright as the diamonds Celina chose to wear later that evening.

"The spotlights are ready, Miss Redman."

Celina turned and faced a member of the lighting crew.  Later that evening, the spotlights would illuminate the red ribbon. "Let's try them out."

The man reached for the cell phone clipped to his belt.  While he gave the men on the roof the go-ahead, Celina looked down at the list on her clipboard and wondered again how she would get everything done in time for the party.

The flowers had yet to be delivered and then arranged on the two hundred tables for eight; the caterers had phoned saying they were late but would be there within the hour, which was three hours ago; the barmen had arrived, but with only half the alcohol she ordered and not a drop of champagne; the walnut dance floor her mother insisted on having was nowhere in sight; and the scaffolding, the damned scaffolding that had taken hours to erect so they could hang the damned ribbon, had to be removed soon, before night fell and the guests arrived.

With such severe time limitations, Celina didn't know how she would pull it all off.  But she would.  All her life she had been trained by her father to work under pressure.  Today was just another challenge.

Hal nodded at her. "Should be any time now," he said.

Celina tucked the clipboard beneath her arm and looked up at the roof.  She was thinking that, at this distance, she would never see if they worked when a switch was flipped and three of the ten spotlights exploded into flames.

For a moment, she couldn't move.

Thousands of shards of jagged glass were hurtling toward her, glinting in the sun.

She could see a great cloud of black smoke billowing on top of the building.

There was fire--roaring, twisting toward the sky.

7

And there was one of the spotlights, flipping through the air, rushing toward her and the ground.

She felt a hand on her arm and was pulled to safety just as the spotlight whooshed past her and slammed onto the sidewalk, where it cracked the cement and burst into a shower of fiery red sparks. For a moment, everything went silent--and then the glass began to hit in a deafening cascade of sound.

She was pressed against the building, frozen in fear as she watched traffic on Fifth veer right, away from the fallen spotlight, and snarl to a halt. Suddenly, there was nothing but the squeal of metal crushing metal, the shrilling of car horns and the frightened cries of passersby, some of whom had been cut from the falling glass.

Stunned, Celina looked at Hal. He was in the street, looking up at the roof, shouting something into his cell phone. His face was flushed. The cords stood out on his neck. There was so much noise, Celina couldn't hear what he was saying. She took a tentative step forward, toward the crushed spotlight, and knew exactly what he was saying--the men on the roof were hurt.

She hurried into the lobby, shot past the waterfall and stepped into her father's private elevator.

The building was too tall. The elevator was too slow. No matter how quickly she raced to the top, it wasn't fast enough.

Finally, the doors opened and she stepped onto the roof.

People were running and shouting and pushing. Some stood motionless in fear and disbelief. Those who had been standing near the spotlights when they exploded were either silent with shock, or crying in pain from the burns that ravaged their bodies.

She moved forward and nearly was run into by someone rushing for help. She watched the man pass, her lips parting when she realized he had no hair. It had been burned off.

She forced herself to focus. She had inherited her father's strength and it was this that she called on now.

Through the smoke that whipped past her in soiled veils of black, she could see the damage--at roof's edge, two of the remaining nine spotlights were engulfed in flames, their wires twisting like angry snakes on the ground beside them. Mark Rand, the man in charge of the lighting, was standing near the spotlights, shouting orders, trying to gain control. Celina went over to him, her legs weak. Although she didn't know what she would do or how she would help, she was damned if she would do nothing.

Rand pointed at one of the burning lights as she approached. "There's a man trapped behind that spotlight. When the lights blew, he fell back and struck his head on the concrete. He's unconscious."

"Why isn't anyone helping him?"

Mark pointed to the tangled mass of writhing wires. "No one's going near them," he said. "It's too dangerous."

"Then turn off the power."

"We can't," he said, and motioned toward the generator at the opposite end of the roof. Although it was still running, it, too, was alight with flames. "It could blow at any moment."

Celina's mind raced. Through the smoke, she could see the young man lying on his stomach, his arms outstretched, the live wires curling inches from his body. She scanned the roof for something that could help him. Anything.

And then she saw it.

She grabbed Mark's arm and they went to the crane that was behind them.

"This is the crane that lifted the lights up here?"

"That's right."

"Then use it to get rid of them."

Mark looked at the spotlights. Their casings were coated with a hard shell of rubber to resist dents. It would not conduct electricity.

He scrambled into the crane.

Celina stood back and watched him bring the enormous steel hook about. It swung swiftly through the smoky air, glinting once in a dim band of sunlight and was upon one of the burning spotlights in what seemed like seconds. It took several tries before he hooked the tip of the spotlight's casing. And when he did, when he finally lifted the spotlight into the air, one of the wires hissing beneath it rested against the fallen man's forearm, sending him into convulsions.

Celina's hands flew to her mouth. She watched the man's head arch back into an impossible position. Reacting instinctively, she rushed forward and knelt beside him--just as

9

Mark Rand began swinging the spotlight over her.

With a start, he pulled back hard on the controls, lifting the spotlight away from Celina with a jerk, causing it to jump and waver on its hook. For one terrible moment, he felt sure it was going to jump the hook and fall on top of her. The spotlight was teetering in the air, no more than ten feet above her, spewing black smoke as it swayed on its metal line. The wires snapping beneath it were almost touching her back. But gradually, he brought the spotlight under control and moved it away from her. When it was far enough away from the generator, the spotlight unplugged itself, the light flashed and it went dark.

A member of the lighting crew went to Celina's side. Together, they pulled the young man to safety. Celina knelt over him. The man's body was sheathed in perspiration. His skin was the color of chalk. She gripped him by the shoulders and gently shook him. She noticed his name sewn into the pocket of his denim work shirt and shouted it once, twice, but there was no response.

Her mind raced. She had been trained in CPR, but that was in college and now she struggled to remember how to perform it. She tilted his head back to clear the airway and then ripped off his shirt, exposing his chest. She looked to see if it was rising and falling, but it wasn't. She listened to see if he was breathing, but he wasn't. She placed the back of her hand to his mouth, but felt nothing. She checked for a pulse in his neck, but found none. She pressed her ear to his chest. Nothing.

For a moment, she thought her own heart had stopped.

He was dead.

Immediately, she covered his mouth with her own, pinched his nose and forced two sharp breaths into his lungs. She checked once more for a pulse, found none and gave several compressions to his chest, wishing she could remember exactly how many she was supposed to administer. She stopped after the twelfth and repeated the procedure. And then she did it again.

But the man didn't respond.

Fighting to remain calm, Celina looked up for help just as the New York City Fire Department stormed the roof, hoses and axes in hand. She turned to her right and saw Mark leaving the crane. The final spotlight was removed and he was coming toward her.

"What's the matter with you?" he shouted. "You could have been killed--" The words died in his mouth when he saw the man lying beside her.

"Get help," she said. *"Move!"*

She bent back over the man, again pressing on his chest, again forcing air into his lungs.

But there was no response.

Panic rising, her shoulder-length blonde hair hanging in her face, she repeated the procedure, knowing that time for this man was running out.

But her efforts seemed in vain. No matter how hard she tried to revive him, the man just lay there, motionless.

And so she went for it.

Raising her fists above her head, she slammed them down onto the man's chest, causing him to jerk slightly upright. He expelled a rush of air. "Breathe!" she shouted.

To her surprise, he did. His eyes fluttered. Color rushed to his cheeks and he gagged and coughed and vomited. Celina felt a surge of elation and turned him onto his side so he wouldn't choke. Tears began streaming down his face as he pulled in great gasps of air. Celina held him on his side. "It's all right," she said. "Just breathe. You're safe now. It's all right."

When the paramedic reached them, she knelt beside Celina, cleaned the vomit from the man's face and covered his nose and mouth with an oxygen mask. Another woman appeared and covered him with a blanket. Celina stood and watched with Mark as relief washed over the man. He drew deeply on the clean air.

For him, the nightmare was over.

"Where did you learn that?" Mark asked.

Celina's face was pale. "My roommate in college had a sister who was a nursing student. She used to teach us things I considered worthless. One of them was how to perform CPR."

"Not so worthless," he said.

Together, they looked at the spotlights Mark had removed. Although they were no longer burning, the air around them was dim with smoke.

"Why did they explode?" she asked.

Before Mark could respond, a fireman approached and answered her question instead. "I'll show you."

She exchanged looks with Mark and stepped over to one of the smoldering lights. There, they watched the man pull two frayed, blackened wires from the now empty light socket. "Do you see these wires?"

They nodded.

"They shouldn't be there." He bent to his knees and asked Celina and Mark to do the same. On the back of the spotlight, he pointed to a small hole where the metal was contorted and twisted out of shape. "This hole shouldn't be there, either."

Celina braced herself for what was coming and the uproar it would cause.

"Off the record?" he said.

"Yes."

"It's not confirmed, but it's obvious. The spotlights were rigged with plastic explosives. When the power was turned on, the electricity came into these two wires and set off the bombs."

"Who would plant three bombs here?" she said.

"That's for you and the police to figure out."

## CHAPTER TWO

George Redman left the limousine, moved to the front of The Redman International Building and was engulfed by reporters.

He pushed through the crowd and tried to ignore the cameras and microphones being thrust in his face. His world was the twin glass doors ahead of him. He would say nothing until he spoke to Celina--but that didn't stop the reporters or their cacophony of voices.

"Can you give us a statement?"

"Do you think this has to do with your plans to take over WestTex? The recent decline in Redman International's stock?"

"Who's responsible for this, Mr. Redman?"

George glanced at the reporter who asked that question and then pressed forward, thinking it was the best question yet. Who was responsible for this?

The crowd was still shouting questions when he entered the building.

Celina was waiting for him beyond the doors and, as George embraced her, he thought she never looked or felt better to him.

"Are you all right?" he asked.

"I'm fine." Knowing her father as well as she did, Celina said, "Really. I'm fine."

George looked around the lobby. Later that evening it would be filled with some of the most influential men and women in the world as they celebrated the grand opening of his building. He had been working toward this day for years. And now this.

"What happened?" he asked.

Celina explained everything to him. When she told him about the man who was trapped behind the spotlight, she raised her hands in apology. "I tried to keep what happened to him from the press, but it was impossible. The reporters got wind of it before I could do anything."

"Don't worry about it," George said. "This wasn't our fault. If anything, they'll be congratulating you for saving that man's life.

Was anyone else hurt?"

"The most severe cases were the two men I told you about over the phone. A Dr. Richards from New York Hospital called twenty minutes ago to tell me that one man will need extensive skin grafting on his neck and face, the other on his hands, arms and chest."

George shook his head. He already was under attack by the media for his proposed takeover of WestTex Incorporated. If this situation wasn't handled properly, he knew he would be besieged for something he wasn't even responsible for.

"So, we're facing lawsuits."

"Not necessarily," Celina said. "I sent Kate and Jim from PR to speak to the families of those who were hurt. If all goes well, each wife will be driving a Lexus by week's end, their kids will have their college educations paid for, money will be in their bank accounts--and we'll have signed documents saying that each family has waived all rights to sue."

Something caught her eye and she turned. George followed her gaze. Across the lobby, three men in dull yellow jackets were stepping into one of the elevators with two large dogs. "Bomb squad," Celina said. "They arrived just after the police and fire department."

"How long will they be?"

She checked her watch. "A full crew is here," she said. "They've already covered the first eighteen floors. With the help of those dogs, I wouldn't be surprised if they're out of here in the next few hours--leaving us time to make a final statement to the press and last-minute preparations for the party."

"If anyone shows," George pointed out.

"They'll show," she said. "If only because they've paid ten grand per couple, they'll show. Besides, when have you ever known one of Mom's parties to fail?"

George raised an eyebrow. She had a point there.

They moved to the bar. "So, who did it?" Celina asked.

"No idea. I've been racking my brain since I got your call."

"I phoned the company who supplied the spotlights and was told that each light was inspected before delivery. If that's true-- and I'm not saying it is--then that can only mean that someone here planted the bombs."

"Have the police questioned the lighting crew?"

"They're being questioned now, but what I can't figure out is why a more powerful bomb wasn't used. The three that went off were low-impact explosives. They were designed to cause only minor damage."

"I've been thinking the same thing."

"So, what is this? A prank?"

George shrugged. "Who knows? Maybe someone hates the design of our building."

Somehow, her father usually managed to keep his sense of humor, even in situations as difficult as this. "What's the word on RRK?" she asked.

"If they were nervous about backing us before, they must be terrified now," he said.

Roberts, Richards, and Kravis--better known as RRK--was the investment group George hired to help finance the takeover of Waste Incorporated. Although George had management, without Ark's $3.75 billion war chest, without their skills and the banks they had locked up, he wouldn't be able to complete this deal on his own.

"I haven't heard a word," he said. "But I'm sure I will by this evening. This is probably the excuse Frank Richards has been waiting for. He's never been in favor of this takeover. If he thinks someone rigged those spotlights to make a statement about our falling stock, or to protest our interest in WestTex, he won't think twice about pulling out--regardless of any deal we have with him."

Celina knew that was true. While there were other banks and investment groups who might be willing to take the risk her father was offering, few were as experienced as RRK when it came to LBOs.

"Have you seen your sister today?" he asked. "Your mother was looking for her earlier. She was supposed to help her prepare for tonight's party."

"And Mom thought she'd show?" Celina tilted her head. "Leana probably doesn't even know what happened here today."

"I need to call your mother," he said. "She made me promise to call as soon as I knew something. If you see Leana, tell her your mother needs her."

Although she knew she wouldn't see Leana until later that evening, Celina agreed and followed her father to the door.

The press was there, cameras and microphones raised. "You can use one of the side entrances," she said.

"And lose their sympathy at the very moment I need it most? Forget it."

And then he was gone, through the doors, swarmed by reporters and finally answering whatever questions he could. Celina watched him for a moment, listened to the crowd's frenzied shouting, but then she stepped away and resumed her work. There was still much to be done before the party.

\* \* \*

The sun was just beginning to set behind Manhattan's jagged horizon when Leana Redman left Washington Square.

She had been in the park since morning, reading the latest edition of Vogue, talking with those people she knew, watching those she didn't.

Now, as she passed the big empty fountain and neared the white arch, she watched the many children playing with their parents, hesitated when she saw a father twirl his young daughter in the air, and then kept walking, oblivious to the man taking pictures of her.

Evening was beginning to descend, but the air was balmy and she was glad to be wearing only shorts and a T-shirt. At twenty-five, Leana Redman had a long, thick mane of curly black hair, which, to her dismay, she had inherited from her father. Although she wasn't considered as beautiful as her twenty-nine-year-old sister, people always looked twice at her. There was something about her that made them look twice.

She left the park and began moving up Fifth. The sidewalks were jammed with people. A group of five teenage boys darted past her on skateboards, screaming and shouting as they shot through the crowd in a colorful blur of red and white and brilliant shades of green.

Leana lifted her face to the warm breeze and tried to focus on the problem ahead of her--tonight's party.  She had planned on not attending when her mother, sensing this, demanded her presence.  "Your father will be expecting your support."

The irony almost made Leana laugh.  *He's never needed it before.*

Four hours ago she was supposed to have met Elizabeth at their Connecticut estate and help her with last-minute preparations for the party.  Why her mother wanted her help was beyond Leana--especially since they both knew that Celina would take care of everything.  *As she always does.*

She stopped at a crowded newspaper stand.  A man moved beside her.  Leana gave him a sidelong glance.  Tall and dark, his face lean and angular, the man wore an unseasonably warm black leather jacket that exposed a broad chest and the sophisticated, 35mm camera hanging around his neck.

Leana sensed she'd seen him before.

It was her turn in line.  Ignoring the many newspapers and magazines that carried front-page pictures of her father, Celina and the new building, she asked the attendant for the latest issue of Interview, paid him and then tucked the magazine into the colorful, oversized Prada handbag that hung at her side.

She looked again at the man in black leather, saw that he was staring at her and she started up Fifth, aware that he had purchased nothing and now was following her.  It wasn't until she glimpsed his reflection in a storefront window that she realized he was taking photos of her.

Leana stopped.  She turned and was about to ask what newspaper he worked for when she saw, tucked between the folds of his black leather jacket, the butt of a revolver.

Startled, she looked at the man's face just as he lowered the camera.  When he smiled at her, she recognized him.  Earlier that morning, in the park, he had been sitting on the bench next to hers.  She thought then that he had been watching her.  Now, she knew that he had.

"Tonight," the man said, "after these pictures are developed, I'm going to pin them to the wall beside my bed--with the others I have of you."  His smile broadened, revealing even white teeth.  "And soon--before you know it, really, Leana--I plan on taking you home with me and showing them to you, myself."

She turned away from him with such speed, the magazine toppled out of her handbag and fell to the pavement. The pages fanned open. Ahead of her, a taxi was dropping off a fare.

Leana rushed to it. The man followed.

"Wait!" she shouted, but the cab already had pulled away. A quick glance over her shoulder confirmed the man was still there. The shiny butt of his revolver glinted in a band of sunlight. Leana was about to shout for help when another cab pulled to the curb. Frantic, she ran toward it, her heart pounding, and stepped inside just as an elderly couple stepped out.

She slammed the door shut and locked it just as the man tried opening the door. His face was only inches from the glass and he looked furious, as if he had been cheated out of a prize. He slapped his hand against the glass and Leana recoiled.

The cab wasn't moving. Leana looked at the driver and saw that he was waiting for a break in traffic. "He's got a gun!" she shouted. "Get me out of here!"

The cabbie looked at the man, saw the rage on his face and punched the accelerator, nearly causing an accident as he cut into traffic and raced toward Washington Square.

Leana looked out the back window. The man was on the sidewalk, his camera hanging around his neck, his arms at his side.

"I didn't know you were in trouble," the cabbie said. "Are you okay? Do you want me to take you to the police?"

She considered it, but thought better of it. "By the time we turn the corner, he'll be gone." She leaned against the cab's torn vinyl seat. "Just drop me off at the new Redman International Building on Fifth and 49th. My car's there."

"I wouldn't count on it."

"What's that supposed to mean?"

"You've gotta be kidding me."

"I don't know what you're talking about."

"Doesn't anyone pay attention to the news anymore?" He spoke slowly. "This morning, three bombs exploded on top of the building."

Leana's face paled. Her father and sister were there today, preparing for tonight's party. "Was anyone hurt?"

"A few people.  One guy would have died if it wasn't for Celina Redman.  She saved his life."

Leana's jaw tightened.  "How?"

"Through quick thinking, the guy on the radio said.  She's a hero."

"What she is is a fucking bitch."

The cabbie stopped for a red light and glanced at her in the rearview mirror, not quite sure he heard her right.  "You know the Redmans, or something?"

Leana wondered again why she had been so concerned for her family's safety.  After all the times her parents ignored her, after all the times they chose Celina over herself, how could she possibly have any feelings for them besides contempt?

"No," she said.  "I don't know them at all."

FIFTH AVENUE

## CHAPTER THREE

High above Fifth Avenue, Louis Ryan was in his corner office, his back to a wall of windows and the new Redman International Building that towered in the near distance.

He was at his desk and gazed at the frosted letters carved into the glass that covered it: Manhattan Enterprises. The company he founded thirty-one years ago was now one of the world's leading conglomerates.

Only Redman International surpassed it.

Earlier that day, Louis' private war against George Redman had begun--Leana Redman was harassed, the spotlights exploded as planned. And now, the gala opening of The Redman International Building was about to begin.

Louis looked up Fifth Avenue, toward the activity surrounding Redman International's red-carpeted entrance. Judging by the crowd of reporters and the string of limousines that snaked down the avenue, one would think that every influential man and woman in the world had come to show their support for George Redman. The fact that Louis did business with many of these men and women made him turn away in disgust.

He looked across the desk at the black-and-white photograph of his wife.

In its heavy silver frame, the photo had faded over the years since Anne's death, but her beauty shined through.

Louis studied her face and thought back to the few years they had shared together. She had been his first love, his champion, his best friend. She had given him his best memories. She also had given him a son and, although he and Michael had their differences, whenever Louis saw him, he was reminded, through Michael's features alone, of his beloved Anne.

The wife George Redman robbed him of.

Louis thought about all that was coming Redman's way. The time was now. At last, George Redman was vulnerable. When Anne died, Louis promised that both he and Michael would make

Redman pay for what he had done to her. He promised to destroy George Redman, his family, the Redman empire. He would make them all feel the pain he had felt for years.

He glanced down at the front page of the Wall Street Journal. The banner headline read:

## REDMAN STOCK PLUNGES TWENTY-THREE POINTS.

### PROPOSED TAKEOVER OF WESTTEX MAKES STOCKHOLDERS NERVOUS.

*Well, that's too bad*, Louis thought.

He opened a desk drawer and reached for the latest issue of People magazine. On the cover was his son, Michael Archer, the movie star and bestselling novelist. Even as he aged, it was clear Michael inherited his looks from his mother, from the dark hair to the cobalt-blue eyes. There wasn't the slightest resemblance of himself in Michael.

Louis wasn't a good looking man and he knew it. *Michael lucked out.*

As he studied his son's face, Louis wondered how Michael would react when he learned that George Redman was responsible for his mother's death. Michael was only three when George Redman murdered his mother. To save his son the pain and anger he had to endure, Louis raised Michael thinking his mother's death was an accident. But despite the tragedy that should have brought them closer together, it had driven them apart because Louis needed to devote his time to Manhattan Enterprises in an effort to secure their futures. They never had been close. In fact, until last week, Louis hadn't seen or heard from Michael in sixteen years.

*And all because of George Redman*, he thought.

He put the magazine down and turned to watch the limousines inch their way down the avenue. He wondered which one his son was in. Last week, when Michael came unannounced to his office, Louis was surprised by the change in him. Michael seemed older to him in person than on film. His eyes had

21

hardened over the years, erasing his former look of innocence. Perhaps struggling in Hollywood had been good for him. Maybe he finally had grown up.

But, of course, he hadn't.

When Michael explained the predicament he was in, that his life was in danger, Louis listened, feeling the same sense of shame and anger he felt when Michael left home for Hollywood at the age of eighteen. Even now, Louis could hear Michael asking him for help. Even now, he could see the look of surprise on Michael's face when told he would only get the help he needed if he went to the opening of Redman International and met Leana Redman.

\* \* \*

In his father's ash-gray Lincoln limousine, Michael Archer looked through the tinted window at the glittering New York skyline and thought he'd rather be anywhere else than here.

He wasn't happy to be back. He hated what he saw. He left this place once and hadn't looked back until a few weeks ago, when he had no choice.

All around him was his father, from Louis' towering office and condominium complexes on Fifth to the lavish hotels he'd passed earlier on Park and Madison. Even if no one knew he was Louis' son, the idea that his father's ego had spread like a disease over this city embarrassed him.

It was ironic, he thought, that now he was being thrust back into a life he had run from. More ironic, still, that his father was the only person who could help him.

On the seat beside him was the manila envelope Louis gave him that evening. Michael reached for it, turned on the light above his head and removed several photographs of Leana Redman.

Most were pictures of her reading in Washington Square, but some had been taken of her standing in line at a newspaper stand. Others were of her running to catch a cab.

Michael studied her face and wondered what his father was getting him into. Why was it so important that he meet Leana

22

Redman?  And why had Louis refused to give him the money he needed if he didn't meet her?

The limousine caught a string of green lights and sailed down Fifth.  Ahead, Michael could see the bright, resilient spotlights fanning across The Redman International Building, illuminating the red ribbon in sharp, brilliant sweeps.

He put the photographs away.  For now, he would do as his father wished.

After the recent threat against his life, he hardly had a choice.

## CHAPTER FOUR

Excitement in the lobby was building.

From his position beside the glimmering waterfall, Vincent Spocatti watched the flurry of activity surrounding him.

Under Elizabeth Redman's direction, uniformed maids were checking place settings, polishing the lobby's gleaming accents, making last-minute touches to the enormous flower arrangements that adorned each of the two hundred tables for eight. Barmen in black dinner jackets were stocking glasses, stocking bottles, stocking ice. Behind him, members of the thirty-four piece band were settling into their seats, preparing for the busy evening ahead.

Considering the bombs that exploded earlier, Spocatti was impressed by how seamlessly everything was coming together. If it weren't for Elizabeth Redman and her daughter, Celina, he knew things wouldn't be going as smoothly.

Elizabeth was moving across the lobby to the bar. Vincent watched her. He thought she was beautiful in her floor-length, black silk gown. Like her daughter Celina, Elizabeth Redman was tall and slender, her blonde hair coming just to her shoulders, framing an oval face that suggested intelligence and a sense of humor. The diamonds at her neck, wrists and ears were competitive, but not aggressive. She knew the crowd she'd invited. She knew how to work them. It was obvious.

As she stepped past him, Spocatti turned and caught a glimpse of himself in the huge mirrored pillar to his right. Where the gun pressed against the breast pocket of his black dinner jacket, there was a slight bulge--but Spocatti paid little attention to it. He was a member of security and had been hired this evening to protect George Redman, his family and their guests from a possible intruder.

The irony almost made him laugh.

At forty-one, Vincent Spocatti was neither a former intelligence officer nor a past member of the FBI. However, he

24

had studied his opposition and employed their tactics himself. He was a computer expert and an international assassin who had amassed a personal fortune with his talents. He had the build of a boxer, the face of a gentleman. His hair was black and cut short, his cheekbones pronounced, the cleft in his chin deep. Years ago, as one of the Army's top boxers, being quick and light on his feet had won him many a fight. After seven years as a private agent, he never had been caught.

Being ruthless helped.

He took in his surroundings. Although security appeared tight, it was sadly loose. After today's bombing, George Redman had hired twenty-five men to stand guard over tonight's gala-- and, as far as Spocatti was concerned, every one of them was an amateur.

With disappointment, he looked at the four men standing guard at the lobby's entrance. Two had their hands in their pockets, one was smoking a cigarette and the other was writing something on a clipboard. Spocatti shook his head. *Never compromise your hands, boys.*

There were other mistakes being made and each made him cringe inwardly. Men were leaving their posts to use the washroom, some were socializing among themselves, and--what made Spocatti particularly uncomfortable--no one in the lobby was paying attention to what was happening beyond the windows.

As unsettling as this might have been under different circumstances, Spocatti actually was relieved. Being surrounded by such incompetence made his job easier. Now he should have no problem slipping into one of the elevators and getting the information Louis Ryan needed on the takeover of WestTex Incorporated.

\* \* \*

Elizabeth Redman was moving again--this time in his direction. Although she seemed unaffected by it, Spocatti sensed by the confident way she held herself that she was very much aware of the power she wielded in this city.

25

She approached with a smile and an extended hand.

"I'm Elizabeth Redman," she said. Her grip was firm. He liked that.

"Antonio Benedetti."

"I've always loved Italy," she said.

*Well, that's rich.* "What can I do for you, Mrs. Redman?"

"Nothing much," she said. "Just see to it that no bombs explode here this evening and I'll be grateful. Can you handle that?"

"Of course."

Elizabeth lifted her head. Her eyes hardened as she studied him. "Maybe," she said. She motioned to the other members of security. "As for these other men, I'm not so sure."

"Neither am I."

"You don't think they're capable of protecting us?"

"To put it plainly, no."

"They're all experienced," she said.

"Perhaps so, but who taught them? I've been watching them make mistakes for the past few hours. They aren't professionals."

"And you are?"

"I am."

There was the deep sound of a bass guitar being plucked behind them. Elizabeth looked at Spocatti and said, "Mr. Benedetti, this morning three bombs exploded on top of this building. Several men were hurt, my daughter nearly killed. Tonight, I think we all know that anything could happen--and it possibly might. With such amateurs on our security staff, it looks as if you're going to have your work cut out for you. I hope everything goes well."

Spocatti watched her walk away, feeling new respect for her. He knew from Louis Ryan that, despite her youthful appearance, she was pushing fifty-five. A graduate of Vassar, she spoke four languages, could talk easily on world affairs and could be as tough as her husband if the need arose. For George Redman's needs, she was the perfect wife.

George and Celina Redman arrived ten minutes before their guests.

They left the family elevator together, Celina kissed her father on the cheek and then started across the lobby without him. She was stunning in her red-sequined dress. Her stride was long and determined, and she moved with her mother's confidence.

Elizabeth was standing at the canopied entrance, speaking to the four members of security stationed there. Celina approached and gave her mother a hug. They stepped back, seemed to compliment one another's appearance, and then Celina turned to one of the guards. Spocatti was surprised to see her pluck a cigarette from the man's hand, drop it into a nearby ashtray and turn him so he faced the windows. She pointed to the street, where a group of reporters were gathered to photograph the guests. Spocatti could almost hear her saying, "Don't let me catch you looking anywhere else but through these windows."

The woman was good. Not only had she saved a life earlier this morning, but she was making an effort that no harm came to anyone this evening. When it came time to kill her, it would be a waste.

George Redman was in a world of his own. He was moving about the lobby, looking with pride at the tables, the flowers, the elaborate place settings. Spocatti knew from Louis Ryan that owning this building on Fifth Avenue was George Redman's dream. He knew how hard the man had worked for it, how happy he was that it was finally his.

Spocatti glanced at his watch. *Enjoy it while you can*, he thought. *Before long, none of this will be yours.*

Behind him, the band began playing "My Blue Heaven." Spocatti looked across the lobby and saw through the windows the first guests alighting from their limousines.

The party was beginning. George and Elizabeth and Celina were at the entrance, waiting to greet, to hug, to be congratulated. It wasn't until Spocatti slipped behind the waterfall and stole into one of the elevators that he realized the youngest daughter wasn't here. The outcast, he thought fleetingly, was missing.

\* \* \*

The elevator doors whispered shut behind him.

Spocatti reached into his jacket pocket and removed the computer-coded card Ryan gave him earlier. He inserted it into the illumined slot on the shiny control panel, punched into the keypad the eight-digit combination he had set to memory, and waited.

For a moment, nothing happened. Then a computerized voice said, "Clearance granted, Mr. Collins. Please select a level." So it was somebody named Collins who sold out to Ryan, Spocatti thought. He pressed the glowing button marked 76.

The elevator began its ascent.

Spocatti removed the card from the slot and withdrew his gun. As the car slowed to a stop, he stepped to one side. The doors slid open. Sensing, judging, he peered out, saw no one and relaxed.

Now for the fun part.

The corridor was long and well furnished. On the ivory walls were paintings by the old masters, the door at the end of the hall was crafted of mahogany, the wood floor gleamed as though it had just been waxed. On a delicate side table, a Tiffany lamp cast amber rainbows of light.

Spocatti leaned back inside the elevator. To any one else, this would have seemed nothing more than a richly appointed corridor. To him, it was an obstacle course.

He holstered his gun, removed a slender pair of infrared glasses from his jacket pocket and put them on. Instantly, everything took on an eerie red glow. He had seen no video cameras in the hallway, but that didn't mean there weren't any. The paintings could be decoys. He would have to risk it.

He looked back into the corridor. Directly in front of the elevator was a thin beam of light that would have been invisible without the glasses. Moving carefully, he dipped beneath it, knowing that if he accidentally severed it, a sensor would detect the difference in temperature and he would not hear the silent alarm as it alerted the police.

He moved on, the web of beams becoming more intricate, more difficult to elude as he neared the door that concealed Redman International's vast cluster of computers. At one point, he had to crawl on his stomach. A moment later, he had to jump twice and roll. *I could have already tripped the alarm and not even know it*, he thought. And the thrill he felt from not knowing

28

charged him.

He reached the door.  Spocatti knew it was reinforced with at least three inches of steel.  Ryan had told him there would be a small keypad at the base of the door that, upon entering a six-digit code, would not only open the door, but turn off all surveillance equipment as well.

He knelt, found the keypad--and saw that it was protected by a series of beams crisscrossing in front of it.  He swore beneath his breath and looked again at his watch.  Ten minutes had passed.  This was taking longer than he anticipated.  *I want to be out of here in thirty*, he thought.

He studied the beams.  Slanting in various angles from floor to ceiling, they formed a grid-like pattern that was so small in design, his fingers would almost certainly sever one of them if he tried reaching through the tiny, diamond-shaped gaps.  He needed something long and thin to stick through the openings and tap out the code.  Like a pencil, perhaps.  Or a pen.  But he had neither.  Mind racing, he looked around the room, but there was nothing here he could use and it infuriated him.  He had come so close.

And then it struck him.  The answer to his problem was on his head.

He removed the glasses from his face and looked at the bows that extended from the green frames. They were long and thin and curved at the end. One would fit perfectly through the tiny gaps.  He snapped off a bow.  Then, while holding the glasses to his eyes with one hand, he gingerly went to work with the other.

It was simple.  In just a few moments, he entered the code he had committed to memory, the infrared beams of light winked off and the door leading to the computer room swung open on its own.

Spocatti withdrew his gun and stood.  He made a quick surveillance of the room and saw nothing inside save for a system of computers he knew little about.  In the twenty-five minutes he had left, he realized he had a lot to learn.

He knew he was in trouble the moment he sat down and turned on one of the computers. As the screen flickered to life, he noticed on the front of the computer an illuminated slot that was like the slot on the elevator's control panel.  And then the following words appeared on the screen: PLEASE INSERT ACCESS CARD.

The only card Louis Ryan gave him was the computer-coded card he had used to access the elevator. He removed it from his jacket pocket, inserted into the machine and waited. The screen went blank. A moment later, a new message flashed on the screen: WELCOME, MR. COLLINS. PLEASE INSERT ACCESS CODE.

Quickly, Spocatti typed in the same eight-digit code he had used in the elevator. The screen winked, a menu appeared and control of the computer became his.

Spocatti's fingers danced over the keys, trying to locate a file that contained information on the takeover of WestTex Incorporated. He went to the directory--and sat back in his chair as hundreds of files began filling the screen.

He was incredulous. He once worked on a system similar to this. As an added security feature, all files were listed by number--not by name--and he knew that an additional security code would be needed to access their information. One that Ryan hadn't given him.

Still, there was a chance that he was wrong. He reached for the mouse that was on the pad to his right and dragged the cursor to one of the files. He double-clicked on the icon and the screen went blank. A message appeared: TO ACCESS Fn E762CC, PLEASE ENTER SECURITY CODE ALPHA.

It was hopeless.

He turned the computer off and looked around the room. There were no file cabinets here, only desks with locked drawers in which he assumed Redman would keep nothing vital. Spocatti knew that everything he needed was in these computers...or safe in Redman's office.

He looked at the time on his watch. He still had twenty minutes before he wanted to be back in the lobby. Ryan had told him that Redman's office was on the third floor of his triplex.

If he hurried....

## CHAPTER FIVE

High above Redman International in her parents' triplex, Leana Redman stood at the end of a long hallway. She was looking out a window and down at the endless line of traffic on Fifth.

In one of the rooms behind her, a clock was striking half past the hour. Leana listened. She now was thirty minutes late for the party. Her parents would be furious and the press would be wondering where she was--which was exactly what Leana wanted.

In no way did she want to be part of this event. And yet she knew she had to go. If she didn't, her parents would disown her. Literally.

*Maybe I'll have a drink first.*

Leana went to the library and bent to the small refrigerator that was at her feet. She removed a bottle of champagne. As she poured herself a glass, she thought again of the man who followed her earlier and wondered if she had made a mistake by not going to the police. For the better part of her life, she had lived in the public eye. Since she could remember, she had dealt with the press. But this man was no member of the press, she was certain of that. This man had a gun.

She put the bottle down onto the bar and remembered his threat: *Tonight, after these pictures are developed, I'm going to pin them to the wall beside my bed--with the others I have of you.* His smile had broadened. *And soon--before you know it, really, Leana--I plan on taking you home with me and showing them to you myself.*

She felt a prickle of fear at the back of her neck. He had called her by name. He said he had other pictures of her. If she saw him again, she'd go to the police.

Leana took a sip of the champagne and glanced around the library. Construction on her father's office was not quite finished and he was using this room in the meantime. On his desk was the usual clutter of coffee-stained papers, computer printouts and

31

reports.

Leana went to the desk, turned on the green-shaded lamp and sat down. While her father never had been a neat man, he was efficient. Leana knew if asked he could find anything he wanted to on this desk. She wondered whether Celina, being close to George as she was, could do the same.

On his desk were several framed photographs of the family. Leana chose one of her and Celina. Here, they were children-- Leana, seven; Celina, eleven--and she was surprised to see how happy they looked. In the meadow behind their Connecticut home, the girls were holding hands, resting against a tree stump and wearing huge straw hats that cast their faces in shadow. Behind them, Elizabeth was laughing, her blonde hair shining in the sun.

Leana couldn't help noticing the pride on her mother's face-- or the adoration on her own as she offered Celina a dandelion. She wondered when her feelings for Celina had changed. The answer came at once: *When Dad began taking her to Redman International.*

It was late. No matter how much she didn't want to go, she had to join the party. Flipping the picture face down on the desk, she turned off the light and left for the bar. As she bent to put the bottle of champagne back into the refrigerator, she caught a glimpse of herself in the windows beside her. She was wearing a simple white dress that left one shoulder bare; her curly dark hair tumbled down her back; and she wore only diamond studs in her ears.

It wasn't until she stood that she noticed something else in the reflection--the door to the library was opening.

She felt a start, turned. The door was almost fully open now. A flag of light spilled into the library, illuminating the many stacks of papers on her father's desk. She was about to ask who was there when a man peered into the room. He did not see her-- Leana was at the opposite end of the room, partly concealed by shadow.

He stood in the doorway, sensing, judging, his concentration intent. Something in his left hand glinted and Leana saw that it was a gun.

She stood completely still, barely breathing. Although she wasn't absolutely certain, he resembled the man who had followed her earlier....

Panic rose in her. She receded deeper into shadow and wondered how he had gotten up here without a card to access the elevator. She watched him enter the room. He didn't walk into it, but eased into it like a cat, his gaze constantly changing as he moved toward her father's desk.

She could not let him see her.

At the end of the bar was a bookcase that extended two feet from the wall. On one side was a small opening she could hide behind. When the man was not looking in her direction, Leana nudged toward it. Her dress rustled when she moved. The man heard it, whirled on his heel and took aim. Leana froze. Their eyes met.

"Who the fuck are you?" she shouted.

The man stepped away from her father's desk and lowered his gun. After a moment's silence, he said, "There you are."

Leana was taken aback. The man was holstering his gun, seemingly oblivious to her fear. "I asked who you are!"

"Antonio Benedetti," he said. "A member of security." He stepped forward and she could see now that he was not the man who had followed her earlier, but one who resembled him. Her heart was pounding fiercely. "What are you doing here?"

"Looking for you," he said. "You're late for the party. Your parents told me to come and find you."

"And you needed a gun for that?"

The man smiled. His teeth were even, white. "Miss Redman," he said, "after what happened here this morning, every member of security is carrying a gun."

She studied him. He was tall and dark, his features sharp and attractive. There was a coolness about him that she found appealing. He stepped over to the door and held it open for her. "Your mother's furious," he said. "If you're not in the lobby soon, she'll probably have me fired. Are you coming?"

Leana hesitated, then started toward the open door. As she walked past the man, she said, "My sister saved a life today. The least I can do is save a job. Let's go."

33

# FIFTH AVENUE

\* \* \*

The elevator dropped like a stone.

As they neared the lobby, Leana looked up at the elevator's lighted dial and watched the floors race by. She heard the crowd's rising din, felt beneath her feet the driving beat of the band and became nervous. She would know few people here. This was her parents' and sister's world, not hers. So, why had she been asked to come?

She looked at the man standing beside her and saw that he was looking at her. Again she thought how handsome he was. She glanced at his left hand and saw no ring. But life had taught her that meant nothing. "What do you think the chances are of this place blowing up tonight?" she asked.

The man smiled. "Less than zero."

"Oh, come on," Leana said. "Don't you think my father has something else planned to capture the world's attention? Like a sniper, perhaps? Or maybe a fire?"

He cocked his head at her. "You think your father rigged those spotlights with explosives?"

"It wouldn't surprise me."

"But people were hurt, your sister nearly killed."

"Quelle domage."

"I still don't see your point. Why would your father want to do something as ridiculous as that? It makes no sense."

"Free publicity, Mr. Benedetti, makes a lot of sense."

He leaned against the wall and studied her. "You don't believe what you're saying, do you?"

Leana's eyes flashed. "That doesn't matter," she said. "It's always interesting to see what other people will believe."

The car slowed to a stop. With the parting of doors came a sudden blast of cool air, music and noise. Leana stood there a moment, undetected, and looked around the crowded room. While she saw no friends of hers, it seemed that wherever she looked, she was reminded of her sister. From the waterfall to her right to the Lalique crystal chandeliers that shined above her head, Celina's influence was clear.

Once, when Redman International was nearing completion, Leana asked her father if she could help decorate the lobby. George said it was a job for professionals. He would never know the hurt Leana felt when it was decided that Celina would decorate the lobby. George would only sense Leana's anger afterwards and pass it off as one of her moods.

They left the elevator. "Well," Benedetti said, "it was nice talking to you."

"And to you," Leana said. "Keep your eye out for any snipers. You never know when one will pop up."

Leana watched him move into the crowd, where this time she saw a few familiar faces in the endless sea of heads. Looking over at her parents and sister, she saw that they were still greeting guests--George laughing, Elizabeth chatting, Celina hugging.

Leana wanted to hurl.

She started toward them, her gaze shifting from George to Elizabeth to Celina. *One of these days, they'll respect me as much as they respect her.* But even as she thought this, she wondered how she'd pull it off. As she took her position next to Celina in the reception line, disappointment, frustration and anger were all clearly expressed by George and Elizabeth--and yet neither said a word.

Leana supposed she should be happy for the way her presence--or lack thereof--had affected them, but she wasn't. In fact, a part of her felt guilty for coming late.

Outside, the paparazzi went suddenly wild as Michael Archer alighted from his limousine and stepped into the lobby. Cameras flashed. The crowd of onlookers cheered. Leana recognized him immediately. "I didn't know Mom sent him an invitation," she said to Celina. "I read one of his books a few months ago."

Celina looked puzzled. "Mom didn't send him an invitation. I went over the guest list twice with her. Michael Archer's name was nowhere on it."

Leana looked at Elizabeth, who was watching Michael Archer shake hands with her husband. She knew her mother had no tolerance for those who crashed parties--especially her own. She wondered how she would handle this.

"I'm sorry," Elizabeth said politely as Michael approached. "But I'm going to have to ask you to leave." Her voice was firm.

She ignored his hand. "This is a private party."

In the silence that fell, George and Celina turned to listen. Leana watched Michael. "I apologize for intruding," he said. "But I understand you're raising money this evening for children with HIV, and I wanted to do something to help." He reached into his jacket pocket and withdrew a slip of paper. He handed it to Elizabeth. "I hope this will."

Elizabeth looked at the check, then coolly back at Michael. "$100,000 is very generous," she said.

"I work in the entertainment industry," he said. "HIV is prevalent there. It's the least I could do. It's a cause I believe in."

Although Leana doubted he knew it, Michael Archer had just handed her mother five million dollars. Perhaps six. Once word got around that he had given her a check for $100,000, the other guests would be scrambling for their checkbooks, desperate not to lose face. Elizabeth knew it, but she didn't show it.

"I apologize," she said to him. "This is very kind of you. We would be pleased to have you stay. Would you?"

The relief that crossed Michael Archer's face was unmistakable. Leana lifted her chin at the same moment he turned to look at her. Their eyes met and Michael smiled. "Mrs. Redman," he said, "it would be my pleasure."

# FIFTH AVENUE

## CHAPTER SIX

The old Buick coughed, wheezed and shook for several moments before it jerked to a halt and died in the heart of Manhattan.

Jack Douglas sat there, numb, as steam rose from the engine and the headlights dimmed into darkness. He knew what was wrong with the car without checking the engine. For weeks now, he had been meaning to have a new radiator and alternator installed, but he was so busy with work, he had put it off. Naturally, both failed him on the night of George Redman's party.

He would have to catch a cab.

He opened the glove compartment, plucked the white, Tiffany-engraved vellum invitation from a mass of crumbled papers, broken pencils and used Kleenex, and searched for his wallet. It wasn't there. He looked on the seat beside him, on the floor, in the pockets of his black dinner jacket and pants, and then remembered leaving it back at his apartment, out in full-view on the kitchen table, just so he wouldn't leave it behind.

He felt a sudden flash of anger. Now he would have to walk.

He left the car where it had died, on the corner of Fifth and 75th Street, and started for The Redman International Building, which was over a mile downtown. He knew his car would get towed, but he didn't care. Tonight, Jack Douglas had more important things on his mind. Tonight might just change the rest of his life.

With the trees of Central Park rustling in the breeze to his right and the elegant limestone and brick buildings at his left, it was easy to get caught up in the aura of Fifth Avenue. Ahead of him, a horse-drawn carriage moved down the avenue at a leisurely pace and Jack could see, in the back of the open hansom cab, the silhouette of a man pouring champagne into a woman's glass. She laughed and Jack smiled. It was sights like these that renewed his faith in the city.

When he first came to New York, he had found it cold and harsh. He came with a Harvard education, which opened doors, but he had little money and no friends. He hated the city then. But as time passed and the city slowly became his own, Jack gradually admitted that if it were not for this city and the people he had met here, he never would be the success he was today.

He had just passed 61st Street when lightning flashed and thunder rippled across the sky. Jack looked up, felt the rising breeze on his face and quickened his step. *It had better not rain,* he thought.

But it did.

When the rain became wind-swept sheets, panic rose in him and he broke into a run, the invitation clutched in his hand, the rain pelting his lowered head. With each passing motorist, he was sprinkled with the spray that flew off their wheels. He ran seven blocks before The Redman International Building came into sight, and when it did, Jack slowed. If George Redman himself hadn't sent him an invitation to tonight's party, he would have passed on this and gone home.

Last week, when he sold an unprecedented $500 million dollars worth of bonds to a client in France, he had become the financial world's most revered species--a Big Swinging Dick. The following morning, when the Journal named him Wall Street's latest financial whiz, every investment firm in Manhattan tried luring him away from Morgan Stanley--but to no avail.

Jack refused the offers, determined to remain loyal to the firm that gave him his start. And then came the invitation from George Redman, asking him to come to the grand opening of the new Redman International Building. "Congratulations on the Journal piece," George wrote on the invitation. "And I hope you'll come to the party. I'd like to discuss a few things with you."

And that was all it took. Redman International was the world's leading conglomerate. If Jack was offered a job there, his career would be set. *So much for loyalty,* he thought.

Rain was beating against the building's shimmering sheets of glass. At the roof, three helicopters circled. A small crowd had gathered outside the building's entrance, most holding cameras--others, Jack sensed, carrying guns.

As much as he didn't want to, Jack knew he had to go through with it. *I just hope Redman has a sense of humor.* He started into the building and handed the doorman his damp invitation.

While the man studied the invitation, Jack stood there, just a few feet beyond the twin gilt doors, his wet clothes dripping on the marble tile, and listened to the silence fall. The band wasn't playing. There was nothing but the rustle of silk, the light din of those who hadn't seen him and the titter of those who had. The doorman looked at him, then at the invitation and seemed to hesitate with indecision. But then he smiled and said, "Have a pleasant evening, Mr. Douglas."

"Right," Jack said, and moved into the lobby.

A waiter stopped beside him. "Champagne, sir?"

"Champagne, sir" was at the end of a ten-foot pole and conveyed the message: "You and your wet clothes and your dirty face are not welcome at this party."

Although he preferred beer, Jack accepted a glass and toasted those who were rude enough to stare. "Lovely evening," he said, and smiled when they turned away. There was a hand on his arm. Jack turned and saw Celina Redman. "You look as if you could use a friend," she said.

This morning, she was on the front page of the Times. While Jack always considered her an attractive woman, he was delighted to find that Celina Redman was even prettier in person. "And a shower," he said after a moment. "I'm afraid I got caught in the rain." He extended a hand, which Celina shook. "I'm Jack Douglas," he said. "Glad to meet you."

Celina returned the smile. "Celina Redman," she said. "That was one hell of a profile the Journal had on you last week. I was impressed. My father invited you personally, didn't he?"

Jack nodded. "Afraid so. My big break and look at me. I'm a mop."

"Don't worry about it," she said. "It shows you have guts."

"I just wish I wasn't wearing them on my jacket and pants." He looked around him. "I should probably clean up before I meet your father."

Celina looked at the dusting of mud and grime on his face and hands, and said, "I'll tell you what--my parents have a triplex on the top floor. If you'd like, you can clean up there and borrow

something of my father's. You look to be about his size." She
motioned toward the bank of elevators beside them. "Why don't
you come with me and I'll see what I can find for you to wear. I'm
sure my father has something."

When they arrived on the seventy-ninth floor, Jack followed
Celina through rooms that looked as though someone had
dismantled a museum to furnish them. And yet the overall effect
was surprisingly warm. Like her.

"There's a bathroom through there," Celina said as they
entered her parents' bedroom. "I'll find you something to wear."

Jack stepped into the bathroom, which smelled faintly of
roses in their prime. He stood before a full-length mirror and
removed his wet jacket, then the damp shirt that clung to his skin.

"I won't be long," he said. "Will you stay?"

Celina stepped out of her father's dressing room with a black
dinner jacket and pants draped over one arm, a crisp white shirt
over the other. "You don't think I'd miss seeing what you look
like dry, do you?" She entered the bathroom and handed him the
clothes. They looked at one another. "Of course, I'll stay."

\* \* \*

Down below in the lobby, Diana Crane, Redman
International's chief corporate attorney, accepted a glass of
champagne from one of the barmen, sipped it and then turned
back to Eric Parker, Redman International's chief financial
officer. He was still talking about the upcoming takeover of
WestTex Incorporated.

Would he never shut up about it? Could he not have a good
time? *Would you pay attention to me, please?*

She listened to him blather on, pretended to be interested and
glanced around the crowded lobby. There was more money and
power in this room than in many Third World countries. Given
her poor upbringing, it still seemed unreal to her that she was
part of this crowd and yet Diana made it a point not to forget her
past. Being part of an event like this made her hard work worth
it.

She finished her champagne and looked at Eric. From the first day they'd met, she'd been attracted to him. Eric Parker was tall and dark, his looks classically Greek, his frame muscular, almost sleek. He had a healthy sense of humor, he was capable of holding an intelligent conversation and he had that incredible financial mind.

For the past two years, Eric Parker also had Celina Redman. And before their recent break-up, there were rumors of marriage.

Lights flashed and the dance floor was plunged into darkness. A murmur rose over the crowd and the band stopped playing. Diana watched with Eric as a piercing beam of light slashed the darkness and cut through the glistening waterfall, sending ripples of blue light across the crowd's expectant faces.

She nudged Eric. "What's this?"

Eric nodded toward the waterfall. "The money shot. Watch."

From behind the waterfall, Elizabeth Redman appeared to walk through it. It was a clever illusion and the crowd cheered. She stood there, elegant in black silk, the diamonds at her neck, wrists and ears winking in the light. George came through the waterfall and was at her side, smiling as the energy in the room began to grow. The spotlight followed them to the center of the dance floor.

Cameras flashed. Society applauded.

"She's beautiful," Diana said.

There was a rustle of ice as Eric finished the last of his Scotch. It was his fourth in less than an hour. "She is," he agreed. "But not as beautiful as her daughter." Eric looked around him. "Where is Celina, anyway? I know I came late, but I thought I'd see her by now."

Diana was exasperated by him. Could he really still have feelings for Celina? After the way she left him? "I'm not sure where she is," she said. "Maybe you'd like another drink to forget?"

Eric handed her his glass. Diana had it refilled--this time without the ice. When the band began playing "One Moment in Time," there was another burst of applause from the crowd as George and Elizabeth started to dance.

Diana was happy for them. *They deserve this*, she thought. *They've worked hard for it.* After a few moments, the spotlight was replaced by the warm glow from chandeliers as other couples joined George and Elizabeth on the dance floor. Soon there was nothing but a swirling mass of glittering dresses and black tuxedos.

Diana reached for Eric's hand. "Let's dance," she said.

Together, they moved about the dance floor, their steps light, graceful. Diana looked up at Eric's face, saw him smiling down at her and she smiled back. He held her closer and Diana wondered if he knew that she was in love with him and had been for years. He lowered his mouth to her ear. Diana tensed and for a moment thought he was going to kiss her. His words were an invasion when he spoke. "When this gets back to her, do you think it'll make her jealous?"

Diana looked up at him, acutely aware of the alcohol on his breath. "What did you say?"

"When this gets back to Celina," he said. "You and me dancing. Do you think she'll be jealous?"

She was incredulous. "I don't know," she said. "Why don't you ask her?" And the music stopped.

* * *

While Jack showered, Celina kicked off her shoes, sat on her parents' bed and allowed her gaze to wander around the bedroom. It had her mother's touch, which meant it was just enough without being overwhelming. Only one thing caught her eye--the photographs of the family framed in silver on the Chippendale side table.

She slid off the bed and chose one of the photographs. It was of her and Eric and they were holding hands outside the old Redman International Building on Madison. Celina could remember the day clearly. Only hours after the picture was taken, she and Eric had made love for the first time. Then, Celina was convinced she was giving herself to a man she would spend the rest of her life with. *Now, I don't know what I want.*

She put the picture back onto the table and wondered if Eric was here. She herself had asked him to come. Although they were no longer seeing each other, it seemed pointless to her that there should be any animosity between them. Celina, in fact, still loved Eric. If he hadn't pressed so hard for marriage, there wouldn't have been a separation.

She wondered why he was in such a hurry. She was twenty-nine years old and too young to marry--let alone to have the children Eric wanted. But she would have them and if Eric could wait, if he could learn to be patient, Celina would have them with him. Until that day, however, Celina planned on living her life--and she would do it single, whether Eric Parker liked it or not.

From across the room, the bathroom door opened and Jack Douglas, freshly showered and wearing George's dinner jacket, stepped into the bedroom. Celina thought how handsome he was. His sandy hair more tousled than groomed, his face rugged and intelligent, Jack Douglas was tall and had an appealingly athletic build. He looked to be somewhere in his early thirties.

He smoothed his hands down the front of the jacket. "What do you think?" he asked.

"Very sophisticated," Celina said. "You clean up well. Now let's go down and find my father. I'm sure he wants to speak to you."

## CHAPTER SEVEN

Leana Redman moved through the crowd and was amused by how the crowd parted for her.

There were faces she recognized and most of them were either stoned on whatever drug was circulating, or had been lifted so many times, a strange, permanent smile was on their lips.

She nodded at a man who made million-dollar-deals during the day and was rumored to frequent sex clubs during the night. She passed a countess who gave hundreds of thousands of dollars to a teenage delinquency fund, and yet was known to steal repeatedly from Bloomingdale's and Saks. To her right was a sheik who loved his many wives--and how their clothes fit his plump body. And to her left, she heard a woman saying, "Brenda? Getting married? That's absurd. Let me tell you something about Brenda. She's so butch, she rolls her own tampons."

Leana looked at the woman who said this and wanted to tell her friends that she might as well be talking about herself. It seemed to her that there was more corruption, drug abuse and twisted social values in New York Society than in any other New York social class.

Across the lobby she could see Harold Baines, Redman International's VP for International Affairs, speaking at a dimly lit corner table with his wife, Helen. Leana smiled. Finally, someone she not only knew, but adored.

Harold had been with Redman International ever since she could remember and they always had been close. When she was a child and had made one of her rare visits to her father's old headquarters on Madison, Harold made it a point to spend time with her. He made her feel special and as though she belonged. Because of the way he treated her, he would always have a warm spot in her heart. While everyone was paying attention to Celina--the daughter who showed promise--Harold intentionally paid attention to her. Leana would always love him for it.

She started in their direction.  The crowd shifted and she saw Harold push back his chair, stand and kiss Helen on the forehead. The lighting above him accented the deep lines on his face, the dark circles beneath his eyes, suggesting an age well past sixty. And yet Harold Baines was fifty-one years old.

Leana waved to him but Harold didn't notice and he stepped into a nearby washroom.  He seemed thinner, older than when she saw him last and Leana noticed he was carrying himself as if the very act of moving required the coordinating of muscles he didn't have the strength to control.  When the door swung shut behind him, she wondered if something was wrong with him. Was he sick?  She was about to walk over and ask Helen when Michael Archer appeared in the crowd.  He approached her--and held out a hand. "Dance?" he asked.

The band was playing "I'll Be Seeing You."  As they danced with the other couples on the dance floor, Leana looked up at Michael and decided to ask a question that was certain to piss him off. "So, tell me," she said. "Why did you really spend $100,000 to come here?"

The question took Michael by surprise.  Hadn't she heard the explanation he gave her mother?  "I thought I already explained that," he said carefully.  "I wanted to help your mother raise money this evening for HIV."

"Bullshit."

"Excuse me?"

"You're going to have to do better than that," Leana said. "That's an explanation my mother would believe, not me."

Michael felt a start, but stilled it.  She couldn't know why he was really here, couldn't know that he had been sent here by his father to meet her.  That was impossible.  Still, he was wary.  She seemed to be looking straight through him.  "A lot of my time is spent with the creative community," he said.  "Some of my friends have the disease, which no longer gets any attention in the press. It's great what your mother's doing.  She'll put HIV back on the front page."

Leana studied his face.  "All right," she said.  "I'll buy that. But you're here for some other reason.  No one gives $100,000 to charity without having some other motivation than mere kindness.  Kindness went belly up in the '40s."  She looked around her. "Is there somebody here you wanted to meet?   A producer, perhaps?  A publisher?"

His arm tightened around her waist.  "I've got those covered," he said.

"Then why are you really here?"

"Why do I have to be here for any particular reason?  Can't I just be a nice guy?"

"No one is nice anymore, Mr. Archer.  Look around you.  See that man over there, the one with the cigar?  Next to him is his wife, who knows that lit cigar goes other places.  Now, what's the reason?"

He saw the humor in her eyes and he softened. *This is a game to her*, he thought. *She knows I'm lying and is just having some fun with it. Relax.* "All right," he said.  "I'll tell you--but on one condition."

"Name it."

"You have to tell me something you're not proud of.  Quid pro quo.  Deal?"

"Deal.  Now, what is it?"

"I don't like giving money to the government," he said, the idea still fresh.  "When I learned your mother was raising money this evening for children with HIV, I saw a chance to write off a hundred grand from my taxes.  Better to help children than to hand it over to adults who behave like children, wouldn't you say?"

Leana nodded.   "Now, that I believe."   She accidentally brushed up against the woman dancing behind her.  Both turned and smiled their apologies.

"Your turn," Michael said.

"I don't think you can handle it."

"Try me."

Her eyes challenged his.  "I'm an addict.  I don't use anymore, but I'm still an addict--that's the label they give you when you leave rehab.  Always and forever an addict.  And, my, how I used to love cocaine.  Loved it.  Still do, really, but I just can't use it or things tend to...collapse."

Suddenly, his game of quid pro quo had lost its appeal.  "I'm sorry," he said.  "That was none of my business."

46

"Oh, everyone knows," Leana said. "It's just another way I've been an embarrassment to my family." She touched his cheek with the back of her hand. "Don't look so glum, chum. It happened while I was at school in Switzerland. I haven't been near the stuff in years."

As they danced, Michael wondered again why his father sent him here tonight. Why was it so important that he meet Leana Redman? He was about to ask her what it was like to grow up in the very atmosphere he escaped from, when a hand descended onto his shoulder. Michael turned his head and saw Harold Baines. "May I?" Harold asked.

Michael reluctantly handed Leana over.

"It was nice meeting you," he said.

Leana smiled. "And you. Maybe you can dip me inappropriately later? Center of the dance floor? Thirty minutes?"

"What do you mean by inappropriately?" he asked.

"It means I'm not wearing any underwear. It means a long, slow dip for the tabloids."

Michael held up his hands and backed away. "Okay," he said. "Thirty minutes. But think about the repercussions in the meantime." He was surprised to find that he liked her.

As Leana watched him leave the dance floor and move into the crowd, she found herself wishing they hadn't been interrupted.

"Do you always put the screws to everyone you meet?" Harold asked.

"Just the cute ones."

"You're wearing no underwear?"

"Of course, I am. That was just to hook him."

"You're amazing," he said. "But I will say that seems like a nice enough young man. Should I recognize him?"

"He's Michael Archer."

"The writer?"

"And movie star. I prefer his books."

"By the look on your face, his looks, as well." He held out a hand. "Dance."

The band was playing an upbeat tune and, as they moved with the other couples, Leana thought Harold seemed different from the man she was concerned about earlier. The lines on his face

47

weren't nearly so deep and he was carrying himself with a greater sense of control. His brown hair gleamed as if he'd wet it down.

"You're looking better," she said.

Harold raised an eyebrow. "Better?"

"When I saw you earlier, you looked as if a mob ambushed you from behind and left you for dead."

"That's kind of you," he said. "And when was that?"

Leana shrugged. "Twenty minutes ago? You stepped into a washroom before I could get your attention."

Harold grasped her by the hand and whirled her about the dance floor. Leana's white sequined dress fanned out and she laughed.

"I think you might need glasses," Harold said. "I've never felt better."

"I'm glad," Leana said. "You had me worried." She looked around her. "Where's Aunt Helen?"

He gave her a look. "Do you really have to ask? She's with your mother, gossiping. Sometimes I can't pull those two apart." He squeezed her hand. "Let's go and have a drink. I haven't seen or talked to you in days--and I want one of your martinis."

"Martinis!"

They left the dance floor and moved over to the bar, which was handling the crowd with ease. She nodded at a young bartender who was so built, he should have been part of security. She had slept with him a week ago and he looked at her now with a smile. "You know what we want, you big lug."

"The Leana Redman special?"

She squeezed Harold's forearm. "Things are looking up, Harold. My father has his own building, I have my own drink. That's fucking progress."

The man started fixing the drinks.

While they waited for them, she noticed Eric Parker leaving the dance floor with Diana Crane. Leana's gaze followed them to the opposite end of the bar where Eric ordered a drink and Diana accepted a glass of champagne from a waiter's tray. She finished it and was sipping her second by the time Eric turned to join her.

"Here you are, Miss Redman."

"It wasn't Miss Redman last week." She winked at him as he blushed. "But manners matter. You've still got my number, right?"

He nodded.

"Then use it," she said. "Like, soon." She accepted the drinks he offered and looked back over at Eric and Diana. They were standing in silence, both nursing their own drinks. Leana noticed that Diana seemed distracted, angry. She wondered why.

She handed Harold his martini. "This will kick your ass to the moon."

"I know it will."

"Good. Let's kick our asses together."

They touched glasses and drank.

"Can we talk in private?" Harold asked. He tossed back the martini and nodded toward Leana's full glass. "You're such an amateur," he said. "Is that the best you can do? Drink up. Something tells me you're not going to like what I have to say."

They followed a wave of instant celebrities and old money past the candlelit buffet table. Ice swans filled with Iranian caviar gleamed orange in the flickering light and Leana could smell a tempting mixture of roast duck, Westphalian ham and salmon mousse. She lingered, but Harold embraced her arm and urged her forward. "This won't take long," he said. "You can eat later."

"I want to eat now."

When they were seated alone at Harold's table, he turned to her and said, "Where were you earlier? You weren't in the reception line when Helen and I passed through it."

*So, that's what this is all about.* "I came late."

"Because of what happened with Celina and the man she helped earlier?"

How well he knew her. "Well, this proves it," she said. "It's still not too late for you to make a career tossing tea leaves."

Harold sighed. Ever since Leana was a child he had tried to instill confidence in her. He had tried to make her see that she was not that different from Celina. Would he never be able to reach her? "Your sister is not better than you, Leana."

"You don't think so? Then tell me why Celina's on the board of this goddamned conglomerate, and I'm not."

"Your sister has worked hard to get where she is."

"If I had been given the opportunities she was given, I also would have worked hard." She titled her head. "So, tell me, why was I shipped off to Switzerland when I could have gone to school here--as Celina did--and work for Redman International--as Celina did."

"You know I don't have the answer to that, Leana."

"I know you don't, but if we're really going to have this conversation again, the story is the same. I'm tired of being the daughter who has accomplished nothing. I'm tired of people thinking I can't accomplish anything. Just once I'd like to be the one getting the attention. Just once I'd like my parents to stand up and notice me."

"Then stop bitching about it and do something," he said. "Do you honestly believe Celina has got to where she is today by sitting on her ass and complaining like a spoiled child?" He didn't wait for an answer. The only way to reach Leana now was by getting her angry. "Of course, she hasn't. Yes, George gave her a chance, but that girl has worked hard and she wouldn't be on the board now if she hadn't earned it. I know George. He wouldn't have allowed it."

"Don't you think I know that?"

"No," Harold said. "I really think you don't. I think you only see what you want to see--and that isn't necessarily the truth."

Leana couldn't keep the edge from her voice. "Why are you saying this to me?"

"Because I should have said it to you years ago, instead of comforting you with words that mean nothing. The only way you're going to make something of yourself in this world is to make it happen yourself. Just because you're George Redman's daughter doesn't mean you should be treated any differently from the rest of us. In fact, it probably means you'll have to work a hell of a lot harder."

"Doing what? I have no skills." She held up a hand. "Check that. I know what it takes to make a killer martini and I know how to fuck strangers. Will that get me a job?"

"Maybe on the streets. What you do have is a college education and interests. The world is yours if you're willing to work hard enough. Your problem is that you're lazy. You've always been lazy, Leana." He checked his watch, hating himself for having been so hard on her, but also knowing this time he might have reached her.

"Listen," he said. "I have to go and find Helen. But I want you to come and see me soon--before Eric and I leave for Iran. Together, we'll see if we can't find something for you to do. You don't necessarily need your father's help to make your mark. Helen and I know most everyone in this town. Maybe I can introduce you to somebody who will give you a chance."

"You'd do that for me?" Leana said.

"Leana, I'd give you to Anna Wintour."

She brought her hands to her chest. "Really?"

"Or Putin."

"What's the difference? They both love fur."

She hugged him.

"Believe it or not, I love you, Leana," Harold said.

## CHAPTER EIGHT

From the bar, Diana Crane watched the couple alight from the elevator and move through the crowd.  She watched Celina laugh, watched the man at her side smile and watched their arms intertwine as they joined George and Elizabeth at the waterfall.

The man was tall and built, his sandy hair cut short, his face rugged and handsome. A few people recognized him along the way, but he didn't seem to notice.  She recognized him from the Journal article--Jack Douglas.  His attention was on Celina and for that, Diana couldn't have been more pleased--or thankful.

She turned to Eric and knew, by the surprised look on his face, that he had been watching them too.

"How'd you like to get out of here?" she said.  "We've made our appearance, shaken hands with all the right people.  George won't miss us."  She took a sip of champagne.  "By the looks of things, neither will Celina."

Eric said nothing.

"I have a car waiting outside for me," Diana said.

"I'm going nowhere with you, Diana."

"It's just for coffee, Eric."

"I doubt that," Eric said.  "Unless you were planning to serve the coffee in bed."

Diana's eyes were like a light suddenly turned to his face. "What's that supposed to mean?"

"It means that I'm tired of you chasing me," he said.  "If you think my seeing Celina with another man is going to make me want to jump into bed with you, you're wrong.  I'm not interested in you.  Never have been.  Never will be.  Now, why don't you do yourself a favor and get lost?  I'm staying here."

He glanced over at Celina.   She was laughing at something Jack said.

Diana placed her half-empty glass of champagne on the bar. "They're a good looking couple," she said.  "I hope it works out for them."  And then she was gone, stepping into the crowd, ignoring

Leana, who had been standing beside them, listening.

"What was that all about?" Leana asked.

Eric shook his head. "You wouldn't understand." He tipped back his drink and studied Leana over the rim. She looked beautiful tonight. "What do you think of the party?" he asked.

She couldn't have heard him right. "What do I think of the party?" she repeated. "Eric, what do you think I think of the party?" She leaned beside him against the bar. From where she stood, she had a clear view of Celina, who was standing with her back to the waterfall, listening to Elizabeth, her red dress among the room's stars.

"I'm sorry," Eric said.

"Forget it." She motioned towards Jack Douglas. "Who's he?"

Eric shrugged. "Damned if I know."

"I just saw them leaving the family elevator together."

"So did everyone else. Do you think they're seeing each other?"

"No idea."

"Now probably isn't the best time for me to find out, is it?"

"If by that you mean going over there and asking Celina in front of Mom and Dad, then, no, I don't think now is the best time to find out. But I would ask her. You have every right to know."

"Why haven't you two ever gotten along?"

Before she could respond, lights in the lobby dimmed, the room fell silent and her father's voice rose above the crowd. Leana skimmed the sea of heads for him. She looked past the band, beyond the waterfall and found him standing in the center of the dance floor, immaculate in his black dinner jacket, a glass of bubbling champagne in his hand--Celina at his side.

"Tonight's a special night for me," George said to the crowd. "Owning a building on Fifth Avenue has been a dream of mine since I was a boy. But dreams come hard and this dream wouldn't have happened without the support of my wife and the help of my daughter, Celina."

He looked at Celina. "If it wasn't for you, we wouldn't be standing here right now. " He touched his glass of champagne to hers. "Here's to many more years of our working together."

The crowd burst into applause. Before Celina could give George a kiss, Leana looked away and asked a barman for a bottle of champagne.  When the man handed her one, she grabbed Eric by the hand and led him into the crowd.

"Where are we going?" he asked.

Leana's answer was as clear as the hurt in her voice.  "To get our minds off Celina."

* * *

They walked down the hallway in silence, Leana slightly ahead of Eric, Eric glancing into the rooms that were on either side of them.  They were in George and Elizabeth's penthouse and as they passed one of the sitting rooms, lightning flashed, illuminating for an instant the family's cat, Isabel, who sat poised and alert on an orange damask sofa.

They stepped into the room that was at the end of the hall.  Leana stopped in the doorway.  She gazed across the library at her father's desk, which was illumined by a green-shaded lamp.  "I thought I turned that light off earlier," she said.

Eric brushed past her and moved into the room.  He dropped into a chair and closed his eyes.  Would the room never stop spinning?

Leana remained in the doorway.  "I know I turned that light off."

"Obviously you didn't, Leana.  The light's still on."

"I don't care if the light's on.  I was here earlier.  Before I left with that man from security, I know I turned that light off."

"So, what are you saying?"

"What do you think I'm saying?  I'm saying that somebody's been here."

"Big deal?  It could have been Celina and her new man."

She hadn't thought of that.  "Maybe."

"Would you please just open that bottle of champagne?  I'm thirsty."

She crossed to where he was sitting and turned on the lamp beside him.  Eric winced from the sudden light and brought up a hand to shield his eyes.  "I think you'd better pass on the champagne," Leana said.  "You look like hell."

54

"I feel like heaven."

"Wait till tomorrow."

She went to the windows that were behind her. In the city's deep glow, sleek black skyscrapers loomed dark against the sky. Eric settled further into his seat.

"You know something, Leana?" he said. "You really are beautiful."

"You know something, Eric? You really are drunk."

"You know what my favorite memory of you is?"

She looked at his reflection in the window. "No."

"You were fifteen years old, I had known you for maybe five months and you told me that you and your best friend at the time--what was her name? Asia Something--were planning on attending Christmas Mass at St. Patrick's Cathedral in the nude. Wearing long jackets, of course."

She turned away from the windows. "Her name is Asia Ward," she said, smiling. "And we're still friends. But cut me some slack. *That's* your favorite memory of me? If it is, I'm more fucked up than I thought I was."

"It's one of them," Eric said. "I can still remember you and Asia sitting between George and Elizabeth, red-faced, trying not to laugh, giving me the eye when no one else was looking. I remember thinking that Celina would never do this, and it was then that I knew you and I would become friends."

Leana popped the cork on the bottle of champagne and brought the bottle to her lips. As she drank, she became aware that Eric was looking at her intently. "You know, Eric," she said, "I have a favorite memory of you."

"And what's that?"

"Do you remember all the letters you wrote to me while I was at school in Switzerland?"

He nodded.

"I was strung out on coke then and you knew. I've never asked you how you knew."

Eric hesitated, his mind fogged by the alcohol, but then he remembered and explained. "That week Celina and I visited? I needed a pen for something and found, in your desk drawer, beneath a pile of papers, a half-empty vial of coke."

Leana closed her eyes. "And you never told anyone," she said. "Not Celina. Not Mom or Dad. You decided to let me handle the problem on my own--which I couldn't. But you had faith in me that I could. All those letters you wrote, encouraging me, letting me know that you were there if I ever needed someone to talk to, did I ever thank you for them? And for keeping my problem to yourself?"

"I'm sure you must have."

Leana smiled. "You're being kind. I was so screwed up, I'm sure I didn't. But I will now. It's what we addicts are supposed to do. Thank you, Eric. Thanks for believing in me when no one else did."

She folded her arms and turned back to the windows. In the reflection of the glass, she watched Eric stand, uncertainly at first, but with greater control as he removed his dinner jacket and flung it over the back of the chair.

Soon he was standing behind her, running his fingers through her hair, brushing his lips against her bare shoulder. Although she knew what was happening was wrong, that it would never amount to anything more than this, Leana didn't resist him. In fact, she welcomed Eric's touch. Right now, more than anything, she needed to be loved and held.

\* \* \*

Across the room, crouched motionless beneath George Redman's desk, Vincent Spocatti listened. The big leather wingback was pressed hard against his chest. His head was twisted down and uncomfortably to the side. His gun was drawn and ready to fire if he had to.

He had been going through the files on Redman's desk when Leana Redman and her friend stepped into the room, taking him by surprise. What infuriated him more than nearly being caught was the fact that he had found nothing here that would be of interest to Louis Ryan. Not one file on Redman's desk had to do with the takeover of WestTex Incorporated.

56

But there were other ways to get the information Ryan needed. And if Ryan was willing to pay Vincent's price, Vincent was more than willing and able to get it for him.

He strained to hear where they were in the room. Although they hadn't spoken for several moments, Spocatti knew what they were doing, could almost hear the sound of their kissing. He wasn't sure how much longer he could stay in this position. The muscles in his neck were beginning to knot, as were the muscles in his back.

And then he heard footfalls on the carpet.

He looked through a small crack in the desk's front panel and saw a ripple of white cloth, a pair of tanned legs, moving in his direction. His hand tightened around the gun. The light above him clicked off. Spocatti tensed, ready to shoot. Leana Redman said, "Remember that, Eric. I turned the light off. I'm not crazy."

"Yes, you are," Eric said. "Now, come on. Let me show you how crazy I can be."

Spocatti waited until he was certain they had left the room before he pushed back the chair, stood and tucked the gun in his holster. As he smoothed his gloved hands down the front of his black dinner jacket, it occurred to him that that was twice this evening that Leana Redman had nearly blown his cover. He stretched his neck, tried to ease a cramp.

*Payback*, he thought as he eased out of the room and stepped into the hall, *is a bitch*.

## CHAPTER NINE

In the lobby, George and Elizabeth Redman moved away from Celina and Jack, and separated as they stepped into the grinning, laughing crowd.

Jack watched them go. "Your father's impressive."

Celina smiled. "He likes you."

"Did I mention that he has good taste?"

"Did I mention that's a horrible line? What did he say to you, anyway? My mother cornered me with gossip and I heard only pieces of the conversation."

Jack shrugged. "He really didn't say much. He said he was pleased that I came, mentioned how nice his clothes looked on me and asked if I'd be interested in coming to your Connecticut home this Sunday afternoon. He never said what for."

"That's obvious," Celina said. "He's going to offer you a job."

Jack didn't want to discuss the possibilities of that until he was sure. "Your father did mention that you have a sister," he said. "I'd like to meet her. See her anywhere?"

"No," Celina said, without bothering to look. "I don't see her. Would you like something to eat? I'm famished."

They stepped over to the crowded, candlelit buffet table. Celina chose one of the small watercress sandwiches. Jack, watching her, sensed a distance. "Why do I feel as if I just said something wrong?"

"Because you're a smart man."

"Want to talk about it?"

"There isn't anything to talk about. My sister and I don't get along. If you want to know why, you'll have to ask her."

Realizing the tone of her voice and the choice of her words too late, she looked at Jack and said, "I'm sorry. I don't mean to sound abrupt, it's just that I don't like discussing my sister. I love Leana. But a long time ago, I stopped wondering why she doesn't feel the same about me."

She motioned toward the dance floor and smiled a smile that never quite reached her eyes. "Would you like to dance?"

Jack nodded and, as they turned to leave, Vincent Spocatti stepped out of the elevator that was to their right. He approached them and showed Celina his security card. "May I have a word with you in private, Miss Redman?" he asked.

\* \* \*

The elevator doors opened and Celina stepped out. She walked briskly down the long hallway. She told Jack that she would be right back and she meant to keep her word--they'd have that dance. Right now, she wondered what Leana wanted. Why would she have a member of security ask her to come here, to their parents' penthouse, when she could have spoken with her just as easily in the lobby?

She passed her father's study, which was empty. She continued down the hall, calling Leana's name once, twice, but only the muffled sound of thunder answered her.

She took the marble staircase to the second floor, searched it, found it empty and climbed the staircase to the third floor, where there were bedrooms, her father's office, and the third-floor library.

She could hear voices coming from the end of the hall.

Celina moved in their direction, finally coming to a stop beside one of the bedroom doors. Although she could hear only pieces of what was being said, she recognized the voice as Leana's and knew at once that she should not be standing here, that something was wrong. Still, she listened. Now the voice was clearer. "Please don't be embarrassed. It happens sometimes. You've just had to much to drink."

Celina moved closer to the door. "Look," Leana said. "Why don't you just lie down? You can sleep here tonight. Mom and Dad won't mind, and I promise they won't know that I was here with you. Neither will Celina. It'll be our secret."

At that moment, Celina stepped into the bedroom. Leana, sitting at the edge of the bed and wearing a thin silk kimono, turned away from Eric and faced her. While Celina noticed that her sister was naked beneath the kimono's brightly colored fabric, she did not see the flash of genuine surprise in Leana's eyes.

She shut the door behind her. "I got your message, Leana. Your friend from security gave it to me."

Startled, Eric sat up in bed. He looked from Celina to Leana, then realized he was naked and drew a sheet to cover himself. "What message?" he said.

Celina's face was composed, but inside, she was furious. She leveled Eric with a look. "I don't want to hear a word from you," she said. "Not one word."

"It's not what you think," Eric said.

"It's exactly what I think," Celina said. "And I don't want to see you again. What we had is over." She looked at Leana, who was standing now, holding the kimono shut with tightly clenched hands. "I just want to know one thing before I leave, Leana--what did I ever do to you to deserve this? Why did you tell that man from security to meet you here?"

Leana shook her head. She felt confused, embarrassed and ashamed. Never had she wanted this to happen. And yet it had. But how?

"Answer me," Celina said. "I have a right to know."

"I don't know what you're talking about," Leana said. "I never gave anyone a message."

The silence stretched between them like a dangerously fraying thread. Celina turned to leave. "I never expected you to tell me the truth," she said. "You always were a liar, Leana. And a coward."

Hand trembling, she opened the door and was about to step through when she stopped and faced her sister a last time. "You can pretend you don't know what I'm talking about, but I know you planned this. I know you told that man to have me meet you here. I think you've been waiting years for this moment. To see me hurt."

Before Leana could say anything more, Celina was gone.

In the silence that passed, Eric looked across the room at Leana. She was dressing. Behind her, Manhattan pushed up a glittering wall of glass and concrete.

"Where are you're going?" he asked.

"After her, of course."

"Don't you think you've done enough?" He slid off the bed.

"I've done nothing, Eric. That's the point."

He looked at her incredulously.

"You call having Celina catch us in bed together nothing? Are you fucking out of your mind?"

"If what she said is true, I call it being set up." She slipped into her dress. There was a tiny rip in the back near the zipper. Earlier, Eric had torn it in haste.

"You know you've ruined whatever chance I might have with her, don't you?"

Leana shot him a fierce warning look. "This was not my doing, Eric. I've told you that. Now, drop it." She stepped into her shoes, walked past him to the dressing table and fixed her hair. She had to speak to Celina, she had to find out who had given her that message, she had to clear her own name.

A thought occurred to her while she brushed her hair. Leana had always wanted to see her sister hurt--but never like this.

"I'm sorry," Eric said. "I know you had nothing to do with this. It's just that--"

"Apology accepted," Leana interrupted. He was drunk. She didn't want to hear him talk. She just wanted to leave this room and find Celina. Quickly.

"Who told her? Who knew we were here?"

She looked at his reflection in the dressing table's mirror. "I'm not sure who told her. But I intend to find out." She turned in front of the mirror, thankful that her hair covered the rip in the back of her dress.

"I'll come with you," Eric said, and Leana noticed as she faced him that he had put on his pants. The rest of his clothes were still on the chair beside him.

"You need to stay here," she said. "Celina can't handle seeing us both right now."

She began to step past him. And as she did so, Eric struck her hard across the face with the belt he had been hiding behind his back.

The blow took Leana by surprise and she fell to the floor, blood spraying from her nose and mouth, spotting the beige carpet. Before she could defend herself, before she even knew what was happening, Eric was straddling her, swinging the belt, raining blows on her thighs, shoulders and breasts.

Her dress ripped from the strain of their struggling. Her cries of pain and help echoed hollowly in the room.

"You fucking bitch!" he shouted. "You knew what she meant to me! You've ruined everything Celina and I could have had together!" He pulled back the belt and struck her once more across the face, leaving her cheek hot and swollen. A dusting of red stars flowered before Leana's eyes as she skated closer to the gray edges of unconsciousness. Somewhere, far in the dark corners of her mind, she realized the blows could kill her.

And then Eric punched her. Hard. In the mouth.

Leana forced herself to think through the daze. If she tried to resist him, he would hurt her worse than he already had. She tried to move her arms, but they were pinned beneath his knees. And then her mind froze. Eric was forcing her legs apart. She felt his hand race up her dress and tear at her underwear. His fingers clawed and searched.

Leana struggled and was about to scream when Eric clamped an open hand over her mouth. She felt wetness and smelled a heady mixture of Scotch and blood. Her blood.

Eric pressed his mouth against her ear. "Just remember," he said, as he ground his hips into hers, "you wanted this."

And then Leana unexpectedly relaxed against him. Eric looked at her with such surprise that he involuntarily relaxed with her. It was then that she made her move.

She bit hard into his hand and shoved him off her when he recoiled. Her heart thundering, her sense of direction shattered, Leana stumbled to her feet. The door was across the room, a million miles away. She ran for it.

Tried to run for it.

Eric grasped her ankle and she lost her balance. The room whirled. Leana knew it was over at the same instant her forehead struck the carpet.

But Eric did nothing. He was on his feet, suddenly aware of what he had done. How could he have lost control like that? What had gotten into him?

He looked at Leana. She was lying motionless on her stomach, her head buried in the crook of her arm. The area of carpet surrounding her was stained with her blood. A wave of nausea overcame him and he wondered how badly she was hurt. She wasn't moving....

He glanced at his watch. How long had Celina been gone? Four minutes? Five? If she had told George what she had seen, he would be coming up here now.

His drunken haze lifting, he stepped over Leana, locked the bedroom door and hurried into his clothes.

Leana waited. She listened to the sound of Eric dressing and peered across the room. Eric was standing before the dressing table, tucking in his shirt, quickly checking his appearance in the oval mirror. He was fully dressed now--except for the belt, which was still clutched in his hand.

He faced her. There was a moment when their eyes met, when a world of hatred passed between them, a universe of rage. And then Eric said calmly, "These are your options--you can either get yourself cleaned up and pretend none of this happened, or you can run to your father and tell him everything." He moved toward her, the belt swinging like a pendulum by his side. "And doing that, Leana, would be a mistake."

As he approached, Leana recoiled, her eyes riveted on the belt. A section of it was stained with her blood. "Get out," she gasped. "I'll call the police."

"You can do whatever you want," Eric said. "But I promise you this--if you do call the police, or go to your father, I'll have a contract put out on you so goddamned fast it'll make your head spin. You hear me? I hope so. Because I will do it. I've got the money and I've got the contacts. If anything happens to me, you die. It's as simple as that."

\* \* \*

The elevator door slid open and Celina hurried out. She slipped through the crowd, avoiding the questioning stares, not stopping until she came upon the twin glass doors that were across the lobby.

Curtains of rain were billowing down the avenue, lashing the windows and the reporters on the sidewalk. Beyond the windows, flashes popped, blinding her. She turned to ask a doorman for an umbrella and came face to face with the man from security who had given her Leana's message.

He nodded at her.

Celina moved in his direction.

"That message you gave me--you're certain it was my sister who asked you to give it to me?"

"I'm positive," he said. "She told me herself that she was your sister."

She had to be certain it was Leana who did this. "Could you describe her to me?"

"She has long dark hair and she's pretty. I only talked to her for a few seconds."

"Do you remember what she was wearing?"

"A white dress, I think. It left one of her shoulders bare."

Celina turned away from the man, her stomach sinking. She was about to leave when she saw her father moving in her direction, sifting through the crowd, his expression grim, businesslike. "We need to talk," he said.

She wanted out of here, but she didn't want to tip him off. She followed him to an area just behind the waterfall.

"I just got through speaking with Richards and Kravins. They're worried about what happened here today. I think they're going to back out of the deal."

"Back out of the deal?" she said. "We've agreed to pay them $125 million in fees plus a twenty percent share of the company. What about Jim Roberts?"

"He said he wants to wait and see what the police find."

"And?"

"If there's even the slightest hint that those spotlights were rigged in protest of our deal with WestTex, he'll side with Richards and Kravins, and they'll pull financing. Richards says it'll be a public relations nightmare if we takeover that company in lieu of what's happening in the Middle East."

"Maybe in the beginning," Celina said. "But when the public learns what we've done, we'll be more than fine."

"At this point, I don't think it matters with them," George said. "They know that until WestTex is ours, our agreement with Iran is only verbal. They feel there's a strong possibility the Navy won't move into the Gulf on the date we've been given. They disagree with the reasons why we're offering twice what WestTex is worth only a month after they pulled their fleet from the Gulf."

"So, let's drop them," Celina said. "Find someone else."

"That's what I was thinking. I'm having lunch with RRK tomorrow. If it falls apart, what if we cut a deal with Ted Frostman at Chase?"

"I like Ted," she said. "He's a good guy. Think he'll play?"

"Maybe. God knows he owes us. I'll set up a meeting with him."

"Sounds like a plan." She was exhausted. "Are we good here? I'd like to go home."

George looked at her in surprise. "Home?" he said. "Are you all right?"

If she told him what had happened, it would ruin his evening.

"Today was a lot," she said. "And I'm feeling every bit of it." She looked over the crowd. "The party will wind down soon. I've spoken to everyone I needed to speak to. If you don't mind, I'd like to call it a day."

It was pouring when she left Redman International. Those members of the press who hadn't been invited inside immediately started taking her picture, their damp, hungry faces looming behind the rapid explosions of light. Some shouted questions, but Celina ignored them and nodded at the short, white-haired doorman standing beneath the canopied entrance.

He spoke sharply into his cell phone, turned to remove an umbrella from a marble stand and opened it with a flourish just as her car pulled up to the curb--long slants of rain illumined in the headlights, the tires throwing up low fans of water.

They hurried towards the limousine and the press followed, recording her exit for the world. She stepped into the back of the car, told the driver to get her out of there and was home fifteen minutes later, packing Eric's belongings.

## CHAPTER TEN

The morning after the party, George Redman was showered, shaved and in his black track suit at a time most people were still in bed asleep. Before meeting Richards, Roberts and Kravins for lunch, he planned on running three miles in Central Park.

He stepped out of his dressing room and moved to where his wife lay motionless in their bed. They had made love last night and the sheets were now twisted impossibly around her pale legs. "I'll see you at breakfast," he said, bending to kiss her on the cheek. "Will you be up?"

Elizabeth murmured something in her sleep, lifted her head from the pillow and kissed him awkwardly on the chin. "You smell good," she said, and turned with a faint groan onto her side. "Don't forget to stretch."

He went to the elevator at the end of the long hallway. The apartment was quiet. Besides Isabel, the family cat, who was washing herself on top of an ormolu table, he was the only one up, which was not surprising considering it was just a little past five.

He stepped into the elevator and pressed a button. As the floors sped by, George wondered again how the meeting with RRK would go. If they decided not to back him, he would have to move fast on Ted Frostman at Chase. He had come too far to miss this deal with WestTex.

The elevator slowed to a stop. The doors slid open and George stepped out, pleased to see the lobby nearly back in order. The cleaning crew had arrived not long after the party ended and they had worked throughout the night.

George left the building, checked the time on his watch, dutifully stretched his legs and started uptown. Soon he was running along the barren paths of Central Park, and musing at how far he had come since graduating from Harvard.

When he graduated in 1977 and moved to Manhattan, it seemed everything he tried failed. Banks were reluctant to trust a newcomer and so they ignored his requests for loans. Instead, they chose to finance the established developer over the rookie. George knew he could go back and work for his father, but that would mean giving up on his dreams. And so he pressed on, determined to find success.

It didn't come. It seemed the harder George tried, the more often he failed. It wasn't until the fall of 1977 that things began to look up.

Louis Ryan, an old college friend, called and told him about Pine Gardens, a 1,000-unit apartment complex that recently had been foreclosed on. Would George be interested in going into a partnership?

George's first mistake was saying that he would. His second was sealing the deal with a handshake. What began as the beginning of his dream, ended with years of fighting Louis Ryan in court--only to lose. Miserably.

He finished his run in just under twenty-four minutes. Winded, he leaned against the trunk of an elm and stretched his legs before leaving the park. The city was coming to life. Cars were shooting down Fifth, rich widows and hip divorcees were walking their well-groomed dogs on retractable leashes and the sun, visible now, gilded the cluster of limestone buildings surrounding Central Park, turning their beige facades to gold.

He bought the Times from a newspaper-vending machine, tucked it beneath his arm without looking at the headline and started down the avenue toward his building, which towered above its neighbors.

Just looking at it filled George with pride. The new Redman International Building was as extravagant in design as its predecessor on Madison Avenue had been conventional. Instead of having four straight sides, the new building sloped gently upward, narrowing from its base to its roof, producing a rather uneasy effect of a hill carved from glass and stone. It trumped everything on Fifth Avenue--especially Louis Ryan's Manhattan Enterprises Building, which was two blocks south.

Before entering Redman International, George stopped and looked at Ryan's building. Despite the years, anger still seized him when he saw it. To this day, he could remember Ryan telling the court that there had never been a partnership between him and George. To this day, George could remember Ryan standing up and calling him a liar for saying so.

* * *

While waiting for Michael to arrive for their eight o'clock appointment, Louis Ryan stood high above Fifth Avenue in his corner office, his hands clasped behind him as he looked out a wall of windows and took inventory of his empire.

From where he stood, he could see the many hotels, condominium and office complexes that he had either owned for years, or were presently under construction. There was the new hotel he was building on the corner of Fifth and 53rd. I would be be the city's largest and already it was six months ahead of schedule and nearly $13 million under budget.

He learned how to control his costs years ago. When they worked together, George Redman taught him well.

On Central Park South, ground was being broken for Louis' new condominium complex. The demolition of the two prewar buildings had been completed four weeks earlier, the foundation one.

He still had to laugh at The Metropolitan Museum of Art, who asked if he would donate the four demi-relief Art Deco friezes that decorated the exterior of each building. At first, Louis agreed, seeing no reason why he shouldn't donate them. If anything, it would be good press and free publicity for the new building. But once he learned that it would take weeks to remove them properly--not to mention hundreds of thousands of his own dollars--Louis had the friezes torn down, not wanting or willing to pay for what he considered worthless art.

He moved away from the window and walked the few steps to his desk. His office was large and filled with things he never had as a child.

Born in the Bronx, Louis came from a poor, working-class family. He looked across the room at his parents' wedding picture. In it, his mother was seated on an antique red velvet chair, her hands arranged in her lap, a faint smile on her lips. She was in the simple, ivory-colored wedding dress her mother and grandmother wore before her. She was seventeen in that photo and Louis thought she was beautiful.

Standing behind her was Nick Ryan, wearing one of the few suits he ever owned. It was dark blue and a few sizes too large for his slim frame, but the smile on his face and the defiant way he held his head made one notice not the suit, but the man himself.

He wished his parents could have witnessed his success. In the fall of 1968, Nick Ryan had been killed while on duty in Vietnam. On the day Louis learned of his father's fate, he quickly learned his own. At the age of thirteen, he was thrust into the position of provider and nothing was the same for him after that. While his mother took in laundry and was a seamstress on the side, Louis worked forty hours a week washing dishes at Cappuccilli's, the Italian restaurant at the end of their block. He pulled straight A's in school. He and his mother planned budgets together and managed to put something aside for a future they were hesitant to face.

As a team, they were invincible. It was in his eighteenth year, only days after Harvard offered him a full scholarship, that his mother became ill. She was tired all the time. There were lumps in her neck and groin. Her joints ached. "I've lost a lot of weight, Louis. There's blood in my stool."

He brought her to the hospital. The doctor was crass, frank and cold. After examining Katherine Ryan, he took her son aside. "There are holes in your mother's bones," he said. "She has cancer. It's beyond treatment. She'll need to be hospitalized, if only to keep her comfortable. That will be expensive. Do you have insurance?"

Louis looked the man squarely in his eyes. "We don't," he said. "But we have money, so you treat her right just the same."

His private hell began then. Times were hard and the hospital was overcrowded. His mother was placed in a room with three other women--each struggling to hang on to lives that were leaving them. Louis wouldn't forget the days that followed--working three jobs so he could afford bills that were scarcely affordable; going without sleep so he could spend time with a woman who no longer resembled his mother; holding her hand because he knew that she was frightened and missing her husband.

He remembered the never-ending stream of specialists injecting poison after poison into a body that was manufacturing poisons of its own. He watched his mother slowly slip away from him. Her skin gradually becoming too large for her body. The experience hardened Louis. Made him see things differently.

At the end of her first week's stay, Katherine, so weakened by the toxins in her system, reached out a hand and gripped Louis's knee. Her voice unusually strong, resolve still burning in her eyes, she spoke calmly and clearly. "I know what you're thinking," she said. "But you won't drop out of school. I won't hear of it."

"Mom--"

"You listen to me, Louis. My life will have been for nothing if you don't succeed. God gave you that scholarship and God gave me this cancer. He'll take me, but He won't take that scholarship. You go to school in the fall. You become a success."

"But the bills--"

"--will take care of themselves." Her face softened. Drugs had clouded her eyes and they now were as grey as the four walls surrounding them. "Don't you see?" she said, squeezing his knee. "Don't you see what you're going to become?"

She died three weeks before he started Harvard. On the night before her death, she said to him in a whisper, "I want to be cremated. If I'm going to die, this cancer is dying with me. I'm not going to let it feed off my body any longer. I'm going to burn it up. I'm going to have the last say."

He granted her wish and scattered her ashes in a park she and his father used to bring him to in upstate New York. It was then that he made a vow--no matter what the costs, he would conquer the business world. He would become the best of the world's best.

His focus was not broken until his Junior year at Harvard, when he met Anne.

He had been walking home one afternoon when he heard what sounded like a woman shouting and several barking dogs. Curious, Louis stopped to listen. For a moment, he thought he was hearing things--there now was nothing but the buzz of traffic and the sound of leafless trees clicking in the stiff March wind.

But then, suddenly, a team of seven dogs rushed around the street corner he was standing at, nearly toppling him as they hurried toward downtown Cambridge. Louis turned and watched them run, their expensive leather leashes whipping behind them like snakes.

And then he saw her.

"For God's sake!" the young woman shouted as she shot around the corner. "Help me catch them!"

Louis ran after her. She was out of breath, her face flushed, her long black hair swinging. Louis was about to ask how they got free when she stopped and her hands flew to her mouth. There was a screech of tires. Undaunted, the dog joined his friends and trotted on--only this time a bit slower as the group weaved through traffic and moved toward the center of town.

"Hurry!" she said.

They began running again, faster this time. Louis's mind raced. "Are they all joined by one leash?" he asked.

"Yes!"

He was running alongside her now. *She's pretty*, he thought. "I'm going to cross the street and head them off. You lure them to me."

Her eyes widened. "How?"

"I don't know--get in front of them, chase them in my direction. When they're close enough, I'll grab their leash and they'll be yours again." He looked across the street and pointed to a cluster of trees. "I'll be over there."

"It won't be that easy."

"It will be," he said. "Go."

He started across the street. "I don't even know your name," he said. "I'm Louis Ryan."

"It's Anne," she said, starting to run again. "Anne Roberts. And I promise if we get these dogs back, you won't regret it!"

It was over dinner that evening that Anne told Louis she walked the dogs to earn extra money for college. Now, remembering that day and those that followed, almost made her death seem as if it hadn't happened, as if George Redman never fouled their lives. But then, as always, Louis remembered that snowy February evening, just days after George lost his final appeal in court, and the first memory shattered.

He leaned forward in his chair and lifted Anne's picture from his desk. When his mother died, he had been powerless to help her. He accepted her death as he accepted his own fate. But his wife's man-made death could be fought. This time he didn't have to accept the unacceptable.

For years Louis fantasized about killing George Redman's wife. For years, he imagined how sweet it would be to take from the man what he assumed was his greatest love. But as time passed and he learned more about his wife's murderer, Louis realized that while Redman loved his wife deeply, he felt perhaps more passionately about Redman International and his daughter, Celina.

They were his life's accomplishments. They hadn't failed him. It was then, as Redman's daughter and his conglomerate matured, that Louis had his awakening. In order to make Redman feel the pain he had felt for years, Louis would take everything from the man, not stopping until his own thirst for revenge was satisfied.

There was a knock at his office door. It was only seven-thirty. Michael wasn't supposed to be here for another half-hour. "Yes?" he said.

The door swung open and his secretary, Judy, stepped into the room. When she saw that he had been studying his wife's picture, she hesitated, remembering a time years ago when she walked in unannounced and caught him weeping while holding it. She turned to leave. "I'm sorry," she said. "I was just coming in to catch up on some work. Jim told me you were here."

She held the current edition of the New York Times in one hand and a steaming cup of coffee in the other. "I was going to give you these."

Louis replaced Anne's picture and managed a smile. "Remind me to give you a raise," he said. "Those are exactly what I need right now. Come in."

"I think you might find the paper interesting," Judy said as she crossed the room to his desk. She was an attractive woman in her middle forties, with short blonde hair and a nose that was just saved from being too wide. She had worked for Louis for nearly twenty years and had become rich because of her ability to keep secrets. "Especially the front page and the business section."

Louis looked up at her, puzzled. "What do you mean?"

Judy placed the coffee down beside him. "This," she said while handing him the paper. There, on the front page, was a picture of the new Redman International Building--complete with a close-up of one of the destroyed spotlights. The banner headline read:


**EXPLOSIVE DAY FOR GEORGE REDMAN**


Before Louis could react, Judy was saying, "And here," as she opened the paper to the business section. There, the headline read:


**REDMAN STOCK CONTINUES PLUNGE;
PLANS TO TAKE OVER WESTTEX CONFIRMED**


Louis skimmed the article that ran beneath the headline before turning to the front page and reading about the three spotlights he had Vincent Spocatti rig with explosives. When he was finished, he looked up at Judy. "And I thought today was going to be a bad day," he said.

## CHAPTER ELEVEN

Michael Archer awoke to the sharp crack of gunfire and the shrill screams of people on the street.

Startled, he sat up in bed and came face to face with his best friend of nearly fourteen years, Rufus, the golden retriever who sat beside him. There was a gnawed plastic dish in his jaws.

Michael slumped back against the mattress and closed his eyes. Already, the morning was warm and muggy. He turned onto his side and looked at what had become his only home--an over-priced one-room apartment on Avenue B that smelled like shit and now was filled with boxes sent from around the world.

Rufus nudged his arm and Michael got up, looking tentatively out the window as he passed it. Down below on the sidewalk, a small crowd of people had gathered around a woman who was face down on the street. Blood was pooling around her head. People were on cell phones, some were taking photos. *Welcome to fucking New York*, he thought.

Michael took the dish from Rufus' mouth and filled it with dry dog food. He watched a cockroach scatter across the countertop and the irony that he now was living in this dump was not lost on him.

At thirty-four, he was one of the more powerful men in Hollywood. His movies made millions at the box office, he had written six blockbuster novels and he had adapted four of them for the screen--all of which he had starred in and produced. To the public, he not only was a fine actor and writer, but also a respected businessman. Through his novels and movies, he led his fans into another world and gave them the escape they desired. He was their king, their shining star, and he was invincible.

They were dead wrong.

The public knew only what Michael Archer allowed them to know. And because of this, they couldn't know that this was now his life--and it was in danger.

The warnings began as small reminders. After a major purchase, his manager and accountants would call and suggest he curb his spending. "You're not the government, Michael," they would say. "Remember, even you have financial limits."

Michael would nod and listen, but he would forget their words and instead remember his beginnings in Hollywood--a time when money was so scarce, he was lucky to eat one meal a day. Then, he hadn't owned a villa in Italy, a brownstone in Boston, an estate in Beverly Hills. Then, Michael had known nothing but the struggle of day to day life and his seedy apartment in West L.A.

To escape from those days, Michael surrounded himself with luxury, often spending more money in a week than many people made in a year. Never did he think his bank accounts would run dry. Until they did.

He had been two weeks in Cairo, vacationing at a high-end resort, when his business manager phoned to tell him that his bank was about to foreclose on each of his three homes. Going as well were the Ferrari, the Lamborghini, both yachts.

He was incredulous.

"If you don't have a minimum of $2 million to cover your debts by this Friday, everything will be taken from you."

"Friday?" Michael said. "That's three days away."

"We've been warning you."

"What are my options?"

"At this point? You've got two."

"What are they?"

"You could go to your father."

"Fuck that."

"Or you could gamble."

It was better than asking his father for the money.

"Where would I go?" he asked. "Apparently, I have no money to place bets--at least not the kind of money I'm going to need."

"You could borrow it," the man said. "A friend of mine runs Aura in Vegas. As a favor to you, I could call and tell him you're coming for a weekend that you're a good risk for a loan."

"And what if I lose and can't pay back the loan?"

"Then you'll be in trouble. This is only a suggestion, Michael, and not one that should be taken lightly. You should go to your father. I recommend that--not the gambling."

But Michael went with the latter.

As promised, borrowing the money was no problem. Paying it back, however, became one. Michael stayed at one of the casino's black jack tables for hours until he lost it all. Now, he owed Stephano Santiago, owner of the casino and capo di capi of Europe's most powerful Syndicate, over $900,000. It was blood money and Michael knew that, if he didn't pay Santiago soon, the man would have him murdered.

A day passed before he received a threatening phone call from one of Santiago's men. Another day passed and he was on a plane headed East toward Manhattan, where he met with his father for the first time in nearly sixteen years.

Seeing his father after all those years was a shock. Louis was older, grayer, heavier than that day Michael left home--and yet he still was a force. Seated at his desk, immaculate in a black silk suit, Louis looked across the room at his son, his eyes as dark and as judgmental as Michael remembered them to be. It didn't take long for Michael to feel uncomfortable. Louis always had been able to make him feel inferior just by looking at him.

Though he didn't want to do it, Michael told his father the predicament he was in. And while Louis said he'd take care of everything, there was that tone in his voice, that calm tone his father used whenever he wanted something.

Now, Michael knew it had to do with the photographs he was given of Leana Redman and the appearance he made last night at George Redman's party. There was a reason his father demanded he meet her and it worried him. His father had a motive behind everything.

He checked his watch and decided he had time to unpack a few more things before meeting with his father. He sat beside Rufus, who knocked his arm with his nose, and reached for a box marked PERSONAL. The first item he pulled from the box was, ironically, his first novel and best-seller.

Michael ran his hand over the faded dust jacket and thought back to when he started the novel. He was eighteen years old, on a bus headed for Hollywood and running away from his father. They had fought the night before and Michael decided then that no matter how hard he tried, he and Louis would never get along. And so he left.

Even now, some sixteen years later, Michael could remember how the fight ended. Louis told Michael that he didn't love him and never had. He said that he wished it was Michael who died, not his mother.

Michael tossed the book aside and dug deeper into the box. When his hands grasped the next object, there was a light tinkling of glass and Michael's heart sank. He knew what it was before he pulled it through the many strands of torn newspaper and held it in his hands. It was a framed photograph of his mother, Anne, something he had cherished since he was three years old. The glass had pierced her face.

Michael was staring at it when a knock came at the door. He put the picture down and glanced at his watch. Puzzled, he looked at Rufus, who now was facing the door, his head cocked in such a way that suggested he too knew they weren't expecting anyone. There was another knock, this one sharper, more urgent, and then the sound of footsteps swiftly moving away.

Michael moved quickly through the maze of boxes and unlocked the door. He opened it wide, stepped into the hall and nearly stumbled over the brilliantly wrapped basket at his feet.

The hallway was cloaked in a network of shadows and for a moment, he heard nothing but his neighbors, who were shouting again at their child. He could sense a presence, knew he was being watched. He stepped back into the safety of his apartment, bolted the door and waited, the sound of his heart filling his mind.

Time seemed to stop. His neighbors continued to shout. And then, from the end of the hallway, came a clatter of metal striking metal as the gate to the freight elevator crashed open and someone stepped inside.

The gate slammed shut and the car hesitated only briefly before it began its noisy, sluggish descent.

Michael opened the door and ran down the hall, eager to see who was inside. But by the time he reached the elevator and gripped the metal bars, the car already was a lost cage of rattling iron shadows.

For a moment, he just stood there, listening to the faint wail of police sirens. Just now, they were coming for the woman who was shot earlier. He wondered if his death would mirror hers. Would a stranger take him by surprise, draw a gun and silence him with a well-placed bullet?

Or did they have something else planned for him?

He returned to his apartment and brought the basket inside. It was cocooned so tightly in sheets of red cellophane that he couldn't see its contents. Rufus nudged his leg and Michael patted his back, reassuring him that everything was all right-- even though he knew it wasn't.

Steeling himself, Michael removed the crimson shield and tossed it aside. The stench was sudden and overwhelming. Michael covered his nose and mouth with the back of his hand and took a step back, the haze of fruit flies lifting in front of him as if they were wavering veils of ash. The basket was filled with rotten plums, peaches that were soft and brown and dimpled with mold, apples that had been gnawed to the core, bananas that were black and alive with maggots.

Michael stared at the filth, knowing who had sent it even before he reached inside and removed the envelope taped to the wicker handle. Inside was a note, precise and neatly typed: "Three weeks, Mr. Archer. That's how old this fruit is, and that's how much longer we're giving you to come up with our money. By then, the sum will be one million dollars. Please have the money by then. If you don't, our generosity will have run out and you'll be giving your mother some unexpected company."

Shaken, Michael crumpled the note and tossed it aside. He had never mentioned his mother's death to anyone, and yet these bastards somehow knew. *But how? And how did they know where I live? I just moved here.*

He looked at his watch and saw with a start that it was seven-thirty. Louis had requested his presence at eight sharp. As Michael rushed out of the apartment, the door locking shut behind him, he realized that if he were late for this meeting, it very well might cost him his life.

## CHAPTER TWELVE

The sun went behind a cloud and a shadow stretched across Manhattan, leaving Louis Ryan's face gray in its presence.

"I want to talk to you about your mother's death."

Michael straightened in his chair. They were in his father's office. Louis was seated behind his desk; Michael in front of it. He thought Louis had asked him here to discuss Leana Redman and the party he had been sent to last night, not his mother.

"Why?"

"There are things you don't know."

"What things?"

"A lot of things." Louis turned in his chair. "But before I begin, I want you to know I realize you should have been told this years ago, when you were young enough to understand it. Maybe, if you knew what I've gone through over the past thirty-one years, we could have been closer--as a father and son should be."

He made an effort to smile but failed, his eyes belying the grief that still lingered within him. "I would have liked that."

Michael raised an eyebrow. That was news to him.

"Do you remember what happened when your mother passed away?"

"She was in a car accident."

Louis stepped to the far right wall of windows, where he watched workers remove the red ribbon from the center of The Redman International Building. "It wasn't an accident. Your mother was murdered and what George Redman did to her was brutal."

Michael couldn't have heard him right. The sudden roaring in his ears dulled his father's words, making it difficult for him to hear everything Louis was saying.

"...George and I were friends at Harvard...."

"...my partner in a development called Pine Gardens...."

"...Yes, I admit I lied in court. I even admit I used George. But I grew up poor. George had all the money in the world. The

79

only reason I asked him to be my partner was because I thought we'd need his father to cosign a loan for us. When I learned I could buy Pine Gardens on my own, I did, and so he sued me...."

Michael shut his eyes. *This isn't happening.*

"For years George tried to get his share of Pine Gardens. For years, he tried to prove we had a partnership. I refused to let him have any of it." He paused. "That decision cost your mother her life."

Michael looked up at his father, his concentration intense.

"Your mother was murdered just two days after Redman lost his final appeal in court. It was late and it was snowing. She was returning home from a friend's house when George blew out her tires with a shotgun. Your mother lost control of the car, skidded in the snow and tumbled over the bridge that led to our house. It was a seventy foot drop. She didn't have a chance...."

Michael looked at his father for some sign of the lie he was sure he was telling, but there was none. It was obvious he was telling the truth. For Michael, it was as if someone had shot him.

"I was never able to prove it," Louis said. "But I know it was him. George Redman killed my wife--your mother. The moment I learned her tires were flattened by a shotgun, I knew it was Redman who pulled the trigger."

"How could you know that?"

"Besides having the perfect motive--wanting revenge against me--George Redman is an excellent marksman. Once, when we were in college, he took me skeet shooting on his father's yacht. Even with the rolling of the waves, George rarely missed. But George is smart. He got rid of whatever gun he used and made certain he had an alibi. When the police questioned him, he told them he was with Judge William Cranston's daughter, Elizabeth Cranston, now Elizabeth Redman, during the night of the shooting.

"I don't know how he did it, but he got Elizabeth to lie for him. Because when the police questioned her, she confirmed it and George was dropped as a suspect. A week later, the police concluded that poachers were hunting in the woods on either side of the bridge. They said a stray shot flattened your mother's tires. Despite pressure from me and a team of lawyers, the case was never reopened and George Redman walked free."

It was as if all those years of never understanding his father came to an end. Now Michael knew why Louis never discussed Anne's death, why he became irritated whenever the subject was brought up, why he, Michael, hadn't been allowed to attend his mother's funeral. Now he understood his father's mood swings and those evenings, as a child, when he heard Louis weeping in his bedroom. Now it all made sense.

"Why didn't you tell me this from the beginning?" Michael asked.

"Too many reasons," Louis said. "But the main reason is that I didn't want to hurt you. You were just a child when Anne died. You barely knew her. How could I tell you then what he did to your mother? If you were me, would you have told your three-year-old son that his mother had been murdered? Would you have brought him to her funeral, knowing how upsetting it would be for him to see her like that? I doubt it. And besides, you wouldn't have understood."

"You could have told me when I was older."

"Agreed," Louis said. "And I wanted to. But every time I tried to tell you, every time I thought the moment was right, I couldn't find the words. I couldn't say that your mother was murdered. It was too difficult. And so I allowed you to live in the comfort of not knowing the truth. I know you won't see it this way, but in a sense, I've spared you the anger I've had to live with for years."

"Why are you telling me now?"

Louis went to his desk and reached for the pack of cigarettes next to his picture of Anne. He shook one out, lit it with a lighter and said in a plume of blue smoke, "Because the time is right."

He handed Michael the newspaper his secretary gave him earlier that morning. As Michael read about the recent, sharp decline in Redman International's stock, Louis said, "Thirty-one years ago, I was unable to put that bastard away for what he did to your mother. Now, with his stock at an all-time low, I finally have the kind of money and power it's going to take to bury him and each member of his family. They'll all pay for what George Redman did to your mother. But I'll need your help."

Before he could react, Michael glimpsed the front-page picture of the spotlight that lay crushed in front of The Redman International Building. For a moment, he just stared at it, his

81

mind making connections he never knew existed. Then he looked up at Louis. "You rigged those spotlights with explosives."

"Let's just say I made it happen."

"But you nearly killed a man."

"Not the right one, Michael. George Redman is still alive."

Michael tossed the paper onto the desk. "You're going to kill him, aren't you?"

"That's the plan. But there are many things to be done before that day, and when it does come, it won't be me pulling the trigger. It will be you. And you'll do it for your Mother. That is, of course, if you still want me to pay off Santiago."

And there it was, the reason his father agreed to help him. Michael shook his head, disappointment, anger and hurt threading through him. Just once couldn't the man help him? Just once couldn't he do the right thing?

He pushed back his chair and stood. "I may be a lot of things, Dad, but I'm no murderer."

Louis' jaw tightened. "You'd better think twice about that, Michael. Your own is about to be committed." He glanced at his desk calendar. "How long has Santiago given you to come up with the money? Two weeks? A month? Your time is running out."

"I'll find another way to get the money."

Louis crushed the cigarette in an ashtray. "Who are you kidding? If you could have gone elsewhere for the money, you would have. You proved I'm your last hope just by coming to me."

He reached inside his desk drawer and removed his personal checkbook. "If you want my help, I'm here--but only if you're willing to help me correct the past."

Michael was about to speak, but then decided it was pointless and left for the door. Before stepping out of the room, he stopped and looked at his father. Louis' eyes were as cold and as bitter as the silence that hung between them. "If George Redman did what you say he did, then he should pay for what he did to Mom. But there are other ways. There's the law. I'll be damned--"

Louis raised a hand. "Don't say any of this to me, Michael. Say it to your mother. She's the one you need to explain this to, not me."

Only his father could make this more difficult than it was. "I'm not a murderer."

"You could be." Louis said. "We all could be."

Michael left the room.

When the door clicked shut, Louis reached for the phone on his desk and punched numbers. Michael would see his side sooner than he expected. "It's Louis, Vincent." He looked at the picture of his wife. He had sworn long ago that he and Michael would avenge her death together. Michael just needed a little stimulation. "I've got another job for you, but you must move quickly."

* * *

Michael knew something was wrong the moment he finished climbing the six flights of stairs and saw that the door to his apartment was ajar.

The first thought that raced through his mind was Rufus. If someone was in the apartment, then why wasn't the dog barking? Had the intruder already left? Michael couldn't be sure.

He started down the hallway, moving slowly, his senses acute. He glimpsed an empty wine bottle lying beside the freight elevator, picked it up and tossed it once between his hands. The bottle was heavy, solid. It could fracture jaws, break noses.

He passed the apartment to his right and heard the sound of a child crying, the tinny blare of a television that was turned too loud. Canned studio laughter wafted through the thin, graying walls--Edith Bunker shouting at Archie.

Michael stopped beside his apartment door, listened, but heard nothing. Surprise was his only chance. Drawing back his foot, hand tightening around the bottle, he gave the door a vicious kick and rushed inside when it crashed open.

The apartment was in shadow. Heart racing, nerves wired, Michael stepped farther into the room, pushing past the sea of cardboard boxes, ready to fight. He called Rufus' name once, twice, but there was no response. He turned toward the open window, moved past the basket of spoiled fruit and stepped over to his bed--where he found his dog's mangled body lying in a bloody heap.

Each of his legs were cleanly chopped off. One was stuffed in his mouth.

For a moment, Michael couldn't move, couldn't speak or react. His heart seemed to slow and then freeze. Lips parting, throat tightening, the bottle dropped from his hand and struck the hardwood floor, where it shattered in dozens of gleaming pieces.

Revulsion cut through him like a blade. Legs weak, mind whirling, he knelt beside his dog, touched his back and tentatively stroked Rufus' tan, bloodied fur.

Already, the dog was beginning to stiffen. His coat was cool. The coppery scent of blood was everywhere. Behind Michael was a box filled with towels, sheets, an assortment of rags and clothes. Moving like an automaton, he reached inside the box, selected a thick, pale-blue towel and draped it over Rufus' back. In numb horror, he watched as it turned dark crimson. It wasn't until he turned to reach for another towel that he saw the envelope taped to the rust-spotted refrigerator.

Michael stared at the envelope. It bore his name in thick bold letters. It seemed to scream out at him, shouting his name across the room.

Again, he became aware of the tinny laughter drifting down the hallway. It was as though someone somewhere was laughing at him.

He covered Rufus with another towel, stood and opened the envelope. Inside was a white piece of paper. Typed on it were these words: "You weren't here so we left an example of what happens when we're ignored. Please have our money soon, Mr. Ryan, or this is just the beginning."

The shock of seeing his real name in print terrified him. How much did these bastards know about him? How far were they willing to go?

Michael tore the note in half and telephoned his father. He needed that money, regardless of the stings that were attached to it. As he waited for someone to answer, he glimpsed the picture of his mother. It was lying askew on the floor, just a few feet away from Rufus' body. Someone had slashed it with a knife.

"Yes?"

"It's Michael. I've changed my mind. I need your help. Just

tell me what I have to do and I'll do it."

Could he commit murder?

"What made you change your mind?"

Michael managed to speak only out of sheer will. "Santiago broke into my apartment and butchered my dog."

"I'm sorry."

"I'll bet you are. Just tell me what you want me to do."

He glanced at the blood-soaked towels that covered his dog and knew that it could be him lying there, knew that if he didn't do as his father asked, it would be him lying there. "I'll do anything."

Including murder?

"Why don't you come to my office tomorrow morning? We'll discuss everything in detail then."

Michael said he'd be there and hung up the phone.

When he knelt beside Rufus, he ran a trembling hand over the dog's back. If he waited, just a moment, it seemed he would understand. "I'm sorry," he said quietly. "This is my fault and I'm sorry."

They said they were giving him three weeks to come up with the money. So, why this? What was the point of killing a harmless dog? Michael covered Rufus with another towel. Then he glanced at the tattered remains of his mother's picture. Anger rose in him, a fury so deep only revenge could pacify it. Maybe it was just as well he help his father.

He could commit murder.

## CHAPTER THIRTEEN

The sun cut through the partly open Venetian blinds and sliced bright bands of gold across Eric Parker's sleeping face, the cream-colored sheets of his four-poster bed, and a section of his bloodstained leather belt, which, along with the rest of his clothes, lay in a crumpled mass at the foot of his bed.

It was late Saturday morning.

He awoke with a headache a little before noon. After fumbling in his bedside table for some aspirin, he sat up in bed, swallowed three Tylenol dry and then walked into the bathroom, where he drank water from the faucet and relieved himself.

As he stood before the toilet, Eric peered at himself in the bathroom mirror, surprised to find that he looked worse than he felt. His eyes were swollen and bloodshot, the pupils still dilated; his hair was a wild mass of dark brown waves; his face, usually smooth and tan, was creased with fine pink lines and he was in need of a shave.

Eric flushed the toilet and turned with a groan away from the mirror. Regardless of how much he'd drank, last night was still fresh in his mind. When Eric left Leana, he took the elevator to the lobby, asked the doorman to get him a cab and then waited for it outside in the rain so there would be no chance of him running into Celina or George.

When a cab finally pulled alongside him, he had stepped soaking wet inside and instructed the cabbie to take him to Redman Place, the condominium complex where many of Redman International's senior executives lived--including himself, Celina and Diana Crane. Not wanting to come across either of them, Eric went straight to his apartment, peeled off his damp clothes and crawled into bed, where he quickly forgot the beating he gave Leana Redman and fell asleep.

Now, standing beneath a hot shower, Eric realized the enormity of what he had done to Leana. Hitting her with that belt had been a grave mistake. If he hadn't threatened her, Eric was

86

certain she would have gone to the police--or to her father--and he now would be in jail, instead of his bathroom.

He wondered how long she would keep quiet. Did she believe him when he said he'd have a contract put out on her? When her anger prevailed--and he knew it would, probably even had--would she risk the chance that he was bluffing and go to the police? Or to George?

Eric stepped out of the shower and was struck with the realization that by hitting Leana, he had given her the power to blackmail him. Leana knew how hard he had struggled to reach the top. She knew how much his reputation and his job at Redman International meant to him.

If she wanted to, she could destroy everything he ever worked for.

\* \* \*

Later, after changing into a pair of dark blue sweat pants and an old, faded football jersey, Eric found it impossible not to think of Celina. His apartment was, in a sense, as much hers as it was his. In his bedroom, on the mantel above the fireplace, were photos of them both--four from their trip to Madrid, two of them holding hands outside the new Redman International Building, and one that was taken just last spring by a professional photographer.

Filling the bookcases on either side of the fireplace were books Celina bought for him "because I think you should read more, Eric. You used to read all the time. Now, all you do is work." When Apple released the iPad, she bought him one. "It's set up for iBooks and Kindle. Just download a sample of a book and if you like it, buy it. Easy."

Fastened to the wall above his bed was the lamp she purchased for his birthday "so you can read in comfort, Eric." And on his dresser were the diamond cufflinks she bought "because I felt like it, Eric."

Her clothes still hung in his closet.

As Eric looked around the room, he wondered if Celina ever

would come here again. After the stunt Leana pulled, he thought it was unlikely.

He needed to explain to her what she'd walked in on last night. If he let too much time pass, more damage would be done.

He went to the living room, picked up the telephone and dialed Celina's number. If she told her father what she had seen, he knew George would fire him--and all those years of struggling to the top would have been for nothing. As the phone rang, his thoughts returned to Leana. If he lost his job because of her, he would make her see that last night was just a party.

There was no answer. Eric replaced the receiver, stepped into a pair of worn moccasins and left for Celina's apartment, which was two floors above his. There was no answer there as well. Either she was out, or she was not answering the door.

He returned to his apartment and dialed the doorman.

"I saw her come in myself, Mr. Parker, at around eleven last night. No, she hasn't left the building. Yes, I'm sure of it. You have a nice day, too, sir."

Eric replaced the receiver. So, she was in her apartment. He considered taking his own key and using it, but thought better of it. She would have nothing to do with him now. If he walked into her apartment unannounced, she would either throw him out herself, or she would have security do it. Eric knew that as well as he knew himself.

It was over. Deep down he knew what he had with Celina was over. And all because of Leana.

He opened two French doors and stepped out onto a terrace that smelled faintly of potted roses and city air. Below him, Fifth Avenue bustled and Central Park sighed, and the sun gilded the tops of shiny limousines and enormous elm trees.

As a boy, owning an apartment in New York City had been a dream. And while he felt that one day his dream would come true, never did he think he would be living on Fifth Avenue. Perhaps on the West side of Manhattan, maybe even in some obscure studio on the East side, but not Fifth Avenue. And never, never with a view of Central Park.

He had paid $25 million for this view. He had handed Manhattan's top interior decorator an additional $10 million so he could say to guests, "It's Art Deco." At the time, he had been convinced the expense was worth it.  When you're a senior executive at one of the world's leading conglomerates--and sleeping with George Redman's daughter--you believe your job is secure and that the money will last forever.

Now that he was faced with the possibility of being fired, Eric wasn't so sure of that.

\* \* \*

The reasons why she hated him--or should hate him, if she could only bring herself to that level--were listed on sheets of white paper and taped to her refrigerator, her desk, her bedroom and office walls.  The effort was immature, sure, but it was effective.

She placed the notes anywhere she could easily see them.  She had spent the better part of the night writing them and now, as Diana Crane taped the final list to her computer screen, she wondered again why she still loved the son of a bitch.

She knew it didn't have to be that way.  She knew that other men found her attractive (hadn't Eric told her so only last night?), and it was this knowledge that kept Diana going. She did not need Eric Parker. She just wanted him.

She left her office and stepped into the sitting room, which was large and airy and bright now with sunlight.  She looked at the latest cover of Business Week, framed in glass and on the wall to her left.  On it were two imposing figures--the new Redman International Building and Diana.  She was standing in front of the building and wearing a crisp black suit, a hard hat and a hungry smile. The caption read: MANHATTAN'S TOUGHEST CORPORATE ATTORNEY?

Diana felt almost amused.  She didn't feel so tough right now.

She looked at the phone on the table beside her, considered calling him and rejected the idea.  *Leave it alone*, she thought. *You can do better.*

But she reached for the phone and dialed his number, anyway.

Eric answered on the third ring.  "Hello?"

He was home.  She felt a rush and was about to speak when

something made her change her mind and hang up.   It was ridiculous, childish, and she knew it.  Disappointed with herself, she left for the kitchen.  She wasn't hungry, but she wanted to keep busy, so eating was the logical choice.

She was deep into a carton of choco-chunk ice cream when the doorbell rang.  Diana listened, hoping whoever was there would go away.  She was in no mood for company.  She had firm plans to finish this ice cream and move on to a box of chocolates.

But the doorbell continued to ring.

She went to the door, knowing she looked like hell in her blue jeans and white sweatshirt, but she didn't care.  Whoever was there would have to accept her the way she was.

She opened the door and found Eric Parker holding two champagne glasses in one hand, and a bottle of Cristal in the other.  He smiled the same crooked smile that had won her heart years ago and Diana found herself hating him for it.

"I came to apologize," he said.  "I was an asshole last night and I'm sorry."  He waited for a reply, but Diana stood firm.  "All right," he said, his smile fading a little.  "What do you say about drinks here and then lunch in my apartment?   We can talk things over, I can tell you what's going on with me and Celina, what's going on with me and you, and then--"

Something caught his eye and he turned to the mirror at Diana's right.  Taped to it was one of her lists.   Eric read the first few entries.  He stopped cold at the fourth.  "You really think I walk like I'm constipated?"

"You're so full of shit, how couldn't you?"

In the silence that passed, they looked at each other--and then began to laugh.  Diana stepped aside, motioning for him to walk through.  "It's like allowing a vampire inside," she said.

"That bad?"

"Worse, but I've got a stake in my bedroom, so I'm covered. Have a seat.  You look like hell.  I'll find the Pepto."

## CHAPTER FOURTEEN

Celina reached for the phone and punched numbers.

While she waited for the line to be answered, she moved across the living room, past the cardboard boxes stacked in the center of the room and stepped out onto the terrace.

It was early Sunday morning and the church bells were ringing across Manhattan. She looked up at the high blue sky, felt the surprisingly fresh breeze on her face and watched the sun begin its slow ascent over the city. Although it had been daylight for hours, the sun was just now making its appearance in midtown.

The line continued to ring.  "Come on," she said aloud. "Somebody answer the phone before I lose my nerve."

The line finally clicked.  "Redman residence."

"Carlos?  It's Celina.  Is my father up yet?"

"He is, Miss Redman."

"May I speak with him, please?"

She had called their Connecticut home.  Since she was a child, her parents always spent Sundays in the country.  Some of her favorite memories were shooting skeet with them both on lazy summer afternoons.

It was a moment before George answered.  "Where have you been?" he asked.  "I've been trying to reach you since yesterday afternoon."

She was surprised by the urgency in his voice.  "I've been here," she said.  "But I haven't been answering the phone.  Is something wrong?"

"Wrong?  Yeah, you could say something is wrong. You could say something is very wrong.  Things have fallen all to hell since I last saw you.  How soon can you get here?"

* * *

91

When she arrived at the Connecticut estate, she found George seated alone in the sunlit breakfast room, sipping black coffee, facing the long array of windows before him.

Celina removed her sunglasses and took the chair opposite him. "What's the problem?"

"Our deal with RRK?" George asked. "It no longer exists. I had lunch with them yesterday afternoon and they've backed out on us. We're going to have to find somebody else to finance the deal."

She wasn't that surprised. "Did they give you a reason for backing out?"

"They gave a whole list of reasons," George said. "All them weak"

"You don't think they're going to try a takeover of their own, do you?"

"That would be stupid. RRK knows we have management. They know any hostile bid could be suicidal."

"That may be so," Celina said. "But they also know we have inside information from your contact in the Navy. They know the only reason we want WestTex is because of that information and our deal with Iran. All of that has to be tempting. They could very well make an offer of their own. And don't forget, they've already secured a commitment from Citibank to help with the financing."

George was quiet a moment, thoughtful.

"It could happen," she said. "I'm not saying that it will, but it could and we should be prepared."

"I know it could," George said. "That's why I called Ted Frostman. He and his brother Nick will be here at noon. I figured the four of us could talk over a game of skeet and see if we can work something out. What do you think?"

After the past two days, the last thing Celina wanted to do was caucus with the Frostman brothers over a game of skeet. She said nothing.

George leaned back in his chair. "Spill it," he said. "You left the party early. Your mother and I aren't fools. What's going on?"

She didn't respond.

"There's a reason you haven't been answering your phone and why you're so quiet now. That reason probably has to do with Eric. Did you two have another argument?"

Celina moved to speak, but she didn't want to get into this. Eric was like a son to George. She knew her father hoped they would marry and have children. She knew he hoped that one day they would head the corporation together.

"It's more than that," she said.

George lifted an eyebrow. Celina hesitated, but then she decided she had to tell him at some point and so she told him everything, her words coming in a rush. George spoke only after she was finished.

"Is that all?" he asked.

"Isn't that enough?"

He peered over his glasses. "That's not what I meant, Celina." His voice was calm, but his face was flush.

"I know," she said. "Yes, I guess that's it." She turned to the windows beside her and waited for him to say something comforting. When he didn't, when there was nothing but a heavy stillness between them, she looked at her father and was surprised by the anger she saw in his eyes. George was furious and Celina immediately regretted telling him anything.

"I shouldn't have told you any of this," she said.

"I'm glad you told me."

"No," she said. "It was a mistake."

"Where is Eric now?"

"Dad...."

"Answer me. Is he at home? In his apartment?"

"I don't know. Do you honestly believe I care where he is now?"

"After devoting the past two years of your life to him, yes, I do think you care." He studied her for a moment. "You're probably still in love with him."

"You can't be serious."

"Of course, I'm serious."

"Is your opinion of me that low?"

"My opinion of you has nothing to do with this--"

"It has everything to do with this. I caught Eric in bed with my sister. When you say that you think I'm still in love with him, it makes me look like a fool. I'm no fool, Dad." But even as she said this, she knew her father was right. She was still in love with Eric.

"Look," George said after a moment. "I'll handle Leana and Eric. All right? I'll take care of them myself. But right now, I want you to forget this ever happened."

"Forget this happened?"

"Ted and Nick Frostman will be here at noon. I need you at your best. If they don't feel comfortable with us, they won't feel comfortable with this deal."

So, it was WestTex that mattered.

She pushed back her chair. "You're incredible," she said. She reached for her sunglasses, walked around the table. "I'll talk to you later."

George looked up at her. "What's your problem?"

"Are you serious?" she said. "If you don't know, then it sure as hell isn't worth discussing." She left the room and started walking down the long hallway. She was aware that he was following her.

"Where are you going?" he asked.

She wanted to put distance between them. She quickened her pace. "I don't know," she said. "To the self-help section at Borders? To psychotherapy? Maybe just a drive off a cliff?"

"Would you stop for a minute? Please?"

Celina kept walking until she reached the entryway. And then she stopped.

"I'm sorry," he said. "I don't know what I was thinking."

A thousand thoughts spun through her mind. "You know something, Dad? I called you this morning because you were the only person I could turn to, because I thought you could help. Never once did I think I'd be leaving feeling worse than when I came. I thought our relationship was a hell of a lot more important than any deal we might have with WestTex."

She went down the brick stairs and stepped into her car. George stood in the open doorway and watched her red Mercedes race down the winding cobblestone driveway to the black iron gates that were at the base of the hill.

It hadn't been his intention to hurt her, but he had and he was angry with himself. He could hear the sound of her car coming to a stop. He imagined the gates opening, welcoming her in a way that he hadn't, and then he heard the roar of the engine as the car shot through.

He wondered where she was going. If she didn't come back for the meeting, he couldn't blame her. He stepped back into the house and went to his office.

\* \* \*

Across the room, on his desk, were three telephones. George chose one and dialed Eric's apartment at Redman Place. The line rang several times before it was answered by a woman--a voice George didn't expect or recognize.

She seemed out of breath.

"Yes?" she said.

"I'm sorry," George said. "I must have dialed the wrong number."

"George?"

He hesitated. The voice was vaguely familiar now. Then he recognized it. "Diana?"

"Yes," she said. "And you didn't dial the wrong number. I'm here with Eric." She was talking very fast. "He needed some legal advice on the presentation he's working on for WestTex. I offered to help."

"I should hope so," George said. "That's your job. Could you put Eric on the line, please?"

"Of course."

He listened to the muffled sound of a hand being placed over the receiver. There was a brief exchange of words, then Eric came on the line.

"George," he said. "This is a surprise."

"Is it?" George said. "Then let me give you another. I know what happened the night of the party. Celina told me everything."

Silence.

"I want your ass out of Redman International by tomorrow morning. You're fired. If you're not out by noon, I'll have you charged with trespassing. And then I'll take it a step further."

# FIFTH AVENUE

* * *

He climbed the stairs two at a time.

Leana's bedroom was on the second floor, next to Celina's old bedroom. As he walked down the hallway, he could see the door to her bedroom was closed.

Or so he thought.

When he knocked on the door, it edged slightly open. George waited a moment, called Leana's name twice and entered the room when there was no answer.

Large cardboard boxes filled with his daughter's clothes crowded the center of the room. Empty bureaus stood with their drawers open. Her closets and walls were bare.

As George glanced around, his anger gave way to a curious feeling of loss and regret. The daughter he had never taken the time to know was leaving home.

He moved around the room, glancing at each box as he passed it. She had packed quickly. Her clothes were stuffed into the boxes. It was clear that she planned on leaving here as soon as possible.

And why not? Leana knew there were no secrets between Celina and him. She knew that sooner or later he would confront her with what she had done. Of course she wanted out. Ever since she was a child, she had dodged responsibility. And now, as George stood in the middle of her bedroom, feeling its emptiness almost as surely as he had felt for years his youngest daughter's rage, he decided that if she wanted to be on her own, she would have to do it on her own. Not with his money.

He came down the stairs and found Carlos, their butler, adjusting a flower arrangement in the entryway. He had worked for the Redmans for nearly twenty years.

"Any idea where Leana is, Carlos? She's not in her bedroom." He had a feeling she might be sitting by the pond behind the stables. It's where Leana went when she wanted to be alone.

Carlos looked surprised. "She left last night, Mr. Redman, before you and Mrs. Redman returned from Manhattan. I thought you knew."

"No," George said. "I didn't know. Are you aware that she's moving out?"

"Yes," he said. "She left yesterday. I offered to help carry her bags to her car, but she insisted on doing it herself. Before she left, she told me that she would send for the rest of her things tomorrow. She asked me not to touch anything until then."

Although Carlos would not tell George this, Leana also had hugged and kissed him goodbye. She told him how much he had meant to her over the years. She said that she felt closer to him than to her own father.

"Did she say where she was going?"

"I asked, Mr. Redman, but she wouldn't say."

"You're positive?" George said. "Did she mention Manhattan?" It would be a place to start looking if she had.

"I'm sorry, Mr. Redman. She didn't."

George sighed. "Tell me if she comes home. And if I'm not here when she comes--*if* she comes--see if you can find out where she's living. Leana's always trusted you and it's important that I know."

"Of course--and Mr. Redman?"

"Yes?"

"This is none of my business, but I'm worried about Miss Redman. She wasn't herself when she left here last night."

This was new. In all the years George had known Carlos, he couldn't remember a time when he ever involved himself in a family matter.

"How wasn't she herself?"

Carlos was silent a moment, the memory of seeing Leana when she returned from the party still fresh in his mind. He had been in his room reading when he heard the front door slam shut. Curious, he had slipped into his black alpaca jacket and went to the entryway. There he found Leana, leaning against the door, her clothes tousled and damp from the rain. Her hair wet, stringy. Her face....

"Carlos?"

The man made his decision and said, "It was her face, Mr. Redman. It was bruised and swollen. There were marks at her throat, her eyes were nearly shut and she was bleeding from her mouth. I checked her car, thinking she'd had an accident, but it was fine.  I think she was beaten."

## CHAPTER FIFTEEN

Leana awoke with a start. Someone was pounding on her bedroom door. She lifted her head from the pillow and winced, the sudden movement causing pain to course through her neck, shoulders and back.

She sat up in bed.

Tried to sit up in bed. The movement took unexpected effort and Leana soon found that her entire body ached. *Eric*, she thought.

She laid back down and turned to look at the clock on the bedside table. The red digital numbers were nowhere to be found. Neither was her bedside table. Puzzlement went through her. And then she remembered.

She wasn't in her bedroom. She was in a suite at The Plaza Hotel.

Last night, before leaving home, she phoned The Plaza and reserved one of the permanent suites Redman International kept for visiting guests. It was here that she would stay until she found an apartment of her own.

The hammering on the door intensified. Leana struggled into a seated position and listened. The sound was coming from the next room. Faintly, she could hear a man's voice. "Open the door, Leana. Now."

She felt a chill. It was her father. But how? She had told no one she was here. How did he find out? And then she knew. She was escorted here last evening by the hotel's manager, a friend of her father's. Although he hadn't mentioned her appearance, the look in the man's eyes reflected his concern. Leana made him promise not to tell her father that she was here. She did not want to deal with George and Elizabeth until the time was right. She hoped the man would keep silent longer.

The pounding stopped and Leana heard what sounded like the jangling of keys beyond the locked door. She stood, glimpsed her reflection in the full-length mirror opposite her and turned away.

As she crossed the room, pain shot through her legs and lodged in her hips. Leana moved through it. She would not let her father see what Eric did to her.

Her back was to George when he stepped into the bedroom. There was a silence and Leana could feel George's hesitation, sense the frown on his face as he glanced around the room.

Last night, she unpacked only one of her suitcases. The other two--and some clothes--cluttered the middle of the room.

"What's going on?" he asked. "What is this?"

Leana was standing at one of the bedroom windows and, in the reflection of the glass, she could see George standing behind her, his hands on his hips. They were as alike as two separate people could ever hope to be. They shared the same blue eyes, the same black hair, the same stubborn temperament. She wondered now, as she often did, how two people so alike could never have grown close.

"Answer me," George said. "What is this?"

"What does it look like?" she said. "I've moved out."

"Mind telling me why?"

"I'm sure you've spoken with Celina. You tell me."

"All right," George said. "Your sister says you slept with Eric. She says you planned it so she would catch you two in bed together. Is that true?"

The tone of his voice said it was and Leana bristled. Couldn't he at least have given her the benefit of the doubt?

"I asked if that was true."

"As a matter of fact, it isn't."

"Which part?"

"Both parts."

"I think you'd better explain yourself."

Was it really so difficult for him to believe her? "There's nothing to explain," she said. "Eric and I did nothing. I didn't set Celina up."

"Bullshit," George said. "Celina saw you two in bed together. She spoke to your friend from security. He identified you as the one who gave him that message. Now, admit it."

She whirled on him. "I'll admit nothing," she said. "And I don't give a shit who that man described. It wasn't me."

And then she saw the look of surprise on George's face and

100

realized what she had just done. In her anger, she had revealed what Eric had done to her.

For a moment, George could only stare. The bruises were dark and they crisscrossed Leana's swollen face. Her upper lip was cut. Her tan had all but disappeared.

"Jesus Christ," he said.

Leana turned away from him, suddenly angry with herself. How could she have been so stupid? How would she ever explain this to him?

"He did this to you, didn't he?" George said.

Leana started to walk past him, toward the open door. As much as she wanted to, she could tell her father nothing. Eric's threat was still fresh in her mind. "I don't know what you're talking about," she said.

"Yes, you do," George said. As she passed, he grabbed her by the arm and twisted her around so they faced each other. "Tell me the truth. Eric did this, didn't he?"

"You're hurting me," she said, trying to release herself from him. "Are you going to rough me up too?"

He loosened his grip on her arm. "Just tell me the truth. Don't lie to me."

"So, I'm a liar now? Let go of my fucking arm."

George wouldn't let go. "Why are you protecting that son of a bitch? Tell me what happened. What did he do to you?"

Leana wrenched her arm free and backed away from him. "He did nothing to me. All right? Nothing. Now, leave it alone."

"Not until you tell me what happened."

She looked at him incredulously. "What the hell do you care? You've never cared about me. You don't even love me. Never have."

"Oh, so it's this again."

"That's right," she said. "It's this again. What an inconvenience it must be for you to hear the truth."

"Your truth."

"Whatever," she said. "It's always been Celina and you know it. But here's the thing, Dad--it stops now. Stay out of my life. I don't want you in it. You bring me down."

George flushed. "You've got a lot of nerve talking to me like that."

"I could say the same for the way I was raised."

"Right," he said. "Everyone should have it as bad as you've had it, Leana. A nice home, the best clothes and schools. Everything you've ever had was the best that money could buy."

"You and your fucking money," she said. "Is that all you're about? Who gives a shit about your money? It's always been you that I wanted, not the damn home, clothes or schools. It's never been any of that. All I ever wanted was your attention. Maybe a sign that I mattered to you. But you were never willing to give it to me. You were always too preoccupied with your business. And your money. And Celina. Let's not forget her."

George regarded his daughter for a moment. He felt angry and hurt, guilty and sad, and he knew it was because Leana was speaking the truth. He wasn't a good father to her--never had been. Just a good provider--that's it.

He left for the adjoining room. Nothing could be solved here now. The air was dirty. "I'm leaving," he said.

Leana followed him to the door. "Good."

"Don't sound so happy," George said. "You're leaving, too." He opened the door and Leana saw two uniformed bellhops waiting in the hall. It was clear by the embarrassment on their young faces that they heard most of the argument.

"Her luggage is in the bedroom," George said to the men, stepped aside so they could retrieve it. He looked at Leana. She was standing with her back to a window, her arms folded, her head lifted just slightly too high. She paid no attention to the bellhops as they crossed in front of her. Her attention was on George.

"You have two options," George said. "You can either have the luggage placed in your car and follow me home--where you belong--or you can hand over the keys to your car, the key to this room and have the luggage brought to the lobby, because you're not staying here. If you want to be on your own, Leana, then you'll have to do it on your own--not with my help. The decision's yours."

Without hesitation, Leana turned to the table beside her and reached for her purse. She retrieved her car keys and the hotel key, and tossed them to her father. Her face was expressionless as she watched him pick them up.

George pocketed the keys. "You're making a mistake," he said.

"That's a matter of opinion."

"No," George said. "That's a matter of fact." He nodded toward her purse. "Hand over your credit cards. I want all of them."

Leana did as she was told, feeling curiously liberated as she emptied the cards from her wallet and handed them over to him. She also took out her cash and tossed it at his feet. He didn't think that she could make it on her own? Fine. She'd show him and everyone else that she could.

George asked the bellhops to pick up the cash and keep it. "I know you have money in the bank," he said to Leana. "There's nothing I can do about that. But I also happen to know it isn't much and you'll soon run out. Maybe then, when you really have nothing, you'll realize just how good you've had it and come home."

"I'm never coming home."

The finality of her words and the cool tone of her voice struck him like a fist. Did she realize what she was saying? How would she make it without him? She hadn't worked a day in her life. "You say that now because you're angry."

"Could your ego get any bigger? Listen closely. I say that now because I'm sick of you, I'm sick of coming in second and because I mean it."

"We'll see," George said. He turned to the bellhops as they re-entered the room. "See to it that she leaves here," he said to the men, and then he was gone, through the door, without looking back.

"I'll need a few minutes," Leana said to the bellhops. "Would you mind bringing back the bags and waiting for me in the hall so I can change? I won't be long."

When she was alone, she sank into a nearby chair and closed her eyes. She felt drained and exhausted. Her father was gone. After all these years, she finally told him how she felt. She finally stood up to him. She should be happy, but she wasn't. She felt like crying.

But she wouldn't cry. She made her decision and she would stick to it. It was time the rest of the world learned that George

Redman had another daughter.  It was time that her father and mother saw what she was capable of.  Leana was determined to make a success of herself--and she would do it without her father's help, without her father's money.  Unlike Celina.

In the bathroom, she ran a brush through her hair, changed into a faded pair of jeans and an oversized white silk shirt, and applied enough makeup to hide the bruises on her cheeks and the base of her nose.  Those around her eyes she concealed with dark sunglasses.  There was nothing she could do about the cut on her lip.  It was small, but it showed.

When she joined the men in the hall, she thanked them for waiting.  They retrieved her bags and she followed them to an elevator.  When they reached the lobby, Leana asked the men to put her bags in a cab while she used a phone.  She had to call Harold Baines.  At the opening of Redman International, he mentioned something about helping her find a job.  Now, she realized that his contacts could be invaluable.

When Harold answered, she told him what happened and asked if she could use one of his guest bedrooms.  "But only until I find a place of my own," she said.  "Yes, I'm all right.  I'll tell you everything when I see you."  She paused.  "And Uncle Harold? Please don't tell Dad that I'll be staying with you.  For once in his life, I want him to worry about me--if that's even possible."

The day was warm and sunny when she left The Plaza.  A breeze ruffled her hair and felt good against her skin.  As Leana came down the stairs and stepped into the waiting cab, she apologized to the bellhops for not having any money to tip them, thanked them for their trouble and left for Harold's townhouse--oblivious to Vincent Spocatti, who was following her in a cab of his own.

## CHAPTER SIXTEEN

"She's staying with Harold Baines. I followed her there myself."

Louis Ryan turned in his chair and watched Spocatti cross the Aubusson rug that led to his desk. For a man who killed people for a living, Louis thought Spocatti dressed and carried himself unusually well. His suits were handmade for him in Italy, his shoes were fitted for him in London. The man moved easily, almost gracefully, despite his muscular bulk.

"And you have someone there watching her now?" Louis asked.

"I have two men," Spocatti said. "Baines lives in a townhouse on the corner of 81st and Fifth. One man is stationed just outside The Met, watching the front entrance. The other is in a van on 81st Street, watching the side entrance and eavesdropping with a directional microphone. The device has an ultra-frequency function that picks up telephone conversations. Everything is linked to a digital recorder. She won't say a word or make a move without our knowing it."

Satisfied, Louis nodded. "You're certain she's staying with him. She could just be paying him a visit."

"She's staying with him," Spocatti said. "I was standing near her when she phoned Baines from the lobby. She asked if she could stay in his guest bedroom until she found a place of her own. I have a feeling they're close."

"How close is close?"

"Father-daughter close. She called him Uncle Harold on the phone and they spent a lot of time with each other at the party."

Louis considered this for a moment. He had met Harold Baines years ago, while at a dinner party for the mayor. Despite the fact that Baines spoke eight languages and was VP of International Affairs for one of the world's leading conglomerates, the man participated in little conversation. He spoke only to those on either side of him--his best friends, George and Elizabeth

Redman.

He thought back to other times he had seen Harold Baines--at functions, banquets and parties. Each time, the man kept to himself and his wife.

"You saw Baines at the opening of Redman International," Louis said. "What's your opinion of him?"

Vincent shrugged. "I only noticed him while he was with Leana, but he seemed to be having a fine time. He and Leana danced--I remember he spun her around the dance floor once-- and they laughed and had a drink afterward."

"So, he was outgoing?"

"Very much so. Why?"

"Each time I've seen Baines, the man has been anything but outgoing. In fact, he's always been completely withdrawn."

"That's not the Harold Baines I saw," Spocatti said. "But maybe he knew he was expected to have his party hat on."

"Maybe."

"Want me to run a check on him?"

"If he's as close to Leana as you say he is, it couldn't hurt," Louis said. "Put your best man on him and tell him to dig."

"Anything else?"

"That depends. Are she and Baines talking now?"

"I can call and find out."

Louis nodded toward the phone on his desk.

"So, call."

Spocatti reached into his jacket pocket and pulled out a cell phone. He dialed. Louis moved to the windows behind him. The sun, not yet above the towering skyscrapers, cast the city in shadow. He checked his watch. Soon, Michael would arrive for their meeting. He wondered how his son would react once told what was expected from him next.

Vincent snapped the phone shut. "They're talking," he said. "And I think you might be interested in what they're talking about."

"What's that?"

"It appears that more went on the night of the party than I originally thought."

"Go on."

"Eric Parker beat Leana Redman with a belt. Her face is a

mess."

"He beat her with a belt?"

"Like her sister, he thinks Leana gave me that message. He accused her of setting him up, of destroying his relationship with Celina." Spocatti shrugged. "He was drunk, he lost control, he took it out on her face."

Louis shook his head. "Redman saw his own daughter like that and still he kicked her out of The Plaza?" He laughed. "What a bastard. Didn't he at least question what happened to her?"

"He did more than question it," Spocatti said. "Redman asked her if Eric Parker was responsible, but Leana's not talking. It seems that Parker threatened to have a contract put out on her if anything happened to him. The guy's smart. If he hadn't threatened her, his ass would be in jail."

"How did Baines react to all this?"

"He's furious. I told you, Leana's like a daughter to him. He wants Parker to pay for what he's done."

"What do you think he'll do?"

"Nothing," Vincent said. "Baines promised to keep quiet. He'll keep his word."

"He'd better," Louis said. "Because if he becomes more involved than he already is, he's going down with the rest of them."

There was a knock at the office door. Michael. Louis called for him to come in. The door swung open and Michael stepped inside. He hesitated in the doorway and looked across the room at Spocatti, then at his father. He obviously thought they'd be alone. Louis wondered how Michael would react if he knew that it was Spocatti who butchered his dog. *Probably not pleasantly.*

He made introductions. "This is Vincent Spocatti. He'll be working with us."

Spocatti took a few steps forward and shook Michael's hand. "It's a pleasure," he said. "I've read most of your books." And then his smile faded into a grimace. "Sorry to hear what happened to your dog. Your father told me. Terrible thing."

Louis caught Michael's glance and motioned toward the chair opposite his desk. Later, he'd tell Spocatti to keep his mouth shut. "Why don't you sit down, Michael?" he said. "This won't take long."

107

"Was it bad?" Spocatti asked. "I mean, about the dog?"

Michael turned to leave. Louis glared at Spocatti and called Michael back.

"Please," he said. "Vincent is just concerned. He has a dog of his own. I promise this won't take long. I know you have other things to do. Would you like coffee?"

Michael would have loved coffee--but not from this man. He shook his head and sat reluctantly in the leather chair.

Louis turned to Spocatti. "How about you? Do you want coffee?"

"I'd love some."

"I thought so." He pressed a button and spoke into an intercom. "Judy, would you bring us two black coffees?"

"I take cream and sugar in mine," Spocatti said.

"Today you don't."

Louis sat at his desk and looked up when Judy arrived with the coffee. She was wearing a crisp white suit that accented her trim figure, and the new diamond bracelet he gave her that morning. As she poured, Louis could smell the faint, lingering scent of her perfume. It reminded him of the perfume Anne used to wear.

When she left, Louis looked across the desk at Michael. The resemblance to his mother was uncanny. From the dark hair to the blue eyes to the square jaw line--it was all the same.

"I telephoned Santiago earlier this morning," he said to Michael. "We've worked out a deal."

Michael straightened. "What kind of deal? What did he say?"

Louis gauged his words carefully. "Among other things, he said he had nothing to do with your dog."

"And you believe that?"

"No," Louis said. "I'm sure Santiago is responsible. I'm also sure it would have been you lying dead on that floor if you hadn't been here talking with me. We can all be thankful for that."

Michael dismissed his father's concern. "What's the deal?"

"In exchange for my word that he'll get his money, he's willing to let you live...for a while, at least."

"What does that mean?"

"It means that I haven't given him my word that he'll get his money--at least not yet. Right now, you're living on borrowed time. A little less than three weeks to be exact. But I wouldn't count on even that much, Michael. After what happened to your dog, I think its safe to assume that Santiago can't be trusted."

"Can you? If I do what you ask, will you give him the money?"

"Of course."

"How come I doubt that?"

"Probably for the same reason I doubt whether you'll complete your end of the bargain. We've been apart too long, Michael. We don't know each other."

"This is some way to get to know each other."

A shadow of anger crossed Louis' face. "I never asked you to leave, Michael. Until your first novel came out, I didn't know where you were living, how you were, or if you were even alive. You dropped me for sixteen years, you changed your name and now, after all this time, you come asking me for help. Don't think you're going to get it without helping me. It doesn't work that way."

*Of course, it doesn't.* "Tell me what you want from me."

"You already know what I expect you to do to George Redman."

Michael said nothing.

"But before that happens, there's something else I want you to do."

"And what is that?"

Louis locked eyes with his son.

"I want you to marry Leana Redman."

# FIFTH AVENUE

## CHAPTER SEVENTEEN

"If you won't stay here permanently, then, for God's sake, Leana, at least let me give you some money. You'll never find a decent apartment in this city with what little you've managed to save over the years. Do you want to live in a dump?"

"If I have to, yes."

Harold Baines made a face and turned away from the window at which he was standing. The early afternoon sun cast a warm glow against his graying hair, the checked shirt he wore, the khaki pants. He sighed. "This new-found pride and determination of yours is wearing me out. Do you want a drink?"

"Too early for me."

"Not for me. I'm going to recreate one of your martinis. Sure you won't join me?"

Leana said she was sure and watched her father's best friend cross to the bar at the opposite end of the library. He seemed thinner to her. At the opening of The Redman International Building, he looked exhausted one moment, vibrant the next. She wondered again if he was ill or if the strain of acquiring WestTex was just taking its toll on him. She was going to bring it up but then thought better of it and allowed her gaze to sweep the library. This was, by far, her favorite room in this house.

Its great length of floor-to-ceiling windows looked out across Fifth to the entire Met, which was jammed with people on the wide expanse of steps, now golden in the sun. Turning, she noted the many photographs in silver frames that rested on the table beside her. Besides the pictures of his own family, two photographs were of her--one as a child, the other taken last summer at a Paris cafe. It had been just her and Harold on that trip, a long weekend in their favorite city.

Next to the photo was the Degas sculpture she had purchased for him at auction in London. It was of a ballerina, her feet in the fifth position, her hands cupped behind her back, the original pink ribbon in her hair. A week before the auction, Harold remarked that he would love to own that particular sculpture because it reminded him of her when she studied ballet as a child. Now, as Harold took the seat opposite her, Leana realized again just how much he meant to her, and how she felt more at home here than in her own home.

"I want you to see a doctor," Harold said.

"I could ask the same of you."

"What's that supposed to mean?"

"It means you don't look well. I told you that the night of the party."

"And I remember telling you I was fine."

"Then explain your weight loss."

"I was getting fat," he said. "And don't tell me you didn't notice. I'm cutting back on everything but martinis and olives. And then there's the deal with WestTex, which has us all pushed against the wall. Who has time to eat?"

She decided she could believe that and backed off. "I just worry," she said.

"And I'm glad you do, but now it's my turn to worry about you. You're my main concern right now. I want you to see a doctor."

"They're just bruises. They'll fade in a week or so."

He shook his head in frustration. "Are you a robot?" he asked. "Has somebody clipped the wires in your brain? I can't believe how you're taking this. The man beats the hell out of you with a belt and you sit there like Little Miss Sunshine telling me the bruises will fade in a week or so. It's unbelievable. Aren't you even angry?"

The question was ridiculous.

"He tried raping you," Harold persisted. "Probably would have killed you if you had given him the chance."

"He also threatened to have a contract put out on me. Do you need to be reminded of that?"

Harold waved a hand. "Eric Parker doesn't have the balls to do something like that."

"And what if he did? You weren't there, Harold. I saw his face. He meant it."

"Bullshit," he said. "That little prick is a pussy."

"Okay," she said. "You've mentioned balls, prick and pussy

over the course of ten seconds. Could you pick more agreeable body parts?"

He knew she was trying to lighten the mood, but Harold was having none of it. He stood and fixed himself another drink, even though he hadn't finished his first.

Leana looked out a window. Why couldn't he understand? She was trying her best to deal with this. She was trying to do what she thought was right. Harold should be proud of her, not angry. "Eric will pay for what he did to me," she said. "Celina will see to that. And if she doesn't, one day I will. But you made a promise and I expect you to keep it. No one, especially my father, is to know what happened to me."

Harold sat back down. "Your father isn't a fool, Leana--he saw you. He already knows. But if he asks me if I know anything, you have my word--I'll play dumb." He changed the subject. "Tell me about your financial situation."

"It's taken care of," Leana said. "Tomorrow morning, I'm going to Mom's jeweler on Park to sell what jewelry I've kept in a safe-deposit box. It'll be enough." She thought of her finest piece of jewelry, the diamond and Mogok ruby necklace, and smiled. "Actually, it'll be plenty. One necklace alone should net a high six-figures."

Harold hadn't known about this. "Do you have anything else you can sell?" If she did, it would put his mind at ease. The thought of the girl living someplace unsafe worried him.

"There's some jewelry back at the house that's mine--but it's in Dad's safe."

"Do you know the combination?"

"I do."

"Then I suggest you take a cab there this afternoon and get what you can. The jewelry is yours, after all, and you won't have to worry about a confrontation with your father. He called earlier. He's meeting with Ted Frostman this afternoon and hopes to strike a deal with him over a game of skeet. He'll never even see you."

"Mom might."

Harold hadn't thought of that. When upset, Elizabeth could be more unreasonable than George. "That's true," he said. "Maybe you should wait. But not for too long. It would be just like George to put the jewelry in another safe, one you don't know the combination to. And that, Leana, is something you can't afford to let happen."

Later, after lunch, he followed Leana to the door. "Don't sit in the park for too long," he warned. "The sun's at its strongest now. You'll burn."

"I tan, Uncle Harold."

"Not in this heat, you won't," he said. "Now, not another word. I'm your father while you're staying with me and you'll do as you're told." He winked at her and they stepped outside, oblivious to the photographs being taken of them from the van across the street. Sensitive microphones recorded their conversation.

"When will you be back?" he asked.

Leana shrugged. "A couple of hours? I just need to be alone and get my head on straight." She lifted the book he gave her. "If this is as good as you say it is, I might be longer."

"Not too long, though."

Leana kissed him on the forehead. His skin seemed unusually warm to her and yet the house was air-conditioned. "You can reach me on my cell. I'll be fine." She touched his cheek with the back of her hand. "Are you sure you're okay? You feel warm."

Harold sighed. "I'm perfect."

*　*　*

Leana had no intention of reading in the park or anywhere else. She had an appointment to keep and she was determined to be on time.

The man she was meeting would have it no other way.

When she was far enough down the avenue and certain Harold could no longer see her, she slipped the book he gave her into the straw handbag that hung at her side, hailed a cab and asked the driver to take her to the meat-packing district.

Traffic was heavy. It seemed an eternity before they reached 14th Street. Leana looked out the cab's open window and saw sleek stores and restaurants where condemned tenement buildings and old warehouses used to be.

Gone were the groups of people in various stages of undress looking for the best deal on heroin, coke, meth and crack. In their place was the hip set. Years ago, when she was still underage, she used to steal down here and go to the gay nightclubs with her friends. It was one of the best times of her life--the clubs were epic in the music they played and the sexual mood they struck. She could go there and dance with some of the hottest men in the city knowing they wanted nothing more from her than to turn it out on the dance floor. And now the bars were mostly gone.

*Fucking Guiliani.*

She paid the cabbie and walked to the end of the block, where there was a group of smartly dressed women moving in her direction and likely going for lunch. A van was parked at the street corner. A woman with a screaming child was doing her best to ignore the tantrum. Leana did as she was told and waited at the corner for five minutes before she hailed another cab and asked the driver to take her to a location on Avenue A. She wasn't sure why this was necessary, but she knew he had his reasons and so she just went with it.

When she arrived at the agreed upon spot, it was one-thirty and she was in a different world, one far away from Fifth. She stepped out of the cab and couldn't help feeling uneasy. The air seemed heavier here and it smelled of the rot coming from the deep piles of trash stacked high along the sidewalk.

She looked at the children playing in the street and wondered what kind of life they would live? With their parents living on welfare and spending their money on drugs and alcohol instead of food and clothing, how would they ever get ahead?

And there it was, right in front of her, the reason he asked to meet here. It was so she would be reminded again of the other side of Manhattan--the side he always accused her of turning her back on.

She thought back to the last day they'd seen each other. It was two years ago, they were walking up Fifth and he shouted that all this was an illusion. The expensive shops, the well-dressed men and women bustling past them on the sidewalk, the horse-drawn carriages parked alongside The Plaza.

This wasn't the life most people knew, certainly not his own. This was about as far from that as she was from reality.

# FIFTH AVENUE

"You want to know what reality is for my people, Leana?" he asked. "Reality is wondering where your next meal is going to come from. Or how you're going to pay next month's rent. Or whether your mother or father will wake drunk the next morning and drag your sorry ass into the same fight they've been having for years--the one that always has to deal with money." He saw the disinterest on her face and reached for her hand. "Let me show you what I mean."

They crossed over to Madison and took a cab uptown--toward Harlem. Leana didn't want to be doing any of this. She looked out a window and saw the expensive boutiques giving way to decrepit tenement buildings; the expensively dressed people to homeless men and women.

She couldn't remember a time when she'd been this far north. When they passed 135th Street, Mario asked the driver to cross over to Fifth Avenue. "We'll get off there," he said. "Where she's comfortable.

Leana turned away from the window as the cab slowed to a stop. "I'm not getting out here."

Mario paid the driver and opened her door. "Yes, you are," he said. "It's Fifth Avenue. Remember? Now, move."

They walked down a street that was not swept clean, but littered with garbage. They passed groups of men and women who didn't have the air of affluence, but poverty. They passed gang members and drug dens, pregnant children and their young boyfriends. And then Leana became aware that she and Mario were the only Caucasian people in sight.

The area was a melting pot of Haitians, Chinese, African Americans, Puerto Ricans, Thais, Cubans, Koreans and Albanians. It was the Third World up here. She reached for Mario's hand and held it tightly in her own. They were approaching a huddle of women. All were middle-aged, poor and angry at the system that had failed them. Their eyes seemed to devour her as she drew closer.

Leana wondered why she felt so threatened. She had done nothing to these women. Their hardships weren't her fault. She should be able to look them straight in the eye.

But she only glanced at them as she passed.

"Seen enough?"

115

Leana saw the sarcastic smile on his lips, the hint of mocking in his eyes and dropped his hand. "I've seen enough," she said. "But let me ask you something, Mario--where do you get off judging me when your Family with a capital fucking F is known to kill people for a living?"

Mario's face flushed. "What my family does has nothing to do with me."

"Exactly," Leana said. "What my father does has nothing to do with me. So you can shove your condescending attitude up your ass, because I'm sick and tired of you telling me how spoiled and shallow I am when you're no better than me."

"I've never said you were spoiled or shallow."

"Maybe not in words, but your actions sure as hell have." She stepped away from him, flagged a cab and was gone before he could say another word. They hadn't spoken since.

Now, looking at these children and knowing what the future held for them, Leana regretted all of it. There was a time when she could have just drawn from the bank account her father kept full for her and written a check to alleviate a good deal of this. And yet she hadn't. Why hadn't she? *And what will Mario think of me now?*

He was on time, of course. In the distance, she saw his car coming down the street and wasn't surprised to find that it was the same car he had two years ago. Here was a man who could own a fleet of Ferraris--and yet he drove a simple black Ford Taurus.

He pulled alongside her. Leana adjusted her sunglasses, hoping the bruises didn't show around her eyes. She knew they did--but just barely--on her face. She didn't want him to see them. At least not yet.

He stepped out of the car, looked at her with that sideways grin of his, and she felt the same thrill she had felt years ago, when they met at a mutual friend's dinner parry. He looked the same. His hair was as thick, dark and as curly as hers. It was just a tad too long, but it helped to softened the squareness of his jaw. His body--that body--seemed more athletic than ever. Mario De Cicco, son of Antonio Gionelli De Cicco, capo di capi of the New York Syndicate, was just as hot as she remembered.

He came around the car and embraced her tightly, kissing her once on each cheek. "It's good to see you," he said. "It's been...what? A year?"

"Two years," she said. "And a lot's happened."

"Then let's go and catch up over lunch. I want you to tell me everything--especially why there are bruises on your face."

As they were leaving, Mario looked around him. "Isn't this place great?" he said. "I chose it just for you."

"What a surprise."

He pointed to one of the tenements across the street. "That's a crack house," he said. "Condemned. Last week, a woman smothered her nine-week-old child there because she was hiding from the cops and didn't want the baby's crying to tip them off. When the cops left, she smoked what crack she had left and dropped the baby into a trash can. It was an elderly woman searching for food who found it. Thank God it was alive."

He looked at Leana. "So, how are things on Fifth?"

Leana fastened her safety-belt. She wouldn't take this lying down. "Everything's shit," she said. "The recession has buried Barney's below Filene's basement. People are reduced to renting the latest Louis instead of buying it. Real estate is in the can--a $30 million penthouse now goes for $20 million. Can you imagine? It's a horror show. The only good news is that now you have no trouble getting a table wherever, whenever." She smiled at him. "Speaking of food, I'm famished. How about that lunch?"

"Fair enough," he said. "I'll treat you to a po-boy."

As they pulled away from the curb, the van that was parked at the street corner followed.

## CHAPTER EIGHTEEN

The bar at Mario's was three-deep in people. Some were watching the Yankees game on the television above the bar. Others were talking excitedly among themselves. It wasn't a large restaurant--it seated only seventy--but the atmosphere was warm, the food was good and the staff was trained to the point of remembering names.

Nestled on Third Avenue, its clientele ranged from the average blue-collar worker to the heads of corporations. When Leana and Mario entered the restaurant, there was a brief lull in the conversation as all turned and said hello to Mario, their faces bright with smiles and respect.

Leana was aware of being watched as they followed a heavyset, dark-haired woman to a back table, which was covered with a plain white tablecloth, simple dishes and flatware. This was clearly Mario's table, Leana thought. It was understated, but positioned so it overlooked the entire restaurant.

Although she felt foolish for keeping them on, she didn't remove her sunglasses.

Mario ordered a bottle of wine. "We'll order lunch later," he said to his Aunt Rosa, winking at her as she left. He noticed Leana looking around the restaurant and asked if she approved.

"It's beautiful," Leana said. "And obviously a success. When did you buy it? You didn't have it when we were together, did you?"

"I bought it last Christmas," he said. "The family needed a place where they could eat in peace, so I opened Mario's. This way, there are no problems."

She decided not to ask what he meant by that. She was glad to see Rosa bringing the wine and happier still when she and Mario fell into conversation. For the next thirty minutes, they talked and drank, recalling things they had forgotten about their affair. It lasted only six months, but it had been powerful.

When Rosa returned, Mario ordered for them. When she left,

he asked Leana if the police learned who rigged the spotlights.

"I wouldn't know," she said.

"You sound as if you couldn't care less."

"That's because I couldn't care less."

"Still having problems at home, huh?"

"Is that even a question?"

She lifted her glass of wine and sipped. There was a time when she told Mario things about her family that she only shared with Harold. They were that close. Mario's understanding, his support and the fact that he didn't judge those feelings was one of the reasons she fell in love with him.

"I moved out of the house last night. I've decided to give it a shot on my own."

Mario looked surprised. "Where's your apartment?"

"I'm staying with friends."

"You moved out of your house without having a place of your own to move into?" His leaned back in his chair. "All right," he said. "Why don't you tell me what's going on and how it's connected to the cut on your lip, the bruises on your face--and those you're trying to hide around your eyes? You called me for a reason. I want to know what it is and how I can help."

Leana removed her glasses and told him everything. She told him what Eric Parker did to her. And she told him about her father's reaction and ultimatum. When she was finished, Mario's anger mirrored her own.

"I've thought a lot about this," she said. "I've thought about the threat Eric made me and I've thought about the consequences. But I can't let him get away with what he did to me--contract or no contract. I'm sure my father will fire him, but that's not enough. Eric will just get a job elsewhere and that will be that."

"It doesn't have to be that way," he said.

"I want him to hurt as much as he hurt me."

"And he should."

"I can't do it alone," she said. "Obviously. Just look at me. Will you help?"

"You had my help the moment he did this to you."

She put her hand on his. "I've got Harold and now I have you. There have been times, over the years, that I've really missed you and regretted ending what we had."

"We can always start over, you know?"

She looked at him with sadness. "I know," she said. "But you're still married, Mario, and I told you once that I'd never come second in your life again. Right now I need you to be my friend. Can you do that?"

He put his thumb over the back of her hand. "I can do that," he said.

\* \* \*

"Will you be needing your car, Mr. Baines?"

Harold descended the mahogany staircase and smiled at the short, gray-haired man standing in the entryway of his townhouse.

"Not necessary, Ted. I'm going for a walk."

He stepped into his office, which was at the foot of the stairs and retrieved the leather briefcase he placed there earlier. He locked the door behind him when he left.

"When Helen gets back from her lunch date, would you tell her that I won't be home for dinner? After my walk, I have a business dinner. I'll be late."

"Of course, Mr. Baines."

When he left his apartment, Harold turned onto 81st Street. A limousine was waiting for him at the street corner. He stepped inside and told the driver to hurry.

Traffic lurched, stopped and lurched all the way to the Lower East Side. The driver shot through two red lights and came close to busting a third. Harold smoothed his hands over the briefcase and closed his eyes. He was only dimly aware of the horns blaring around them. The driver slowed to a stop in front of a building near Houston.

Harold looked out a window and watched a scene that was so far removed from his life on Fifth Avenue, it disquieted him.

People were scoring crack, dealing crack, doing crack. He saw an elderly woman slump against the side of a deserted bus and tie a rubber tube to her upper arm. He looked away before she could inject the heroin and glanced at the building that was to his right.

He checked the address to make sure this was the correct place, saw that it was and told the driver to return in three hours.

"Wait for me if I'm not here," he said to the man, and stepped out of the car just in time to see a van and two Bentleys slowing to a stop in front of him. Harold thought the cars looked ridiculous here. It wasn't often that this part of town saw automobiles worth $500,000.

But that was part of the fun.

He entered the building. Inside, leaning against a yellowing wall, was a tall, dark-haired man dressed in tight black leather pants and nothing else. He was handsome and built, his face and chest clean-shaven, his nipples pierced.

The man lit a joint, inhaled deeply, held the smoke and exhaled it in Harold's face. Nothing was going to hurry him.

He cocked his head towards the briefcase in Harold's hand. "That your membership card?"

Harold nodded.

"Then hand it over."

Harold did as he was told and parted with ten thousand dollars.

He walked up a flight of stairs. The lights were dim and trippy dance music pounded down at him from the floor above. Faintly, he could hear someone screaming, then laughing, then crying. A woman...?

He climbed the stairs faster, the familiar rush of excitement beginning to flood his senses. The second floor was an empty shell. The windows were closed and blackened with spray paint. The track lights were soft spots of red that strobed in time with the music. Metal cages filled with naked, writhing bodies acted as walls. The air was a heady mixture of alcohol and sweat.

Harold joined a line of men and women removing their clothes and handing them over to the clothes check. He recognized a famous actor, the CEO of a powerful conglomerate, a U.S. Senator, two priests. He began unbuttoning his shirt.

The place was crowded. He moved naked through the room, nodding at men with secrets, with pasts--men like himself.

In one of the steel cages, a man was wrapped in plastic from head to foot. Soon his master would start the bandaging. Beyond the steel cage was a wading pool filled with urine. In it lay a woman on her back who was staring up at the circle of ten men masturbating above her. She snapped at their cocks with a whip, waited impatiently for them to explode on top of her. In shadowy corners, solitary men high on whatever drug was circulating preened, posed and prowled. And finally, in the last steel cage, was Harold's reason for being there.

The man standing beside the black leather sling was naked save for the executioner's hood he wore. He was tall and grossly overweight, his back and chest covered with coarse dark hair. A single latex glove was stretched up his right arm. It glistened with lubricant.

Harold had reserved him specifically for the thickness of his forearms.

He nodded at the man as he approached. As he settled himself into the sling, thoughts of Helen, George and Leana shot through his mind. He thought of his three kids, of his life at Redman International. And then he winced as the man's fingers-- then fist and forearm--began forcing its way inside of him.

He began to perspire. His eyes watered. He felt a sudden flash of guilt and was about to stop this when the man held a coke inhaler to his nostril.

Harold met the man's gaze and breathed in deeply. There was a medicinal rush and he nearly gagged. He hadn't snorted cocaine since the night of the party--just moments before he danced with Leana. The fact that she had noticed a change in him and suspected something was still too difficult and terrifying for him to believe. If anyone learned of his other life, Harold wasn't sure what he would do.

The man twisted his fist and shoved it further in. "I can feel your heart beating, pig," he said. "Want me to stop it?"

Harold took another hit off the inhaler. And another. He felt no pain now, only a sweet, gray, misty bliss. This wasn't just coke. It was laced with something else. Harold welcomed it. He started to float.

He focused on the man standing above him and saw only his dark eyes framed by the black hood. Harold thought they were the most beautiful eyes he had ever seen. He tried lifting a hand to remove the hood, but in spite of the floating sensation, his arm was oddly heavy and he could lift it only a few inches from the sling.

Over and over again, the man was saying: "...like to get fucked, don't you...like to get fucked, don't you...like to get...."

Harold closed his eyes. He was sailing now, his body on a higher plain as the man's arm went elbow-deep. He had waited four weeks for this, four long weeks, and he was pleased to be here, happy to have spent the money. It was all worth it.

\* \* \*

"How'd you like me to ram my cock up your ass?"

Standing at the rear of the dimly lit room, his back to one of the metal cages, Vincent Spocatti turned away from Harold Baines only long enough to look at the woman standing beside him. She was tall, fit and attractive. In this light, her hair was red and it curled around the tips of her naked breasts.

"My dick is big," the woman said. "The priest loved it. It'll make you scream."

He was aware of the woman's hand moving between her legs. Spocatti looked down and saw the enormous dildo jutting from her vagina. It was black and slick with lubricant and God knows what else. Her hand stroked it in time with the music.

"You've got rhythm," he said.

"I've got more than that."

"Talent?"

"I've been told that."

"Too bad I need to pass," he said. "I prefer to be shit on--by men." He ran a finger along his lower lip. "I like a brown mouth."

"No worries," she said. "I'm not into that, anyway. I hear Frank's good at it, though."

"Who is Frank?"

"The guy squatting over that man's mouth over there."

Spocatti looked through the gloom, caught the scene. "Promising."

"He has a good rep."

And she had a sophisticated air about her. Though she was trying for the gutter, the tone of her voice carried with it a whiff of privilege.  He wondered who she was when she wasn't just the pretty woman with the fake cock jutting from her vagina.  He nodded toward Harold, who was writhing, peaking.  "I think my friend over there would love to have a piece of you."

The woman squinted through the flickering red light.  When she saw Harold, recognition flashed on her face and her hand stopped caressing the rubber penis.  She stared at Harold.

"Your friend is an asshole," she said.  "Two months ago, he pissed in my mouth after I told him not to."

Spocatti felt a spark.  "Just the piss?"

"That's right.  He strapped me to that fucking sling and pissed in my mouth.  I can handle plenty, but not piss.  It crosses a line.  It's not for me."

"We all have our limits.  How long ago was this?"

The woman shrugged.  "I don't know. Two months ago?"

"How often does he come here?"

"*Here?*"  She looked at him quizzically.  "This is our first time here."  She tilted her head.  "Are you new to this?"

Spocatti admitted he was.

"We move around a lot," she said.  "Have they told you that?"

"Not yet," he said.  "The other group I belong to has one specific place they meet."  He let a beat of silence pass.  "How often have you seen him in places like this?"

"You make our club sound like a disease."

"That's not what I meant--"

"Are you a cop?"

"No," Spocatti said.  "I'm definitely not a cop."

"You'd have to tell me if you were."

"I'm not a cop."

"Then why all the questions?  What is this?  A fucking inquisition?"

He was about to speak when she held up a hand.  "Never mind," she said.  "I don't want to know."  She removed the dildo from her vagina and pointed it at Harold Baines.  "I've been a member of this club for years now--and so has he."

She turned to leave.  "If you don't mind, I'm going find somebody who came here to fuck, not talk."

As she walked away, Spocatti glanced with bemusement around the room, seeing things he'd only heard about, only read about, but had never actually seen.   The thought that these people, these members of New York society, had paid actual money to come here was laughable to him.

To gain entrance, all Vincent had to do was show the doorman his gun.

He returned his attention to Harold Baines.   The man was moaning now, his head lolling from side to side.  Spocatti checked his watch and wondered how much longer Baines would be.   He hoped not too much longer.   Vincent wanted to tell Louis Ryan everything by nightfall.

## CHAPTER NINETEEN

The young man who worked for Redman Place glanced down at the three cardboard boxes stacked in the entryway of Celina's apartment.  He picked up two, calculated their weight to be around sixty pounds apiece, looked at the rest and then looked back at her.  "He came back from Redman International an hour ago.  I just finished helping him carry a bunch of boxes up to his apartment?"

Curiosity flickered in Celina's eyes.  What would Eric be doing at Redman International on a Sunday?  "How many boxes?"

"Eight?"

"Do you know what was in them?"

The young man shrugged.  "Office supplies?"

"Office supplies?"

"Maybe not.  I don't know.  I only caught a glimpse."  He looked at his watch.  "Look, Miss Redman, if I'm going to deliver these boxes to him, I should probably get going.  My break's over in another ten minutes."

Celina turned to the table beside her and reached for her purse.  She removed a $50 bill, glanced at him, and then removed another.  "Don't worry about being late," she said.  "You work in receiving here, don't you?  I'll phone Jake and tell him to give you the rest of the day off--with pay."  She handed him the money.  "And this is for you.  Thanks for the information, Dan.  I appreciate it."

"My pleasure."  And he was gone with the first of Eric's belongings.

She moved through her apartment.  Every room, every corridor, was quiet and mysterious and changed.  Her home seemed foreign to her now.  The rooms were weirdly bare.  Although she had never paid much attention to them before, Celina now was acutely aware that the photographs of Eric and her no longer rested on side tables or hung on walls.  Now they were packed away in boxes.

She stepped into her bedroom. The bed, the antique chairs and tables Eric bought for her while abroad on business all remained, as did the shelves of hardcover books they once read in bed. The books and the chairs and the tables would stay, she decided. Celina needed some tangible proof that what she and Eric had was real.

As she turned to leave, she caught a glimpse of herself in the bedroom's full-length mirror. She was an unfamiliar woman who no longer looked happy, but years wiser than she had only days ago.

She closed the door behind her when she left the room. It was getting late. She wondered if her father had finished shooting with the Frostmans. When she left him that morning, she returned to Manhattan and packed the rest of Eric's clothes. Although the job took only a few minutes, it had seemed to her like a lifetime.

She wondered if George was angry with her for not returning. After the way he treated her, she decided, for the first time in her life, that she didn't really care. The phone rang just as Dan was leaving with the final box. Celina answered it in the living room.

"Where have you been?" George asked. "We missed you this afternoon."

It was not anger she heard in his voice, but something else. Regret...? "I've been here," Celina said. "Cleaning."

"Since when?"

"Since I decided to get rid of Eric's things."

A silence passed. Celina dropped into a chair covered in glazed cream chintz and said, "What's up, Dad? Why are you calling?"

"Two reasons. First, I wanted to apologize for what happened earlier. I never should have reacted the way I did and I'm sorry. Forgive me?"

Sometimes her father sounded so formal it amused her. "There's nothing to forgive," she said, wanting to put it behind her. "Let's just forget about it, okay?"

"Sounds good to me."

"How'd your meeting go with the Frostmans?"

"Only Ted came," George said. "And it went fine. But we'll discuss that later. I'm calling for another reason."

"What's that?"

"I don't think we should discuss it over the phone."

"Why not?"

"It's about your sister."

A part of her recoiled. "Whatever Leana has done now--"

"She was beaten."

"Beaten?"

"Eric did it the night of the party--probably not long after you left the room. If I had known that earlier this morning, he would be in the hospital now, instead of just looking for a job."

Things were moving too quickly. Her mind tried to grasp what her father was saying. "You fired him?"

"Of course, I fired him," George said. "And that's just the beginning. Now, look. I don't want to discuss this over the phone. Can you come out to the house, or not?"

*  *  *

They were in George's study. After thirty minutes of long silences and raised voices, the room had gone quiet. Celina looked from her father to her mother and then back at George. He was seated at his desk, his face flushed. Few times in her life had she seen him so upset.

"If we press charges against the son of a bitch," George said, "if we bring him to court, our name and Leana's will be dragged through every rag on the newspaper stand. And for what? So Eric can walk free because no one witnessed the beating?"

Elizabeth frowned down at him. She had just returned from a charity luncheon when George led her into his study, saying they needed to talk.

"What about our daughter?" she said. "Isn't she witness enough?"

"It'll be his word against Leana's."

"So? Leana will win. Diana Crane will see to that. She'll put that man behind bars."

George thought back to earlier that morning, when Diana answered Eric's phone. He was almost certain they had been in bed together when he called. And if that was the case, if Diana was sleeping with Eric, she would hardly try her best to defend Leana against him in court.

He looked at Elizabeth and said guardedly, "I don't think that would be possible."

"Why not?"

"I have my reasons."

"What reasons?"

"Reasons you don't have to concern yourself with."

He saw the confusion on Celina's face and glared at his wife. He would tell her later--away from Celina. "What matters is this," he said. "Leana would lose no matter who represented her in court. Eric Parker has lived a model life. Our daughter's bout with cocaine was once the center of a media circus. The defense would make it a point to remind the court of that, and her word would become worthless."

"I saw them in that room together," Celina said. "In front of Eric, I accused Leana of setting us up. That's got to be worth something, Dad. It's a motive, for God's sake."

"What you two seem to be forgetting is this--Leana's not talking. I'm convinced she never wanted anyone to know about this."

"But why?" Elizabeth said. "Why couldn't she have come to us?"

"Because she's angry," Celina said. "She's angry with us, angry at life. Leana always has been."

"I don't understand why. We've given that girl everything."

"Except love," George said.

Elizabeth, a woman who was known and revered for her poise and grace, turned to George without a shred of it. "Are you saying I don't love my daughter?"

"You love Leana as much as I do. What I'm saying is that we paid very little attention to her while she was growing up and Leana's angry because of it." He looked at the picture of Leana that was on his desk and noticed for the first time that it was neatly tucked behind his pictures of Celina and Elizabeth. He wondered if that's how Leana saw herself--being neatly tucked away in a silver frame--and decided it probably was.

He looked at his wife and daughter. "Leana didn't come to us because she doesn't love us. I think there are two reasons. She doesn't trust us. And I think Eric threatened her."

"Threatened her?"

George nodded at Celina. "I'm fairly certain of it."

Elizabeth watched her husband. It was obvious he already had made decisions concerning Eric Parker and his future. She knew his temper and right now, it frightened her. Once, many years ago, losing control of it had nearly sent him to prison.

"George," she said firmly. "I want to know what you're going to do."

George met her gaze with his own. "Something I should have done this morning," he said, and reached for the phone.

\* \* \*

Celina wasted no time in leaving. She didn't want to know who her father called or how it might affect Eric Parker.

After kissing her mother goodbye, she left the house. Her father caught her as she was stepping into her car. "Where are you going?" he called from the porch.

Celina felt a flash of disappointment. Who had he spoken to so quickly? "I have a few errands I need to run and then I'm going home," she said.

"Jack Douglas will be here in another half hour," George said. "Why don't you come back for the meeting? You might find it interesting."

In all the confusion, Celina had forgotten about Jack Douglas and his meeting with her father. Although the last thing she wanted to do now was attend a meeting that might take hours, a part of her wanted to see Jack again.

"Why would I find it interesting?" she asked.

"Because I'm going to offer him Eric's job."

"I'll be there," she said.

\* \* \*

Traffic in town was heavier than she anticipated and she was forty minutes late for the meeting.

After parking her car behind an old Buick she supposed belonged to Jack Douglas, she hurried into the house and went to her father's office.

Jack Douglas was there, his back to a sunlit window, reading a file on WestTex Incorporated, the large shipping corporation based in Corpus Christi, Texas. In that brief moment before he realized she was there, Celina saw on his face a look of relaxed concentration.

To her surprise, he wasn't wearing a suit, but tan pants and a white Polo shirt. His sandy-colored hair was more tousled than groomed, and on his face was a day's growth of beard. She sensed in him a man who was comfortable with himself, unaware of his good looks and somebody who refused to put on airs.

She thought back to the night of the party. Although he arrived soaking wet, there had been an unmistakable, refreshing poise about him, a directress and sense of humor she admired. She remembered liking him very much.

She glanced around the room, noted that her father wasn't there and cleared her throat. She smiled when Jack looked up. "How are you?" she asked.

Jack closed the folder and placed it on the table beside him. He was silent for a moment, thoughtful. Then he looked at her with a grin. "Drier than when we first met?"

Celina laughed and stepped into the room. As she crossed to her father's desk, she became aware of herself. She wondered how she looked. She wondered why she cared. "I owe you an apology," she said, while sitting in her father's leather wingback. "I meant to return for that dance, but something came up and I had to leave unexpectedly."

"Don't worry about it," Jack said. "I left not long after you, anyway."

"You saw me leave?"

Jack nodded. "I would have gone after you, but you seemed pretty upset. Is everything all right?"

If he had seen her in that state, she could hardly lie. "It wasn't, but I'm fine now. Thank you for asking."

At that moment, George stepped into the room. Celina looked at him and felt relieved. She didn't want to discuss that evening with anyone.

"You're here," George said to Celina. "Good. Then we can get started." He looked at Jack. "Have you told her the good news?"

"We didn't get around to it."

"Then we should now. Jack accepted my offer, Celina. He'll be taking Eric's place as our chief financial officer."

A wave of feelings assailed her. She felt a sense of loss--not the happiness she had been anticipating. Eric was gone. He really was gone. It was as if the past two years of her life had meant nothing. But there was another feeling and she couldn't deny that it was a sense of relief.

She managed a smile--and knew by the change in Jack's expression that he could sense it wasn't genuine. She felt uncomfortable. She wondered why she came. She wondered why she still had feelings for Eric. She should hate him for what he did to her and to Leana. So, why did she miss him?

"That's great," she said to Jack. "Congratulations."

Jack said nothing. He looked away from her and faced George, who was opening a file on WestTex. Celina sensed this meeting was going to pass slowly, but business was business, so she sucked it up.

They discussed the takeover of WestTex, which owned seventy-one tankers and twelve super-tankers. The company shipped anything from oil out of the Persian Gulf to coffee beans out of Colombia. Eighty-six percent of their business was strictly international and it was not uncommon for most of WestTex's fleet to be in international waters at the same time.

As Jack thumbed through the file, he learned that while business at WestTex was good, it was being affected by the instability in the Middle East. He also learned that George Redman was about to pay $10 billion for a company that, according to these figures, was worth half that.

He looked at George, who was seated across from him, and found himself at a loss for words. Why would a man whose stock was at an all-time low pay twice what WestTex was worth when the company had just pulled its entire fleet from the Gulf and whose situation was worsening in the wake of the Iraq and

Afghanistan wars?  No wonder the press was hounding him.  No wonder his stockholders were so damned nervous.  The man could lose everything if he took over WestTex.

And then it occurred to him.  George Redman was no fool.  He obviously knew something the press and his stockholders didn't know, something that had the power of making him millions. Jack couldn't help a smile.

"So, what do you think?" George asked.  He was sitting in his chair, legs crossed, hands clasped behind his head.  The late afternoon sun cast a warm glow against one side of his face, leaving the other side in shadow.

"If you weren't George Redman, I'd say you were a fool to even consider this takeover."

"Mind explaining why?"

"Not at all.  With your stock at an embarrassing low, you've agreed to pay $10 billion for a company that's worth half that."

George shrugged.  "WestTex can support itself."

"Not if the Middle East remains in the can."

"WestTex isn't just about the Middle East."

"According to these papers, more than sixty percent of its business is done in the Middle East."

"So, we turn things around.  Find other avenues.  Explore other ventures."

"Insurance prices have soared since the wars.  What profits that could have been made are now no longer worth the risks."

Jack lifted the folder from his lap.  "It says here that because of each war, WestTex and other shipping companies are pulling their tankers from the Gulf.  That's a sixty percent drop in business for WestTex.  And with that kind of decline, there's no way in hell it can support the $10 billion you're willing to pay for it, no matter what avenues or ventures you have in mind.  The money is in oil."

George suppressed a smile.  "So, why do you think I'm going through with it?"

"I think you know something the public doesn't," Jack said.  "I think once this takeover is complete, you're going to be the one laughing--not the press.  Am I right?"

"I hope so."

"Mind filling me in?"

133

"Absolutely. You're an employee now. What is said in this room stays in this room."

"Of course."

George left his chair and stepped to one of the large casement windows behind him. Acres upon acres of green lawns and rolling hills stretched out as far as he could see.

"You're perfectly right," he said to Jack. "Under ordinary circumstances, this takeover would be the end of me and Redman International. Not only can't WestTex support itself at the price I've agreed to pay for it, but after spending nearly $1.5 billion on the new building, I would never be able to afford it." He smiled. "But, luckily, that isn't the case."

"Why's that?"

"Because of my deal with Iran," George said. "The deal no one knows about." He turned to Celina, who was sitting beside Jack. "This is your area. Why don't you take it from here?

Celina began with the basics. "Two weeks ago, my father and I met with a group of Iranian officials to see if we could work out a deal that would make us one of Iran's chief exporters of oil. For a lot of reasons, few are willing to go near them."

"Except for you and a few others," Jack said. "But why?"

"We're willing to take the risk because of two factors," Celina said. "First is the price we'll be paying for the oil. Iran has guaranteed us a price so low, the revenues we'll earn from hauling and selling the oil should pay off WestTex in less than five years. That's over two billion dollars a year. In a sense, we can't afford not to go Iran."

The kind of money they were discussing was astronomical. "What's the other reason?" Jack asked.

"It was recently announced that the U.S. would do what they did during the Gulf War. Our country plans to send the Navy into the Gulf to provide military escorts for dozens of American-flagged tankers. For security reasons, the exact date wasn't given. It's been kept top secret. No one--not Iran nor Iraq, nor any other oil or shipping company--knows the date but us."

"How did you find out?"

"I have contacts at the State and Defense Department," George said. "I called in a few favors and was given the date."

"So, what you're saying is that, with the Navy in the Gulf, the risks will be fewer and insurance prices will go down."

"Exactly," George said. "Making the venture profitable."

"If that date was made public, every oil and shipping corporation in the world would be scrambling to export oil out of the Gulf."

Celina smiled. "But instead, most are scrambling to get out of it."

"It's not all a gilded road," George said. "There are problems-- major ones. Just yesterday afternoon, RRK, the investment group we hired to help finance the deal, pulled out. They felt the risks were too great to get involved, the deal with Iran too shaky because our agreement with them is verbal."

"Verbal?"

"That's right," George said. "Verbal."

"I'm not sure what to think about that."

"That's because you don't have the biggest set of balls in this room. Earlier this afternoon, I met with Ted Frostman from Chase. We talked over a game of skeet, I told them the pros and cons of taking over the company and he's agreed to work with us."

Celina didn't know this. "Dad, that's terrific," she said.

"Don't get excited just yet," George said. "We've yet to discuss fees and the terms of the deal--but Ted did assure me that he can get a commitment from Chase and, if for some reason that falls through, word's out that Peter Cohen at Morgan Stanley is looking for an LBO--he might be interested."

George looked at Jack. "What do you think?"

Jack's former boss was Peter Cohen, Morgan's chairman and chief executive. "I think Peter would be very interested," he said. "Morgan is still trying to get back into the LBO business and I happen to know that Peter is under pressure to save their third-quarter earnings, which are expected to be down. A one-shot injection of, say, $100 to $200 million might be the opportunity he's been waiting for."

"Good," George said. "Because we have to move fast. If I wait much longer, Iran could learn of the Navy's move--and if that happens, there's no question they'll withdraw their offer."

He stepped away from the window and sat in his chair. There was a sudden energy about George, a vitality that glimmered in his eyes and animated his features. "My sources at the State and

Defense departments say that the Navy will begin its move on July 21. I've already spoken to my contacts at Lloyds, and they've agreed to cut their insurance rates in half when the Navy is stationed in the Gulf."

"Where do I come into all this?" Jack asked.

"Besides your connections at Morgan Stanley, which might prove invaluable. On the day WestTex becomes ours, you, Celina and Harold Baines will be signing the final papers in Iran. It's all just a formality, really--by then, the papers will have been drawn up and vetted. But obviously, it's an important formality. If I take over WestTex without having secured this deal with Iran, I could lose everything I've ever worked for if they decide to back out."

"Why don't you just complete the deal with Iran first?"

George looked wistful. "I wish I could, but Iran won't allow it. Only when WestTex is ours will they sign the final papers. They refuse to commit themselves otherwise."

Jack couldn't still a sense of apprehension. The risk this man was taking was great. He found himself admiring Redman, but also wondering how the man slept at night. "Are you sure this is the right move?" he asked.

"No," George said. "But I didn't get where I am without taking risks. I think this one is calculated. I feel good about it, so I'm going for it." He stood. "I think you and Harold should meet before the trip. How does dinner sound?"

"Fine," Jack said. "I'm free anytime." He looked at Celina, who was flipping through a file on WestTex. He had been waiting all afternoon for a moment like this. "Why don't you join us?" he asked casually.

Celina looked at him, surprised and speechless. She was about to refuse when her father said, "That's a good idea. This way, you all can get to know one another before the trip."

* * *

Eric Parker was there, but now only in the back of her mind. As her dinner date with Jack drew nearer, Celina found herself thinking more and more about him.

At board meetings, he would enter her thoughts by surprise. At business dinners, she would remember his smile and how they first met. In cabs headed cross-town, her mind would wander into his personal life. When he wasn't at work, how did he spend his time? He seemed athletic. Was he on a team of some sort? Did he belong to a gym? And where did he live? Near her? On the West side? Downtown?

And her thoughts deepened. She wondered if he was seeing anyone.

She began to imagine the kind of woman he was interested in. She would be pretty, of course, but not beautiful. Somehow, she sensed that looks were less important to him than intelligence. And he would want someone who had a sense of humor; someone witty like himself, but not cutting. As the days passed, she imagined endless possibilities--but then, on the eve of their dinner date, she put an end to it.

*This is crazy*, she thought. *Not only have I just ended a relationship, but once WestTex and the deal with Iran is secured, there will be more problems, more responsibilities and less time for me. This man should be furthest from my mind.*

She was thinking this as she slipped into the black silk dress she purchased earlier that morning at Saks. *Besides, it isn't as though we're going to be alone at dinner. Harold will be there. I'm simply a businesswoman attending a business dinner with my business colleagues.*

She stepped in front of the bedroom mirror. The dress was short and chic and clung to her body, exposing her tanned shoulders, accenting her long legs. Studying herself, she wondered what had happened to the businesswoman, wondered what Jack Douglas would think if she arrived at the restaurant looking like this.

She reached into her closet and removed a black Chanel jacket. She put it on and turned before the mirror, inspecting the more conservative version. "That's more like it," she said.

But when she left her apartment, it was without the jacket.

\* \* \*

137

When she arrived at the restaurant, she was led by the captain into a room filled with bouquets of fresh flowers, people dining at elegantly appointed tables, a man playing piano in the center of the warmly lit room. Jack Douglas was already seated at their table and he stood as she approached.

"You look terrific," he said.

Celina thanked him and, as the captain pulled out her chair and she sat down, she noted the expensive navy blue suit Jack wore, his recently trimmed hair. "You don't look so bad yourself," she said. "Harold's not with you?"

Jack shook his head. "I thought he'd be with you." He looked at the captain, who was standing beside them, and asked Celina what she would like to drink. "A bottle of champagne?"

Celina regarded him with a smile--this man did not drink champagne. Although he seemed perfectly at ease at this restaurant, she sensed he would rather be dining at a Village cafe, cutting into a thick steak, drinking a cold beer. "I was thinking more on the line of having a beer," she said. "Does that sound all right with you?"

Delighted, Jack grinned. "Sounds fine to me," he said. "But I drink from the bottle."

"What a coincidence. So do I."

And it was that simple.

The beers came and they began to talk.

"Why'd you leave Morgan?" Celina asked. "You made a name for yourself. Things were happening. Why leave?"

Jack shrugged. "The pressure wasn't worth the money and the money wasn't worth the hassle of putting up with a room full of bond traders--most of whom would kill their mother if they thought her life would cut a better deal."

He look a long pull from his beer. "Besides, there's a lot going down that nobody knows about. A lot of inside deals. I've been offered an obscene amount of money for a whisper of information, but I don't want any part of it. These people haven't learned. When Wall Street collapses again--and it will, before you know it, really--I didn't want to be anywhere near the place when the concrete begins to fall."

He straightened. "So tell me about yourself," he said. "When did you decide that working at Redman International was for you?"

"You're assuming I had a choice," Celina said. "When I was a kid, my father used to bring me to each month's board meeting. I'd sit in a special corner chair while he hammered out deal after deal. He was mesmerizing. The board loved him. At night, I'd pretend I was him. I'd stand in front of my bedroom mirror and mimic the way he stood before the board--arms crossed, feet spaced firmly apart--pretending I was the one in charge. Believe me, I know it sounds cheesy, but at the time I was enthralled. My father was my hero."

"Is he now?"

Although she said, "Yes, of course," Celina wasn't sure. After the incident with Eric Parker and her father's reaction to it, her feelings had shifted toward George in ways she couldn't quite describe.

The conversation turned and they laughed and joked about how they met and how Jack was planning on buying a new car. They talked with ease, as if they were old friends catching up over dinner. From time to time, Jack would touch Celina's hand to make a point. From time to time, Celina would do the same.

When the waiter brought the second round of beers, Celina excused herself and left to use her cell phone. She called Harold at home. It was his wife, Helen, who answered.

"He should be there, Celina," the woman said. "He left over an hour ago." A silence followed. Celina could hear the sudden whistling of a tea kettle coming from Helen's kitchen. "Maybe he's at the office," Helen said. "He did mention stopping by there."

But Harold wasn't in his office. And he wasn't with her father.

"How long have you been waiting?" George asked.

"An hour," Celina said. "And I'm getting tired of waiting. Where do you think he is?"

George didn't know.

"If this wasn't becoming a habit of his, Dad, I'd be worried. But it is becoming a habit. First he decides not to show for two board meetings, and now this. What's going on with him? Harold's never acted like this before. That man used to be on time for everything."

"He may have just forgotten, Celina. The deals with WestTex and Iran have doubled his workload. He's not as young as you."

"True," she said. "But my workload has tripled and you don't see me missing a business dinner."

"I'm not going to defend him."

"I don't expect you to. You know how I feel about Harold. But I do expect you to talk to him. Somebody has to."

She severed the connection and forced herself to relax. She was damned if Harold's absence was going to ruin this evening.

She returned to the table. Jack looked up at her as she approached. "We might as well eat," she said. "It looks as though he won't be coming."

"Did you find out where he is?"

"No," she said. "And at this point, I really don't care. I'd rather have dinner alone with you, anyway." She picked up the menu and flipped through it, aware that Jack was looking at her intently. "The salmon here is wonderful," she said. "I'm having that."

* * *

Later, after dessert and coffee, Celina said, "It's still early. Would you like to come back to my apartment for a nightcap? We can continue the conversation there."

Jack said he would like that very much.

* * *

The evening was so warm, they decided to walk.

"You haven't mentioned your family," Celina said. "What do your parents do?"

They were walking up Fifth, stopping from time to time to glance at the illumined store windows. Jack reached out and held Celina's hand. "They're retired," he said. "Dad worked forty years at a Pittsburgh steel mill before he sold the house and moved to

West Palm with my mother. They live in this little house near the ocean. My mother calls once a week to tell me that Dad is driving her crazy. My father calls twice a week threatening divorce'"

"So, they're happy?" Celina said.

"Excessively."

"Any brothers or sisters?"

"One sister," Jack said. "Her name is Lisa. She's a nurse."

When they passed 59th Street and her apartment complex came into sight, the first thing Celina noticed were the flashing red and blue lights surrounding it. As they drew nearer, she counted six police cars and one ambulance. A crowd had gathered outside Redman Place and traffic was lined up the street. Sirens gave chill to the warm night air.

"What's going on?" Jack asked.

Celina didn't know. She immediately thought back to the bombs that exploded on top of Redman International and couldn't still a twinge of fear. The police still hadn't learned who rigged the spotlights with explosives. "I don't know," she said.

They hurried up the avenue. Car horns were sounding and people were talking excitedly, their voices rising. Celina tried to grasp what they were saying, tried to make sense of it, but it was impossible in the confusion.

The ambulance was parked in front of the building--lights flashing, sirens now quiet. A team of ten officers kept the crowd at bay. Jack led Celina toward the building's entrance. His grip was strong, firm, and she was thankful for it.

When they reached the front of the crowd, they were in time to see two paramedics wheeling a man out on a stretcher. Celina knew it was a man by the arm that dangled to one side. It was muscular, bloody and bruised. An IV dripped life into it.

As the paramedics neared them, her stomach tensed and she squeezed Jack's hand harder. She leaned forward but could not see the man's face as he passed. It was partly covered by a bloody sheet.

She noticed that one of the man's legs was quivering. She also noticed that the other leg was twisted horribly beneath the sheet.

Celina knew almost everyone in this building. It was here that many of Redman International's senior executives lived. She turned to one of the officers and was about to ask who had been hurt when, from inside the building, a woman shouted, "Wait!"

To her surprise, Celina watched Diana Crane rush from the building.

There was a bandage on her forehead.  One eye was slightly swollen.  Celina heard Diana say, "I'm going with him."  She watched in disbelief as the woman climbed into the back of the ambulance.  No one objected.

The paramedics were lifting the stretcher.  Celina knew it was Eric lying there even before the sheet fell to one side and revealed his broken face.

For a moment, she couldn't speak, couldn't move or react.  Her mind began making connections.  She remembered her father calling a week ago and saying, "Leana's been beaten, Celina.  Eric did it the night of the party--probably not long after you left the room.  If I had known that earlier this morning, Eric would be in the hospital now, instead of just looking for a job."

She knew her father was responsible for this.  She was sure of it.

Why else would he have asked Elizabeth and her to leave the room before making that call?

The ambulance's doors slammed shut.  The sound broke Celina's reverie and she saw that the vehicle was preparing to leave.  She was about to run forward and ask what hospital they were taking him to when she caught sight of her sister in the crowd.

For a moment, Celina could only stare.

Arms crossed, face grim, Leana was standing across from her, sandwiched between two tall, muscular men.  She was wearing dark glasses, a black pant suit, no jewelry.  Her hair was pulled away from her face.

Celina called out her name.

Alarmed, Leana turned in her direction.  Their eyes met.  Leana took a step back.

Celina called out her name again.

Leana ignored her.  She spoke to the men beside her, they looked at Celina and quickly led Leana away.

She was gone at the same moment the ambulance screamed to life.

# FIFTH AVENUE

## CHAPTER TWENTY

The first thing Mario noticed when he arrived at the modest-looking brownstone on 12th Street was his father's black Lincoln limousine shimmering in the fluorescent glow of a streetlamp. Instinctively, he looked across the street at his home and saw the three men standing guard at the brick entrance.

Something was wrong. His father only visited on Sundays.

He parked the Taurus behind his father's car, stepped out and slammed the door shut. He crossed the street and nodded at the men as he approached. "What's up, Nicky?" he said. "Why's my father here?"

The man shrugged, even though Mario sensed he knew exactly why Antonio De Cicco had taken the time and trouble to drive all the way into the city from his Todt Hill mansion on Staten Island. "Didn't say. He don't look too happy, though. Wants to see you inside."

Mario entered the house. It was his wife who met him at the door. Tall and slender with fiery red hair, the years had almost been as kind to Lucia De Cicco as her plastic surgeon had.

She greeted him with a smile and a slap across the face. Mario's head snapped to the side and his cheek burned. When he turned back to look at her, Lucia's smile had dissolved.

"What the hell's the matter with you?" he said.

She raised a hand to hit him again, but Mario grasped her arms and held them at her sides. She writhed beneath his touch. Her eyes blazed. "Let go of me!"

"Why did you hit me?"

She nodded toward the library, which was to her right. A lock of her carefully dyed hair fell into her face. "Your father's in there. I'll let him tell you."

She wrenched her arms free and hurried up the staircase that led to their bedroom. Mario watched her go, realizing that this was the first time she had stood up to him.

143

# FIFTH AVENUE

He went to the library. The large mahogany door creaked when he entered the room. In the fluorescent glow of an enormous saltwater aquarium, he saw the faint but familiar images of paintings, furniture and urns. He looked for his father and found him sitting beside the aquarium in a leather chair.

Blue light rippled in waves across his tanned face, making him look oddly like a living corpse. A cloud of cigar smoke hung in the air above his bald head.

His voice came unexpectedly. "Close the door and sit down. This won't take long."

Mario did as he was told and shut the door, feeling contempt for this man he never loved--but also fear. He sat opposite his father and noticed that while Antonio was shorter, he seemed to be sitting slightly higher.

De Cicco leaned back in the leather wingback and began tapping his knuckles against the side of the aquarium. The fish jumped, skidded away. Mario looked at his father and knew now why the man was here.

"You've disappointed me, Mario," De Cicco said. "You're not thinkin' with your head, anymore." His knuckles struck the aquarium harder. Water sloshed. "You're thinkin' with your cock."

Mario glanced at the aquarium. Of the seventy-six fish filling the tank, one alone was worth twenty thousand dollars. It was so rare, it had taken him nearly eight months to obtain it. The others were almost as rare.

"It's not what you think."

"It's exactly what I think. You're bangin' that Redman cunt again."

"You're wrong."

"You call having lunch with that whore in your Family's own restaurant not seeing her?"

"She's not a whore. And that restaurant belongs to me."

"Bought with Family money."

"Bought with my money--for the Family."

The shadow of what looked like a small grey shark crossed Antonio De Cicco's face. He cracked a knuckle against the aquarium and the fish darted away. "I told you two years ago what would happen if you started seeing her again. I warned you.

You've disgraced Lucia for the last time. You know how I feel about that girl. She's like a daughter to me--her father is my best friend--and I'll be damned if you're going to hurt her just because you like the way that Redman bitch sucks your cock."

"You've got it wrong," Mario said firmly. "I haven't seen Leana since we broke it off two years ago. She came to me. She's in trouble. She asked a favor of me. That's the extent of our relationship."

"Bullshit."

"It isn't bullshit. It's the truth. Do you really believe I'd bring Leana to the restaurant if I was sleeping with her? Aunt Rosa waited on us, for God's sake. Do you think I'm stupid? Listen to yourself. You know me better than that. What you're saying doesn't make sense."

De Cicco was silent a moment. When he rose from his chair, he looked at the aquarium, considered it for a moment, then stepped away from it and Mario, his hands in his pockets.

"I'm gonna talk with Lucia," he said after a moment. "Calm her down, tell her everything's all right."

He faced his son. "But if I find out that you've been lyin' to me, that you been fucking that little shit slut behind your wife's back, I'll kill her myself. I promised you that years ago and I mean it as much now as I did then. You will not hurt Lucia. You will not embarrass your children--my grandchildren. Because if you do, you might as well have loaded the gun and murdered Leana Redman yourself."

**BOOK TWO**
**SECOND WEEK**

**FIFTH AYENUE**
**CHAPTER TWENTY-ONE**

Swinging out through the big brass and glass doors of Harold's townhouse on 81st Street, Leana looked up at the buttery morning sun, felt the warmth on her face and decided she would walk to most of her appointments instead of taking a cab. There were a few apartments in the Village she wanted to look at and she had to sell her jewelry to her mother's jeweler on Park.

She was beginning to feel better about herself. Not only had the bruises on her face faded and the cut on her lip healed, but she was full of resolve and a measure of hope. For the first time in her life, she was doing something productive. Soon, she would have an apartment of her own and enough money to furnish it comfortably. At breakfast, Harold mentioned something about finding her a job.

And Mario was back in her life.

He called earlier that morning and asked her to dinner. He said they needed to talk, that it was important they talk and that they must talk soon. Leana agreed, but under the condition that she pay for the meal. Although a part of her wanted much more than a friendship with Mario, Leana was determined to keep their relationship simple. She would not sleep with Mario while he was married.

*But I'll think about it.*

She continued walking until she came upon a crowded newspaper vending machine. The crowd shifted and she was able to glimpse the front page of *The Daily News*. A chill threaded through her. The headline and recent pictures of Eric Parker screamed out at her:

# FIFTH AVENUE

## EX-REDMAN FINANCIAL CHIEF
## BEATEN IN APARTMENT

Leana stared at the headline, then at the photos of Eric. One showed him being wheeled out of the building on a stretcher. She studied the fine lines of his face and saw that it was broken.

She remembered the shock of seeing Celina last night. She remembered Mario's men hurrying her away from the crowd and into a limousine. She remembered the shrill of the ambulance as it raced past them.

She wondered what Celina was thinking this morning and decided she didn't care. *I didn't do anything to Eric.*

Sensing someone standing behind her, she turned and faced a rugged-looking man in a dark suit and dark glasses. His hair was black and cut short. He was looking at the headline as well.

Their eyes met and he shook his head in disgust. "You're not even safe in your own home anymore," Vincent Spocatti said.

The man seemed vaguely familiar to her. She had the feeling that she'd seen him before, but couldn't place where.

She shrugged. "Maybe he deserved it."

"You can't be serious."

"I happen to know the man," Leana said. "And I am serious. He deserved it."

And she started for the Village, leaving Spocatti intrigued.

* * *

She had appointments to see two apartments--one studio and one loft. It was the loft that caught Leana's eye.

Overlooking Washington Square, her favorite place in New York, the loft was large and sunny and located on the fifth floor of a prewar building. It had promise, and a few issues that could be fixed--it needed fresh paint, two of its windows were cracked and the carpet was worn and in need of updating. *Hardwood would work in here,* she thought. *Maybe polished concrete.*

147

Despite its flaws, the loft had character, a sense of style. Her mind began to picture plants, clean ivory walls, paintings. *I could make this place my own.*

The owner of the building, a thin woman who hadn't stopped smiling, was standing in the middle of the living space, making sweeping movements with her arms. Copper bracelets winked and jangled.

"What furniture's here is yours," she said, as if that would tip the balance. "The bed, the desk, the table and chairs--all yours. Some freak artist left them and the smell of cat piss behind. If I hadn't had the carpets cleaned, you wouldn't be able to stand it in here." She wrinkled her nose, sniffed, and looked uncertainly at Leana. "You can't smell the piss, can you?"

"I can smell it," Leana said. *And I also can smell your desperation.*

She stepped over to a window and watched a group of children run past the empty fountain to a flock of pigeons. The birds took flight in a dizzying cloud of gray and black and white, and the children cheered. Leana thought back to the last day she had been in the park. It was the day the bombs exploded on top of her father's building.

It was the day the man had followed and harassed her.

She wondered if she made a mistake by not going to the police and filing a report on him, but decided she hadn't. They wouldn't have caught him, but she decided if she did see him again, she at least would go to the police and get it on record.

The woman was standing behind her. "Beautiful view, isn't it?"

It was, and Leana said so.

"There was a time, on a clear day, that you could see to the World Trade Center." The woman actually stopped and genuflected. She kissed her fingers and closed her eyes, as if to pray.

Leana was as sensitive as anyone about that day, the people who died there or were otherwise affected by it, but this was overkill. This was a show. *Give me a fucking break.*

The woman crossed her arms--jangle, jangle. "So, what do you think? It's originally $20,000 a month, but you look like a nice girl, one who won't cause me too many problems, so I'll let you have it for $18,500--plus deposit." She snapped a piece of gum and looked up at the ceiling. "That's $37,000--up front, of course."

Leana barely had that in her savings account. She knew her financial situation would improve once she sold her jewelry, but she didn't want to give any more money to this woman than she had to. "That's too much," she said. "Especially since your former tenant couldn't keep his cats in check. My price is $10,000."

"No way," the woman said.

"Then let's get real. You've got a problem here--take a whiff. It's the reason this place isn't moving. It's the reason someone like me is going to have to get someone in here and get the smell out. What's your best price?"

The woman turned and when she did, she breathed in through her nose. "No less than "$15,000."

"Okay," Leana said. "So, $12,500 and you've got yourself a deal right now. I'll cut you a check for $25,000 and we're both happy." Leana looked around the space. "You also need to agree to repair those windows, pay for half the painting costs, and throw in a couple of fans. Ironically, the air in here would kill a cat."

The woman tried to look affronted, but Leana saw relief in her eyes.

"Fans, windows and paint I can handle."

"I thought you could."

She studied Leana for a moment. "You're tough. And you've got a good business sense, too. I like that in a woman. What did you say your last name was again?"

"I didn't," Leana said. "But it's Redman."

Something in the woman's eyes flashed and she lifted her chin. "I thought I recognized you," she said. "Are you as tough as you father and sister?"

"I'm tougher."

"So, you are."

She wrote the woman a check.

\* \* \*

Later, at the bank, she followed the assistant manager to a vault that was surrounded by rows of gleaming safe-deposit boxes.

As the man went to the back of the room and stooped to insert a key into one of the boxes, Leana remained in the doorway, thinking of the seven pieces of jewelry she kept here. Although each was a major piece in its own right, nothing compared to the diamond and Mogok ruby necklace. It was this piece that would fetch the highest price when she sold it later that afternoon.

It was this piece that would furnish her new apartment and buy her food.

The manager cleared his throat. Leana looked at him and saw that he was waiting for her to insert her own key. She apologized and crossed to where he was standing. She unlocked her side of the box and carried it to the small table that was at her left. The manager followed.

"I'd like to be alone," Leana said. The man's gaze flicked up to hers. Hesitation crossed his face and she sensed he wanted to stay and see what was inside the box. He didn't move.

"Do you mind?" Leana said. The man bowed slightly and left the room.

Leana watched him go. He went no further than the entrance to the vault, where he crossed his arms and watched her from there.

She turned her back to him and opened the box.

Inside were seven black velvet cases of various sizes. Leana chose one of the cases, opened it and was greeted with a brilliant flash of diamonds. She looked into another case and was rewarded with a glimmer of sapphires. In the third was the diamond and Mogok ruby necklace.

She lifted the necklace from its case and held it to her neck. Its coolness and the sheer weight of the stones warmed her. *For awhile, at least, you're going to give me time to make my mark.*

After checking the other cases and tucking them in her oversized straw handbag, she slid the box back into place, locked it and left the bank with an armed guard at her side.

The sun was bright and the heat oppressive--it rising in waves from the street.  Three young boys on rollerblades darted through the crowds on the sidewalk, nearly toppling an elderly woman.

Leana wasted no time leaving.  She stepped to the curb, flagged a cab, got one on the fourth try and left for the jeweler on Park.

To be certain he wouldn't lose her, Vincent Spocatti, who was waiting for her outside the bank, did the same.

* * *

Quimby et Cie Jewelers was an elegant establishment, with a liveried doorman on the outside and two armed guards on the inside.  Some of the wealthiest people in the world bought and sold their jewelry here, and they had to have an appointment to do so.

Leana was met at the door by Philip Quimby, the owner and her mother's good friend. He was a small, impeccably dressed man with short graying hair and blue eyes that were just this side of being unnaturally too blue.  She noticed the shop was empty, as it should be.  "It's good to see you, Leana," he said, in a slightly nasal voice.  "Let's go to my office.  We'll have tea there."

His office was large and impressive, paneled in dark wood and decorated in quiet good taste.  Paintings by the old masters tiled the walls.  He offered tea.  When Leana declined, he said, "Well, then, at least a martini?"

"Only if you're having one."

"As if I'm not," he said.

He made the drinks, handed one to her and motioned toward the two Queen Anne chairs arranged at the center of the room. They sat.  Leana sipped.  Few things were better than a cold martini on a hot day.

"So," he said.  "What do you have for me?"

Leana put the martini on a side table, opened her handbag and removed the seven velvet cases.  She placed them on the table in front of them.  "These," she said.  "All were purchased here."

"I would hope so."  He had known her since she was a child and winked at her.  "Let's see if I remember them."

151

One by one, Philip Quimby opened the cases. Diamonds and emeralds and rubies blazed. "Goodness!" he said. "Heavens!" He brought a hand to his chest and looked sideways at her. "You expect cash for these? Today?"

"If it's possible."

"I don't think so," he said. "The banks will be closing soon. All those lazy clerks and vice presidents and stupid little bank managers will be going home. But I'll see what I can do. Naturally."

"If you want them--and if we come to a price--I'll need the money today. Could you do me a favor and have someone make a call and let them know a transaction will be forthcoming?"

"Anything for you." He lifted a phone and gave the instructions to whoever answered. Then he inserted an eyepiece and removed an enormous canary yellow diamond ring from its case. He held it up to the light and turned it around with his slender fingers.

"Hmmm," he said, and reached for the diamond and Mogok ruby necklace. He glanced at Leana and studied the rest. When he finished, his face was slightly flushed.

"Is something wrong?" Leana asked.

One magnified eye turned to her. "You purchased these here?"

"You know I did. You sold them all to me."

"Not these, I didn't."

"Excuse me...?"

"They're fake," Philip Quimby said. "Nothing but cut glass and cubic zirconium. Every last one of them."

She felt the blood drain from her face. "That's impossible."

"I'm afraid not, Leana."

"But there's more than a million dollars' worth of jewelry there."

He plucked a white envelope from his jacket pocket and handed it to her. "Your father sent this to me," he said. "He called and told me not to open it unless for some reason I should see you. Now, look. I don't know what's going on here and I don't care to know. It's none of my business. But something tells me you'll find the answers to your questions in that envelope."

Leana tore into it. Inside was a note.

Leana:

I told you if you wanted to make it on your own, you'd have to do it on your own and not with my money. The originals, along with the rest of your jewelry, are at home where they-- and you--belong. Why don't you stop this foolishness and come home? You've taken this far enough.

--Dad

Leana read the note twice before folding it in half and putting it in her handbag. Her father was convinced she couldn't make it on her own. Convinced. She felt the beginnings of a spear sink into her heart. What was it about her that made him think she was such a failure?

She lifted one of the necklaces. "Are these worth anything?"

Quimby's eyes sparkled with renewed interest.

"They're excellent counterfeits," he said. "Only an experienced eye like mine could tell they're fake. I would have no problem selling them, especially to the Hollywood set. You think what they are wearing on the red carpet is real? Get real. They wear these."

"How much are you offering?"

He sat poised and ready on the edge of the Queen Anne chair. "Twenty thousand."

"Make it thirty and you've got a deal."

\* \* \*

She ended up with twenty-five.

When Leana returned to Harold's townhouse later that afternoon, she found him seated alone in his study, leaning back in a chair, flipping through a file on WestTex. She managed a smile when he looked up at her. "I need someone to talk to," she said. "Do you have a few minutes?"

"Of course, I do."

He motioned toward the sofa that was in the corner of the room and asked her to sit down. "Tell me everything," he said, sitting beside her. "Tell me why you're upset."

Leana rested her head on his shoulder and told him what had happened.

"But how did George get a key to your safe-deposit box?"

"My father doesn't need a key, Harold. He's George Redman."

"But it's illegal."

"He's George Redman."

"And you think one of the bank's assistant manager's helped him?"

"He probably paid off their mortgage for their trouble."

"What are you going to do?"

"What can I do?"

"Go and ask your father for the originals. They are yours, after all."

"And give him the pleasure of seeing me grovel? Forget it. I'll make my own money."

"How?"

"This morning you mentioned something about finding me a job. That sounds like a good place to start making money to me."

"I've been having seconds thoughts about that job," Harold said.

Leana pulled away from him. "Why?"

"I'm not sure it's right for you."

"Let me be the judge of that," she said. "Harold, please, if you've found something, anything, you have to let me know what it is. I have to be given a chance."

"You really are determined to make it, aren't you?"

"If I accomplish nothing else, I want the world to know that George Redman has another daughter--one who is smarter, tougher and more successful than Celina ever could become."

"That's going to be quite an accomplishment," he said. "You do realize that don't you?"

"I do," Leana said. "I know Celina's good. In a way, I almost admire her--she had the chance to learn from Dad. But that doesn't mean it's impossible. It doesn't mean that she's smarter than me."

"No," Harold said. "It doesn't." He reached into his jacket pocket and removed a card with an address on it. He handed it to Leana. "If you want the job, be at this address by four this afternoon."

\* \* \*

She was fifteen minutes early for the appointment.

When Leana arrived at the towering office building, she took an elevator to the sixty-seventh floor, gave the secretary her name and was escorted to a reception area that was quiet, cool and sparsely decorated. The walls were steel gray. The long array of windows behind her looked out at Manhattan.

Knowing the impression she gave was critical, she chose a fitted black Dior suit. She wore just enough make-up to cover what was left of the bruising, her hair was pulled away from her face and she wore no perfume.

She felt like a fraud.

From her seat at the rear of the reception area, Leana watched the steady stream of activity in the enormous room beyond. At a desk piled high with papers, one man was typing frantically into a computer while a woman impatiently directed him. Behind them, two secretaries were digging through file cabinets in search of something that seemingly couldn't be found. At still another table, someone stopped yelling into a phone only long enough to shout, "Quiet!" to a group of people who could care less.

Leana found herself envying these people.

At five minutes to four, filled with nervous tension, feelings of insecurity and thoughts of pending failure, she went to the ladies' room that was across the hall. Each of the three stalls was occupied. As she turned to wash her hands in the marble vanity, she glimpsed herself in the mirror before her. She was very much a young woman whose appearance gave the cool impression of professionalism, but whose eyes revealed a hint of intimidation and fear.

Although Leana hated to admit it, she wished she was at Redman International now and working with her father.

155

She left the bathroom and returned to her seat in the reception area.  At precisely four o'clock, the secretary came for her.  "We're ready, Miss Redman."

Leana left her seat.  Her shoes clicked on the marble-tiled floor as she followed the woman down a long corridor.  *This isn't going to work.  He's going to see right through me.*

But then she remembered all those years of wanting to prove to her father that she could become a success and neared the office with a feeling of determination.   Once, as a child, she overheard George telling Celina that if she worked very hard, the world could be hers.  *Why can't that apply to me?*

They entered the office.  Leana stood behind the secretary and took in the room.  A painting of a young couple hung above a fully stocked bar; an elaborate model of a future high-rise was near a Ming vase; through the wall of windows to her right, she could see The Redman International Building, towering like a beacon in the afternoon sun.

Leana's gaze lingered on her father's building for a moment before she turned to the man seated across the room at the enormous mahogany table.  His back was to her.  The secretary said, "Leana Redman to see you, sir."

Louis Ryan turned in his chair and faced George Redman's daughter.

Their eyes met.  In each other, they saw the future.

Smiling, he stood.  "I'm glad you could come, Leana," he said. "Last night, Harold Baines was kind enough to miss a dinner engagement with your sister so he could tell me about you."  He motioned toward the chair opposite him.  "Please sit down?"

Leana did.  And the meeting began.

*  *  *

"I don't believe in wasting time," Louis said.  "So, I'm going to come to the point.  You don't mind, do you?"

"I prefer getting to the point," Leana said.  "It's why I'm here."

She watched him move to a window that looked uptown.  He pointed at a tall structure cocooned in scaffolding.   "Are you familiar with the new hotel I'm building on the corner of Fifth and 53rd? That's it over there."

Leana nodded. "Once finished, it's supposed to be the city's largest."

"That's right," Louis said. "And I bet it pisses your father off that I'm its owner and not him."

"I have no idea what my father thinks."

"Oh, come on," he said.

"Sorry. I wouldn't know."

"Of course, you do. Your father makes it a point to own the biggest and the best of everything in this city. All of New York knows that. He must be furious that soon I'll be running the largest hotel in Manhattan, not him."

"What does any of this have to do with me, Mr. Ryan?"

"It's Louis," he said. "And I'm getting to that."

He walked to his desk and sat. He lit a cigarette, exhaled and looked at Leana through the screen of gray-blue smoke. "You don't get along with your father, do you?"

Leana met his unwavering gaze with her own. "That's none of your business."

"Maybe not," he said. "But it's not exactly a secret."

She let the silence linger.

"How old are you, Leana?"

"Twenty-five."

"And your sister?"

She hesitated. "Twenty-nine."

"That isn't much of an age difference."

"I guess it isn't."

"Last night Harold told me that Celina was just a young girl when your father began taking her to board meetings at Redman International. He neglected to say how old you were."

"That's because my father never took me to board meetings at Redman International."

"Really?" he said. "That's odd. Certainly you must have worked there at some point."

"No," Leana said. "Never."

"Then you didn't have any interest in the business?"

"I didn't say that."

"Then what are you saying?"

She knew he was trying to get her angry, but she didn't understand why. "I guess I'm saying that my father didn't want me around."

"And why is that?"

"I'm not sure."

"Are you incompetent?"

"Are you serious?"

"Isn't it true that, in your father's eyes, you never could quite compare to Celina? That you didn't measure up? Isn't that why you were shipped off to Switzerland all those years?" His shrugged. "Isn't that why you got addicted to cocaine?"

Leana stood. "You can go to hell."

"I probably will," Louis said. "But while I'm still on this earth, you'd better let me help you while I can. Now, sit down and cut out the sulking bullshit."

Leana left for the exit. *What was Harold thinking sending me here?*

Louis waited for her to cross the room and grasp the door handle before he called out to her. "I could put you on top, you know. I could make you the envy of this town, bigger than your sister Celina ever could hope to become."

The temptation was great, but Leana opened the door and left the office. She wouldn't be treated like this by anyone.

She moved down the hall toward the wall of elevators, passing the same groups of men and women she envied earlier but no longer envied now. Some seemed to recognize her along the way and she sensed them staring, as if they were wondering why George Redman's daughter was here, of all places.

Behind her, a door opened. And then his voice: "Leana."

She was on the cold rails of her control now, making steady progress toward the elevators.

"Leana." There was a new note in his voice. "Please come back so we can talk. There was a reason for what I said."

She turned to him. He was standing just outside his office, smiling a smile that was not sarcastic, but apologetic. *What in God's name do I want this bad?*

When she returned to his office, she found him fixing them a drink at the bar. Ice rattled as he poured what looked like vodka into two short glasses. He tried to hand her one of the glasses, but instead put it on the counter when she refused it.

"I meant what I said, you know. I can--and will--put you on top." He took a drink. "You'd like that, wouldn't you?" He raised a hand. "No need to answer--I can see it in your eyes. You're angry as hell and I can't say that I blame you. Your father gave your sister the world and he left you with nothing. It hurts. I get it."

"Why are you doing this to me?"

"Because I hate your father. He's fortunate enough to have had two beautiful daughters and stupid enough to have treated only one of them fairly. My father used to treat me the same way your father treats you. My brother was the star--not me. When Harold came last night and told me your story, I decided I wanted to help."

"If you want to help me so badly, then why did you put me through that?"

"Because I needed to see if you had it in you to stand up to me--which you did." He looked toward the picture of a woman that rested on his desk. "If I didn't think you had guts, Leana, I could never offer you the position I'm about to offer you."

"And what position is that?"

"The new hotel I'm building?" Louis said. "I want you to run it for me."

\* \* \*

Like the waiters who worked there, the restaurant on 56th Street was chic, charming and Italian. When Leana arrived, she checked her watch, saw that she was a few minutes early for her dinner date with Mario and went to the crowded oak bar that was to the right of the lobby.

The buzz of conversation was noticeably louder there and it surrounded her. Leana sat on a wooden stool, ordered a glass of white wine and amused herself by watching the people. She was feeling very, very giddy. *I just agreed to run the largest hotel in Manhattan--and I know zip about the hotel business. So, I'm crazy. And so what if I am?*

The restaurant was filled with couples. Leana turned and saw people of all ages talking and laughing and smiling. At one of the corner tables, she noticed a young woman speaking to an older man. They resembled each other. The woman was talking quickly and her features were animated.

Leana wondered if they were father and daughter. She wondered what news the woman was sharing and couldn't help feeling a stab of envy. Although she knew her father loathed Louis Ryan, Leana decided there was nothing more in the world she would like right now than to share with her father her own exciting news.

She looked away from the couple, knowing that day wouldn't come. While her sister shared a life with her father, Leana had shared only his house.

It was getting late. Mario usually was punctual. She wondered where he was. She had just ordered her second glass of wine when a man in a dark blue suit placed a hand on the stool beside her.

"Is this seat taken?" he asked.

Leana was about to say it was when she noticed it was Michael Archer. She felt an initial start, but stilled it. "Now, this," she said coolly, "is a surprise."

Michael smiled. "I could say the same."

"It's good to see you," Leana said. "What brings you here?"

"Good food and a beautiful woman." She glanced behind him and he added, "Who ultimately stood me up."

"Oh, please. Who stands you up?"

"It's true," he said. "And it always happens with models. Care to offer some insight?"

"Just let me be clear on this," she said. "You date models?"

"Sometimes."

"That's the saddest thing I've heard all day."

"Maybe a drink will make you feel better?"

Leana lifted her full glass of wine. "Too late," she said. "But let me buy you one. It will help cheer you up from your model malaise. What would you like? Something without calories?"

He laughed. "Anything cold," he said. "The heat is murder today."

He caught the barman's attention and ordered a beer. When it arrived, he took a long swallow and thanked Leana.

"My pleasure."

"What brings you here?" he asked. "I'm not interrupting something, am I?"

"You're not interrupting a thing. I'm supposed to be meeting a friend for dinner, but he's late. I'm beginning to wonder if I've been stood up, too."

"How late is late?"

"Thirty minutes late."

Michael lifted an eyebrow. "You've got that kind of patience? I was leaving after waiting only twenty minutes."

"Oh, you novelists," she said. "Oh, you movie stars. So busy. So little time."

He couldn't help a smile. "Have you given him a call?"

"No," Leana said. "But that isn't a bad idea."

She excused herself to use her cell phone. She was reaching into her purse for it when a waiter tapped her on the shoulder. "Leana Redman?"

Leana looked at the man. "Yes?"

"Message for you." He handed her a slip of paper and left.

Leana knew the note was from Mario before she opened it.

Leana:

I tried calling you at Harold's but you were out. I'm not going to be able to make dinner tonight. I forgot it's Lucia's birthday and I need to spend it with her and the kids. Especially because of the kids. I swear I'll make this up to you. Try not to be angry. I'll explain everything when I get in touch with you.

--Mario

Leana crumpled the note and dropped it in an ashtray. So, now he was lying to her. She knew Lucia's birthday was only a week after her own--and that wasn't for another five months.

She tried to still a twinge of anger, but couldn't. She should have known that he would let her down. Sooner or later, most men did. She wondered why she thought she could trust him in the first place. *He's married*, she thought. *When am I going to get it? Married men and Leana Redman equals poison. Time to move on.*

When she returned to the bar, Michael was signing the back of a cocktail napkin for one of the waitresses. Leana watched him. He seemed comfortable with his celebrity, at ease and unaffected by it. She knew he was attracted to her. She sensed that the night of the party. But she was attracted to him, too.

She waited for the waitress to leave before approaching him.

"Can I also have your autograph?" she asked. "It would mean the world to me, Mr. Archer. I'd do anything to get it."

"Where do you want it."

She waved a hand, sat down and reached for her glass of wine. "Since my ass obviously is a target tonight, you could put it there."

"What does that mean."

"Apparently, I've been stood up, too, which is a shame because I'm starving. So how about me buying you dinner?"

"You already bought me a drink. My turn."

"No," she said as they slid off their barstools. "I asked first. But please, do me a favor and order of the children's menu." She placed a hand on his shoulder. "Money got a little tight today."

\* \* \*

Vincent Spocatti waited for them to be seated before leaving his seat at the end of the bar. He phoned Louis Ryan, who answered on the second ring. "This is Ryan."

"They're ordering dinner."

"Good," Louis said. "And I assume Mr. De Cicco won't be bothering them during their meal?"

"I doubt it," Spocatti said. "Not after the package I sent his wife."

Spocatti was full of surprises. "What was in it?"

"Three dozen black roses and a note saying if she'd like to join her mother in hell, please feel free to step out of her home."

He spotted the note Leana tossed into the ashtray and reached for it. He uncrumpled it and read it to Louis. "Obviously, Mario is keeping an eye on his wife as we speak."

"How did Leana react?"

"How do you think? She is having dinner with Michael, Louis."

"Let's hope sparks fly," Louis said. "Because if they don't and if I don't hear wedding bells soon, I'm not paying Santiago a dime and my son will go to hell."

## CHAPTER TWENTY-TWO

While Leana was having dinner with Michael, Celina was phoning George and asking him to meet her for a drink. "I don't care if you're busy. I need to talk to you. Be at Houlihan's on 56th and Lex in an hour. It's important."

She arrived at the popular bar ten minutes early.

The bar itself was three deep in people--most of whom were either posing or prowling, or throwing their heads back in comic relief.

Celina's glance swept the pandemonium for George. She saw young businessmen in thousand-dollar suits struggling to look sophisticated and successful young businesswomen sipping white wine and trying to kick the traces of cocaine. She didn't see George and she was glad. Celina wanted to see her father come in, wanted to watch him in that one moment before he knew she was watching.

She shouldered her way to the bar. One of the women recognized her and there was an audible whisper across the crowd: "Celina Redman...."

People turned and stared and Celina heard Eric Parker's name mentioned more than once. She focused her attention on the barman. She ordered a martini and turned to look across a wooden divider, where people sat talking and drinking. A couple was just leaving a corner table, making it now the only available table in the place.

Celina paid for the drink and moved toward the table. She sat--and was surprised by how tired she was.

All day long, she and her father had been caucusing with Ted Frostman about the feasibility of taking over WestTex Incorporated. While he was enthusiastic, there were some at Chase who were more cautious. They wanted to run their own due diligence. They wanted to unleash on the company their own team of lawyers and accountants. They wanted to speak to Iran themselves. Until they knew every nook and cranny of WestTex,

164

until they were certain the deal with Iran would not fall through, they would not commit themselves to this takeover.

And Celina couldn't blame them. There was too much at risk, but time wasn't a luxury in this deal and Frostman and Chase knew it. If they couldn't give her father a commitment soon, George would have to try again and look elsewhere for financing.

She happened to be watching the doors when George stepped into the bar.

He looked tan and lean and was wearing the same comfortable style of clothing he always wore after work--khaki pants, white cotton shirt, brown leather loafers.

He went to the bar. People stepped aside, the conversation around him faltered, and he knew it. He had just caught the bartender's eye when a young man in an expensively tailored gray suit approached him. He thrust out his hand, shook George's and spoke to the bartender. Two drinks appeared in what seemed like a matter of seconds. They touched glasses, drank and George listened patiently as the man made his pitch.

Celina couldn't help a smile. Although it happened more frequently than he liked, her father never shied away from such situations. He often said this was how he found some of his best employees.

She wondered if George felt that way now. He had met and hired Eric Parker at a bar like this.

The young man left with a smile stamped on his face and George turned to look for Celina. When he spotted her, he held her gaze for a moment, nodded to acknowledge he had seen her and came across the room. Celina could sense in him a slight annoyance at having been called away from home.

He took the seat opposite her. "This is quite a place," George said. "Loud and full...and young. You come here often?"

"Eric and I used to." ·

He accepted this with a nod.

"Let me come right to the point."

"Go for it."

"I want to know if you had anything to do with what happened to Eric last night."

The tension was quick to form, and it stretched between them. George looked at Celina, but his face remained expressionless.

He didn't answer.

"I was there when they wheeled Eric out of Redman Place," Celina said. "I saw them lift him into the back of an ambulance. I saw Diana Crane join him. I want to know if you had anything to do with it."

"What does your heart tell you?"

"Don't play games with me, Dad."

"I'm not playing games with you."

"Then just answer the question."

"Not until you answer mine."

At that moment, she felt a bitterness toward her father she had never before felt--and it frightened her. She thought of the argument they had the other morning and realized they no longer were as close as they once were. Something had shifted. She knew she could stop this, but she wouldn't. Celina had to know the truth, no matter what she might lose because of it.

"All right," she said. "My heart says there is no way you could have done this."

"Then why are we here?"

"Because the rest of me feels differently."

"Well," George said. "I'm sorry to hear that." He finished his drink and stood. "I'll see you tomorrow, Celina."

"Where are you going?"

"Back home to your mother."

"But you haven't answered my question."

"And I don't intend to. It's ludicrous."

"Then answer this for me, Dad. If you had nothing to do with what happened to Eric, who did you call that day in your study?"

George looked down at her. Celina met his gaze with her own. She wouldn't look away.

"You want to know who I phoned that day in my study?"

"Yes. I want to know."

George placed his hands on the table and leaned forward. His face was only inches from hers when he spoke. "I phoned a friend of mine who's going to see to it that Eric Parker never works in this town again. That's what I did to Eric, Celina. I destroyed his professional career. Nothing else." He straightened. "Satisfied?"

She knew he was telling her the truth. She could see it on his face.

George turned to leave.

"Wait," Celina said. "There's something I have to tell you. Something that's important."

"What is it?"

"It's about Leana."

There was a guarded look in his eyes. "What about Leana?"

"She was there last night. I saw her in the crowd."

George looked around them, likely to judge if anyone was listening. He reclaimed his seat. "Go on," he said.

"She was with two men. I noticed her after they wheeled Eric out of Redman Place."

"Did she see you?"

"I called out her name to make sure of it."

"What did she do?"

"She spoke to the men beside her, they looked at me and hurried her away from the crowd. When they lifted Eric into that ambulance, I swear to God she was smiling."

George reached for his empty glass of Scotch and wished it was full. "What did the men look like?"

Celina read his mind. "They looked like friends of Mario De Cicco's to me."

"Do you think she's seeing him again?"

"I wouldn't put anything past Leana."

"Neither would I." He pushed back his chair.

"There's more," Celina said. "This morning, I spoke to the doormen who were on duty last night."

"And?"

"Each of them mentioned talking with Leana. My guess is that she distracted them so her friends could get to Eric." There was a silence. "I didn't want to tell you any of this, but I thought you should know. If one of those doormen tells the police that Leana was there during the time of the attack, she could get into serious trouble--especially if Eric learns she was there. There's no telling what he'd do if he makes that connection."

"What makes you think he hasn't already?"

George stood and turned to leave, but then he stopped and faced his daughter. "I'm going to be honest with you, Celina. One thing still bothers me."

"What's that?"

"The fact that you knew all this and still thought I was responsible for what happened to Eric."

\* \* \*

Later, in his office at Redman Place, George spoke separately to the same three doormen Leana spoke to the night Eric was beaten.

One was a Mexican, the other two Hispanics. The message he gave each was the same--George had friends at the Department of Immigration. If even one of them mentioned to the police that they spoke to Leana the night of the beating, he would see to it that all were deported to their respective countries the following week.

## CHAPTER TWENTY-THREE

For three days there was nothing but darkness and haze and a terrible, unrelenting pain that came in waves and consumed him. From time to time, during those moments when the haze lifted slightly, he became aware of sounds--a door swinging open, men talking, a woman sobbing. And then darkness.

He dreamed.

He was in his bedroom, making love to Diana and suddenly there was no longer a sheet covering them. Before he could react, before he could even think, there was a hand on the back of his neck and he was being pulled, lifted, thrown. At the same instant his head struck the bureau, he heard Diana scream. There were two distinct slaps, followed by a muffled cry. And then nothing as she fell silent.

Eric struggled to his feet, groped for a light switch, turned it on. There were two men, both in black. One had a handful of Diana's hair and was dragging her from the room. Blood seeped from her forehead and mouth, staining her skin. She was unconscious.

Eric looked to his right. The other man was coming at him. He was tall and solid and walked without hesitation or hurry. In his hand, Eric saw his own baseball bat--the one he kept in the front hall, the one he used on Sunday afternoons in the Park, the one he once hit a grand slam with. Leana was at that game. She had sat beneath the shade of an elm, cheering along with the rest of the crowd.

Leana....

He took a step back, stumbled to the floor and watched the baseball bat descend to bash in the side of his head. He lifted a hand to shield his face, but the attacker instead swung lower and the bat struck Eric's leg, splintering the bone.

Eric screamed. He turned onto his side, clawed at the carpet, tried to move, tried to run, but it was useless--the pain was overwhelming.

169

He looked down at his leg and saw that it was horribly twisted. A broken bone jetted from the torn flesh. A wave of nausea seized him. Bile rose in his mouth and he gagged. The man tossed the bat aside, grabbed Eric by the head and started clubbing his face with his fist. Each blow sent Eric into an abyss that was deeper than any nightmare he had ever fallen in.

But even in sleep, Eric knew this nightmare was reality. When he woke on the fourth day, the hospital room was in shadow. He became aware of sounds again. He heard the faint hum of an air conditioner, the familiar tapping of rain against a window he couldn't see. He turned his head.

Tried to turn his head.

The action sent sharp knives of pain throughout his body. He moaned.

Across the room, someone, a woman: "Eric?"

His lips parted. They felt as dry and as swollen as his tongue and throat. It took everything he had to force out one word: "Celina?"

"No," the voice said. "It's Diana."

She came across the room and sat in the white vinyl chair that was beside his bed. After pressing a button to alert the nurse, she reached for his hand and held it in her own. "You're going to be all right," she said. "You're in for a rough ride, but you're awake now and you're going to be all right."

He tried to speak again, but Diana put a finger to his lips. "Try not to talk or move. You've had an operation on your leg. It's in a cast now, but the doctors say you'll eventually be fine. All you have to do is rest and concentrate on getting better. I'll take care of everything else."

The nurse stepped into the room. Diana turned to her. "He's awake," she said. "And he's in pain. Can you get something for him?"

The woman stepped over to the bed and checked Eric's chart. "I'm sorry," she said. "He isn't due for another shot until four."

"I don't care if he isn't due for another shot until next week," Diana said evenly. "He's in pain. Part of your job is pain management. Now, either you move your ass and manage that pain, or I'll get your supervisor." She cocked her head. "You won't want that to happen."

The nurse said she'd speak to the doctor and left the room.

Diana turned back to Eric and saw that he was looking at her intently. "I'll be all right," she said. "It's just a black eye and a scrape on the forehead. I've been dealt worse blows than this in my life."

Eric wondered if that was true. Although he had known Diana for years, he knew surprisingly little about her. He knew she came from a small city in Maine, knew her father died at an early age, knew what a struggle it had been for her to complete college and earn her law degree. Beyond that, it was as if she was just another one of the many faceless people he had met in his life. Only this faceless person was in love with him and now caring for him. He wondered if she sensed that he didn't love her, that he never had and never would, that the only reason he stepped into her life was because he was lonely and wanted to make Celina jealous.

He felt a twinge of guilt. There was no question that somehow Diana saved his life. He should feel grateful for what she's done for him, and he was, though not in the way she wanted him to be. Eric still loved Celina.

Diana was smiling down at him, her hand still squeezing his. She was a strong woman--he knew that--and although he never fully liked her, he did respect her. She was a good lawyer. She appeared to be a good person. But when he fully ended it with her, he wondered how good she would be then.

Diana stood. "There's something I want to show you," she said, turning on a light.

Eric winced. He saw the flowers only after his eyes adjusted. The room was literally filled with bouquets of flowers. Diana plucked a rose from its vase and Eric looked questioningly at her.

"A lot of people care about you," she said. "These have been arriving for the past four days. But there's no more room for them. I hope you don't mind, but I told the nurse to start sending whatever else comes to those patients who haven't received flowers."

"Who sent...?" His voice was a rasp, his lips barely able to move. "Did you collect the cards?"

"Of course," Diana said. "They're all in that drawer. But most are from Louis Ryan. He's been here half a dozen times and he's pretty concerned about you."

She stepped over to the bed and looked down at him. "Considering the way George feels about him, I had no idea that you and Louis Ryan were such good friends."

Neither had Eric.

* * *

Diana had just left for Redman International when the doctor stepped into the room.

He was middle-aged with a deep tan, deeper brown eyes and hair that had gone prematurely white. His name was Dr. Robert Hutchins and he checked Eric's chart closely. "You have a broken leg, two cracked ribs, and a multitude of cuts and bruises. Otherwise, you're in perfect health."

Eric attempted to sit up, but failed. He tried to clear his throat and was surprised that even that was difficult. Earlier, they had given him a cup of hot tea with honey, a generous shot of Demerol and now it was easier for him to speak.

"When can I get out of here?"

"That depends on you."

"Start packing my bags."

"Maybe I should rephrase that," Hutchins said. "You'll leave here when your body allows you to. The men who attacked you knew what they were doing. Your leg was broken in three places. I think they wanted to make sure you wouldn't walk again."

It was a moment before Eric could speak. "Will I?"

The doctor hesitated. "You'll walk," he said. "But it will be awhile before you can do so without a limp. You were struck in the leg with a baseball bat and your femur splintered, causing nerve and muscle damage. As you know, we had to operate. You now have a steel pin in your leg." He drew back the sheet and pinched Eric's big toe. He watched Eric's face and waited for a reaction. There was none.

He pinched harder, this time digging in with his fingernails. Nothing.

"I want you to try wiggling your toes for me, Eric."

Eric lifted his head slightly and looked down at his leg. It was elevated and in a cast. His toes were a shade darker than the bruises had been on Leana's face.

The sight startled him.

"I know," Hutchins said. "But some discoloration is normal. They'll look better in a week. Now, try wiggling them."

When Eric couldn't, he eased his head back onto the pillow. With tightly shut eyes, he said, "I'm going to fucking kill her."

"Excuse me?"

"Nothing," he said, and tried again to wiggle his toes. He couldn't. No matter how hard he tried, he couldn't move them.

"Okay, Eric," the doctor said. "Come on. Try moving them for me."

"I have been."

Hutchins glanced at him. There was a look of fear on Eric's face--only slightly masked by a look of rage.

Wordlessly, Hutchins replaced the sheet. "How much of that night do you remember?"

*Everything.* "Nothing."

"Any idea who could have done this to you?"

*I know.* "None," he said.

"When you woke earlier, we had to call the police. They're waiting outside. They want to question you, but if you feel that you're too weak to do it, just tell me and they'll be gone for now."

"I'll talk to them eventually," Eric said. "But later? I want to go back to sleep. I doubt if I'll be of any help, anyway." *I'll take care of that bitch myself.*

"How are you feeling?"

"How do you think I'm feeling? I'm in fucking pain."

He watched Hutchins prepare a syringe and inject it into the IV. "Sleep," he said. "This will help." He clicked the empty syringe into the biohazard box and touched Eric's shoulder. "You're going to be all right," he said. "But I'm not going to lie to you. The worst is yet to come. It'll be months before you regain full use of your leg--and you'll only get that far if you work very hard in rehab. So, I want you to get as much rest as possible. You're going to need it."

# FIFTH AVENUE

* * *

He woke at midnight.

The rain had stopped, the sky was clear and moonlight cut into his room from the window opposite his bed.

He looked down the length of his cast to his foot. In the silver light of the moon, the bruises on his toes looked black. He tried moving his toes, couldn't, and tried harder. They remained still.

Eric closed his eyes and prayed to a God he hadn't prayed to in years. He made promises no man could ever be expected to keep and opened his eyes. He tried but still couldn't move his toes. It was as if they were no longer a part of his body. He wondered if he would ever walk again.

It was at that moment he made his decision. He reached for the phone that was on the table next to him, grimaced from a sudden stab of pain in his left shoulder, and punched numbers. A moment passed before a familiar voice answered.

After explaining in detail what had happened, Eric told the man exactly what he wanted from him. There was a silence.

"You're sure?" the man said.

"I'm sure," Eric said.

"And you understand once I've set things into motion, you can't change your mind. We go through channels, many of which are anonymous. This is an irreversible decision on your part. You need to understand that."

"I understand that," Eric said. "That's why I called you."

"Any particular way you want it done?"

"I couldn't care less how it's done, Sal--but I do expect her to suffer before she dies."

"Suffering is additional."

"Then charge me for it."

"We'll be in touch," the man said. "And don't worry. We'll make her life a living hell."

## CHAPTER TWENTY-FOUR

The phone rang three times before Leana looked at the clock on her bedside table.  It was 7:15 A.M. and her apartment was ablaze with early-morning sunlight.

She sat up in bed and wondered who would call at this hour of the morning.  She thought of a number of possibilities and realized the only person she really wanted to hear from was Michael Archer.  But he rarely phoned.  Lately, he almost always chose to stop by instead.

When the phone entered its fifth ring, Leana answered it--and the line went dead.  That was twice since last evening someone had called and hung up on her.  She wondered if Mario somehow got her number and was calling to see if she was in and safe, but didn't want to talk.  But she cast that idea aside.  If Mario wanted to talk to her, he'd talk.

She replaced the receiver, slid under the covers and wondered how he was.  She hadn't seen him since the night Eric was beaten; hadn't heard from him since the note she received in the restaurant.

Although she was angry with him for lying to her, she missed him, though not enough to call.  She would leave that up to Mario.

She looked around her new apartment.

In a matter of days, she and Michael Archer had transformed the loft into a place she now was proud to call home.  No longer were the walls a dull, lifeless gray--they now were ivory bright.  The furniture the previous tenant left behind was gone--Michael had it hauled away--and the broken windows were replaced with fresh panes of glass.  Although there still was much to be done-- furniture to buy, curtains to hang, floors to clean and wax--she was looking forward to the work, perhaps because she knew Michael would be there to help her.

She wondered if he planned on stopping by later.  Since the night they had dinner, he had come by every morning to help with the painting.  They spent their days painting and talking and listening to music on the iPod and Bose dock Michael bought as a housewarming gift.

She learned about his life in Hollywood, how difficult it had been for him to write and publish his first novel, and the details of his parents' death.

"What's it like without them?" she asked.

"I miss my mother," he said. "She died when I was young. But my father?" He shrugged. "Not so much. We didn't get along."

Evenings were best. After calling it a day, they would clean up and take to the city.

Michael showed Leana a side of New York she hadn't seen. They dined at small family restaurants in the Village, went to poetry readings, browsed the many art galleries. They went to see a play at the Cherry Lane Theater, had a beer and a game of darts at the Kettle of Fish, and walked the streets, looking up at the buildings and discussing how different the architecture looked at night.

Now, as Leana thought of her new job, of the opportunities it offered and how she felt about Michael, she realized she was approaching an unfamiliar kind of happiness. Not since her relationship with Mario had she felt this vital. She was in an apartment of her own, soon she would begin work for Louis Ryan and she had a great man in her life. For the first time in years, she was experiencing something hopeful. Leana decided it wouldn't be something she would let go of easily.

The telephone rang again. Leana considered ignoring it, but sat up in bed and snatched the receiver from its hook. "Hello," she said.

"Look out your window."

"Who is this?"

"Just look out your window. Hurry up before I get a ticket."

It was Louis Ryan.

Leana stepped out of bed and moved across the room. She hadn't finished unpacking and had to push cardboard boxes out of her way to get to the window.

She parted the blinds.

Down below, double-parked on Fifth, was Louis. He was standing beside a sleek new Mercedes Gullwing, his crown of graying hair stirring in the rising breeze.

His arms were lifted, spread wide. In one hand, he held a bouquet of roses, in the other he held a cell phone. Leana lifted the window and leaned out. "You're insane," she said into the phone. "What are you doing here?"

"Dropping off your new car," Louis said. "Just my way of saying thanks for taking the job."

She felt a thrill. "My new car--you can't be serious!"

"I'm dead serious," he said. "The car's yours--along with my appreciation. You're moving into a powerful position. This car fits the image of that position. People will expect you to be driving something like it."

"They'll hate me for it. Look at those doors!"

Louis shrugged. He tossed the roses and the phone onto the dash and pushed the door down until it clicked shut. He flagged a cab. As one rolled to a stop beside him, he nodded toward the gleaming Mercedes. "The car's running," he shouted. "I didn't have time to find a parking space for it. Unless you want someone to steal it, I suggest you get down here now and find a place to park it."

"But I'm not dressed!"

Louis Ryan didn't care. He was gone.

Leana dressed quickly. She went to her bureau, pulled on a pair of shorts, changed her nightshirt for a crisp, white T-shirt, and stepped into a pair of worn moccasins. Feeling like a child on Christmas morning, she fled her apartment, darted down the five flights of stairs and burst out of the building.

At this hour of the morning, the sidewalks were nearly deserted. Only a few people wearing NYU sweatshirts were jogging down Fifth toward Washington Square.

Leana went to the car. She ran a hand along the slick black surface, felt the smooth hum of the engine, lifted the driver's side door up and down, and couldn't help a smile--the car was a work of art.

As she slipped inside, she reached for the roses and buried her nose in them. Only three years ago she had been in a drug rehab clinic, ready to give up on a life she was convinced was no longer worth living. Now, she was sitting in the new Mercedes Gullwing her employer purchased for her, and soon she would start managing New York City's largest hotel. The change of events was incredible to her.

The cell phone Ryan left behind burst into sound. It was on the passenger seat. Leana reached for it. "I love it," she said.

Louis laughed. She could hear traffic rushing past him and sensed he had the window down. "I'm glad," he said. "And believe me--you'll earn it. Now, look--I'm on my way to the hotel. Why don't you throw the car into gear and meet me there? I think it's time you see where you're going to make your success."

She panicked. "I don't know how to use this thing. It's too powerful. Can your hear the engine? It's roaring."

"Purring," he said. "That car purrs. But you can get it to roar."

"I'll have to change," she said. "And take a shower--"

"Nonsense," Louis said. "You look perfectly fine the way you are. And, besides, it'll just be the two of us. Promise."

\* \* \*

The hotel seemed to touch the sky.

When Leana pulled in front of it, she looked up at its enormous sheets of mirrored glass, at the ultra-modern exterior glass elevators shooting up and down its sides and felt a rush of adrenaline when she noted that the scaffolding had been removed.

Although Louis said work would be completed soon on the 4,000-room hotel, she had no idea it was this close to completion. And then reality struck. *I'm going to be running this place in a matter of days.*

Although her father owned a fleet of hotels, Leana knew nothing about the hotel business. But she knew it would be okay. *Harold will help me.*

With the exception of the exterior glass elevators, perhaps the most striking part of the building was its sign--it was sleek and modern, so smooth in its conception, it looked as if it was designed with the next century in mind. Centered above the entrance, shining in the sun, were three words in ten-foot steel letters:

## The Hotel Fifth

Leana looked at the sign and felt a chill--then a shot of determination--dart up her spine. *I'm going to do this*, she thought. *Failing isn't an option.*

She put the car into gear and was about to leave for the underground garage when she noticed a man in an immaculate gray suit walking swiftly toward her, his smile almost as dazzling as the hotel's sign. "Miss Redman," he said. "Welcome."

He moved to her side of the car and extended a hand, which Leana shook. "Zack Anderson," he said. "Your new assistant."

"It's a pleasure to meet you," Leana said, and quickly became aware of her appearance. Louis said it would be just the two of them here and so she hadn't changed her clothes. But this man, this man who was at least twice her age, looked as if he just stepped off the cover of GQ--and he would be working for her.

"Is Louis here?" she asked.

"He's inside," Zack said. "Just beyond those doors. Would you like me to park the car for you."

Leana thanked him and stepped out of the car. Before he slipped inside, she noticed him noticing her wrinkled shorts, her T-shirt and worn moccasins, and couldn't help wishing she had changed into something more appropriate before leaving home. He lowered the door and Leana watched him run his hands along the leather steering wheel, watched him envy the plush cream interior.

Before he sped off, she said, "Can I ask you something?"

He checked his hair in the rearview mirror. "You can ask me anything," he said casually, without bothering to look at her. "It's why I'm here."

It was at that moment she decided she didn't like him. He was too smooth, too helpful and there was a whiff of condescension about him. *He thinks I'm just another pretty face,* she thought. *So, I'll need to prove him wrong, too.* "How long have you been in this business?" she asked.

179

"Twenty-three years" he said swiftly. "And I have to be honest with you, Miss Redman--one of these days, I hope to have your job."

\* \* \*

Louis Ryan was nowhere in sight when Leana entered the hotel. She waited by the revolving glass and steel doors for several moments before she climbed the small flight of stairs that led to the lobby--which left her stunned.

It was huge, cavernous and filled with seven floors of shops and restaurants and bars. People were hurrying about her. Escalators zigzagged to the atrium's glass ceiling. An enormous indoor waterfall rippled in the center of the room, glinting and casting rainbows of light on the gray marble walls, dividing an open-air restaurant filled with exotic flowers and plants. Not only was this lobby bigger than Redman International's, the way it was positioned in the room made it superior in every way.

She turned her attention to the people bustling past her, watched the hustle and commotion, and became fascinated by how seamlessly everything was coming together.

Men were pushing racks of clothes, polishing glass, wheeling cartons of food across the great expanse of carpet. Women were shouting orders, arranging window displays, shooting past her in crisp, designer outfits.

One woman called to a friend. "We're opening Wednesday and we're booked. Tell me how we're going to be finished in time when we're having a party the night before. This is going to be impossible."

*We'll see about that,* Leana thought and moved further into the room.

As she looked around, it occurred to her that she could see herself managing this place and turning it into the success she promised Louis Ryan it would become.

There was a hand on her arm. Leana turned and saw Zack Anderson. "So, what do you think?" he asked.

"It's beautiful," Leana said.

He laughed softly. "I guess we're not on the same wavelength," he said. "I know it's beautiful. This lobby alone set Mr. Ryan and his investors back a cool $300 million. I was just wondering if you think you're going to be able to manage it."

He was patronizing her. Leana felt a flash of irritation, but stilled it. She smiled at him. "I don't see how I can go wrong, Mr. Anderson. With you taking direction from me and doing all my leg work, how could I fail?"

Zack Anderson's smile faded. Leana squeezed his arm. "I understand there are several gyms here," she said. "May I offer a tip?"

"Of course."

"Start using them. To keep up with me, you're going to have to improve your cardio, not to mention your attitude. I can't have an assistant who can't keep up. And I won't have an assistant whose ego is so big, it could fill this space and squeeze everyone else out of it. Are we clear?"

He was about to answer when something caught his eye and he turned. The smile she had wiped clean from his face resurfaced. "Well, well," he said. "So they decided to come, after all."

Leana followed his gaze. Across the room, moving leisurely in their direction, was Louis Ryan--and he was surrounded by a small group of people in business suits.

"Who are they?" she asked.

Zack Anderson looked surprised. "Who are they?" he repeated. "Miss Redman, just how much do you know about this job?"

"Not as much as I'd like," she admitted. "But that's what you're here for, Zack. Now, tell me--who are they?"

"His investors," the man said. "The people you'll be working for."

He glanced at her scuffed shoes, at her shorts and tousled jet hair, and his smile broadened. "I'll tell Mr. Ryan that you're here so he can make introductions."

\* \* \*

181

Things always had a way of falling into place for Louis Ryan.

When he asked Leana to meet him here this morning, he genuinely thought no one of any real importance would be at the hotel--certainly not at this hour of the morning. And so he told her to come as she was.

Now, as he and his group of investors followed Zack Anderson toward the waterfall, he couldn't have been happier that all that had changed. Just seeing the embarrassment on Leana Redman's face when he introduced her to his partners was worth whatever mistrust she undoubtedly would feel toward him.

They stopped to admire the waterfall. The way it was designed, the water seemed to fall from nowhere though it flowed from a concealed location high above. There was no rippling of the water, just a wide, pure band seamlessly falling into a lighted abyss. As they passed the waterfall, Louis expected to see Leana waiting beyond it, but she wasn't there. He looked around him, but didn't see her. "Where is she?" he said quietly to Anderson. "I thought you said she was here."

The man looked surprised. "She was," he said. "I left her just a moment ago."

"Then where is she now?"

"I'm here," Leana said.

Both men turned.

Walking swiftly in their direction, dressed in an immaculate red Dior suit and matching red shoes, was Leana, her hair tied neatly away from her face, a diamond brooch glimmering on her lapel. She was coming from the direction of the Dior store, where two women stood at the doors and admired how the suit fit.

As she breezed past Louis and Zack and began introducing herself to the small group behind them, there was something in her eyes, something in the defiant way she held her head, that made each man feel as though they just lost a serious game of chess to a woman they assumed was an amateur.

Leana looked away from the group, fixed her gaze on her assistant, then at the man who had become her boss. "Would everyone like coffee?" she asked

A few said they'd love coffee.

"Perfect," she said. "Zack isn't exactly gifted behind the pot, so it's good news that we have Starbucks here." She looked at Zack. "All you need to do is take their order and make sure you get it right. This time, please don't make a mistake." She turned to the group and held out her hands. "Sometimes he gets ahead of himself and makes errors in judgment, especially when it comes to people."

They chuckled. And at that moment, with the heat searing between her and Zack, it was a wonder the waterfall didn't start to boil.

When he was finished taking orders, Leana said, "How does everyone feel about a tour? I've yet to see this place for myself and I just found out we're opening Wednesday. I'm eager to see the hotel for myself."

She leveled Louis with a look. "Shall we?"

\* \* \*

The hotel had four restaurants, five bars, two nightclubs and a theater that seated 3,000 and rivaled anything on Broadway.

In the atrium were name-brand shops of every type, for every taste, but not necessarily for every budget. There was an Olympic-size pool on the roof, a gym on every fifth floor and a small army of personal trainers who were under the advisement of the hotel's five physicians. If guests stayed a week at The Hotel Fifth, there was no reason why they couldn't go home looking and feeling better than they had in years.

As Leana followed Louis and his investors through those rooms he chose to show, even she, a woman who had spent time in some of the world's great luxury hotels, was impressed. Each room offered spectacular views of the city.

"Obviously we're targeting an upscale market," Louis said. "And so each guest will be pampered. Fresh flowers when they arrive in their rooms, an assortment of fruit, a complimentary bottle of champagne. Transportation by our suite of limousines and Bentleys will be available on a first-come, first-served basis. For the business person, we have everything they need--wireless, printers and fax machines, and a spacious, well-lit writing area. For those seeking computer equipment, laptops are available at no cost. For those on vacation, we've provided stylists for the women, tailors for the men." He was beginning to sound more like a well-rehearsed PR person than the chairman of a multi-billion dollar corporation.

Leana stepped onto the terrace, lifted a hand to shield her eyes from the sun and wondered again why Ryan had taken the risk of asking her to run such a hotel. More than once it had occurred to her that he might be using her to anger her father, and while Leana didn't like the feeling, she accepted it because she, too, took the job for the same reason--sticking it to George.

She sensed someone standing behind her. It was Louis. He was standing in the doorway, hands clasped behind him, the sun reflecting off his glasses, making his eyes seem like gleaming spheres. "Pretty boring stuff, huh?"

Leana smiled.

"You won't have to hear more," he said. "We're alone now. Zack's going to finish the rest of the tour."

"That's good," she said. "Zack is so...capable."

"He's an arrogant prick," Louis said. "But he's the best at what he does. When you're in a pinch, he'll have your back. That's why I keep him. That's why you'll come to like him."

"We'll see."

He moved to the railing she was standing at and leaned against it. They were on the fortieth floor and the city stretched out before them. "So, what's the problem?" he asked. "You're quiet."

Leana decided that if she was going to work for this man, she was going to be honest with him.

"I got this job because you wanted to piss off my father, didn't I?"

"Now what makes you think that?"

Leana raised a hand. "Look," she said. "Can we just cut the bullshit? We both know that you and my father would like to see each other dead. We both know that my father is going to be furious when he learns I've taken this job. That'll make you happy. Frankly, it also will make me happy. Very happy. Do you understand what I'm saying?"

Louis lifted his head.  Behind his glasses, his eyes narrowed slightly, almost as if he were seeing her in a different light, putting her in a different league. "I do," he said.

"I just don't want you to think that I don't know what's going on here," Leana said. "Because I do.  But I promise you this, Louis--this hotel will become a success under my leadership.  It will become the only hotel to stay at in this city.  I know the right people to ask for help when I need it.  And I also know when to trust my gut when they aren't available. Are we clear on that?"

"Perfectly."

"Good," Leana said.  "So, if there's nothing more, I have to return this outfit to the boutique on the first floor.  Before I was ambushed by your group of investors, I told the manager she'd have it back within the hour." She clicked her tongue.  "And to think you said it was going to be just the two of us this morning."

"I thought it was going to be," he said truthfully.  "Seeing them here was as much a surprise to you as it was to me."  He nodded at the brooch.  "What are you going to do with that?"

Leana lifted her lapel and looked down at the dazzling swirl of diamonds.  "Oh, this?  This is going to be charged to you.  So is the suit.  J'adore Dior.  The car's nice, Louis, and I appreciate it.  But now that we've come to a mutual understanding about why I'm really here, I think you'll agree they're worth it when my father learns that the car, the suit and this brooch came from you."

As she moved past him, she leaned into him.  "You want me to play dirty?  It comes at a cost.  But you can afford it.  See you."

\* \* \*

On the drive back to her apartment, Leana allowed herself a well-deserved smile.  She had been put on the spot and she handled herself well.  She doubted whether her sister could have done better.

After finding a rare parking space along Fifth, she grabbed the roses off the seat beside her and raced up the five flights of stairs to her apartment--stopping abruptly when she saw the man waiting outside her apartment door.

He turned to her.

"Leana Redman?" he said.

Leana took a step back down the stairs, ready to bolt if he tried something. She did not give her name. "How did you get up here?" she said.

The man was short, wiry and had blond spiky hair. He nodded past her, motioning down the stairs. "The door was open."

"What do you want?"

"If you're Leana Redman, I got a package for you--but you need to sign first."

He thrust out a clipboard with some papers on it and Leana noticed for the first time the gift-wrapped package that was at his feet. Still wary, she signed where she was told and took the package when he handed it to her.

The man didn't move. Instead, he just looked at her and waited with his hands on his hips. He attempted what she supposed was a smile.

Leana got the hint and moved past him. "Sorry," she said. "My purse is inside. Could you give me a minute?"

She unlocked her apartment door and closed it when she went inside. She dropped the roses and the package onto a counter top, and reached for her purse on a side table. She removed a twenty, went back to the door and handed it to the man. "Thanks," she said, and shut the door in his face. She locked it twice and dead bolted it once. He gave her the creeps.

The box was heavy for its size.

As she crossed the room to her bed, she shook it. Something inside rattled. She couldn't imagine what it was or who it was from. *Not Louis again....*

She sat at the foot of her bed, curled her legs around her and began removing the pink wrapping paper. When she opened the box, a scent of her favorite perfume drifted to her--the perfume Michael gave her yesterday as a gift. Smiling, she removed sheet upon sheet of red tissue paper, not stopping until she had gripped the object that was at the bottom of the box.

For a moment, she froze. The object was a gun.

Leana released it, the coolness of the metal lingering like a poison on her palm and fingertips.

Inside was a note.

Miss Redman:

I've been asked to watch you for some time now and I must say that it's going to be a shame to kill you. Never have I seen such a remarkably beautiful young woman. This morning, while you were sitting in your new car, I had to still an urge to press against your back the very gun that's in this box and take you home with me. I can only imagine how exquisite your legs would feel around my back, can only dream how sweet our love-making would be.

But that won't be. My job is to kill you. Allow me to apologize now. When I take your life, it won't be with pleasure.

And that is why I'm giving you an opportunity--take the gun, press it against your temple and pull the trigger. It will weigh much less heavily on my mind knowing you had the good sense to take your own life and I can guarantee you that it will be far less painful. Sometimes, when people don't take my advice, I can become quite....brutal. Especially when I've been paid more to be brutal.

It really is a perfect day for a suicide, wouldn't you say? The sun is shining, the birds are singing, the gun is loaded. Please make the right decision, Miss Redman. Someone as pretty as you should be spared as much pain as possible.

I'm giving you twenty-four hours to make your decision. Any time after that and you're fair game. Oh, and please don't do anything foolish like telling someone about this. If you do, I'll know--and neither of us wants that.

Leana crumpled the note and dropped it in the box.
Her breathing was uneven.
Perspiration shimmered on her forehead.
Eric was behind this. She was sure of it.

She looked at the phone. She should call Mario and tell him everything. But she couldn't. If she did, there was no doubt that somehow this man would find out.

She felt suddenly and entirely alone. There was fear, but it was a different kind of fear from the fear she felt when Eric beat her. She knew then that he wouldn't kill her. She knew now that he wanted her dead.

She looked at her watch and saw that it was getting late. She wondered where Michael was. She wondered if he had already come by and found her gone.

Her head was spinning.

*I'm giving you twenty-four hours to make your decision. Any time after that and you're fair game.*

## CHAPTER TWENTY-FIVE

From the Mercedes' cool interior, the three men watched Michael Archer walk down the busy sidewalk, watched him shift a bag of groceries from one arm to the other, and watched him stop to say hello to an elderly woman pushing a rusty shopping cart.

Only after he entered the brick tenement on Avenue B did they make their move.

One by one, they stepped out of the car. Doors opened, clicked shut. Two men were tall and muscular, their dark hair slicked back into shiny ponytails. The other man was slightly older, wiser-looking, with short graying hair and pale skin--the glass of his silver spectacles flashed white in the hazy, early-morning sun.

His name was Ethan Cain, he was an international assassin and he had been hired yesterday morning by Stephano Santiago. While he hadn't met Santiago in person, the $125 thousand dollars Santiago deposited into Cain's Swiss bank account was perhaps the only introduction he would ever need.

His instructions were simple--remind Michael Archer that in one week a certain gambling debt was due. Use whatever force was necessary.

Cain had his own ideas about that.

Although he was American, he had lived the better part of his life in Paris and spoke in French to the two men beside him. "Archer's apartment is on the sixth floor. Try not to kill him."

They crossed the street and entered the building. Inside it was dark and musty. The air smelled of alcohol and cigarette smoke. Cain glanced down both ends of a long corridor, saw peeling wallpaper, a cat urinating in a shadowy corner, a woman stepping half-naked into her apartment. He also saw two stairwells and a service elevator. He gave his men their instructions.

When they separated, it was Cain who took the elevator. As he rose in the rattling iron cage to Michael Archer's apartment, he reached inside his black leather jacket and felt the gun he concealed there earlier. Its steely coolness sent a rush of anticipation up his spine and he wondered if Archer would give him an excuse to use it.

He hoped so. It had been a week since he'd taken a life.

They met on the sixth floor. In one of the apartments, someone was playing a stereo so loudly that the walls and floor literally vibrated with the sounds of heavy metal music. This pleased Cain. It was a sign to let him know that Archer was in his apartment. Earlier, he had given the man playing the music five hundred dollars to be a lookout.

They started down the hall. Cain's senses were acute. He was aware of sights and sounds and smells he normally would have ignored. Later, as always, he'd be able to describe--in detail-- exactly how the job went down.

They stopped at the door at the end of the hall. Cain withdrew his gun, took a step back. There was a silence while he and his men stood looking at one another. Then Cain nodded at the taller of the two men and winced as the door was kicked open.

They rushed inside, ready for anything.

But the room was empty.

Incredulous, Cain stood in the middle of the small living space. As the driving beat of the hard rock music enveloped him, he saw on a side table the sack of groceries Archer had with him on the street and knew that he'd been here.

He looked around the room. How did Archer leave when all three exits were covered? Was he still in here, hiding?

Cain threw open a closet door, shoved aside a rack of clothes. Nothing. His gaze swept the room. Boxes filled with Archer's belongings cluttered a floor that was scarred with a million heel marks. Sunlight from an open window played across a bed that had been slept in. A pair of torn, faded curtains moved in the breeze.

And then Cain knew. Knew.

He went to the window and looked out. Archer was hurrying down the fire escape, rapidly approaching street-level, his footsteps deadened by the music thundering from the hallway.

Somehow, he had seen them. Cain raised his gun, had an impulse to shoot, but stilled it. There were too many people on the street.  He would have to take Archer another way.

He fled the apartment with his men.

\* \* \*

The streets were thronged with people.  Michael pushed his way through them, shot through traffic, got nudged in the hip by a moving car and kept running.  Not once did he look behind him until he reached the corner of East Houston.  And there they were, closing in, hands in outsized pockets, unseen weapons gripped--just as he had feared.

He ran faster.

Since Rufus' death, he had taken precautions.  He knew his father was correct.  No matter what Santiago promised, the man couldn't be trusted.  And so, whether leaving his apartment--or returning to it--Michael always found an excuse to stop and glance around.

Today, the excuse was saying hello to the elderly woman with the rusty shopping cart.  If he hadn't stopped to say hello to her, he never would have seen the three men watching him from the Mercedes.  And if he hadn't rushed up the steps to his apartment and looked out his only window, he wouldn't have seen those men leaving the Mercedes to cross the street.

He turned up First Avenue, looked over his shoulder.  The men were still there, closer than before, threading their way through the crowds on the sidewalk.  Michael knew that as long as they kept him in sight, they could force him to keep running blindly, not knowing which street or alley he took might lead to a dead end where he could no longer run.

He felt a sudden, overwhelming sense of rage.  They had killed his dog.  Did they think they could kill him, too?  Right here in the open?

And then he thought of the woman who was shot dead outside his apartment.  Of course they could kill him here.  In these crowds, they could fire three or four muted gunshots at close range and escape in the resulting chaos.

He was moving faster, his mind racing. Why were they here? He still had a week to come up with the money. He didn't think they wanted to kill him, but he was certain they wanted to hurt him.

He was running so quickly now, the people on the street gave him looks ranging from annoyance to indifference to surprise and even a sense of fear. Lower First Avenue was a mecca of stores and shops. If he could somehow slip unnoticed into one of the shops, he could wait a few minutes and then leave for a place where he knew he would be reasonably safe--Leana Redman's apartment.

But he cast it idea aside. The moment they couldn't see him was the moment they started searching each shop for him.

The men were fifty feet behind him. Desperation rose in him. Michael's legs were beginning to cramp. He bumped into a woman stepping out of a Laundromat and sent her clean clothes flying--a rainbow of color was tossed into the air. He stumbled, righted himself and began wondering if this was worth it. *Why run?* he thought. *Sooner or later, they'll find me.*

But he wouldn't give up.

An intersection was approaching. The light was red and cars were racing by. He couldn't cross. He looked left, then right....and was surprised to see a van rounding the corner and screeching to a stop in front of him.

Car horns blared and there was the sudden stench of burnt rubber in the air. Then the van's passenger door shot open. Michael recognized the driver instantly.

"Get in!" Vincent Spocatti shouted.

Michael did as he was told and the van shot forward

He tried to catch his breath. The muscles in his legs and lower back ached. He looked at Spocatti, saw him glancing in the rearview mirror, saw the determined set of his jaw and knew it wasn't over.

"They're following us, aren't they?"

Spocatti didn't answer. He jerked the van to the left.

Michael looked out the rear window. A cab was following them at a dangerously close distance. He turned back to Spocatti. "Can you lose them?"

"The driver probably has a gun to his head.  Shut up and let me concentrate."

"Just one question."

Spocatti gritted his teeth.

"You were following me.  You must have been.  Why?"

"Your father told me to."

"Why?"

"That's two questions," Spocatti said.  "If you ask one more, I'm throwing your ass out of here."

They hurtled across 21st Street.  Traffic was dangerously light.

Michael looked out the rear window, saw the cab trying to pull alongside them and was about to speak when Spocatti spun the wheel to the right.  There was a sudden scraping of metal against metal, the blaring of a car horn and the cab was behind them again, front end dented.

Tires screaming, they turned onto Second Avenue. Although traffic was heavier here, the cab was able to pull alongside them. Michael looked down at the cab.  At the same moment he saw a glint of steel from the cab's rear side window, Spocatti darted right, busted a red light and swung onto 19th Street, leaving a traffic cop blowing her whistle.

The cab followed.

"We're not going to lose them," Spocatti said.  "The driver is too skilled.  To stay alive, he'll do anything those men tell him to do.  I won't be able to lose them unless you listen very closely to me and do exactly as I say."

Michael was surprised by how calm Spocatti sounded--how measured and precise his words were.  "What do you want me to do?"

Vincent told him what he wanted him to do.

Michael told him he'd be shot.

"No, you won't.  If those men wanted you dead, they would have killed you earlier. Now, move."

Michael moved to the back of the van, pushing his way through a sea of large cardboard boxes.  He looked out the front window.  They were rapidly approaching Third Avenue.  Traffic was backed up 19th Street and the light at the end was red.  If it didn't turn green soon, there would be no escape--no matter how well Spocatti drove, no matter how well Michael did as he was told.

Michael braced himself by gripping a rusty steel rod bolted to the metal wall behind him. He waited, adrenaline pumping. Never in his life had he been filled with so much hatred or fear-- hate for his father, hate for Santiago, hate for these men chasing them, fear for his life.

He remembered his dog's brutal death and the fear turned to rage.

The light at the end of the street turned green, traffic lurched forward and Spocatti said, "Do it now, Michael."

Michael tightened his grip on the steel rod, threw open the door with his free hand and was struck by the sudden suction of wind. He glimpsed the startled expressions on the men in the cab, saw them reach for their guns, and then he began kicking out the boxes that surrounded him, one after the other, in a steady stream of cardboard.

The driver was overwhelmed.

He swerved left, then right, attempting to dodge the boxes, but he wasn't that skilled. The boxes struck the hood of the car, rolled over the windshield, obscuring the driver's vision. Michael turned to kick out more boxes--but as he swung around, the steel rod he was holding onto suddenly gave way and he toppled out of the van, his head and shoulder striking the pavement.

He rolled, the cab screeching to a stop behind him. As he lay there, stunned, his body screaming with pain, he watched in disbelief as Spocatti shot around the corner to Third Avenue, leaving him alone. He turned his head toward the people on the sidewalk. They were either standing back in shock or hurrying past him, heads slightly lowered. No one would help him. He had to get out of there.

He tried to struggle to his feet, but he was too weak. He heard the distant shrill of police sirens, the sudden opening of car doors, the controlled voice of a man saying, "Put him in the back."

At the same moment Michael recognized the man's accent as French, strong hands lifted him from the pavement and shoved him into the back of the cab. Michael knew it was over when his eyes met Ethan Cain's.

# FIFTH AVENUE

### \* \* \*

They drove back to Michael's apartment.

The city sped by, flashing vignettes briefly framed by the window, but Michael didn't notice. He was sitting between two men in the back of the cab who looked like twins with their slick jet ponytails and oversized bodies. The other man, the older and seemingly wiser of the three, sat in front, smiling over his shoulder at Michael, pressing a gun against the cabbie's side.

Michael was paralyzed by fear. There was a roaring in his ears that had nothing to do with the sound of the cab's engines. *If they're not going to kill me, then they're going to hurt me. Badly.*

He closed his eyes. His head and shoulder ached from the fall. There seemed to be no strength left in his body. He wondered how much more of this he could take. What was his limit? Whatever it was, Michael knew he was approaching it.

The cab driver, an Iranian, was whispering something in a language Michael didn't recognize or understand. He listened. The man was repeating the same phrases over and over. It was a form of chant. And then Michael knew. The man had been confronted with death several times today and he was praying. Michael wondered what God could save them from this.

A window was open and he could hear the fading shrill of the police sirens. The cabbie was losing them. Michael wondered where Spocatti went. They slowed to a stop outside his apartment building. Cain said something in French to his men and looked at Michael. "Understand this," he said. "We will kill you if you try to escape again. Do you understand me? I'll put a bullet through your head myself."

"I doubt that," Michael said. "I have a week to come up with the money. If Santiago wanted me dead, you would have killed me when I fell out of the--"

His words were cut short by a crushing blow to the stomach. Michael doubled over in pain and two fists slammed hard against the small of his back.

For a moment, he couldn't move or breathe--then Cain grabbed a handful of his hair and jerked him into an upright position.

"Listen to me," he said, his accent stronger than before. "It would be very easy for me to tell Santiago that you pulled a gun on me and I had to shoot you in self-defense. Don't for one minute think I won't do it."

Michael spat in his face.

Cain pulled back a hand and was about to strike when the cabbie's voice suddenly rose and his praying became hysterical. Cain looked at the man, grimaced and reached into his jacket pocket. He removed a silencer, attached it to his gun and glanced out the windows. No one on the street was looking in their direction.

Like a flash, he covered the driver's mouth with one hand, jammed the gun into the man's stomach with the other and fired four shots in rapid succession. The cabbie's eyes grew huge with sorrow and disbelief, a wet, clotted gasp escaped his lips, and he slumped forward, dead.

Cain turned to Michael.

"Here's what's going to happen," he said. "We're going to cross this street and enter your apartment and you're going to act like we're friends. Because if you don't, if you make even one false move, I'm blowing your fucking head off. Got it?"

Michael was pale with fear. He nodded.

Satisfied, Cain turned to the man seated at Michael's right. "You're coming with me," he said. "And if you even sense he's about to try something, I want you to shoot him. Understand?"

The man smiled. He understood.

"And you," Cain said to the other man. "I want you to get rid of the driver and the cab. Dump them both someplace close and hurry back." He opened the door and stepped out into the morning sun. "I might need you to dispose of another body."

\* \* \*

They entered Michael's apartment.

"Sit down," Cain said. "We'll talk in a minute."

While Cain went to the window to see if the cab had left, Michael glanced around the small room, looked at his unmade bed and went to it. His legs were trembling as he sat--both from exhaustion and a sudden surge of hope.

Beneath the mattress would be the loaded gun he purchased a week ago for protection. He could almost feel its steely hardness pressing against his thigh. Earlier, there was no time to grab the gun before he fled his apartment. Now, if he could somehow slide a hand under the mattress without being seen, he could kill these men and leave before the other returned.

He looked over at the man blocking the doorway, saw the hard, probing eyes taking in every inch of him and turned away, afraid that his secret would be revealed on his face. There was no question that this man would kill him if he went for the gun. *If I don't get him first.*

He glanced across the room at Cain, who was leaning out the open window, his jacket slightly parted. Between the shimmering folds of black leather, Michael could see the man's shoulder holster and gun. *There's no way I'll be able to shoot them both,* he thought. *No matter how quick I am, it won't happen.*

Still, he knew if the opportunity presented itself, he would take the chance.

"You know," Cain said as he turned away from the window and leaned against the sill, "I'm a big fan of yours. I've seen your films, read your books. You're quite big in Europe."

Michael had to turn slightly to look at him. He used the motion as an opportunity to lift himself and position his hand closer to the gun.

"Yesterday, when I got the call from Santiago, I have to tell you I was disappointed. Not because I was being given the opportunity to kill you--that has been surprisingly challenging-- but because someone I respected so much had allowed themselves to get caught up in something so stupid. With all of your novels and films, with all of your financial success--how could you possibly have run out of money? Unless you were so careless as to have spent it all--which the fan in me seriously wants to doubt--then where did it all go?"

Although that very question had troubled Michael for weeks, he remained silent, watchful, wondering where Cain was taking this.

Cain shrugged. He stepped away from the window and started pacing the room. "I don't know," he said. "Maybe you did spend it all. Maybe you became so comfortable with your success, that you took all the books and all the films and all the money for granted. If that's the case, Mr. Archer, then someone should teach you a lesson in handling money."

There was a silence. Cain stopped pacing and removed from his jacket pocket a small box of matches and a pack of Gitanes cigarettes. He struck a match, lit the cigarette and shook out the flame. It wasn't until he turned to look for a place to put the match that he stopped to look at the desk beside Michael's bed. On it were several empty cans of Diet Coke, innumerable magazine and newspaper clippings, a typewriter and a small stack of neatly typed pages that resembled a manuscript.

Cain tossed the match to the floor. He picked up the stack of papers, thumbed through them and looked sideways at Michael. "This is the new book you're working on?"

Michael didn't answer. When he first learned what his father wanted in return for paying off Santiago, he started writing the book, knowing that if he gave his agent several chapters and a proposal, she would be able to sell it--and he himself could pay off Santiago.

Ninety pages were written. Before today's event, he planned on finishing the proposal tomorrow morning, knowing that if his agent could sell it before week's end, he would be rid of his father forever. And now this man held it in his hands--the only existing result of his hard work. As Cain began reading the novel's first chapter out loud, Michael lowered his hand to his side. The gun was inches away.

**FIFTH AVENUE**

A novel by:

Michael Archer

# FIFTH AVENUE

**BOOK ONE**
**FIRST WEEK**

**CHAPTER ONE**

July
New York City

The bombs, placed high above Fifth Avenue on the roof of The Redman International Building, would explode in five minutes.

Now, with its mirrored walls of glass reflecting Fifth Avenue's thick, late-morning traffic, the building itself seemed alive with movement.

On scaffolding at the building's middle, men and women were hanging the enormous red velvet ribbon that would soon cover sixteen of Redman International's seventy-nine stories. High above on the roof, a lighting crew was moving ten spotlights into position. And inside, fifty skilled decorators were turning the lobby into a festive ballroom.

Celina Redman, who was in charge of organizing the event, stood before the building with her arms folded. Streams of people were brushing past her on the sidewalk, some glancing up at the red ribbon, others stopping to glance in surprise at her. She tried to ignore them, tried to focus on her work and become one with the crowd, but it was difficult. Just that morning, her face and this building had been on the cover of every major paper in New York.

\* \* \*

While Cain read, Michael glanced at the man standing in the doorway, saw that his attention was on Cain, and started to slide a hand under the mattress.

But it wouldn't fit.  The weight of his body was pressing the mattress and box spring together.  He turned slightly, carefully, and shifted his weight onto one thigh.  The mattress lifted an inch and he was able to force a hand inside.  He could feel the cool butt of the gun.  His fingertips pressed against it.  He looked up at Cain, saw that his concentration was still focused on the manuscript and knew that if he was going to do this, the time was now.  At the same moment he wrapped his fingers around the gun, Cain finished reading the first chapter.

He looked at him. "What is this?" he asked. "Nonfiction?"

For a moment, Michael couldn't move or speak.  Cain was standing diagonally across from him, no more than ten feet away.  Neither he nor the man in the doorway could see where his hand was.  He leaned forward, using the action to pull out the gun.  The bed creaked.  Michael began to sweat.

"That's debatable," he said.

"It says here that it's a novel.  If that's so, then how can you use these names?  These events and these places?"

Michael shrugged.  The gun was now pressed against his thigh, hidden from sight. "That's a problem for my lawyers to figure out.  If things get out of hand, maybe I'll use a pseudonym for protection."

"It's a shame," Cain said. "I bet this would have been a good read."

Michael tightened his grip on the gun. *Would have been?*

"And I bet you would have made a bundle--probably even enough money to pay off Santiago." He looked at Michael. "Isn't that what this is for?  These chapters, this letter of proposal?  A last ditch effort to pay off Santiago?  I'm not a stupid man, Mr. Archer.  I can see right through you.  The fear in your eyes is only slightly masked by your hatred of me.  But I can understand that.  I hold in my hand hours upon hours of your hard work.  If I destroyed this, and if you were unable to pay off Santiago, he would rehire me and I would come back in a week to finish a job that I should have been allowed to finish today."

He looked thoughtfully at the manuscript.

"Actually, I could use the extra money.  There's a little villa in Nice that I'd love to spend my winters at."

Motionless, Michael watched Cain hold the manuscript over the metal waste basket at his feet. And then the man dropped the pages into the basket. The sound they made was like the rapid beating of wings.

Before Michael could react, Cain reached into his jacket pocket, removed the box of matches, struck one against the side of the box and dropped it into the can. There was a moment when Michael thought the match had gone out, but then a flickering yellow flower began to bloom.

And he knew it was time.

He leapt to his feet, revealed the gun and aimed it at a surprised Ethan Cain. He glanced over at the man standing at the door and saw that his gun was drawn and pointed directly at him. "You shoot, and so do I," Michael said. He turned back to Cain. "Put out the fire. Now."

Cain backed away from the basket, his hands at his sides, the fire burning in the glass of his spectacles. "No," he said.

"Do it!" Michael shouted.

"No."

The fire grew in intensity. He didn't have much time. He kicked the metal basket in an attempt to tip it over and knock out the fire, but the basket spun across the hardwood floor like a fiery comet, stopping with a metallic clank beneath the open window, where the curtains moved in the air.

There was a sudden burst of orange as the curtains ignited. With fresh air coming into the room, the fire had its fuel and it used it to roar and churn. It tasted the dry, cheap fabric and it twisted with surprising speed toward the stained ceiling, not stopping until that, too, was alight with fire.

And still the fire grew, creeping along the walls and ceiling, destroying everything it touched. Michael turned to Cain, who was staring at him, his gaze unwavering, daring. There was a bitter smile on his lips. Bits of fire and sparks were falling all around him from the ceiling. The heat and smoke were becoming unbearable.

Michael lifted the gun to the man's head, cocked the trigger and heard a similar sound from across the room. He knew that if he pulled the trigger, his life would end too. After all he had been through, he wondered if that was such a bad thing.

201

"You don't have the guts to do it, do you?" Cain said.

Michael's eyes began to water. He wasn't sure if it was from the smoke filling the room, or from the fact that he was facing certain death. He wondered if his father ever really loved him. And then he realized it didn't matter.

He pulled the trigger.

There were two explosions.

Cain's chest erupted in a cloud of blood and he went down like a tenpin. Michael collapsed to his knees and fell to one side. As he lay there, his breathing slowing, the heat from the fire warming his already paling face, he knew he was dying. As bright as the room was, Michael was losing sight of it.

Breathing wasn't an option.

He choked on his last few breaths and swore his father to hell.

He was floating now, lifting, no longer a part of his body. He saw his mother's face but couldn't hear her voice.

And then there was a flash of bright light and a sudden, terrible darkness.

## CHAPTER TWENTY-SIX

"There's this little party tonight," Celina said, steeling herself while she leaned through the doorway of Jack Douglas' office at Redman International. "It's in honor of two events--the work Countess Castellani has done for HIV research, and the recent discovery of twelve Monet paintings in the attic of a famous Parisian brothel. Now, look. I know you dislike these types of events, but it's being held on Anastassios Fondaras' yacht, which is the largest private yacht in the world, so that alone should be interesting. I was wondering if you'd like to join me."

Jack grinned. "Did you just say, Countess Castellani?"

"That's what I said."

"Is she a real person or a reality star?"

"I don't know how to answer that--parts of her are real. And she's very nice in a complicated way."

He groaned.

"It's for a good cause."

"Agreed."

"And you'll like Anastassios."

"What is it with these names?"

"They're the international set."

"Oh," he said. "Well, I'm the American set."

"They're good people. They just have titles."

"How much did they pay for those titles."

"Depends on the method of payment. Are we talking cash or something else?"

"Let's not go there."

She cracked a smile. "I know it sounds ridiculous, but it is what it is. I don't want to go either, but I have no choice."

He was seated at the desk that used to belong to Eric Parker, feet up and crossed on the shiny wood surface. Empty coffee cups and paperwork concerning the takeover of WestTex surrounded him. "If I go, can I borrow your father's dinner jacket again?"

"Only if your car breaks down and it rains."

"Then I'd better start praying for both," he said. "Everything I own is at the cleaner's." He lifted his feet from the desk and stood. "Can I ask you a question?"

"Shoot."

"If you hate these events so much, why do you go to them?"

"Because it makes my father happy," she said, stepping into the room. "He always said you never know when or where you'll strike a deal. And these are the sorts of events where deals are made."

"All right," Jack said. "I can see that. But something tells me you want more out of life than just striking a deal." There was a silence while he glanced out the windows before him. Even at this height, the buzz and activity of midtown was noticeable.

"Have you ever been bungee jumping?" he asked.

"Excuse me?"

"Bungee jumping. You strap a heavy elastic cord around your ankles, dive off a cliff or a bridge, and plummet to a body of water, usually a river or stream. It's fun. Just when you think you're about to hit the water, the bungee slows your fall and you snap away from it, bouncing back into mid-air, where you start to fall again."

Celina looked at him. "You do this?"

"I sky dive too."

"What are you, Indiana Jones?"

"I was thinking more of a Jason Bourne."

"I can't believe I'm hearing this."

"I just like to live."

"Sounds to me like a good way to die."

"Oh, come on," he said. "It's completely safe. Where's your sense of adventure? Look--I'll tell you what. I'll go to this party with you tonight if you go bungee jumping with me tomorrow morning. There's this place in Upstate New York that I go to with friends. Very peaceful. Just trees and birds and mosquitoes--not a building or a takeover in sight. And I can guarantee you that after the jump, you'll never look at life the same way again. You game?"

Celina saw the challenge in his eyes and nodded. "I'm game," she said. "But we do it blindfolded."

Jack laughed. "Lady, you got yourself a deal."

# FIFTH AVENUE

*  *  *

When Celina returned to her office, she found her father there, near her desk, arms folded. "I just got off the phone with Ted Frostman," he said.

Celina remained in the doorway. They had waited days to hear back from him. "And?"

"We've got them," he said. "Ted called a few minutes ago to say that Chase has run its due diligence, and that the right people are impressed. They want to back us."

Celina felt as though a weight had been lifted from her. They were coming down to the wire. Within a week, the exact date of the Navy's move into the Gulf would become public. If WestTex wasn't theirs by then, the deal with Iran would collapse and they would have to call off everything. And lose billions in the process.

She went to her desk and sat. "Tell me what you know. Do we have a commitment from Chase?"

George started to pace, energy coming off him in waves. "Not yet. First, they want to discuss fees, our deal with management, the possibility of outside investors, etcetera."

"How comfortable are they with Iran?"

"That's the sticky spot," George said. "Big surprise there. Some feel the deal is too shaky. A few nearly backed out because of it."

Celina understood that. Even she was concerned with the verbal agreement her father had secured with Iran. On more than one occasion, she wondered what would happen if, on the day WestTex became theirs, Iran decided to back out. *We would lose everything*, she thought.

"The good news is that they know I'd never risk Redman International if I didn't feel this deal was going to fly. I'm meeting with Ted and a few select members of Chase today."

"Want me to come along?"

"I don't think so," he said. "You've got enough work to keep you busy here."

Celina looked at the files stacked on her desk, at the reports she had yet to read. *That*, she thought, *is an understatement.*

"I'll tell you what happened later," he said. "You're going to the Fondaras party, right?"

"Jack's coming with me."

George lifted an eyebrow. "Really...?" he said.

"It's not what you think. We're just friends."

"Of course."

"I didn't want to go alone."

"Who would?"

A beat of silence passed. The moment stretched.

"But he is kind of cute, isn't he?" Celina said.

There was a mischievous look in George's eyes when he started toward the door. "Wait until I tell your mother," he said.

\* \* \*

Clouds were moving in from the west when Celina and Jack left the limousine and started up the ramp to the Crystal Princess. Jack was in black dinner jacket, Celina was in a simple white evening dress. A river-cooled breeze that smelled faintly of salt was in the air, as were the light sounds of an orchestra.

A group of reporters were gathered along each side of the red-carpeted ramp. Cameras flashing, microphones raised, the paparazzi called out to them as they passed.

"You're looking great, Celina. Would you turn this way, please?"

"Word's out you're leaving for Iran soon. Does this have to do with the takeover of WestTex?"

"Can you at least give us your reaction on what happened to Eric Parker."

That got her. Celina squeezed Jack's hand and put a smile on her face as he handed an elegantly uniformed butler the Tiffany-engraved vellum invitation for Celina Redman and Guest.

As they stood there, she became aware of people looking at her. She heard Eric Parker's name mentioned more than once and though she tried to ignore it, she couldn't. She was beginning to wonder if coming to this party was a good idea when the butler led them to the reception line and called out their names.

206

Anastassios Fondaras, the Greek shipping tycoon and their billionaire host, held out his arms to Celina as she and Jack approached.

"Celina," he said, enveloping her in a hug. "It's been what? A year? Two?"

A camera flashed as Fondaras kissed Celina's cheek.

"Two, I think," Celina said. She pulled back so they stood at arm's length. "And look at you," she said. "I've never seen you so tan. Retirement is suiting you, Anastassios."

"Retirement?" Anastassios Fondaras said with a shrug. "Retirement is a term I use so I can sleep an extra hour each morning without feeling guilty. You don't think I'd give up control of my ships just because I've passed the golden age of sixty-five, do you?"

"I hope not."

"Your parents are here somewhere," Fondaras said with a glance around the deck. "Haven't seen either of them in years. They looked wonderful. Your mother looks better each time I see her." When his gaze settled back on Celina, something in his eyes darkened. "Rumor has it that your father's planning a move into the shipping business."

*It's more than just a rumor*, Celina thought. *And you know it.* She nodded, and hated that she was made to feel somewhat guarded. Although Fondaras was a friend, he was cunning when it came to discussing business and she never trusted him because of it.

"Tough business," Anastassios said. "Lots of competition out there--including me."

"I think there's enough trade to go around, don't you?"

"I've never thought there was enough trade to go around."

"It's a big world, Anastassios."

"Not with me on it, it isn't."

"I can promise WestTex won't infringe on your business."

"Don't be ridiculous. How could you possibly promise me that?"

"You'll see soon."

"I'd rather see now."

"That's impossible."

There was an uncomfortable silence.  Celina kept her gaze on his.

"I don't like playing games, Celina."

"It's business, Anastassios.  We're all in it to win.  It's why I respect you so much.  But my father and I never play games."

"Except for those you win?"

She didn't reply.

Anastassios shrugged, as if the conversation now meant little to him.  Still, a hard look remained in his eyes.  "I just hope no one gets their toes stepped on," he said.

*So do I*, Celina thought and turned to Jack.  "I'm sorry," she said.  "Where are my manners?  This is my friend, Jack Douglas."

Fondaras nodded at Jack.  "I've read about you," he said. "You're the man who sold $350 million worth of bonds a few weeks ago, right?  Became a Big Swinging Dick at Morgan?  I was thinking of hiring you myself, but I see that Redman beat me to it."  He turned to Celina.  "Let's hope that doesn't become a habit. Have either of you met my good friend Lady Alexa Ionesco from Spain?"

Lady Alexa Ionesco from Spain was a tall reed of a woman with dark hair pulled back into a chignon, black eyes that reflected a curious intelligence, and lips that were oddly full, likely from a few too many injections.  Celina thought back to her conversation with Jack and was willing to bet that her title-- unlike the ropes of diamonds that blazed at her neck, wrists and ears--was fake.

As they made small talk, she wondered if this woman, who was dressed in a stunning red dress and who was at least thirty years Fondaras' junior, stood a chance with him.  Divorced twice, widowed once, Anastassios Fondaras was one of the world's most eligible bachelors.  And he knew it.

"I think you're darling," Lady Ionesco said.  The way she said "darling" made it sound as if she'd taken the word and stretched it like a rubber band.

Celina took her hand.  The woman warbled a bit.  *And I think you need to lay off the booze.*  "You're very kind."

"Have you ever been to Turkey in the fall?"

"I think only in springtime."

"Fall is best. Fall is a must. Fall is the new spring. You must come. Promise me, you'll come. I own a fantastic little cottage there--fifty rooms along the ocean, fifteen servants, three pools, a garden to die for--but we make do." She glanced at Jack. "There's plenty of room."

"Of course," Celina said. "Let's have lunch sometime and look at our calendars."

"Mine's impossible," Lady Ionesco sighed. "My assistant put everything on one of those little iPad things for me, thinking it would organize a life that can't be organized. He still doesn't know who I am. He still doesn't get that there is no order to the world in which we move. He thinks my life can be squeezed--squeezed!--into something shiny and slick. And now, naturally, the situation is worse than ever." She tossed her head back and cackled out two words. "Technology! God!"

In an effort to steady her, Anastassios put a hand on her back.

"Anastassios," she said, her head rolling toward the ceiling. "That chandelier. I never noticed it before. It's sublime."

"It's Lalique."

"It's terrifique!"

"You about ready for a drink?" Jack asked Celina. He looked at Lady Ionesco. "We just came from the city and I have to say, a drink is in order."

"Try the champagne," Lady Ionesco said. "It's divine. And then try a Manhattan. God, I love a Manhattan. So '20s. So now. So forever."

Celina gave Anastassios a kiss on each cheek, and then did the same with Lady Ionesco, who said too loudly, "Turkey! Fall! Lunch!"

As they stepped away from them and moved into the crowd, Celina said, "You handled yourself well."

"I barely said a word. You, however, were impressive. That woman is a mess and that man is a clever son of a bitch."

"He's a lot more than that," Celina said as they followed a wave of instant celebrities and old money to an aft bar that was teeming with people anxious to forget the pressures of the world in which they lived.

While Jack ordered drinks, Celina glanced around the polished deck.

The first person her gaze settled upon was the last person she expected to see here--Louis Ryan. Celina remembered that Ryan, who was ousted by society because of his refusal to donate money to charity, once was quoted by a newspaper as saying: "My mother used to tell me that charity begins at home. If that's the case, I own eight homes, and that's where my money goes."

She watched Ryan and wondered why he received an invitation to this event, where money almost certainly would be expected from him to help combat that forgotten disease, HIV, which was becoming hot again among the charity set. Standing alone near the twenty piece orchestra, he was sipping a glass of champagne and watching the guests giggle and hug and push.

Celina wondered if her father had seen him yet.

She turned to look for George and came face to face with Diana Crane, who was standing near Celina, her back to the bar, a glass of bubbling champagne in her hand. There was a silence while the two women stood looking at one another. Appraising one another. Then Diana stepped forward. "Hello, Celina."

Celina nodded. She noticed the fading bruise around Diana's eye, the carefully concealed scrape on her forehead and couldn't help wondering what she and Eric had gone through the night they were attacked.

"That's a beautiful necklace you're wearing," she said.

Diana brought a hand to her neck and her fingers tip-toed over hundreds of carats of diamonds and rubies and sapphires. "Thank you," she said. "Eric gave it to me."

It was a casual remark, not a slam, and Celina felt a kind of sadness for Diana, not anger. She wondered how such an intelligent woman could fall for someone like Eric. And then she checked herself. *Why not? I did.*

She decided to at least deliver a warning.

"I remember when Eric bought it for me," Celina said. "We were in Milan, vacationing, and I was struck by the size and the clarity of the stones. You do realize that the stones are flawless, don't you?"

It was a moment before Diana could speak. Her fingers pressed against the necklace, the stones cutting into her flesh. "Eric bought this for you?" she said.

Celina nodded. "Three years ago, I think. I sent it--and others like it--back to him when we broke up. I think it looks better on you, though. The sapphires bring out the blue in your eyes."

Diana Crane turned and walked away. Celina felt a twinge of guilt as she watched her leave. "I had to do it," she said aloud. "He gave her that necklace and made her think he bought it for her. What a bastard."

"Who's a bastard?"

Celina put her hand on Jack's arm. She wondered how long he had been standing behind her, wondered just how much he'd heard. "It's not important," she said, taking the glass of champagne he offered. She sipped--and noted it wasn't champagne. It was beer. "You really are too much," she said.

"Would you rather have drunk from the can?"

"We have in the past. Why stop now?"

"Good point," Jack said. "Next time, I'll ask for a six-pack."

"You do that," Celina said and, acting on impulse, she leaned forward and kissed him on the cheek. "You know what I'd like to do right now?"

Jack shook his head.

"I'd like to dance with you before this floating palace casts off. What do you say?"

They danced slowly at first, Jack's hand gently embracing hers, Celina's cheek touching his, each aware of the other's body. Couples Anastassios had flown in from around the world were twirling around them, some laughing, others talking--all enjoying the orchestra.

Celina was aware of people looking at them from the surrounding tables, but she made an effort to ignore them. She was happy to be here with Jack. She was glad to have him in her life.

"Isn't that Harold Baines over there?" Jack asked.

Celina followed Jack's gaze with her own. Standing with his back to the railing, drink in hand, was Harold. He was talking with Louis Ryan. She nodded, surprised to see the two men together.

"I wonder what he and Ryan are arguing about?"

"What makes you think they're arguing?"

211

"Harold raised his voice a moment ago," Jack said. "I heard him. And look at Ryan's face--it's as red as that woman's dress. They're arguing."

The music became softer, slower and Jack held her closer. Celina looked away from Harold at the same moment Harold stormed away from Louis Ryan. She brushed her cheek against Jack's, smelled his cologne and felt the warmth of his body through the thin material of her dress. She wondered if he was as aware of these things as she was. She wondered if she was on his mind as often as he was on hers. She wondered if he was as attracted to her as she was to him.

Gradually, she began to lose herself in him and the dance. He was speaking to her. His voice was a low rumble above the lapping of the waves and the faint roar of the engines as the ship cast off. She heard him mention something about the yacht and the guests, about the thickening storm clouds and the threat of rain, but she was unable to follow what he was saying. As far as Celina was concerned, they could be anywhere in the world.

"Am I boring you?" Jack asked after awhile. They had been dancing for nearly twenty minutes. "Is something wrong?"

Celina pulled back and knew he had asked her a question she hadn't heard. She felt embarrassed. "No. I--my mind was elsewhere. Sorry."

Jack was no fool. He leaned forward and kissed her on the mouth. Celina kissed him back, only dimly aware of the murmurs rippling through the crowd. There was no question what would happen next.

"Come with me," he said, taking her hand.

They found a staircase that went below ship and followed a narrow passage to its end. As they turned onto a wider passage and began looking for one of the staterooms, Celina thought that she never wanted a man more than she wanted this man.

It came to her then that this would be only the second man she had ever been with, and the thought exhilarated her. She sensed that it would be different with Jack than it had been with Eric. She sensed it would be better.

They stopped in front of a door that was at the end of the hall. Jack opened it and stepped inside. Across the room, seated naked at the foot of a large four-poster bed, was Harold Baines, a rubber tube tied to the sunken flesh of his upper left arm, the needle of a syringe buried in the fold.

Seated behind him was a young man, his legs wrapped around the shadow of Harold's thinning waist, his waiter's uniform cast carelessly to the floor.

There was a moment when Harold's eyes met Jack's, when shock registered on each man's face, then Jack quickly closed the door before Celina could see.

"What's the matter?" she asked.

"Nothing," he said.

She went for the door. Jack reached for her hand and pulled her toward him. He kissed her on the forehead, then on the mouth. "We're getting ahead of ourselves," he said. "Anyone could walk in on us here and we'd regret it. Here isn't the place. Let's wait."

* * *

"This must be some sort of joke," Elizabeth Redman said in a whisper to her husband. "He can't be seated here. He can't be seated at our table. Anastassios knows better. He never would have allowed it."

"Don't be so sure," George said, looking away from Louis Ryan, who was seated opposite them. "Anastassios knows I'm trying to buy WestTex. He knows I'm going to be competition. This is exactly something he would do."

"Well, I can't believe it. The man doesn't even belong here. What does Louis Ryan care about the discovery of twelve Monet paintings? What does he care about HIV and AIDS? Just look at him," she said in a low voice. "Sitting there, smiling, as if he doesn't know that we're here. As if he doesn't remember what he put us through all those years ago. You murdering his wife. Ridiculous."

George squeezed her hand. It was a moment before he could dispel the image of Anne Ryan that flashed before his eyes. "Look," he said quietly. "It's been a long time since we've seen him. This was bound to happen someday. Why don't we just ignore him and enjoy ourselves?"

"I've got a better idea. Why don't we just leave?"

"Because we're on a boat in the middle of the Hudson. We can't leave."

"Oh, please, George. Somewhere on this floating island there's a helicopter. We can tell Anastassios that there has been an emergency." She looked around her. Everyone was either sitting down to dinner, or preparing to. The air was a hum of voices. "Where is Celina sitting? Maybe she and Jack wouldn't mind switching tables with us."

"I haven't seen Celina."

"And I haven't seen Harold. Look at poor Helen over there, sitting by herself, having to talk to that awful Mamie Fitzbergen and listen to one of her dull conversations about how splashes of Holy water are restoring her youth. You'd think Harold would be more considerate of her."

"Something isn't right with Harold," he said. "He seems distracted lately. Not himself. I'm going to talk to him soon and see if anything is wrong."

"And when you do," Louis Ryan said from across the table. "Make sure you give him my thanks."

His voice cut across the table like a blade. Silence lingered as those seated at the Redman table--and those seated at the tables surrounding it--stopped talking and started listening.

Elizabeth and George turned to Ryan. It was clear by his amused expression that he had been listening to them.

"What do you mean by that, Louis?" George asked.

Louis lowered his chin and peered over his eyeglasses. "I wish I could put it in simpler terms, George, but I can't. It means that I'd like you to give Harold my thanks."

George ignored the sarcasm and kept his tone light. "What for?"

"For finding someone to run my new hotel for me."

George hadn't become successful in this crowd without possessing the ability to act. He remained calm, even though denial was rising up in him that his best friend would talk to this man. "It's good that you and Harold have been chatting."

"Actually, we had a meeting," Louis said. "And I have to hand it to him--I couldn't be happier with his choice." He smiled. "Of course, I should probably be thanking you and Elizabeth, as well. Without your efforts, the young woman Harold brought to my attention wouldn't be alive today."

George was slipping, beginning not to care. "Maybe we should talk about this later?" he said. "Another time?" He held up his glass of champagne, lifted it to Louis and drank. "For me, talking business ended a few hours ago."

It was as if the suggestion went unheard.

Louis eased back in his chair and said, "What strikes me about this young woman is how closely she resembles my dead wife. Do you remember Anne, George? Do you remember how long and dark her hair was? How tan she would get in the summer? How beautiful and stubborn and strong she was? How alive she was?" He paused. "Probably not. I would imagine that killing someone and getting away with it must force a person to stuff down any memory of it. I, on the other hand, have never forgotten."

At the same instant a reporter stepped forward to take their picture, Louis leaned forward and locked eyes with George. The camera flashed.

Elizabeth Redman looked at the reporter with such hatred and stood so quickly that her chair toppled over and crashed to the hardwood deck.

Excitement rippled through the crowd.

The reporter took another picture. And another.

George reached out and gripped Elizabeth's hand before she did something she would later regret.

"You've got a lot of nerve, Ryan," he said.

"You don't even know just how much nerve," Louis said. "The person I'm talking about is your daughter, Leana. I've hired her to run my new hotel for me. She starts next week."

## CHAPTER TWENTY-SEVEN

While her parents and sister were dining on the world's largest privately owned yacht, Leana was standing at the corner of Mulberry and Prince. It was dark, a light rain was falling and traffic from the two streets hummed in her ears.

Twelve hours had passed since she was sent the gun. Twelve hours of decisions and indecisions had passed through her mind. Twelve hours left to go before the man carried out his threat.

She glanced around her.

Age-worn brick buildings lined the block. Somewhere in the distance, a woman was crying, shouting, screaming. Leana was aware of the men passing her on the street, and she was aware that they were aware of her. Although she had gone through great lengths to come to this spot and not be followed, she knew that any one of these men could be the man who sent her the gun.

She removed her cell phone from her inside jacket pocket and felt the gun she concealed there earlier. If for some reason the man decided to make his move tonight, she would kill him with his own gun. *If I get the chance.*

She punched numbers. There was a click and the line began to ring. She waited for someone to answer. Rain whipped against her in sheets, soaking her clothes, chilling her to the bone. She could no longer hear the woman screaming. It was as if her voice had been snuffed. A man walking past her slowed his pace and smiled a smile that had long since ceased being a smile.

Leana turned away. She felt the gun pressed against her ribcage. She began to tremble.

Finally, the line was answered by a woman. Leana recognized the voice instantly and knew that once she spoke, the woman would recognize her voice as well. Still, she didn't hesitate to ask for the one man she should have phoned earlier--the only man who could now help her. "I need to speak to Mario," she said to his wife. "Tell him it's Leana Redman. Tell him it's urgent."

But the line went dead.

\* \* \*

"Who was that on the phone?"

Lucia De Cicco turned in surprise as Mario entered the kitchen from the foyer. His hair, face and black leather jacket were dripping from the rain. In his hand was the gallon of ice cream she asked him to get.

"I asked who that was."

"It was no one," she said. "Whoever was there hung up."

She moved away from the phone, carefully wiping clean from her face any sign of the anger she felt only moments before. Lucia knew that if she was going to keep her husband, she would have to still whatever rage and jealousy was within her and pretend a woman by the name of Leana Redman didn't exist.

"You know I don't want you answering the phone," Mario said as he removed his coat and shoes. "Not after what happened last week."

It was a moment before Lucia could dispel the image of the three dozen black roses she received by messenger. "I don't want to talk about that."

"Don't you think it's about time we did?"

"As a matter of fact, I don't."

In her bare feet, she crossed the room and took the ice cream from her husband's hands. For years, she was a woman who moved with the confidence beauty inspires, but now she seemed oddly aware of it and herself.

"What kind did you get?"

"Heath Bar Crunch," he said. "And don't change the subject. We're going to talk about this."

She went to the large island that dominated the center of the kitchen, removed two bowls from a cupboard, a silver spoon from a drawer. As she began scooping the ice cream into the bowls, she looked at Mario, then over at the phone, which was across the room. Mario took the stool opposite her. She sensed him staring at her and said, "Look, Mario. I've spoken with your father, I've talked to your brothers. As far as I'm concerned, what happened last week never happened."

"But it did happen."

She focused on the ice cream.

"You were sent a death threat, Lucia. Somebody wants to kill you and we need to talk about it."

She glared at him. "And for what? Because of something I did? No, Mario. Because of something you or your goddamned family did. How do you think it makes me feel knowing I might be dead in a week because of my association with this family?"

"That'll never happen--"

"Really?" she said. "You can promise me that? You can promise our children that?"

"Lucia, please."

"Look," she said. "You wanted to discuss this, so let's discuss it. I want to know what you're going to say to the children when they see their mother shot dead because she wanted to open a window for some air. How are you going to explain the holes in my body? The blood on my face? I'm scared to death and you haven't once comforted me. I lie in bed at night wondering when I'll be able to leave my home again, but realize I might never be able to because it could mean my death."

Mario was about to speak when the phone rang. Lucia looked at her husband, saw him turning on the stool.

She knew who was on that phone. She began to cross the room, but Mario was suddenly beside her, intercepting.

"You're not answering it," he said. "Forget it."

He reached for the receiver at the same moment Lucia asked him not to answer it. But Mario did answer it, a brief conversation was held, and he hung up the phone, furious.

"You lied to me," he said. "That was Leana who called a few minutes ago. She's in trouble. She said you hung up on her. Why?"

"You know why."

"That isn't an excuse."

"I'm your wife. I don't owe you an excuse when another woman calls--especially that woman."

"Like hell you don't," he said. "She's in trouble."

He reached for his jacket and put it on while stepping into his shoes. He was angry with her, but he would deal with it later. Leana needed him.

"Where are you going, Mario?"

"I'm meeting her at a shelter on Prince Street."

"No, you aren't."

"Lucia--"

"I'll call your father," she said. "I'll tell him where you're going."

"You can do whatever you want. My father knows the situation. He knows I'd only be going to help her."

"Not if I tell him differently."

Silence hit the room.

Mario looked at his wife and thought of all the years he had wasted with her; all the years that were gone and he could never get back. "What's that supposed to mean?" he asked.

"It means I'll tell him you're sleeping with her," she said. "It means I'll tell him I caught you in bed with her. That the children caught you in bed with her."

Mario took a step toward her.

Lucia stood firm. In her eyes was a defiance that would not be shattered by intimidation. "He trusts me more than he trusts you. He'll believe it all and he'll kill her. He told me so himself. He'll kill her, Mario."

"You'd actually do that? You'd destroy my relationship with my father. You'd lie to have an innocent person killed?"

There was no hesitation when she said, "You're fucking right I would."

Mario knew that whatever love and respect he once felt for her was gone. He was finished with her. "Then I suggest you pick up the phone and start dialing, Lucia, because I'm leaving."

He stepped past her and moved toward the door. Lucia went to the phone. Hands trembling, her pride and her marriage threatened, she picked up the receiver and started dialing.

"I'd give some thought to that, Lucia," Mario said from the door. "Because if any harm comes to Leana or myself, I swear on my mother's grave it will be the biggest mistake of your life."

\* \* \*

# FIFTH AVENUE

When Leana arrived at the shelter on Prince Street, she found it crowded with men, women and children. Volunteers circulated with hot coffee and sandwiches, soup and rolls. Fluorescent lights winked and buzzed, casting a harsh glow on an even harsher reality.

She went to the rear of the shelter, chose a seat at the only empty table and watched the entrance. She wanted to see Mario come in, wanted to watch him walk toward her, wanted to feel the reassurance his presence would bring. Only then would she feel reasonably safe.

As she sat there, her thoughts turned to Michael and she wondered, as she had throughout the day, where he was and why he hadn't phoned or come by the apartment. Although only a day had passed since they were together, she was surprised by how much she missed him.

A woman carrying a pot of hot coffee and a bag of Styrofoam cups stopped beside her table and sat down. "You're new," she said. "My name is Karen. Welcome."

Leana felt self-conscious. She didn't belong here. Her father was one of the richest men in the country. This woman's time should be spent with someone who needed the attention. "Thank you," she said.

"Would you like some coffee? You look cold in those wet clothes."

"No, thank you," Leana said. "I don't want to be any trouble."

"It's no trouble at all. Here. Let me pour you a cup."

"But I didn't come here for that. I came here to meet someone."

The woman lifted her head. Leana noticed her noticing the expensive clothes she wore, the diamond and gold watch Harold gave as a Christmas gift and suddenly wished she was somewhere else.

"I see," the woman said. She poured Leana a cup of coffee anyway and handed it to her. "Look," she said. "We all have problems. If you feel uncomfortable accepting this--which you shouldn't--maybe you'd like to give a donation when you leave. But that's up to you. This coffee will warm you up and, if nothing else, that makes me feel good."

She stood. "Now, how about a blanket while you're waiting for your friend?"

Leana was touched by the woman's kindness. "I'd love a blanket," she said.

When she was alone, she looked more closely around the shelter. Leana knew that for many of these people, what they were eating here was probably their first meal of the day. In a corner of the room, she saw one of the volunteers bathing a young child while its mother, preoccupied with her other two children, looked on. She wondered where this woman and her children would sleep tonight. Had they found space at a shelter, or was it the street for them after this?

She took a sip of coffee and knew that Mario chose to meet here on purpose. Even now, with a threat against her life, he refused to let her forget how fortunate she was.

When the woman returned with the blanket, Leana wrapped it around her shoulders, thanked her and asked, "Where do these people go at night, once they're finished eating?"

The woman leaned against the table. "By now all the shelters are full," she said. "And so they go back to their spots on the streets."

Leana looked across the room. She could not imagine that woman and her children sleeping alone on the streets. "How do they survive there? How do they live?"

"Many don't survive there. Many don't live."

The woman said it so matter-of-factly, Leana was taken aback. "Those children over there with that woman. Do they go to school?"

"Some do. But even if they don't, that doesn't mean they're not bright. Every child you see in this room--except for the smaller ones--knows how to take care of himself. If they are hungry and there isn't a food shelter nearby, then they know which restaurants throw out the cleanest trash. If they want a bed for the night, they know to start looking early at the shelters instead of looking late. If they have no money, they either beg, borrow or steal--usually steal." The woman shrugged. "It's a way of life for them," she said. "While some are angry as hell at the system, you'd be surprised by how many have accepted their situation."

Leana couldn't imagine accepting any of this. She couldn't imagine living without a home, or going to bed hungry, or sleeping in a cardboard box. She couldn't imagine picking through a garbage can for food.

She looked around the room and a feeling of shame overcame her. Had she really had it so bad as a child?

There was the sound of a door being shut and Leana looked up to see Mario coming toward her. Never in her life had she been more happy to see him.

"That your friend?" the woman asked.

"Yes," Leana said. "That's my friend."

"You're a lucky woman. He's one of my favorite people. Do you realize he comes here once a week with either a carload of food or a check to buy food?"

"It wouldn't surprise me." The woman left and Leana kept looking at Mario, who was now weaving through the tables.

"My car's outside," Mario said, after giving Leana a hug. "I want you to come with me. We're moving you out of your apartment."

Leana hadn't expected this. She began to protest. "But where will I go?"

"That's taken care of."

"There's got to be another way, Mario. I love that apartment."

"More than your life? Let's go."

Reluctantly, Leana went with him. As they left the shelter and stepped into the night, the two men waiting outside the entrance fell in step behind them. Leana knew that these men, like herself and Mario, were armed.

Traffic was barely moving on Prince. Cars were double-parked and people were cutting through traffic. Mario's black Taurus was parked at the street corner, shimmering in the falling rain.

They sat in the back, Mario's men in the front. The moment the door was shut behind them, Leana reached over and held Mario tightly. "It's going to be all right," he said. "Just do as I say."

"I'm scared."

"There's no need to be. Just do as I say."

They rode in silence, each secure in the other's arms. She put her head on his shoulder.

"On the phone you mentioned a note," Mario said. "I want to see it. Do you have it with you?"

"It's at my apartment."

"Along with the gun?"

"No. I have that with me."

He was pleased by this. He released her from the embrace and asked to see it.

Leana removed the gun from her inside jacket pocket. It felt cold and heavy and threatening in her hands. She gave it to Mario. "Is it loaded?"

He checked. "It's loaded. Where do you live?"

Leana told him. Mario leaned forward and gave the driver directions. He wanted that note. Before killing Eric Parker, he planned on nailing it to the man's forehead.

\* \* \*

After securing the apartment, Mario told his men to wait for them in the hall. "We won't be long," he said. "Make sure no one comes near here."

He closed the door and looked across the room at Leana. She was removing the note from her bedside table. Watching her now, he felt the same deep love, the same strong physical attraction, the same sense of wanting to protect her, that he felt when they were together for those brief six months.

He thought of Lucia then and realized that whatever love he once felt for her was nothing compared to the love he felt for Leana. And how could it ever compare? With Leana, love came naturally. With Lucia, their lives had been arranged by their fathers from birth. It always was known that Antonio De Cicco's first-born son would marry Giovanni Buscetta's first-born daughter.

For Lucia Buscetta, the marriage was a welcome event--her attraction to Mario De Cicco was great. For Mario, the marriage was a cruelty imposed on him by his father. At the age of eighteen, he was told to marry a girl he barely knew, let alone loved. Then, as now, there was nothing he could do about the arrangement.

At least not while his father was alive.

"Here it is," Leana said.

"Let me see it."

Leana waited until he finished reading it. "Well?"

"When were you sent this?"

"A little after nine-thirty this morning."

"Who gave it to you?"

"A messenger?"

"What did he look like?"

"I don't remember."

"Try to remember."

She thought back. Although only hours had passed since she'd seen the man, she was surprised at how difficult it was to conjure an image of him. "He was blond," she said after a while. "And he had an earring."

"Was it the guy who chased you that day in the park?"

"No," Leana said. "That man had dark hair. And, besides, I'd never forget what he looked like."

"What kind of earring was this messenger wearing?"

"A small gold hoop, I think."

"Which ear?"

"Right. No, left." She looked at him. "Left."

"Was he tall?"

"He actually was kind of short."

"Did he seem nervous?"

"Not at all. He actually seemed impatient with me, as if he had a thousand other errands to run."

"What else can you remember?"

"Nothing. It happened so quickly, I'm surprised I remember as much as I do. Why is this so important?"

"It's important because whoever delivered this note and that gun to you might be the man who's been hired to kill you." He saw fear cross her face and said, "Look--why don't you start packing? The sooner we're out of here, the sooner you can move into your new apartment."

He leaned forward and kissed her on the cheek, then on the lips. She was scared and his heart went out to her. "I promise you'll like it. It has lots of windows and high ceilings and hardwood floors and a kitchen that's bigger than this whole apartment."

"What good will a big kitchen do me?" Leana said. "I can't cook." She thought of all the terrible pots of coffee she had made for Michael and said, "I can't even make a pot of coffee without screwing it up."

"So?" Mario said, smiling. "We'll drink tea. And you don't have to worry about dinner. I'll cook for you--just like old times. Okay?"

Leana thought of his wife and children, thought of all the times they had been separated in the past because of them, and decided that she didn't want it to be like old times. It was time for her to have something real. A relationship with Mario couldn't be. Circumstances would always prevent it. She made the mistake of falling in love with a married man and foolishly thought that something good would come from it.

Her mind went to Michael. What would he think when he came here and found her gone? She had no way of getting in touch with him. Michael always called her. On her cell, it always said that his was a private number. Worse, they always met at her apartment. For the first time, she realized how absurd that was. They were together so much and yet he hadn't given her his number or told her where he lived.

Mario placed his hand on her arm. "We should leave," he said. "Is there anything you want to bring with you?"

Leana went to a bureau across the room.

She pulled out shirts and pants and shorts and underwear, tossing them all into the suitcase Mario held open for her. She did not see the clothes. She did not see what personal items she tossed into the bag. She saw only Michael and Eric, Louis, Celina and her parents, and could not believe how much her life had changed in the two short weeks since the opening of The Redman International Building.

She wondered if her life would ever be what she'd dreamt it to be and decided it would. *I will make it*, Leana thought. *I will make it to the top.* And then a thought occurred to her. *If I live.*

"You ready?" Mario asked.

"There's something I want to give you," she said, walking the few steps to her bed. Hidden beneath it was a locked metal box. Leana lifted it onto the bed and removed a key from her bedside table. She unlocked the box. Inside were pictures of her mother and her father and Celina, old letters from old friends--and the $25,000 check Philip Quimby gave in exchange for the counterfeit jewels.

She handed the check to Mario. "Tonight, I saw a woman whose sole possessions were her three hungry children and a few torn garbage bags filled with God knows what. I might be leaving my home tonight, but I'm leaving to move into another home that will keep me warm and dry. That woman and her children should be so lucky."

She nodded toward the check. "Would you donate that to the shelter and see to it that it's put to good use?"

Mario looked touched. "Of course, I will."

"I start work soon," she said, and saw by the change in Mario's expression that he knew nothing about this. "We haven't discussed that yet," she said. "I was going to tell you about it over dinner that night--but you didn't show. Where were you, anyway?"

He was about to tell her the truth, but then decided now wasn't the time to tell her about the threat against Lucia's life. "I told you I was with Lucia," he said. "It was her birthday."

Leana shook her head in disappointment. "No, it wasn't, Mario. Lucia's birthday is a week after my own. I haven't forgotten that. So, why the lie?"

He was surprised she knew. "I'm sorry," he said. "I didn't want to, but there's a reason for it. Something happened at home."

"What's happened at home?"

"I'll tell you later. Right now, I want to know about this job."

Leana stilled the wave of stubbornness rising within her. He was helping her now. She decided to answer the question. "Louis Ryan asked me to manage his new hotel. I start next week."

"Louis Ryan?" Mario said. "The developer?"

"Yes," Leana said. "The developer."

"But the man's a crook," Mario said. "Everyone knows that. And your father hates him." His last words lingered in the air. "Which is why you took the job."

"Maybe," Leana said. "But the job also is a great opportunity. It was Harold who suggested it, Mario."

"Your father's own best friend suggested this?"

"He set up the appointment."

Mario was incredulous. "Something isn't right here, Leana. You've got to see that."

"Everything's perfectly right," she said. "Harold wouldn't have suggested that I meet Louis if it wasn't. Now, look. I don't want to discuss this now. If you want to do so later, fine. What's more important is that soon I'll have an income of my own. I'll finally be independent. That's a big step for me, Mario. Don't ruin it."

Mario tried to accept what she'd just told him--but he couldn't. He couldn't believe she was going to work for Louis Ryan. Did the woman have no sense? All of Manhattan knew how Louis Ryan and George Redman felt about each other. He knew that if Leana took this job, sooner or later she would take the brunt of that hatred.

*So, we'll talk later*, he thought.

When they left the apartment, they walked swiftly to Mario's car. It was parked at the curbside, perhaps 500 feet away. In the distance, the Washington Arch glowed and the faint sounds of a reggae band carried in the breeze.

They had just reached the car when someone called out Leana's name from across the street. Leana turned and glimpsed the person at the same moment Mario opened the car's rear passenger door and shoved her inside.

She slid across shiny black vinyl. Her head struck the driver's side headrest and she was aware of a sharp pain in her left shoulder.

Mario withdrew his gun, leaned into position.

His men followed suit.

Someone on the sidewalk--a woman--screamed at the sight of the drawn guns. Leana lifted her head and looked out the side window. Standing frozen in the middle of Fifth Avenue, traffic curling to a stop around him, was Michael Archer.

227

## CHAPTER TWENTY-EIGHT

At midnight that evening, Louis Ryan left the party on Anastassios Fondaras' yacht, returned to his office at Manhattan Enterprises and locked in a wall safe the DVD Fondaras gave him upon leaving the ship.

He fixed himself a drink, finished it and fixed himself another.

He walked the few steps to his desk and sat. He stared at the glittering facade of the Redman International Building and sipped.

He waited.

The knock came at twelve-thirty. Ryan glanced at his watch. It was about time Spocatti showed. Louis hadn't seen or heard from him all day.

"Come in," he called.

The door swung open and Spocatti stepped inside. As usual, he was dressed in black. He approached Louis' desk.

During the weeks they had come to know each other, a deep respect had grown between the two men. While Louis admired Spocatti's mind and intellect, Spocatti felt a strong sense of camaraderie toward Louis. As far as he was concerned, anyone who could make his own son believe that a person by the name of Stephano Santiago actually existed deserved respect.

"I assume everything went well," Louis said.

Spocatti stopped fifteen feet before reaching Louis' desk. Instinct made him move left while he stared at the floor-to-ceiling windows behind Ryan.

"There were a few problems," he said. "And I'll tell you about them when you either move away from the windows, or close the drapes."

Louis wrinkled his brow. "You think I'm at risk?'

"Anyone who has wealth and power is at risk, Louis. Especially those as hated as you. Why open yourself to a potential sniper when you can prevent it?"

"Because I happen to like the view," Louis said, but he opened a desk drawer and flipped a switch, anyway. The curtains whispered shut. "Now that I'm safe from predators, tell me what happened."

"Cain and his men are dead."

Louis sat motionless. Vincent told him everything--about the chase, the cab driver, Michael's manuscript, the fire.

"Michael had a gun?"

"Hidden beneath his bed."

"And he shot Cain?"

"He killed Cain--at the same moment I killed the man who was blocking the doorway to his apartment. I told you we couldn't trust Cain, Louis. I warned you not to use him. The man made his own rules, would kill for the hell of it. If I hadn't gone on a hunch to Michael's apartment, your son would be dead. I saved his life after Cain burned the manuscript Michael was working on. By the time I reached him, the apartment was in flames and Michael had passed out from the smoke in the room. I had to carry him out of the building."

Things were moving too quickly. Louis only hired Cain to frighten Michael, to strengthen his belief in a man by the name of Stephano Santiago. None of this was supposed to have happened.

"Did anyone see you carry him out of the building?"

"Lot's of people saw me. Some wanted to help."

"Did anyone recognize Michael?"

"I can't be sure of that. There was too much confusion."

"Where did you bring him?"

"To my apartment. I tried reaching you but you were out." Spocatti shot him a look. "Where were you tonight?"

"Doesn't matter. How long did Michael stay with you?"

"Until his lungs cleared. They were filled with smoke."

There wasn't a trace of concern on Louis' face. Michael was alive. That's what mattered.

"Where is he now?"

"On a plane headed to Europe with Leana."

"And?"

"Michael is scared. He needs the money and he's ready to marry. Leana's the challenge."

"She'll marry him," Louis said. "She has to."

Although Spocatti had wondered for weeks why this marriage was so important to Ryan, he decided not to ask why.

"What about Mario De Cicco?" Louis asked.

"He's going to be a problem."

"How much of a problem?"

Spocatti shrugged. "Depends on how much you wanted to use Eric Parker. Next time you send him roses, it might be to his grave."

"What does that mean?"

"It means that Parker went through with his threat. He had a contract put out on Leana Redman."

"He did what?"

"Relax," Spocatti said. "De Cicco found out about it. He'll use his contacts to have it canceled, he'll track down Parker and he'll kill him himself."

"How do you know all this?"

"Technology is a wonderful thing, Louis."

"What else have you heard?"

"Plenty. Seems De Cicco's concerned about you. He doesn't like the fact that you're going to be Leana's new employer. He's angry about it and told his men to get a complete rundown on you and Michael by the end of the week."

"He doesn't know Michael's my son, does he?"

"Not now," Spocatti said. "But if his men dig deep enough, he will. Right now, he's more concerned with the reason Harold Baines sent Leana to you. He knows Harold is George Redman's best friend. He knows something isn't right. He's a smart man."

"Not as smart as me."

"That remains to be seen."

"Don't forget," Louis said, "I've got you."

"And he's got the Mafia. Things are changing, Louis. Things aren't as simple as they once were. Things are getting serious."

"It's nothing we can't handle."

"We're talking about the Mafia, Louis."

"And I'm talking about an extra $10 million if you stay with me. That's over and above the money I've already offered you. Half will be in your Swiss account by the end of next week. You'll get the other half when Redman is dead."

There was a silence.

230

"You said you were the best, Vincent."

"I am, Louis--but the best are never fools, not even for money." He corrected himself. "Especially not for money."

"I need to know if you're still in," Louis said.

Spocatti weighed the situation, had a few ideas and then he nodded. "I want that money in my account by tomorrow morning. Not next week."

"Done."

"And from now on, we do things my way."

"I can't agree to that."

"Then we compromise. It's my ass out there. I'm not losing it for you."

"No one's asked you to."

Spocatti laughed. "Right," he said. "So, what do you want me to do next?"

Louis told him.

*　*　*

From the doorway of her husband's study, Elizabeth Redman stood removing her jewelry while George, standing at the far right wall of windows, finished the last of his Scotch.

"Are you all right?" she asked.

It was a moment before he turned to her. "Not really."

She walked over to where he was standing and put her arms around him. "You can talk to me," she said. "I'm always here for you."

"I know you are." He kissed the back of her hand.

"Last night, in your sleep, you said Leana's name twice. You're worried about her, aren't you?"

George nodded.

"Do you think it's true what Louis said about her tonight?"

"I don't know," George said. "But I was planning on finding out when you came in." He released himself from the embrace and walked to his desk. He picked up a phone and started dialing.

Elizabeth stepped to his side. "Who are you calling?"

"Who do you think?"

231

"Don't you think it's a little late to call?  Helen might be in bed.  You'll disturb them."

"I don't care if I disturb them.  If Harold's been speaking to Louis Ryan about my daughter, I want to know about it."

"You know you can't believe a word Ryan says."

"I understand that," he said.  "But I also know my daughter.  And you've seen how Harold's been acting lately.  There's a reason behind it and this might be it."

"Why didn't you just confront him about it on the ship?" she said.  "We could be beyond this now."

The line started ringing.  "Because I was too angry," George said.  "And making one scene was enough."

"You're not angry now?"

George shot her a look.  The line clicked and Harold answered the phone.  "It's George.  Can you come to my office?  I need to see you. Yes, tonight."

* * *

"What's the problem?"

George turned in his chair and looked across his office at Harold Baines, who had just stepped inside and now was standing in shadow.

"I'm not sure," he said.  "But I think you can help me figure it out."  He motioned toward the chair opposite his desk.  "Why don't you have a seat?  We have a lot to talk about."

Harold hesitated for a moment, but then came across the room.

"Want a drink?"

As he sat, Harold looked at George.  Although he was nervous, a part of him even frightened of this meeting, he somehow managed to keep his features neutral.  "Are you having one?"

"I've already had several.  One more isn't going to kill me. What do you want?"

"What you're having."

George crossed to the bar.

232

Harold turned in his chair. He looked at his best friend and wondered if Jack Douglas told him what he'd seen on Anastassios Fondaras' ship.

He was frightened. He wasn't sure how he would handle the situation if it arose. Never had Harold been confronted with his homosexuality. Never had anyone called him on his drug problem. He always was discreet, careful. But recently, he had been preoccupied, forgetful. Sometimes, he felt as if he were losing control of his life. The deals with WestTex and Iran, his increasing dependency on heroin and coke, all were devouring what little structure and routine he once had.

For years he had been living a lie. For years he had been miserable because of it. The drugs and the sex were an escape from a life he was becoming convinced was no longer worth living. He did not love his wife or his children because he barely knew them. The only people he cared about were the people who had never let him down--George and Leana. And now he couldn't face them because he had betrayed them both. What kind of a man was he?

"We've been friends too long for bullshit," George said from the bar. "So, I'll just get to it. I spoke to Louis Ryan tonight--or, rather, he spoke to me. He told me something I'm not sure I believe."

Harold sat motionless in his chair. In the windows before him, the city gleamed.

George walked over with the drinks. "He said you two have become friendly. He said that, thanks to you, Leana's going to be running his new hotel for him." George stopped beside Harold and handed him his martini. "I want to know if that's true."

Harold put his glass down on the table beside him. If he lied to George now, he knew that it would destroy what had taken thirty years to build.

"Obviously, it's not true."

George sat in his chair. He leaned toward his desk and rested his head in his hands. He felt drained, exhausted--but relieved, as well.

"I didn't think you had," he said, straightening. "But I had to ask. I hope I didn't offend you."

"You didn't offend me," Harold said.

233

"I had to know."

"I understand."

There was a silence while the two men drank.

Harold returned his gaze to the view out the windows. As he sat there, numb, he watched two helicopters sail over a city he was beginning to hate. It was a city that, like so many other things in his life, held little appeal for him anymore.

He looked at George and knew that nothing could ever assuage the guilt he felt for having betrayed him and his family. Nothing could fill the deep emptiness that had become his life-- not friendship, not love, not truth.

He wondered how much longer he could live a lie. He wondered at what point his world would begin to crumble.

"This takeover has been difficult on you, hasn't it?" George said.

"What do you mean?"

"You've lost weight," George said. "A lot of weight. Helen tells Elizabeth that you're not eating well. I noticed that at tonight's dinner. You hardly touched the food on your plate. Is there something wrong? Are you not well?"

"It's just my ulcers," Harold said. "I admit I'll feel better once this takeover is complete."

"You're sure there's nothing else?"

"Nothing I can't handle with a little thought," Harold said.

George leaned back in his chair, curious to know what Harold meant by that. He decided to let it pass. "I met with Frostman today," he said.

Harold looked surprised--and then perhaps a little vulnerable. "I didn't miss a meeting, did I?"

"This time you didn't. I met with him alone." He finished his drink and stood. "Chase is onboard, but they've struck a tough deal. But so have I. I think it's one I can live with. One we all can live with."

"What's their money going to cost?"

"Eight percent."

Harold raised an eyebrow. "Not bad. Who gets senior debt?"

"We do," George said. "But for that, they'll end up with a thirty-five percent share of WestTex."

Harold shook his head. "You're going to have a hard a time

234

getting board approval on that."

"I know," George said. "But that's their deal and we're running out of time. The board will have to accept it--or we lose billions."

"What if this falls through?" Harold asked.

George seemed almost defeated when he said, "I guess we approach someone else."

*  *  *

Later, when Harold left Redman International, the black Mercedes limousine that had been waiting on 50th Street started its engine, cut into traffic and cruised to a stop beside him.

Harold stepped away from the curb at the same moment the limousine's rear door shot open and Vincent Spocatti stepped out.

Harold felt a shock.

Calmly, Spocatti pressed a gun against his side. "Get into the car, Harold. Your day isn't over yet."

## CHAPTER TWENTY-NINE

"How about a nightcap?"

Jack turned from the painting of irises he was admiring in the foyer of Celina's apartment and moved into the living room, where she was standing at a bar. They had just returned from Anastassios Fondaras' party and it was late.

"Do you have any beer?"

"As a matter of fact, I do." She bent to the small refrigerator that was at her feet, reached inside for something light, which she knew he liked, and then looked at Jack. In her eyes was a spark of humor. "Would you like me to pour it in a champagne glass?"

Although Jack smiled, he seemed distracted as he loosened and removed his black bow tie. "This time, the bottle's fine."

He came over to where she was standing and took it from her. He looked at her for a moment, moved to speak, but then sipped his beer.

Celina turned back to the bar and poured herself a glass of wine. She was confused about what happened earlier on the yacht and more than a little angry with Jack, but she didn't want it to show. She wanted to make love to this man and yet she wasn't sure if he wanted the same. *Why did he stop it from happening at the party? He asked me to follow him below ship and then he stopped it. Why?*

"Nervous about tomorrow morning's jump?"

Celina turned and saw that he had removed his jacket--it now was draped over the chair beside them. He waited for an answer, his gaze meeting hers levelly.

"A little," she said. "It's not every day I jump off a bridge with a rubber band strapped to my ankles." She lifted an eyebrow. "What made you ask?"

"Your hands are trembling."

"Can I ask you something?"

"Shoot."

"Tonight, on the yacht, you asked me to follow you below ship.

236

I went with you because I wanted to be with you. But when we arrived at that stateroom, you stopped us from going inside. Why?"

Her question hung in the air. Although she didn't enjoy being so blunt with him, she wanted an answer. She wanted to know why he hadn't gone through with it--especially considering he had asked her to follow him.

"It's not what you're thinking," Jack said.

"And what am I thinking?"

"That I didn't want to make love to you. That I changed my mind." He looked at her. "That's not so."

"Then what happened?"

"We couldn't have entered that room even if we wanted to."

"Why?"

"Because two other people had a similar idea."

She hadn't expected this. Surprise reflected in her eyes. "Who was in there?"

A shadow of indecision crossed his face. He wasn't sure just how much he should tell her. If he told her what he had seen in that split second before he closed the stateroom's door, it would not only destroy Harold Baines' career, but his life as well. He made his decision. "I'm not sure who they were," he said.

"But you said you saw two people."

"It was dark. I couldn't make out their faces, only that they were men and they were indisposed."

Color rose in her cheeks. "They were having sex?"

When he shrugged, Celina laughed.

"What's so funny?"

"I don't know," she said. "Maybe I'm jealous that they beat us to it."

He put down his beer on the table beside him and took a step toward her, his last image of Harold Baines fading. "Anything you want to do about that jealousy?"

"Depends on what you have in mind."

Wordlessly, Jack pulled her to him. They kissed and Celina knew from the passion in that kiss that there was no turning back now.

She placed her wine glass on the bar, put her hand in his and led him across the living room to her bedroom. There, the city glowed in the windows just beyond the bed. Celina turned to him. Jack moved to her, his mouth found hers again and they began to kiss.

Only this time it was a different kiss. This time it wasn't as gentle as it was in the living room. Her hands went to his hips, his to her breasts and then to the small of her back. He pulled her closer to him and she felt his erection running up the length of his groin.

Things weren't moving fast enough. Jack turned Celina and began removing her dress, his lips kissing each area of newly exposed skin. Celina shuddered at the roughness of his shaved chin, the warm breath and moist tongue on her back, the strong hands working their way down to the curve of her buttocks. Just when she thought she couldn't stand it any longer, he unfastened the last button and her dress rippled to her feet.

She turned to him, naked, her breasts full with anticipation. She felt vulnerable yet alive. Jack's gaze roamed over her body and she saw on his face a flash of excitement. She wasn't wearing underwear.

He leaned forward and brought his head down to her breasts. Celina's head fell back and she moaned as Jack's lips found one of her nipples. The waves of pleasure that assailed her were intense. As if sensing her impatience, Jack guided her to the carpet and lay on top of her. She felt how hard he was, how big he was, and suddenly it was she who wanted to be the explorer.

Pushing him off her, Celina straddled him, her breasts only inches from his face. She saw him smile--an intimate, knowing smile--and she heard him gasp when she gave his shirt a quick, brutal tug. Buttons popped and the material separated, exposing his muscular, hairy chest. She stared at him for a moment, her excitement rising, then she dropped her head to his chest and covered one of his nipples with her mouth.

Jack's back arched. "Jesus," he said.

She wanted him naked. She sat up, reached down, removed his shoes and socks, then unbuckled his pants. She grabbed at the material and tugged. Jack raised his hips and his pants came off. She threw them aside and they struck a table top, where they slipped into a framed photograph of herself taken years ago in London.

It fell to the floor. There was the sound of glass splintering.

Celina paid little attention to it--all she saw was Jack. His face was flushed. She knew he was excited and that fueled her to push the limits further. Lowering her head to the waistband of his shorts, she bit the fabric and pulled them off with her teeth. With a flick of her wrist, they sailed across the room, a shadow striking one of the windows.

His penis was unusually large. Celina stared at it, transfixed. Extending from a thatch of dark-brown hair, it lay an inch above his belly button and throbbed in time with each of his uneven breaths. She reached down to touch it. Jack's breathing became hoarse, his body taut with anticipation. Watching her admire it seemed to inflame him.

But Celina didn't touch it. Instead, she met his gaze with her own and licked the area of skin directly surrounding it. Jack grabbed a handful of her hair. Celina sank on top of him and her nipples brushed the base of his penis. She liked it a little rough. She sensed he did, too.

Suddenly, she stood and went to the table that was across the room. Incredulous, Jack watched her go. "What are you doing?" he said. "Come back here."

"Wait," Celina whispered. "Just...wait."

When she struck the match, her face burst into brilliant, glowing bloom. She lit the candle that was in her hand, blew out the match and started toward him. With the city twinkling in the windows behind her and the candle burning in her hand, she was radiant.

She straddled him again and tossed her hair away from her face with a quick flick of her head. Her eyes seemed to challenge his when she looked down at him. "Do you trust me, Jack?"

Jack looked at her, then at the candle flickering in her hand. He knew what she had in mind and it thrilled him. "I trust you," he said.

She held the candle over his chest, tipped it slightly and allowed the flame to melt the wax. "I've never done this before," she said. "But I've always wanted to. Do you think it will hurt?" Before he could respond, she turned the candle onto its side and watched the shimmering droplets of wax rain down onto his chest.

Jack caught his breath and winced, the hot wax rolling towards his stomach in thin rivers. It pooled in his belly button and spilled onto the beige carpet. It wasn't painful, but it was exhilarating.

And then Celina blew out the candle.

Rising up the length of his body, grinding her body hard against his, she found his mouth with her own and they kissed. Jack reached down and grasped himself. Celina raised her hips and parted her legs.

"Are you ready?" he asked.

"Probably not." She touched his face. "Just go easy. What you've got down there should be studied."

Just as he was about to enter her, they searched one another's eyes. They were having the same thought, that if they went through with this, nothing would be the same between them again. While there was an attraction in the past, their lives had been professional up to this point. They would still have to work with one another at Redman International, still have to confer at board meetings, still have to act as though there was nothing between them, although there was more than just something there. They were in love.

And so Celina lifted her hips higher, allowing him to gently push inside of her. *He's too big,* she thought. But everything that happened after that initial pain became a blur to her. She wanted this. She wanted Jack. She wanted him in her life.

As they rocked together on the carpet, his thrusts became deeper, faster, more demanding. Spasms coursed through her. Her fingernails dug into his back. Her hand clutched a handful of his hair and she pulled. He pushed her hands away and pinned her arms at her sides. He covered one of her nipples with his mouth and bit gently. She arched her back. Her nipple was so full, it felt as if it might burst.

She looked up at his face and realized that he was as close as she was. Wanting him deeper inside of her, she countered each of his thrusts with her own until there was nothing but their release.

Later, after they showered together, they made love again. As Celina drifted off to sleep, her body secure in Jack's arms, she realized how much she missed having a man in her bed at night. She moved closer to him and kissed his chest. His heart was still racing, but the sound of it soothed her to sleep.

# FIFTH AVENUE

## CHAPTER THIRTY

"You look a little piqued, Harold. Seem a little tense. Want a drink before we begin?"

Harold Baines turned from the window he was standing at and looked across the office at Louis Ryan, who was pouring vodka into a glass of crackling ice. "It's a full bar," he said. "I can't imagine there isn't something here that wouldn't appeal to you."

He put the bottle of vodka down and took a sip of the cold Absolut. "Or maybe beer's more your style," he said. "Isn't that what they serve at those sex clubs you go to? Isn't beer the choice of drink while someone's pissing on you or shoving their fist up your ass? If it is, and if that's what you prefer, then I'm afraid I can offer you none here."

"Go to hell, Ryan."

"I'm already there, Harold," Louis said, and pointed to the chair opposite his desk. "Sit down. What I have to say won't take long."

Harold sat. Through the windows before him, he could see The Redman International Building towering amid the Manhattan skyline. He thought of the meeting he had just had with George Redman, of the friendship he had betrayed, and looked away, his guilt and self-hate overwhelming.

He listened as Ryan stepped behind him.

"I want you to tell me everything you know about the takeover of WestTex Incorporated."

Harold turned in his chair, perhaps too quickly because he became dizzy. It was a moment before he could focus on Louis--and when he did, when the room finally righted itself, he saw that the man was standing beside a large television.

"I want you to start from the beginning," Louis said. "I want dates, facts, figures. I want to know the terms of the deal, and I want to know everyone's part in it--that includes yourself, George, Celina, Jack Douglas, the entire board. But most of all, I want you

242

to tell me why Redman is doing it. I want to know why he's taking over a company whose profits have plummeted since the Middle East went to hell.  I want to know why he's willing to pay twice what WestTex is worth when he knows goddamned well their profits are down--way down--and can't possibly support the $10 billion he's willing to pay for it.  It must be something good for him to risk everything he's ever worked for, and I want to know what it is--now--because time is running out."

The two men stared at each other.  Louis tipped back his drink and sipped, a confident man moving in for the kill.

And then Harold stood.  He couldn't do this to George.  He couldn't allow this to go any further than it already had.  He walked to the doors that were across the room.

Tried to walk.

His limbs became oddly weak, the muscles in his legs unable to hold him.  Another wave of dizziness overcame him, he listed slightly to the right and reached out a hand to steady himself on a Chippendale table.

Tried to reach.

The world blurred and he collapsed to the floor.

"What's the matter with you?"

Harold closed his eyes, the pressure inside his head building. He tried to shake off a wave of nausea, failed and put a hand over his mouth.  He began vomiting through his fingers, vomiting onto his clothes, vomiting onto Louis' priceless Aubusson rug.

Ryan took a hesitant step forward, not sure what to do. Harold studied his vomit-stained hand as though it were an object that had materialized from another place, another time.  The smell reached his nose, his stomach clenched and he doubled over again, making a gagging sound.

And Louis knew.

"You're addicted to it, aren't you, Harold?" he said.  "You're addicted to whatever the hell drug you're on.  How long has it been since you had your last fix?"

Harold didn't hear him.  The roaring in his head was too loud. He fished a handkerchief from his inside jacket pocket and wiped his mouth and hands.  His throat was burning, his heartbeat and breathing were erratic.  Dazed and disoriented, he pushed himself into a seated position and looked around the room.

For a moment, he didn't know who or where he was. For a moment, he knew nothing.

But as he sat there, the color gradually returned to his face.

"Pull yourself together," Louis said, still slightly shaken. He took a step back, wanting to put distance between them. "This isn't going to work with me."

Again, Harold looked around the room, recognition reflecting in his eyes only after Louis came into focus. He struggled to his feet, tried to regain his composure, and walked the few steps to a suede-upholstered sofa, where he sat, exhausted.

Time passed. When the man's breathing returned to normal, Louis said, "Talk."

Hostility radiated from Harold like summer heat from a city street. "Give me some water."

"Not until you tell me what you know about WestTex."

The universe of rage welling within Harold eclipsed whatever nausea he felt. In a controlled voice, he said, "Either you give me a glass of fucking water or I'll end this now, call the police and tell them what I know."

"I wouldn't count on that," Louis said. He stepped to the television that was behind him, turned it on and pushed play on a DVD player. The screen flickered to life.

Motionless, Harold sat watching and what he saw was himself. Naked. A young man was kneeling in front of him and sucking his cock. He recognized the scene, remembered the room.

Somehow, he had been taped sleeping with the waiter on Anastassios Fondaras' yacht. Somehow, he had been taped shooting heroin into his left arm. Somehow, he had been taped hurrying into his clothes after Jack Douglas entered the room and took him by surprise.

"Anastassios is a friend of mine," Louis said, watching the screen. "Like me, he has an interest in George Redman--only for different reasons. When I told him there was a way to obtain information on the takeover of WestTex Incorporated--not to mention why Redman is doing it--he said he'd gladly help me get that information, so long as it was made available to him. You, Harold, were kind enough to accept that young waiter's advances and follow him into the stateroom filled with the concealed video equipment. If you hadn't, I wouldn't have had anything tangible to nail you with."

He clicked off the television.

Harold continued staring at a picture that was no longer there.

Ryan went to the bar, poured water into a tall glass of ice, grabbed a small towel and handed each to the man who had aged thirty years on his sofa.

"Clean yourself up," he said. "You've got vomit on your jacket. And have your drink. When you're finished, you're going to tell me everything you know about WestTex, starting from the beginning, or a copy of that DVD goes to your wife, your children, George and Elizabeth, the press. It'll destroy you."

He went to his desk, where there was a digital voice recorder. He pointed it toward Harold and pressed record.

"Start talking," he said. "Now."

\* \* \*

Later that evening, when he was alone, Louis stared into the dark silence of his office. He was numb. If what Harold Baines had just told him was true, Redman's plan was nothing short of brilliant.

If he took over WestTex under these circumstances, the man's power would soar. If he took over WestTex under different circumstances, the man's power could plummet.

That is, of course, if what Harold Baines just told him was true.

He left his chair and went to the bank of windows to the right of him. He looked hard at the Redman International Building and felt the familiar coil of hatred unwind in his stomach. As much as he wanted to believe Baines, he knew he couldn't. The man was George Redman's best friend.

He needed someone who could get the information verified, someone who worked at Redman International and wanted to see Redman burn every bit as much as he did. But who? He stood in thought, his mind whirling with possibilities.

245

And then he knew exactly who could get the information he needed.

# FIFTH AVENUE

## BOOK THREE
## THIRD WEEK

### CHAPTER THIRTY-ONE

The following morning, at precisely the same time Celina Redman was leaving to go bungee jumping with Jack Douglas in upstate New York, and only hours before George Redman left Redman International for his three-mile run in Central Park, Eric Parker was being wheeled out of New York Hospital to a gray stretch limousine that was double-parked at a discreet side entrance.

There were no reporters--Diana Crane had seen to that--and as the chauffeur came around to help the nurse lift him into the back seat, Eric thought that the day he stepped foot back into this hospital would be far too soon. It was time to go home.

Diana already was seated in the back, facing traffic. She wore a black Chanel suit that came just to her knees, the diamond brooch Eric gave her the night they were attacked and a matching diamond tennis bracelet that also was from Eric.

Her legs, sheathed in black stockings, were crossed. Because his leg was extended in a cast, Eric had to sit sideways on the seat facing her. Diana did not look at him once as he was hoisted from the wheelchair and into the back, and there was no conversation once the door shut behind him.

She had been cool toward him since her arrival that morning.

"Is there something wrong?" Eric asked. He knew she had been to Anastassios Fondaras' party and wondered if something had happened. Celina, George and Elizabeth were there.

"Nothing is wrong," Diana said.

"Then why aren't you speaking to me?"

"You really don't want to know, Eric."

*Fucking women.* "Yes, I do."

"Then we'll discuss it later--not here."

The limousine swung out of the hospital.

Eric turned away from her and looked out a window. On today of all days, he didn't need to deal with a moody woman. Only an hour ago, he learned that because he no longer was an employee of Redman International, he also no longer was under their insurance plan and would have to pay all medical expenses himself--which were rapidly approaching the six figure mark, and would certainly top that number considering the months of rehabilitation he still had to endure. Although money wasn't a problem for him now, the idea of having to pay for something George Redman's daughter did to him was infuriating.

The limousine caught a string of green lights and sailed across 69th Street to Fifth. Eric watched men and women and children stroll down the streets and avenues, walking their dogs on retractable neon leashes, jogging with iPods clipped to their waists.

He rolled down a window and breathed in the smells of the city. He would be back soon. The city would be his once again and he would be back on top--only this time without the prestige of Redman International.

When they turned onto Fifth, Diana reached in her purse for her cell phone and started punching numbers. "I'm going to call ahead to Redman Place and make sure no unexpected visitors are waiting for us," she said.

Eric looked at her. "I thought you already took care of the press."

"I did," Diana said. "That's why no one greeted us at the hospital. But things can go wrong, Eric, so I'm calling ahead to be safe."

*Whatever.* Eric turned back to the window. All he wanted to do now was go home, grab a cold beer from the fridge and crawl into his own bed. At this point, he couldn't care less about the press. His mind was more preoccupied with the possibility that he might see Celina or George while they were wheeling him across the lobby. He was on crutches, but they were so awkward to use, he felt they made him look more like a cripple than a wheelchair did.

And Eric did not want to appear weak should he run into George or Celina.

248

Diana snapped her phone shut. She looked out a window. Eric watched her--something in her features had changed. The fingers of her right hand were toying with the brooch he once gave Celina.

"What is it?" he asked.

"There's a problem."

"What kind of problem? Is the press there?"

"It has nothing to do with the press."

"Then what is it?"

She took a breath and let it out all at once. Whatever anger he sensed coming from her earlier was now an emotion he couldn't quite define. "Diana--"

"It's your apartment," she said.

* * *

Before the pipes burst, the apartment was one of the most sought after in Manhattan for its view of Central Park. It was valued well into the millions. His collection of paintings, antique furniture and sculptures bought anonymously at auction was worth more.

But now, as Eric wheeled through the half-foot of water that already was ruining the hardwood floors, he realized that figure had dropped dramatically overnight.

His apartment was ruined.

He turned to Sam Mitchell, the manager of Redman Place, a man he had been friends with for years--but who now was curiously distant toward him.

"What happened, Sam?"

"Several pipes burst, Mr. Parker." The man's sudden formality hung in the air. Mitchell always called Eric by his first name. Now, Eric could only wonder how many other people George Redman had turned against him.

"I can see that, Sam. Mind telling me why?"

"Our men are still working on it. We won't know until the end of the day."

He wheeled over to the terrace, where Diana stood with her shoes in her hands. She fought for a smile, couldn't manage it and looked away. Water dripped onto them from the vacant hole that used to be a ceiling. His cast, the very cast his doctors warned him not to get wet, was soaked.

"How many other tenants went through this?" Eric asked.

"None, Mr. Parker."

"You mean to tell me mine was the only apartment whose pipes burst?"

"That's correct."

"But how can that be?"

"We won't know until our investigation is complete."

"I want to know now."

"We're working as fast as we can."

"Pipes don't burst in the middle of summer. In this building, they wouldn't burst even in the deepest of winter. I need to know what's going on. Now."

The man said nothing.

Diana placed a hand on his shoulder. Eric shrugged it off and wheeled away. He felt like hurling something right now, but stilled the impulse. Water sloshed at his feet.

"I assume my insurance will cover this," he said, moving toward the bedroom that no longer was a bedroom--maintenance had torn it apart to get to one of the burst pipes. "The paintings alone are worth a fortune. They can't be replaced. And the furniture--all one of a kind, all bought at auction. Are you getting the picture, Sam? Are you hearing me?"

"You're not going to like what I have to say."

"Say it. Nothing can faze me now."

"I hope that's so," Mitchell said, "because when you were terminated from Redman International, you lost your insurance coverage on your apartment. As you know, as a senior employee, it was paid for by the organization. But with your recent termination, Mr. Redman canceled it."

Eric was speechless. Diana mouthed--but did not say--the word "terminated.'"

"I'm afraid that's not all," Mitchell said. "The water is leaking through to the apartment below yours. It has destroyed Mrs. Aldrich's van Gogh and each of her prized Monets--not to mention the Henry VIII furniture that has been in her family for years and is considered priceless. She told me her insurance company plans to sue you. She told me to tell you to get a good lawyer."

"None of this makes sense," Diana said. "This isn't Eric's fault. Your insurance will cover it. This has to do with the building itself, not with Eric Parker."

Mitchell's words were measured. "While it's true that our insurance covers our original systems, the problem is that it appears that the trouble started in Mr. Parker's master bathroom, which he remodeled two years ago. If the report finds that to be the source of the problem, then we're dealing with plumbing that was altered by a third party. And it releases us from responsibility."

"No, it doesn't," Diana said. "The plumbing was up to code. It passed all inspections--yours and the city's. You signed off on that."

Sam held out his hands. "Look," he said. "I know this is difficult. I know everyone is upset. But when you read the document we signed with Mr. Parker, you'll note a clause that releases us from all responsibilities when any alterations are made to our original systems."

"Then the plumbing company is responsible."

"Maybe," Mitchell said. "But we're two years out from that remodel. If it were a month, you'd have a strong case. But two years?" He shook his head. "I doubt it."

Eric shot Diana a look. What he saw in her face was defeat. *Redman bankrupted me.*

There was a silence while Mitchell moved across the room to an Art Deco table that was beside a shiny black bar. On it were four vases filled with red roses. "There is at least one bright note to all this, Mr. Parker," he said. "These roses arrived this morning as a welcome home gift. They're from Louis Ryan."

* * *

"George is behind this. You know it as well as I do."

Diana entered her living room with a pot of hot coffee in one hand, two coffee mugs in the other. She was fresh from the shower and now wore a white terry bathrobe. Her hair, curling around her face in slick dark waves, was wet.

"He's responsible for those pipes bursting."

"We have to talk, Eric," she said, sitting in the chair opposite him and arranging the mugs on an end table. "Things aren't adding up."

"What things?"

She poured the coffee, handed him one of the steaming mugs and took a sip from her own. She seemed very tired when she said, "You've been lying to me."

Eric was about to speak, but Diana held up a hand, silencing him. "Right now I'm going to do the talking. You're going to shut up and listen. When I ask you a question, you'll answer it and you'll answer it honestly. If you lie to me, Eric, I'll know. It's what I do. It's that special gift that I get paid so much for. And if you do lie to me, that will be a mistake you will regret, because as far as I see it, you need me now--and I've just about had it with you."

She eased back in her chair.

In the window behind her, Manhattan was cloaked in a blanket of haze and smog. There was only the slightest hint of the sun behind the screen of clouds. She reached into the pocket of her robe and pulled out a rectangular black velvet box. She handed it to Eric and waited for him to open it. With the parting of velvet came a brilliant flash of diamonds and sapphires and rubies.

He looked at her.

"You can have your jewelry back," she said. "I saw Celina at the Fondaras party and she recognized the necklace I was wearing as one that used to belong to her. She said you bought it for her in Milan, I think, and that the stones were perfect. She said she sent it back to you along with the others that are in that box." Her voice dropped a note. "She said the sapphires brought out the blue in my eyes. Wasn't that nice of her?"

She sipped her coffee. "Actually, it wasn't. In fact, it was embarrassing. I can't tell you how many people overheard the conversation, but even if one person overheard it on that ship and at that party, all of Manhattan knows by now and I'm probably a laughingstock--something I never deserved."

"Diana--"

"Shut up, Eric. Just shut up. Are you as tired of your voice as I am? After all I've done for you, you at least owe me the courtesy of sitting there and listening."

He decided to stay quiet.

"You said you bought that jewelry for me because you loved me. How do you think it makes me feel knowing that your love is a farce?" She didn't wait for an answer because she didn't want another lie. She moved to the next subject. "You told me that you quit Redman International. You told me that because you were no longer seeing Celina, it was too difficult for you to continue working there and so you quit. Quit. I believed you because I always considered you an honest man. But you're not. An hour ago, Sam Mitchell said that George terminated you. I want to know why."

"That's none of your business."

She willed herself to remain calm. "If you lied to me, then it is my business. I've invested a lot of time and concern and love in you. I was beaten in your apartment by two men who wanted to hurt you for a reason you somehow can't explain. If it wasn't for me, you'd probably still be lying in your own blood. If I hadn't called in a number of favors, your name still would be at the top of the tabloids. You owe me the truth and you're going to spill it. If you don't, you can get out of here and out of my life. It's really that simple."

Eric reached for his crutches, struggled to his feet and moved to the windows that were at the opposite end of the room. He looked out at the city while she looked at him.

She deserved the truth. But how could he tell her that what began as a terrible mistake during the night of Redman International's opening had snowballed into a nightmare he couldn't let go of until Leana Redman paid for what she did to him?

The doctors still were not sure if he would regain full use of his leg. The damage done to his muscles and nerves was more severe than they originally thought. It was only right that Leana pay and he planned on going forward with that. Still, he had to tell Diana something. She now was the only person he could count on. Without an apartment or an income, how would he survive? Lawsuits were coming. At the very least, he needed her guidance.

He moved in her direction. "It's true," he said. "I was fired from Redman International."

"Why?"

"Because I was stupid."

"What a surprise. How stupid?"

"I almost slept with Leana the night of Redman International's opening. We would have gone through with it, but I was so drunk, I couldn't get it up." He reclaimed his seat. "Is that frank enough for you? She was putting me to bed and telling me to forget about my limp cock when Celina stepped into the room. We were in George and Elizabeth's penthouse. How she found us there is obvious. Someone tipped her off."

"Well, that's a shame," Diana said. The tone of her voice dropped the temperature in the room a good ten degrees.

"It meant nothing, Diana. We were both drunk and angry at life and Celina. It was a mistake."

"A rather large one, I'd say." And the room dropped another ten degrees.

"Celina must have told George," Eric said. "And then he fired me. That's all."

"Who attacked us that night?"

"That I don't know. It could have been anyone. It could have been a burglary."

"Oh, please," she said--and the room started to heat up. "It wasn't a burglary and you know it. Nothing was missing from your apartment. I checked on that the day after you were admitted to the hospital. Those men somehow slipped past security and entered your apartment, which was locked. The police reports show that the door was not opened with force and that the lock wasn't picked. Whoever did it had a key."

A silence passed.

"Tell me the truth," she said. "Who did it?"

*Friends of Leana's.* "I don't know."

"I don't believe you."

"Do you honestly believe I'd let whoever did this to me--to us--get away with it if I knew who they were?  Give me a break, for Christ's sake.  If I knew who was responsible for shattering my fucking leg, Diana, I'd bypass the police and take care of them myself."

At least that rang true.  "You've got to have some idea," she said.

"Take your pick," he said.  "I've pissed off a lot of people during my years at Redman International.  I've made a lot of enemies, especially while working on the deal with WestTex.  You know that as well as I do.  It could be anyone."

She leaned back in her chair.  So, maybe he didn't know.  Did she care?  She didn't know that either and a part of her hated herself for not knowing.  She finished the last of her coffee and poured another cup.  "So, what are you going to do now?"

"What do you mean?" Eric said.  "I was hoping I could stay here."

"I'll bet you were."

"Only until my apartment is repaired."

"Really?" she said.  "That's presumptuous.  And fixing your apartment will take months.  I don't see it happening.  I don't see you here."  She nodded at the jewelry.  "Sell those.  That should put a roof over your head."

"I need your help."

"I know you do."

"I'd like to stay here."

"Tell me," she said.  "How do you plan on paying for the repairs on your apartment?  You have hospital bills to pay, lawyer fees to pay and, if you lose the case, a ruined van Gogh, two botched Monets and destroyed Henry VIII furniture to buy.  I don't see how you're going to pay for the apartment, Eric, let alone the rest of it."

"Looks like I'm going to have to get a job."

She wanted to laugh.  "Well, God knows you're a catch, Eric.  Naturally, any reasonable person will overlook the fact that George sent you packing, they'll overlook the headlines you've been making, and they'll just hire you just because you're the great Eric Parker."

"One man will."

"And who is that?"

"You've seen the roses Louis Ryan has been sending me.  He obviously wants me at Manhattan Enterprises.  He's also got as much money as George--and we all know how those two feel about each other.  If I play my cards right, I might get myself out of this mess completely."

## CHAPTER THIRTY-TWO

"Do exactly as I say and you won't get hurt."

His voice was unnerving. Celina stood at the edge of the footbridge, a bungee cord no larger than the size of her wrist strapped to her ankles, a blindfold covering her eyes. Although she couldn't see the river twisting below her, she could sense the coolness of the water just as she could sense the sheerness of this height.

She clenched her teeth and waited for her instructions.

"I'm not comfortable with you wearing that blindfold," the man standing behind her said. His name was Steve Simpson and his company, Vertigo Fever, owned the footbridge they were standing on. "No one's worn one before--not Jack, not even myself. I don't think it's a good idea."

Celina removed the blindfold and looked at the man. Although she was nervous about jumping, a part of her even frightened, she tried to appear calm. "That may be so," she said. "But you've told me time and again that this sport is safe."

"It is safe," Simpson said.

"Then what difference does wearing a blindfold make?"

"Probably none. But you're a beginner and it's a 320-foot drop. I'm not comfortable with it."

"So, I can't wear it?"

"I didn't say that."

"Then what are you saying?"

"I'm saying that I would feel a hell of a lot more comfortable if someone with experience put the blindfold on and jumped first-- like Jack. That way I can see how it goes and hopefully feel more comfortable with it."

Celina was about to speak when Jack held up a hand. He looked at Simpson and said with a grin, "I wish I could go first, Steve. But she won't let me."

"Won't let you?"

"That's right."

"Why not?"

"Because we tossed a coin before we left the city and it came up heads. She jumps first."

"I don't believe this."

Celina crossed her arms. For a moment, her fear of jumping was replaced by impatience. She wanted this over with. "Believe it," she said. "Now, can we get on with this? I'm sure these other people would like a chance to jump."

Simpson looked at the group of twelve other jumpers who were waiting behind them, saw the impatience on their faces and made his decision. "Forget it," he said to Celina. "Either you jump without the blindfold, or you don't jump at all."

Celina felt her face flush. This was ridiculous! What harm was there in wearing a stupid blindfold? Before she could protest, a tall man with dark hair and sharp features stepped away from the group of other jumpers and said, "I have a suggestion."

Celina looked at the man. He was wearing a black T-shirt, white shorts and dark sunglasses. He looked familiar to her, though she hadn't noticed him on the walk up. "What's that?" she asked.

"Why don't I jump first? I'm experienced, you'll still be able to jump before your friend and I'll wear the blindfold so Steve here can judge for himself if it's safe."

Celina turned to Steve. "Well?" she said. "What do you think?"

"Depends on how long he's been jumping."

"Two years," Vincent Spocatti said. "At a park in Texas."

* * *

"My partner is in a raft anchored beneath the bridge," Simpson said to Spocatti. "If you lean forward, you can see him."

Spocatti gripped the footbridge's wooden handrail, leaned forward and saw bobbing in the river an orange raft that seated eight. The man sitting in it waved up to them. Although it was difficult to tell from this height, the man looked half Spocatti's

258

size.

"You about ready?" Simpson asked.

Spocatti nodded.

"Take a deep breath if you're nervous."

"I'm not nervous."

Simpson had noticed this. Even experienced jumpers started to sweat a little when it came time to jump. This one would be wearing a blindfold for the first time--and yet he seemed absolutely cool.

"You sure you want to wear that blindfold?"

Spocatti glanced over at Celina, who was standing behind him with her arm around Jack. She smiled at him. He smiled back, relieved she hadn't recognized him from the opening of The Redman International Building. He supposed the sunglasses, strapped to his head, helped.

"I'm sure," he said.

"Then let's do it."

Simpson knelt, wrapped a nylon strap around Spocatti's ankles, pulled it tight and snapped a series of buckles. While the bungee was being hooked to the strap, Spocatti glanced downriver. Parked in a discreet clearing next to one of the park's many dirt roads, two of his men were waiting for him in a Range Rover.

Simpson stood and slapped him on the back, indicating it was time to jump. Holding onto the railing with one hand, Spocatti lowered the blindfold with the other. With the sudden darkness, his senses became acute. He could hear the river roiling beneath him, the cry of a crow flying overhead. Against his thigh, he could feel the small pocketknife he had zipped into one of his pockets.

If Celina gave him too much trouble, he would carve her a new necklace.

"I'm going to count down from five," Simpson said. "When I'm finished, I want you to dive out as far as you can. Understand?"

Spocatti nodded.

The countdown began.

When Simpson reached zero, Spocatti pushed off the bridge without hesitation and plummeted to the river in a graceful arc. Celina moved forward with the crowd and watched. His arms

outstretched, his head lifted high, Spocatti seemed to be flying--
then the bungee went taut and cracked him like a whip.

He didn't scream or yell or shout. There was no whoop of joy
or exhilaration. He simply shot back toward the bridge and began
to bounce. It was over in less than a minute. He was lowered to
the raft.

When the bungee and blindfold were pulled back, Simpson
looked at Celina. Her face was pale. She was squeezing Jack's
arm with one hand, swatting a mosquito with the other.

"I'm satisfied," he said. "You next?"

"Is that even a question?" Celina asked. "Piece of cake."

"Try to concentrate," Simpson said to her. "Push everything
from your mind and think only of the jump. Nothing is going to
happen to you. I promise you that. Soon you'll be safe in the raft
and wearing what we jumpers call the post-bungee grin."

Although she heard little of what he said, Celina took a deep
breath and nodded. Once again, she was standing at the edge of
the footbridge, holding onto the rail behind her with tightly
clenched hands. In the raft below, Spocatti and Simpson's
assistant were looking up. They seemed a thousand miles away.

Celina put the blindfold in place and wondered why she was
doing this. Why did she always have to prove to herself and to
others that she was every bit as strong, every bit as brave, every
bit as smart as a man? *So, I need therapy. Great.*

She felt a hand on her arm. "Are you all right?" Jack asked.

"I'm fine," she lied.

"You sure you want to go through with this?"

"Mmm-hmm."

"Want to have lunch with me later?"

"Mmm-hmm."

"I love you," he said.

Celina gave a start. She couldn't have heard him right. But
when he squeezed her arm and gently kissed her cheek, she knew
she had. *He loves me*, she thought. If there'd been time, she
would have told him that she loved him too. But before she could,
Jack stepped aside so Simpson could strap the bungee to her
ankles.

"Okay, Celina," he said. "I'm going to count down from five.
Just jump out as far as you can and the cord will do the rest. You

ready?"

She nodded.

"All right, then. Here we go."

And he began to count.

Celina's mind whirled. With each number spoken, she felt her heart beat a little faster, her breathing become a little shallower, her hands grip the rail a little tighter. She wondered what would happen if the cord broke. She thought of the raft and the security it represented. She thought of her father, her mother and even Leana. She thought of last night with Jack, of the words he just spoke to her. And then, at the same moment Simpson shouted "Jump!" and she leapt into the air, she realized she had to pee.

It was a nightmare.

The wind whipped through her hair and snatched the blindfold from her face. She saw trees, rocks and water racing toward her. Her stomach lurched. Her bladder went. The world blurred. And the bungee went taut.

She stopped just short of hitting the river, there was an instant when her eyes met Spocatti's, and then she was being catapulted away from him and the attendant and the raft, toes first, toward the bridge--where she began to plummet again.

When the bouncing finally stopped and the attendant helped her into the raft, Spocatti took her by the hand and led her to one of the wooden seats, where she sat, exhausted.

"Fun, isn't it?" he asked.

Celina was about to say it hadn't been fun at all--it had been horrifying--when Spocatti suddenly slipped, fell hard against the side of the raft and capsized it, sending them all into the water.

* * *

"Something's wrong," Jack said. "They're in the water. The raft's upside down."

Simpson joined him at the rail and leaned forward as far as he could. In the river below, he could see only the swiftly moving water and the anchored, upturned raft.

No bodies.

"I don't see Celina," Jack said. "Where is she?"

Simpson could only stare as those waiting to jump joined them at the rail.

"Where the hell is your attendant, Steve? Where's the man who jumped first?"

"I don't see them."

Jack climbed quickly over the rail. "Strap the other bungee to my ankles."

"Jack--"

"Move!"

Simpson did as he was told, moving like an automaton while his mind tried to make sense of the situation. "I don't like this," he said to Jack as he pulled the nylon strap tight. "It's dangerous. There's no one down there to release you."

"I'll release myself. Just get me down there."

He looked at the strap, then at the fraying bungee cord that was attached to it and coiled beside him. "Ready?" he said to Steve.

At the same instant Simpson nodded, Jack jumped.

\* \* \*

She was trapped beneath the raft, her legs tangled in the rope that was attached to the anchor.

Her mouth was barely above the rushing water. Her breathing was sharp with fright.

She held onto the wooden seat above her so she wouldn't be pulled under by the current or by the weight of the anchor.

Below her, Spocatti and Simpson's assistant, Alex Stevens, were trying to free her. With each tug on the rope that bound her legs, her hands slipped a little on the slick seat. She held on as tightly as she could, knowing that if she let go, she would have little strength to fight the anchor as it pulled her down.

There was another tug on the rope. And another. Celina closed her eyes and prayed as her hands slipped and she sank a little deeper into the river.

The water level flowed over her mouth, cutting off her breath for an instant until she remembered she could breathe through her nose.  She let out a small cry of despair and her mouth filled with water.  She choked on it and began to cough.  She struggled against what she feared was the inevitable.

There was a sudden flurry of activity in the water.  Bubbles burst to the top as Spocatti and Alex surfaced, their dark hair as slick and as shiny as seal skin.  While Alex gasped for air, Spocatti swam calmly behind Celina and lifted her up so she could get a more sturdy grip on the wooden bench.

He turned to Alex.  "Go to the shore and get something to cut the rope with.  If we don't do something soon, the weight of the anchor and the pressure on her legs will cut off her circulation."

Alex shook his head.  "I'm not allowed to leave.  It's against regulations."

"Fuck regulations," Spocatti said.  "If we don't do something soon, this woman will be in serious trouble."

Alex glanced at Celina and saw that she was having difficulty breathing.  A mixture of fear and exhaustion was stamped on her face.  He looked at Spocatti.  "Why don't you swim to shore?" he said.  "I'll stay with her."

"I can't swim to shore," Spocatti said.  "I've hurt my leg."

"It was fine a moment ago."

"That's where you're wrong, pal.  I twisted it when I fell.  I just don't show pain as easily as you do.  Now, either move your ass and get something to help this woman, or we'll see you in court."

The two men stared at one another.  Then Alex made his decision and dived beneath the surface, leaving Spocatti alone with Celina.

He swam in front of her.  "Do you have any feeling left in your legs?"

"Some," she said.  "But they're tingling.  And they're colder than the rest of me.  What happened?"

"My guess is that while you were struggling to free yourself from the rope, the anchor shifted off something--probably a ledge--to a deeper part of the river.  Until it reaches solid ground, the weight is going to continue to pull you down."

"How far down."

He didn't answer. Instead, he looked up at the rope that was secured to the raft. Although slightly frayed and swollen with water, the rope looked solid enough. "As long as this rope is attached to the raft, you aren't in danger of sinking too far beneath the surface. Certainly no more than a foot."

"I can drown in a foot of water," Celina said.

"That's true," Spocatti said. "So if I were you, I wouldn't let go of the bench."

He glanced down at the water, then briefly at his watch. Alex had been gone a little over a minute. "Can you move your legs at all?" he asked.

She tried, then shook her head. "The anchor's too heavy."

"All right, then," he said. "I'm going under to see if I can alleviate some of the pressure. Just hold on."

Celina nodded and watched him dive below the surface.

She waited, her grip becoming weak on the wooden plank, her body shivering. She wondered what Jack was doing and hoped that he was all right and not thinking the worst. She wondered where Alex was and how much longer he would be.

She was lifting herself up to get a more secure grip on the bench when a tremendous pull came on her legs, straining all muscles, causing something in her right knee to give.

She gasped.

Her hands scrambled not to lose their grip on the bench and she screamed. There came another pull on her leg. And another. Celina fought each one, her entire body straining, adrenaline surging. It was the fourth and most brutal tug that cracked the wooden plank she was holding onto.

Spocatti surfaced, pocket knife in hand.

Reaching above Celina's head, he grabbed the rope, severed it with the knife and then followed Celina as she plummeted like a rock to the river's mucky bottom.

* * *

When the bouncing finally slowed, Jack pulled himself up, released the nylon strap with one hand while holding onto the cord with the other and dropped into the river, where he immediately kicked off his shoes so he could swim.

His head light from the fall, he treaded water, the current pulling him downstream while he tried to make sense of his surroundings. He looked around and saw that he was about ten meters from the raft. He swam as quickly as he could toward it-- and saw that the raft was floating downstream.

Jack looked about him. In the distance, moving toward shore, he saw Simpson's assistant struggling against the current.

There was no sign of Celina or the man who had jumped first.

He lifted his head from the water and shouted after Alex. "Where are they?"

Alex turned. He spotted Jack in the water, surprise crossed his face, then he glimpsed the bungee as it was being lifted to the bridge. "They're under the raft," he called--and only then did he notice that the raft was drifting downstream.

He stared after it, the confusion in his eyes gradually giving way to fear. There was no sign of Celina or the man who told him to come to shore. No sign of them at all.

At the same moment Jack disappeared beneath the surface, Alex dived.

\* \* \*

Celina struggled as she sank.

Arms flailing, fists striking blows on Spocatti's flesh, she struggled, the need to breathe rising, becoming paramount.

Eyes wide open in fear, she was aware of a flurry of bubbles racing past her, the river's increasing debris as she neared bottom, and Spocatti as he fastened around her legs the rope he just severed from the raft.

The anchor struck bottom with a muffled thud. Celina looked down through the swirling murk, grabbed a handful of Spocatti's hair and began pulling. She wanted to hurt him, stop him, kill him. She tried to dig at his eyes, but Spocatti twisted wildly to the right and his hair slipped through her weakening grasp.

Celina looked up as he kicked away.

She didn't understand any of this. She didn't understand why he wanted her dead.

Her chest ready to explode from lack of oxygen, she bent to release the rope. Her hands and fingers grasped and pulled and tugged.

But it was no use. Spocatti had bound her legs together too tightly. She couldn't loosen the rope. In one terrible, outraged scream, she jerked upward and released what oxygen was left in her lungs. A furious whirlwind of bubbles hurled forth from her mouth and spun to the surface.

And then she inhaled, reflexively, filling her lungs with a horribly wet coolness.

Celina choked, sucked in more water, and her hands began clawing at her throat as every muscle, as every sense, rejected what she'd just done. *I don't want to die!*

But the choking ended. Fading images turned to black, her eyes saw nothing and she started to list in the wavering current.

\* \* \*

As Jack swam down, down toward the muffled scream, he glimpsed to his right a streak of black, a flurry of white and the rapid scissoring of legs.

For an instant, his gaze lingered on the departing figure and the maze of bubbles that spiraled in its wake. Then he continued downward, the need to breathe rising, his concentration focused and intent.

It was Celina's hair Jack noticed first.

Fanning out in a half-circle, the light blonde was in sharp contrast to the river's dark, mucky-brown bottom. Reaching out a hand, he grabbed hold of her arm and lifted her to the surface.

Tried to lift her to the surface.

Her body was unusually heavy, unusually still. As hard as he tried, as hard as he kicked, he could only lift her a few feet off the river's bottom.

He swam down so they were facing each other and he noticed in horror that her mouth and eyes were open. Every part of his

266

body rejected what he saw before him. Celina's mouth hung slackly. Her eyes were frozen in sightlessness. She was staring at something that wasn't there.

He needed air. In one last attempt to lift her to the surface, he put his arms around her...and felt the rope that was secured to her legs.

He glanced down, saw the rope, saw the anchor lying on the pebbly muck, and knew. Knew.

His chest was on fire. If he didn't get air soon, he felt sure his lungs would burst. He bent down and worked on the rope--his hands pulled, pried and searched.

But it was no use. No matter how hard he tried, he could not loosen the rope. He could not free her. He could do nothing for her now and it tore him apart. This was his fault. This had been his idea.

With one brutal thrust off the river floor, he hurtled to the surface, kicking furiously, wildly--and leaving Celina behind in a whirlpool of bubbles.

# FIFTH AVENUE

## CHAPTER THIRTY-THREE

The first thing George Redman thought when he returned from his run in Central Park and saw the crowd of reporters gathered outside his building on Fifth Avenue was that someone must have leaked another story about the takeover of WestTex Incorporated--this one probably pertaining to his new partnership with Frostman and Chase.

During the past week, the press had been relentless. They phoned, they emailed, they Twittered and they even sent notes via messenger in an effort to obtain interviews. One particularly aggressive reporter somehow slipped past security and stormed his office, demanding that his stockholders deserved to know why he wanted to take over a shipping company whose stock had plummeted since the wars in the Middle East.

It was as exhausting as it was stressful and George had had enough. *They might be bitching now,* he thought, *but it won't be long before they're saying how they had faith in me all along.*

He slowed his stride, considered taking one of the side entrances, but thought better of it. Each entrance would be covered by a group of reporters, word would be texted in seconds of his whereabouts and he would be surrounded in spite of his efforts. And so he quickened his pace, readied himself for the assault, determined to get past them and through the doors and into his penthouse as soon as possible.

It was a female reporter standing at the rear of the crowd who first spotted him. George watched her turn to the cameraman at her right and say something in a sharp voice. By the time the man had his video camera on his shoulder, three dozen other reporters were charging forward, microphones and cameras raised, faces set in determination....and some other emotion George couldn't define.

They enveloped him in waves, first from the front, then from the sides and back. Strobes of light went off like exploding stars. George squinted from the glare and hurried forward. All week

268

long he had increased security around himself and taken precautions against this very thing happening. But this morning, he thought he would be able to sneak out without incident. A nice jog in Central Park was all he wanted, with no one but himself and the trees and the other joggers for company. *Naive*, he thought.

He listened, but couldn't distinguish what the crowd was saying. The roar of questions was too loud, too fervent for him to decipher, but not once did he hear mention of WestTex.

Confused, he pushed toward the doors and heard Celina's name mentioned once. Twice.

He shouldered his way past a reporter, striking him by accident in the chest and he heard the man say that he was sorry. So very sorry.

*For being in my way?*

George turned to the crowd. Lightning seemed to light the morning sky as seventy cameras went off in rapid succession. Traffic slowed on Fifth as curious drivers tried to see what was unfolding in front of his building. Horns blared. Someone shouted something from a passing car.

A chill raced up his spine--something was wrong. The reporters were silent, expectant, their eyes searching his. They were just standing there, waiting for him to say something, although he didn't know what.

It was the man he had struck in the chest who broke the silence. "I think I speak for all of us, Mr., Redman, when I say how sorry we are."

"For what?" George said. "Sorry for what?"

Glances were exchanged.

The reporter who stepped forward now took a step back.

Beyond the crowd, two police cars pulled to the curb. Although there were no accompanying sirens, their lights were flashing.

"Would one of you please tell me what is going on here?"

Nobody said anything. There was the sound of car doors being slammed shut. At the same moment George saw Jack Douglas leave one of the police cars--face drawn, clothes rumpled--a voice from the back of the crowd said: "It's Celina, Mr. Redman. We thought you knew. She drowned earlier this morning. Her body was sent to the Medical Examiner's Office on

First."

And the frenzy began.

\* \* \*

The silence in the room was deafening.

"I'm sorry, Mr. Redman."

George squeezed Elizabeth's hand harder, drawing on it for strength, but finding little there. Her hand was as cold as the ice in her stare. Her breathing was uneven. She learned the news only moments before he, Jack and the police stepped into the penthouse.

George found her in the second-floor living room, the phone on its side and next to her feet. Her face was pale as talc. Her eyes burned with an odd mixture of emptiness, sorrow, rage and disbelief. Helen Baines was still calling her name into the phone, still asking if she were all right, when George bent to pick it up.

He released his grip from her hand, put his arm around her and pulled her close to him. He kissed her and said they would get through this. It was one of the few lies he had ever told her and not for one minute did Elizabeth believe it. Her face crumpled, she glared at him through tears and then looked at the detective who was sitting on the sofa opposite them.

"I'm sorry," he said again.

"I want to know what happened," she said to the man in a thick voice. "You tell me what happened to my daughter."

Lieutenant Vic Greenfield, the detective assigned to the case, glanced at George, saw that he also was ready for answers and stood. "She was bungee jumping with Mr. Douglas--"

"I know that," Elizabeth said sharply. "Celina and I talked about it at last night's party. I told her that I thought it was a foolish idea. I told her I didn't want her to do it, but she said she had no choice."

Her eyes hardened on Jack, who was sitting across the room, running a hand through his hair. Although his face was flushed, his eyes wet with grief, Elizabeth saw no remorse on the man's face, only her own anger and loss reflected on it. "She said she had no choice because she made a deal with Mr. Douglas that she would do it. My daughter never backed down on her word, Lieutenant. Not ever."

"Perhaps you should know that Mr. Douglas himself nearly drowned while trying to save your daughter's life. If it weren't for a man by the name of Alex Stevens, he wouldn't be sitting here right now."

Elizabeth gave the detective a look of loathing. "That would suit me fine, Mr. Greenfield. As far as I'm concerned, he's responsible for her death."

"Elizabeth," George said.

"It's true."

"It's not true. You know how Celina was."

"If she hadn't gone with him, she would be alive now."

"This was an accident."

"No, it wasn't," Jack said from across the room. "It was murder."

Elizabeth looked at Jack at the same moment Isadora, the family cat, strolled into the living room and began washing herself in a slim band of sunlight. She gave the animal a look as gray as driftwood and said in a low voice to Jack, "What did you just say?"

"I said it was murder."

Before anyone could speak, the Lieutenant intervened and told George and Elizabeth everything. He told them about Celina's jump, how she was lowered successfully to the raft and how the raft capsized when the first jumper--a man they had not yet identified and were still searching for--apparently slipped and fell, sending all aboard into the water.

He told them that by struggling to stay afloat, Celina's legs got tangled in the rope secured to the raft's anchor. He told them about Jack's efforts to save her.

Although George listened, hearing every detail of his daughter's death and the attempt to rescue her, he found it difficult to concentrate. He was numb. He was not sure how much more of this he could take. The pressure and the grief and the anger building within him were beginning to take their toll. His daughter was dead. Celina was murdered. It all seemed unreal to him. Just yesterday they were together. She was vibrant and excited by what was happening in the company and by what was happening in her life with Jack.

Now she was gone. Somebody stole her from him.

From the bottom of his gut, his fury took control of him. He had power and he would use that power. Some of his closest friends were the leaders of countries. His daughter was dead, but he was alive and with his contacts, with his billions, he could make his enemies tremble.

Looking hard at the Lieutenant, he said, "I want to know what happened to the son of a bitch who's responsible for this."

"We're still looking for him, Mr. Redman."

"You mean to tell me no one standing on that footbridge saw him swim away from the raft?"

"That's correct," he said. "We questioned the witnesses, but there was so much confusion, no one could recall seeing anyone swim away. Many thought he also drowned."

"Well, he didn't," George said. "He's out there right now-- free. And I want him caught. Do you understand me?"

The Lieutenant's jaw tightened. "Of course, Mr. Redman."

George's stomach felt as though someone had driven nails into it. "Whoever rigged those spotlights with explosive is the person responsible for my daughter's death."

"We can't be sure of that," the man said guardedly. "But we've considered it."

"You're telling me you don't see the parallel?"

"Until we have more information, it's under consideration."

"Here's something else to consider," George said, rising from his seat. "I've been waiting weeks for you to find out who was behind those explosives, but you've come back with nothing. Not one thing. Tell me why."

"It was done professionally," the man said. "Whoever tapped those lights left no leads."

"They're there," George said. "You and your incompetent team of men just haven't looked hard enough."

The man's face flushed. The two uniformed cops standing behind him exchanged glances. "With all due respect, Mr. Redman, we've looked damned hard."

"Bullshit," George said. "Whoever's responsible for those lights exploding is responsible for my daughter's death and they're still out there. Free. Probably getting ready to do something else to my family. So, why don't you get off your asses and do something about it before that happens?"

The Lieutenant turned to his men and nodded toward the door. He moved to follow, but then stopped and looked at George. "I understand that you're upset, Mr. Redman," he said. "And my heart goes out to you and your family. But nobody here killed your daughter. Keep that in mind next time you talk to us."

He was gone before George could say another word.

* * *

It was a moment before anyone in the room spoke.

In the distance, George could hear telephones ringing. He imagined his staff saying that Mr. and Mrs. Redman had no comment at this time.

He looked over at Jack. The man was sitting with his elbows on his knees, his face in his hands. He was shivering. *I know you tried to help her*, he thought. *I don't blame you.*

Elizabeth broke the silence. Her features were oddly calm. "We need to be with her, George," she said. "She's our daughter and we have to go. I don't want her there alone. If they'll let me, I'll stay the night with her."

She was in shock. He could see it on her face, hear it in her voice and he wished that there was something he could do or say that would take away her pain. But he wasn't that clever.

On the table next to Elizabeth, the phone rang. It was their personal line. No one but intimate friends and the immediate family knew the number but themselves.

George reached past Elizabeth and answered it, knowing this would be one of many calls they would take in the coming days.

It was Harold Baines. To George's surprise, he didn't mention Celina, but instead told George to quickly turn on a television. George found the remote on a desk and pointed it at the television across the room. He pushed the power button and asked Harold which channel. Harold told him and George was surprised that he was being directed to an entertainment channel.

The sound came on before the picture.

George heard the familiar voice of a woman. Then Leana was on the screen. She was standing beside Michael Archer.

They were holding hands. Their smiles lit the screen. He and Elizabeth and Jack listened as an announcer reported their recent marriage.

Elizabeth put a hand to her mouth.

There was a sound bite. "We're very happy," Leana said.

George dropped into a chair. For the first time, he noticed that Leana was wearing a white dress, that Archer was wearing an immaculate charcoal-gray suit. Beyond them were mountains and a harbor filled with white yachts. There, the sun was shining.

"Are you still there?" Harold asked.

"Yes," George said.

"I wanted you to know before the press caught you off guard again. I'm sure this was taped earlier. They're obviously in Monte Carlo. That's the Palace behind them."

George was silent.

"Has she contacted you yet?" Harold asked.

"I haven't heard a word from her since the day I threw her out of the Plaza."

"She doesn't know what happened to Celina, George. Leana would have called if she'd heard anything. It's still too soon."

George said nothing.

He hung up the phone at the same moment Elizabeth turned off the television.

## CHAPTER THIRTY-FOUR

"You sure you don't want something to rest your leg on?"

In the bright, afternoon light, Eric Parker looked across the shiny mahogany desk at Louis Ryan. The man was leaning back in his chair, hands clasped behind his head, legs crossed. He was wearing khaki pants, a lightweight cotton sweater and tan moccasins.

He was staring at Eric. Although Eric couldn't be absolutely certain, there was something in Ryan's eyes that made him wonder if the man really cared if he was uncomfortable or not.

He didn't want to appear weak. He was sitting in the chair opposite Ryan, his broken leg, newly cast after the other cast was ruined by the water in his apartment, extended painfully to the floor. Not only had his doctor told him to keep the cast dry, but he also told Eric to keep it elevated at all times, which he certainly wasn't doing now.

*I'm batting a thousand*, Eric thought, and he considered asking Ryan for another chair or a hassock. But his pride wouldn't allow him to.

"I'm fine," he said, with a forced smile. "Really."

Louis shrugged. "I don't believe you," he said. "But it's your leg. Do you want a drink before we begin?"

Eric nodded. A shot of booze would do him good right now. Not only did Ryan just call him a liar, but his leg felt as if it was on fire and he was nervous as hell. Earlier, when he phoned Ryan from Diana's apartment, he did not anticipate meeting so soon with the man. Perhaps in a week, he thought, but not on the day he returned home from the hospital and found his apartment under six inches of water.

Still, he was glad to be here. Not only was the meeting helping to take his mind off his problems at home, but soon Eric would learn why Louis Ryan had been sending him dozens of roses since his arrival at New York Hospital.

"What would you like?" Louis asked, rising. "I have everything."

"Scotch?"

"Fine."

He watched Ryan walk to the bar across the room. He wondered what the man wanted from him. Louis knew for years that he had been an executive at Redman International. Was it that? Did Ryan want information of some sort? Or did it have to do with Celina? All of Manhattan knew they were once an item. Did this meeting have something to do with her? Or did it have to do with George? The rivalry between the two men was infamous. With such similar corporations, they were in constant battle with one another and for years the press made it seem as if they were in a private war--which they were.

But while the press made it appear that their hatred for one another stemmed purely from business matters, Eric knew differently. Years ago, in a moment of confidence, Celina told him that George was once thought responsible for the death of Louis' wife. While Eric himself didn't believe that George was capable of murder, he never ruled out the possibility. There had been too many times over the years when George's feelings for Louis Ryan surpassed the point of mere hatred and become something colder, darker and more personal.

He watched Louis pour Scotch into two short glasses of ice. *I don't know why you asked me here,* he thought, *but if you want me bad enough, it's going to cost you.*

Louis came over with the drinks. Eric accepted his and they touched glasses. "To the future," Louis said, and they sipped. Eric felt a hot flash of liquid fire shoot down his throat and bloom in his stomach. He took another sip and began to relax. Ryan stepped over to a wall of windows that looked uptown. To Eric, he seemed consumed by The Redman International Building.

Eric leaned forward. The group of reporters he passed earlier were still gathered in front of the building's entrance. Although he wasn't sure why they were there, he assumed it had to do with the takeover of WestTex.

"I want you to help me destroy George Redman," Louis said.

Eric looked at the man, not sure if he had heard him right. Louis was still facing the windows. The sun beating through the

276

glass turned his silvery crown of hair to gold.

"You'll be paid an obscene amount of money for what little I want from you," Louis said simply. He left the window and reclaimed his seat. "In fact, even after you pay off your hospital bills, refinish your apartment and replace your neighbor's paintings and her Henry VIII furniture, you'll be set for life."

Eric was speechless. How did Ryan know about his apartment? About the destroyed paintings and furniture? The pipes burst only that morning.

Louis opened a desk drawer and removed a slip of paper. He handed it to Eric and Eric saw that it was a check. His eyebrows rose--the amount was indeed obscene. "And how will I earn this?" he asked.

Louis sat down. "I need you to confirm some information I received concerning the takeover of WestTex Incorporated. All you have to do is copy a few files for me and that check is yours."

"Confirm?" Eric said. "Then you've already been in contact with somebody from Redman International?"

Louis casually waved a hand.

"Who?"

"Doesn't matter. What matters is that I don't trust this person. Unlike yourself, he doesn't want to see Redman burn."

*So, it's a man.* "What makes you think I do?"

"Because you hate George," Louis said. "I think we both know that Redman has destroyed your reputation. You couldn't get a job in this city even if you wanted to flip burgers. It's also obvious that Redman is behind the pipes bursting in your apartment. He canceled your insurance for a reason. He wants you out of his building and out of New York."

"How do you know all this?"

Louis sipped his drink and met Eric's gaze levelly. "There's nothing I don't know about you, Eric. Not the beating you gave Leana Redman the night of Redman International's opening, nor the contract you put out on her while you were in the hospital."

Eric could only stare. If the man wanted to, he could blackmail him with this information.

"So," Louis said. "We have a deal?"

## CHAPTER THIRTY-FIVE

From the great semicircular balcony of their corner suite at the Hotel de Paris, Leana stood looking down at the crowded port of Monte Carlo. It was late afternoon, the sun was setting and in the distance on a jutting, rocky promontory, she could see the Palace, framed beyond by a deepening-blue sky and the Mediterranean.

The air was cool, clean and smelled of salt. Dozens of yachts and sail boats were returning to the harbor after a day at sea. All around her, the charming Edwardian villas she had come to love as a child were a refreshing change from the skyscrapers of Manhattan.

It was still difficult for her to believe that only yesterday she had been in New York, single and living a nightmare.

Behind her, she heard a faint groan and the rustling of sheets. She turned to look across the room at the bed and found Michael settling onto his stomach, his arms outstretched, his face turned to hers. He was breathing soundly and Leana thought that he was beautiful.

She was glad he could sleep. For her, sleep hadn't come. Everything that led to them coming across the Atlantic to this hotel room was still whirling in her mind.

It seemed unreal that she married Michael only that morning and that they made love all afternoon. Last night, Mario nearly killed him. If she hadn't looked up from the car's back seat and seen Michael standing in traffic, if she hadn't screamed for Mario to not shoot, she knew that either he or one of his men would have done so.

And Michael would be dead now.

The idea that her association with Mario might have led to Michael's death was something she didn't want to face. Michael came into her life at its darkest point and he lifted it. All those days they spent cleaning and painting her apartment--and going out on the town when they were too exhausted to continue--

278

meant the world to her. He had changed her life for the better and she loved him for it.

Today, marrying Michael had felt right, regardless of how briefly she'd known him. Leana knew she would never have a relationship with Mario. She knew he would never leave his wife for her. His father wouldn't permit it. If she had gone with him to the apartment he offered, if she had allowed him to come in and out of her life as he had in the past, she knew she would have been miserable.

And so she left with Michael. To her surprise, Mario didn't put up a fight. Instead, he held her, kissed her and told her that the situation with Eric Parker would be taken care of while she was gone. Leana knew what that meant and the thought chilled her.

Mario was going to kill him.

*  *  *

It was in the cab that Michael proposed.

After she told him about the gun, the note and the contact Eric Parker put on her, he surprised her by removing two airline tickets from his inside jacket pocket. "You know I love you," he said. "You're too smart not to know it. Marry me. We'll fly to Europe. You'll be safe there. You'll be safe with me. We'll get away from this and we'll be happy. I promise."

It was all so easy.

Leana was so frightened by what was happening in her life, so confused and worried about her future, she realized that she wanted to leave New York, that she didn't want to return until Eric Parker--and his contract--had been dealt with. She would be too scared living there otherwise.

Without giving it another thought, she took the small Tiffany box he gave her, opened it and found inside one of the largest solitaire diamonds she'd ever seen. "Of course, I'll marry you."

It was morning when they arrived in Nice. Rested from the trip over, they rented a car, drove the short distance to Monte Carlo and checked into their hotel suite only long enough to take a shower. It was then, while Michael undressed, that Leana noticed the dark bruises on his back, stomach and shoulders. Alarmed, she asked him what happened.

"I was mugged," he said simply.

"Mugged? When?"

He put a finger to her lips. "It happened yesterday morning. Three guys jumped me on Avenue B." He shrugged. "They didn't get much money and I'm still alive. That's what matters."

"What were you doing on Avenue B?"

"Research for a book."

"You're taking this awfully calmly."

"Don't forget I'm an actor."

She put her arms lightly around him.

"Did you go to the police?"

"What good would that have done?"

He was right, of course. Leana recalled her own experience when the man harassed her in Washington Square. She felt the same as Michael. The police could do little in situations such as this. There were too many people in the city and not enough officers to make a difference. "Why didn't you tell me this sooner?" she asked.

"I didn't want to worry you."

"You should have," she said. "Are you all right?"

"In a few hours we'll be married," he said. "I've never felt better."

"You'd better not be acting now," she said.

At Cartier, they bought their wedding rings--two simple bands of platinum. At a men's clothing store, Michael found a charcoal-gray suit and black loafers. And at a small boutique, Leana bought a simple yet elegant white silk dress. Although it was not the wedding dress of her childhood dreams, she accepted this because she knew now that dreams rarely came true. And so what if they didn't? Too many things had gone wrong in her life. She felt lucky to have found a man who wanted to spend his life with her.

When they had everything they needed, they went to the crowded port, chartered a yacht and were wed by the yacht's captain in international waters at sea. Now, as dark clouds moved in from the west, eclipsing the setting sun, Leana left the balcony and stepped into the bedroom, her hair stirring in the rising breeze.

She closed the French doors. Michael was still asleep. Despite the diminishing light, she could see the bruises on his back and thought how painful they looked. She wondered how he could move, let alone sleep. But as she stood there looking at him, she realized just how tired she was. For the first time since their arrival, she felt as though she could actually sleep.

She checked her watch and decided to lie down for a half hour before calling the front desk and making dinner reservations. She removed her black silk kimono and snuggled into bed beside Michael. His body was warm, his breathing heavy. She closed her eyes and began to drift.

* * *

She was awakened hours later by the sound of rain beating against glass.

Leana stretched in the dark and checked the digital clock on the bedside table. Three hours had passed. She closed her eyes with a groan. "I can't believe I slept this late," she said aloud. She turned to wake Michael, but his side of the bed was empty. She sat up, looked around the dark room and saw a flag of light coming from beneath the closed bathroom door. She heard running water. He was in the shower. She was tempted to settle back onto the warm sheets and go back to sleep, but they hadn't eaten since morning and she was hungry.

She turned on the lamp beside her and looked through the windows. Rain was whipping against the glass. There was no going out in this weather. Although the hotel had a restaurant she loved, she didn't feel like putting it together and leaving their suite. *Room service it is*, she thought, and reached for the phone.

As she lifted the receiver to her ear, she didn't hear a dial tone, but a male voice saying: "...paid Santiago half this morning. He'll get the rest of the money you owe him when you finish the job and kill her father--"

281

The voice abruptly stopped. Leana sat there, puzzled--she knew that voice. She strained to hear something more, but only the hum of static was left on the line.

"Michael?" she said. "Are you on the phone?"

There was silence, then the sound of someone taking a breath. Leana replaced the receiver. She sat motionless and felt uneasy. The voice she heard wasn't Michael's, yet she was almost certain she had heard it before. But where?

She quickly picked up the phone and held it to her ear. Now, there was nothing but a deep dial tone. Whoever was on the line had hung up.

Her kimono was at the foot of the bed. Leana put it on and went to the bathroom door. She listened. She could hear Michael humming, could sense the moist heat in the room beyond. She tried the doorknob, turned it and found it unlocked.

She was surprised by this. For some reason, she was expecting to find the door locked.

She opened the door. Steam poured out of the bathroom and curled around her feet. Leana stepped quietly into the room and looked at the phone that was on the wall beside the shower. She checked it and found that it was dry. She looked at the shower. She could see Michael beyond the frosted glass doors, could see him rubbing a washcloth over his muscular frame. His back was to her and he continued to hum, seemingly unaware of her presence.

Leana was about to tap on the glass and ask him what was going on when the phone suddenly rang. She drew a sharp breath. Michael stopped humming and turned off the water. She watched him open the shower door and leisurely fumble for a towel on the rack outside.

There were none. They had used both towels earlier that morning and they were now lying across the room in a wet heap. The phone rang again. Michael said, "Shit!," and started to push open the glass separation.

"Do you want me to answer it?" she said.

"Jesus!" His hand jerked back and struck the shower door. "Leana? What are you doing in here? I thought you were asleep. Christ, you scared me."

The phone entered its third ring, began its fourth. The sound echoed in the large bathroom. "Can you get that?" he asked.

She was confused. She was certain he was going to insist on answering it himself. Had the lines somehow gotten crossed in the storm and she heard someone else's conversation? She couldn't be sure, but she knew she'd heard that voice before.

The phone rang again. Michael said tentatively, "Honey...?"

Leana reached for the phone, not sure what to expect. The press had tracked them down earlier, but the front desk had been given specific instructions to screen all calls. Mr. and Mrs. Archer did not wish to be disturbed by any member of the press.

*Then who is calling? Nobody knows we're here.*

She answered the phone. A man's voice. "Leana?"

"Yes?"

"It's Harold. Thank God, I found you."

"Harold?" She looked at Michael. "Is something wrong?"

"You need to come home immediately. Something terrible has happened. Your parents need you."

"Since when?"

Harold paused. "It's your sister, Leana."

## CHAPTER THIRTY-SIX

He entered her apartment not as guest, but as intruder. It was an odd feeling and one he wasn't comfortable with. The woman, after all, was in love with him.

With the help of one of his crutches, Eric eased the door shut behind him and listened. He was standing in the foyer of Diana's apartment and he could hear a television playing in the distance. It sounded as if it was coming from the kitchen. Or from one of the rooms upstairs.

Was she home? She said she would be out most of the day. *If you're going to stay here, I'm going to have to buy food? What do you want?*

He made a list and she left. It was then that he phoned Louis Ryan and left for their appointment.

He moved out of the foyer and into the living room, catching a glimpse of himself in the mirror she had taped a list of his faults to. He looked tense beneath the purplish bruises on his face, and if she was here, he knew she would notice and ask him what was wrong.

*Calm down.*

The living room was empty. To his right was the winding staircase that led to the second-floor bedrooms and Diana's office. Eric looked up and called her name once, twice, but there was no reply.

The kitchen was at the end of a long hallway. Awkwardly, he moved toward it, the rubber tips of his crutches catching on the carpet, the sound of the television growing louder. There was no one in the dining room as he passed it. He opened a door and saw that the bathroom was empty.

When he reached the kitchen's closed swinging doors, he listened and heard not only the television, but also running water. He closed his eyes. She was home. She was fucking home. Now what was he going to do? Ryan wanted that information immediately.

284

He turned and looked back down the hallway, toward the living room. For a moment, he considered sneaking into Diana's office, locking the door behind him and getting the files Ryan needed. But that would be stupid. If Diana ever went to her office and learned what he was doing, his ass would be behind bars for the next twenty years. He would have to wait and get the information later.

Parting the kitchen doors with his shoulder, he stepped through.

Tried to step through.

In front of the doors was an overturned bag of groceries, their contents spilled. Eric looked around the room, saw a small wooden table on its side and another bag of groceries on the floor. Alarmed, he went to the island that was in the center of the kitchen and turned off the running water--the television seemed to grow louder. He looked at the screen, saw that she had it on CNN and clicked it off. It wasn't until he turned to look once more around the room that he saw the note stuck to the refrigerator.

He plucked it off. In a hurried scrawl, she'd written these words: "George called an emergency board meeting. I don't know when I'll be home. Call me immediately at the office."

Eric read the note twice, wondering what had happened and why George would call an emergency board meeting on a Saturday afternoon. He was tempted to call and ask her what was going on, but there was no time. He dropped the note into a wastebasket and left the kitchen.

As fast as he could, he moved down the hallway toward the living room. Leg throbbing, head aching, one single thought revolved in his mind: *The sooner Ryan has that information, the sooner that check is mine.*

In the living room, he was faced with his first obstacle--the tall, winding staircase.

Eric looked up at it with dread and wondered how he would get to the top of it without falling and breaking his neck. He took one stair at a time, moving carefully, his crutches slipping twice on the varnished wood.

By the time he reached the upper level, four minutes had passed and he was out of breath. His forehead shimmered with

perspiration and he wiped it off with the back of his hand. Her
office was through the door to his right. Eric glanced at his watch
and wondered how much longer she would be. Hours? Minutes?

He stepped into the sun-filled room. File cabinets were along
the wall to his left. At his right were bookcases filled with law
books. On gleaming glass tables were computers, printers,
telephones, fax machines and photocopiers. The office was large,
but it wasn't overdone. Like Diana, it was practical and efficient.
Essentially, it was a smaller version of her corner office at
Redman International and Eric knew that everything she kept
there, she had files of here. For convenience.

He went to the computer that was in the center of the room.

As he sat in the leather chair and lowered his crutches to the
floor, it occurred to him once more how ridiculous this was.
There was not one thing Eric didn't know about the takeover of
WestTex Incorporated. He and Diana discussed it every day. If
Ryan had only listened to him, he now would have the
information he needed confirmed. But the man trusted no one.
He insisted on having hard copies of every file Eric could get his
hands on--and Eric was in no position to argue.

He turned on the computer. The screen flashed a message:
ENTER PASSWORD.

Eric opened the top drawer of Diana's desk. Inside, between
two piles of neatly stacked papers, was an envelope slightly larger
than the size of a credit card. Eric removed the envelope and
closed the drawer. Inside, on a slip of paper, was Diana's
password, just where it had been a month ago, when his own
computer died and he phoned to ask if he could come down to her
apartment and finish the report on her computer.

Like his own, the machine was linked to Redman
International's main cluster of computers. It was then that she'd
shown him where she kept her password, a combination of twenty
letters and numbers no one could remember. *Not even me*, Diana
said. *And you know how good my memory is.*

He entered the code, the screen winked and control of the
computer became his.

His fingers danced over the keyboard. He went to the menu,
brought up the directory and hundreds of files began filling the
screen. The files he needed were halfway down the screen and

listed in code.  If you knew it, the code was simple to understand. Any file that began with an asterisk and ended with the letter "T" was a file that contained information on the takeover of WestTex Incorporated.

Although there were only twelve files, each one contained hundreds of pages of information--clearly too much to print out on Diana's printer in the short amount of time he felt he had left. And so Eric opened a side drawer and removed one of her flash drives.  He inserted it into the machine's USB port and the computer buzzed, whirred and hummed.  He reached for the mouse that was on the pad to his right and moved the cursor to one of the files.  He clicked on the icon, dragged it to the drive icon--and a new message appeared:

**TO COPY FILE *FA#IB!$S@*T**
**ENTER SECURITY CODE BETA**

Eric stared at the screen in disbelief.  As an added security feature, Redman International changed their security codes every three months, which must have happened recently.  When he last had access to the system, it was code ALPHA.  Not BETA.  BETA hadn't fucking existed.  Without a code to enter into the computer, he wouldn't be able to transfer the files onto the disk.

There had to be a way around this.  The system was tight, but not airtight.

A thought occurred to him.  Whenever Redman International changed their security codes, an email was sent to employees giving them the option of coming up with their own security code, one they would have less trouble remembering.  The idea was that if they had gotten this far, they were indeed an employee of Redman International and so security became somewhat more lax.

The code could be anything they wished.  Eric wondered if Diana was anything like him and Celina, and just used her old code out of laziness.  He knew the code she gave him before was her middle name--Marie.  He entered it into the computer.

And the screen winked.

# FIFTH AVENUE

* * *

The emergency board meeting ended almost as quickly as it began.

Diana Crane snapped her black crocodile briefcase shut, rose from her seat and went with the other directors to where George stood at the head of the mahogany table. "I just received a call from Ted Frostman," he said only moments ago. "And we have a commitment from Chase to go forward. Now, more than ever, the deals with WestTex and Iran must go through. For Celina."

As Diana watched Harold Baines and the other directors pay their regrets to George, she was struck once more by the reality that Celina Redman had been murdered only that morning.

George extended a hand when she approached. His face seemed cast in stone, his eyes empty and void of feeling. Awkwardly, Diana moved his hand aside and gave him a tentative hug. "I'm so sorry," she said. "I'll miss her."

George didn't hug her back.

Diana pulled away from him and saw that his eyes had narrowed slightly. He seemed to be looking straight through her.

"Is there anything I can do?" she asked.

"No."

"Are you sure?"

"From what I hear, your hands are pretty full these days, Diana. Just take Celina's place and fly to Iran with Jack and Harold. Get the papers signed. Make the trip a success. That's all I ask."

*And then you can go home to Eric.*

Although George didn't say those words, Diana knew he was thinking them. She had shown no loyalty to Redman International by dating Eric Parker so soon after he was fired. She had shown no loyalty to the Redman family by dating Eric so soon after Celina ended her relationship with him. She deserved his cool reception now and she accepted it.

As she left the boardroom and walked down the hallway to her office, she felt oddly removed from the unusual quiet, from the senior secretaries sitting at their desks, from the tears being shed.

She had dealt with death when her own father died and she would deal with this now. Since work always had been her escape, Diana would throw herself into this deal. She would make certain the contracts were unbreakable, that each deal went smoothly.

Her secretary was waiting for her in her office. The woman was standing in the center of the room, her face slightly flushed. She too had been crying. Diana squeezed her arm as she passed. "I'll tell you what," she said. "Pour each of us half a cup of coffee. I've got a bottle of brandy in that desk for the other half. We can use it."

The woman managed a smile and left the room.

As Diana watched her leave, she wondered if something was wrong with herself. Why couldn't she feel the pain and loss these other people felt? Before Eric, she had been friends with Celina for years--close friends. Was she really so cold that she couldn't show--let alone feel--any other emotion besides relief? Was Eric Parker so important to her that she felt no loss for a woman she once held in such high esteem?

Best not to deal with this now. Dealing meant coming to terms with who she was as a person and Diana wasn't ready for that. She expected she wouldn't like the outcome.

She went to her desk. If she was going to take Celina's place on this trip, there were files she had to familiarize herself with before leaving.

She turned on her computer, pulled a slip of paper from the back of a drawer and entered her password. She hit return and the computer did something it never had done. A message appeared in the center of the screen:

**\*\*ACCESS DENIED\*\***
**TERMINAL B IN OPERATION**

Diana stared at the screen, confused. Terminal B was her computer at home--and this computer was saying that it was in use. *But that's impossible*, she thought. *I shut it down this morning.*

289

She entered her password again, thinking she'd made a mistake the first time. She knew that only one of her computers could be used at a time. It was an added security feature that let the user know if somebody else was on their system.

The screen flashed and again she was denied access.

For a moment, she remained puzzled. And then realization struck.

She once gave Eric her password. His computer wasn't working and he needed to use her computer to finish a report.

A chill went through her.

Right now, a former Redman International executive was using her computer.

\* \* \*

Eric stared at the computer. "Come on," he said aloud. "Come on...."

A message appeared on the screen: ACCESS DENIED.

He looked at the message with resentment, knowing he would never get the information Louis Ryan needed and that the check wouldn't be his.

Enraged, he slammed a fist hard against the side of the computer--and sat back in surprise as the screen flashed and sparks erupted from the back. As the screen turned in on itself, fading rapidly to black, he realized he'd just broken her computer.

Now she would know he had been using it.

Frantic, he unplugged the machine in case of fire and looked around the room, knowing she could be home at any moment. He was about to say to hell with this, to hell with Ryan and leave the office when he glimpsed the long line of file cabinets across the room. He wondered if the information he needed was there, already stored for him in neat files....

Grimacing, he reached for his crutches and went to the nearest cabinet. He tugged on one of the four drawers and found it locked. That was no surprise, but with any luck, perhaps somewhere in this room were the keys to unlock them.

He went back to her desk.

He opened the top drawer, carefully moved aside stacks of papers and found no set of keys. He opened the drawers to his right, found nothing but thick, deep green folders, and then he opened the drawer to his left. Gleaming inside was a slick black crocodile briefcase, one of several Diana owned. Eric was about to move it aside and look underneath it when he stopped. And wondered.

He removed the briefcase and put it on the desk. The briefcase was unlocked and he opened it. Crammed inside were files on the takeover of WestTex Incorporated.

His heart lifted.

He quickly scanned the hundreds of pages of information and saw that everything Ryan needed was there, in this briefcase. Not believing his luck, he reached for one of the phones beside the computer and punched Ryan's number. The man answered on the second ring.

"What took you so long, Eric?"

Eric ignored the sarcasm. Things were different now. Now it was he who had the upper hand--not Ryan. "I have everything you've requested," he said. "But time is running out. She'll be back shortly. How soon before you can have somebody here to pick it up?"

"Ten minutes."

"I said shortly," Eric said. "Make it five. And here's something else, Ryan. I want that check tripled or there's no deal."

There was a silence.

"Answer me," Eric said. "It's all here. But it's triple or nothing."

"You're out of your mind," Louis said. "I'm not paying you--"

"The information's worth ten times that amount and you know it," Eric interrupted. "Now, what's it going to be? You're down to four minutes."

"All right," Louis said. "I'll triple it."

Eric smiled grimly, his stomach tense. Now for the bluff. "And, Louis, in case you decide not to come through with that check, and in case anything happens to me, I want you to know that before I called you, I called a friend about this. If he reads my obituary, the world soon will be reading yours. Remember that. Don't fuck this up. Don't fuck with me. I've already set things into motion should anything happen."

He severed the connection and dialed the front desk.

"This is Eric Parker," he said to one of the doormen on duty. "I'm expecting friends. No need to call me when they arrive. Just send them up to Diana Crane's apartment."

He put down the phone, removed the files from Diana's briefcase and substituted them for the files he had seen in the drawers to his right. The folders were an identical deep green. He snapped the briefcase shut and put it back as he had found it. By the time Diana realized the switch, Eric hoped to be somewhere in Europe, perhaps Switzerland, with the money Louis Ryan owed him.

He tucked the folders beneath his arm and reached for his crutches. No sooner had he left the room and tackled the winding staircase that he heard someone ringing the doorbell.

He hesitated, wondering if Ryan had believed his bluff. He knew there was a chance that he might open that door and take a series of bullets in the chest.

It was a risk he'd have to take.

He went to the door and looked through the peephole. Standing in the hallway was a tall, rugged-looking man in his early thirties with tousled dark hair. He was wearing an unseasonably warm black leather jacket. His hands were cupped behind his back.

Eric wished the man's hands weren't concealed, but he opened the door anyway.

They stared at each other.

The man in the hallway looked at the folders beneath Eric's arm, then at the cast on his leg, the bruises on his face. The edge of his mouth lifted into a smile.

Eric held out a hand for the check.

The man's smile faded. He reached into his jacket pocket, removed the check and handed it to Eric. "Give me the files," he said.

Eric unfolded the check and saw that the amount had indeed been tripled. Relief overcame him.

He gave the man the files and closed the door in his face, locking it quickly.

It was over.

He pressed his back against the door as elation swept through him.

He was now worth ninety million dollars.

## CHAPTER THIRTY-SEVEN

Diana moved quickly down the hallway, perhaps too quickly given the crisis she was leaving, because all eyes were on her as she hurried toward the bank of elevators.

Why was Eric on her computer?  What was he hoping to find?  Was he just bored and using it to see how things were working out with the deals he left behind when George fired him?  Or were there other reasons?

She was about to reach the elevators when someone behind her called out her name.  She turned and saw Jack Douglas.  He was standing just outside his office.  On his face was a look of concern and curiosity.

"Are you all right?" he asked.

She needed to get out of there.

"I'm fine."  She pressed a button on the elevator.

"No, you're not," he said, coming toward her.  "Something's wrong.  What is it?"

"It's really nothing--

"What is it?"

She looked at him.  Tall and muscular, his body as rugged as steel.  Regardless of what Eric was up to, she decided having someone like Jack accompany her to her apartment might be a good idea.  She motioned him over.

"Will this remain between us?" she asked.

He nodded.

"I'm depending on that," she said, and so she took the risk.  "Eric Parker is staying with me.  I just learned he's on my computer, which is connected to Redman International's main database and which obviously has created a major security breach since Eric no longer works here."

The doors to the elevator whisked open.

"I don't know what he's doing," she said.  "But he received no permission from me to use that computer.  I'm concerned."

"Do you want me to come with you?"

294

She nodded and they stepped inside. "This is going to sound stupid," she said. "But do you have access to a gun?"

The question surprised him. "No," he said. "But why would I need a gun?"

Diana pressed a button and looked at him as the elevator dropped. "Because if he's doing what I think he's doing, we might need it and the police."

\* \* \*

For Eric Parker, there was only escape.

He left the door and went to gather his things. On a table, he placed the check next to his watch and wallet and then he went to the staircase--that fucking winding staircase--and started to climb the stairs that led to the guest bedroom Diana offered him.

It was a struggle to reach the top, but he made it and went to the bedroom, where he grabbed a duffel bag and started tossing clothes into it.

He didn't need everything, just enough to get him on a plane and out of the country. In the bathroom, he took only what was necessary. In his briefcase, he checked to make sure his passport was there. He went back to the bedroom and picked up the phone. He called his travel agent and ordered a first class ticket to Switzerland. A flight was leaving in two hours. The e-ticket would be waiting for him at the ticket counter.

Perfect.

He dialed the front desk. "It's Eric Parker. Would you hail a cab for me? I'll be down in 10 minutes."

As he replaced the receiver, he heard a door open and click shut. It came from downstairs. A rush of panic shot through him, but he stilled it.

She was home.

Eric thought about how he would handle this and decided there was only one way. Get out of this bedroom, get down the stairs and face her.

He was leaving. She didn't have to know where he was going. By the time he got to the airport, she'd likely learn that he'd

gotten into her computer. But at that point, it wouldn't matter--
he'd be well on his way to a country that would protect him.

He snatched his duffel bag, tossed it over his shoulder and
grabbed his crutches. This wouldn't go well, but he'd keep it brief.
He was out of there.

He went to the bedroom door, opened it and took a step back.

Standing just beyond the door wasn't Diana. It was Mario De
Cicco and with him were two men, each holding guns now pointed
at Eric's face.

\* \* \*

De Cicco moved into the room with such force, Eric staggered
back. His cast caught on the floor, he nearly fell, but he reached
for a chair and righted himself so he wouldn't go down.

De Cicco glanced at the duffle bag. "Going somewhere?"

Eric said nothing. He noticed that De Cicco and his men were
wearing gloves. On their feet were paper booties that covered
their shoes. He felt a rush of fear and knew why they were here.
They were going to kill him.

"Answer the question, Eric. Are you going somewhere?"

"I'm going back to my apartment. What the fuck is it with
you?"

"When you put out a contract on Leana Redman, it means
everything to me." He moved toward Eric, knowing this needed
to be brief.

"How did you get up here?" Eric said.

"They let us in. Apparently, you were expecting friends. We
just breezed through, so thanks for that." He moved closer to
him. "Beating Leana Redman was your first mistake, Eric.
Taking out that contract was your final mistake." He stepped
aside. "Walk through the door."

"Fuck you."

One of De Cicco's men lifted his gun and pointed it at Eric's
head.

"This can go one of two ways, Eric," Mario said. "You can go
through that door by yourself or you can have me drag your ass

through it by your broken leg. Your choice. One will be less painful. Now choose."

There was no choice. He let go of the chair, grabbed his crutches and started moving past De Cicco to the door. What De Cicco didn't know is that just beyond that door was a desk. On top of it was an iron statue of a woman. It was about eighteen inches tall and just heavy enough to do serious damage to a skull.

If he timed this right, if he grabbed the statue, swung it at De Cicco's head and shut the door before the others could follow, he might have a chance to get to Diana's room, lock the door, go to her bathroom, lock that door and call security for help.

He knew it was a long shot, but it was all he had.

\* \* \*

At Redman International, Jack and Diana left the building, flagged a cab, got one on their fifth try and told the driver to take them to Redman Place.

"There's a hundred dollars in it for you if you hurry," Diana said. She opened her handbag, removed the money and dropped it on the driver's front seat. "It's an emergency."

The driver stepped on it, but traffic on Fifth was thick. He tried to maneuver through the clogged thoroughfare, but it was difficult and there wasn't much he could do. "I'll do my best," he said. "But this is bullshit. Look at these assholes. They don't know how to drive."

"Just try," Diana said. She looked at Jack. "We might be too late."

"You don't know that."

"I know Eric."

The driver found an opening and raced through it. Redman Place was a five-minute drive. If this man was aggressive enough, they could be there in three.

\* \* \*

297

"Let's go, Eric.  If you don't step it up, I'll help."

Eric looked at De Cicco as he passed him.  He focused all of his concentration on what was beyond that door and where the statue was on the desk.  It would be to the far right.  He would need to drop a crutch, grab the statue and then turn to swing it.

He moved through the door, shot a sideways glance and saw it sitting there.

And everything slowed.

He dropped the crutch under his right armpit, leaned in to reach for the statue and grabbed it.  He turn to swing it so he could bash in the side of De Cicco's head but instead he was being propelled forward.  Somebody had shoved him.  He sailed through the air and crashed onto the floor.  His head struck wood and for a moment, he blacked out.

He was being shaken.

He opened his eyes and saw De Cicco leaning over him.  "Get up."

His eyes fluttered and he saw movement across the room. One of the men was carefully putting the statue back in place with his gloved hands.

"Get up."

He made an effort to move, but a searing pain shot through his shoulder, which was dislocated.  De Cicco saw the problem, grabbed Eric by the shirt and easily picked him up so he was standing.

Eric's shoulder was drooping.  The pain was unbearable.  He was about to shout when one of De Cicco's men came behind him and covered his mouth with a hand.

"You can live or you can die," Mario said.  "Your choice.  To live, you need to tell me who you called to put the contract on Leana."

Without hesitation, Eric jerked his head away to free his mouth and blurted out the person's name.

Without hesitation, Mario De Cicco grabbed Eric again and lifted him to the top of the staircase.  And right there, on Eric's face, was the shock of what was about to happen to him.  He tried to struggle, tried to get this man off him, but it was useless.  De Cicco leaned close to Eric's ear.  "You fucked with the wrong

person.  Nobody touches Leana Redman.  When they do, just look
at what happens."

\* \* \*

The cab swung in front of Redman Place.  Eric and Diana
rushed out.  She tossed another hundred through the passenger's
side window, thanked the driver and ran with Eric to the
revolving doors.

Across the lobby was the bank of elevators.  They hurried
toward them, pressed the button and waited for one of the doors
to open.

\* \* \*

"You told me you'd let me live!" Eric shouted.

"I lied," De Cicco said.  "Ain't that a bitch?"

"Here's your bitch," Eric said.  "It's Leana Fucking Redman.
Tell her for me that she can burn in hell.  Tell her for me that she
can--"

But before Eric could finish speaking, De Cicco pushed him
down the winding staircase.

Mario and his men moved forward to watch him fall.  They
watched his body twist and bend in unnatural angles as he
toppled down the staircase, they watched his cast catch on a rung
and snap it in half, and they watched what happened when he
suddenly flipped over and his neck came down hard on the
banister.

It wasn't the wood that cracked--the banister could sustain
the impact.  Instead, it was the bones in Eric's neck that cracked
and the sound they made was like wood splintering in the room.
As Eric Parker continued to fall, the men noted the difference in
how he fell.  He now was a rag doll.  As he fell to the bottom of the
steps, there was no life in him--just momentum behind him.  He
was dead and lying in a growing pool of his own blood by the time

he hit the floor.

"Let's move," De Cicco said.

The men hurried down the stairs, Mario placed a gloved finger on Eric Parker's neck, felt no pulse and joined his men as they checked the room to make certain no trace of themselves was there. They were backing out of the room and looking for any signs of a struggle when Mario brushed against a side table. He looked down and saw Parker's watch and wallet, and what looked to be a check.

He lifted the check, read the amount, looked at the name of the corporation listed on it and then looked back in surprise at Parker. What was World Enterprises? Who was behind it? Why had they paid Parker $90 million? What had he done to earn it?

Mario pocketed the check. Since there was no asking Eric Parker now, they left the room, found the stairs and began rushing down them just as an elevator door whisked open. De Cicco and his men were three floors down when they heard a woman, her voice high and shrill, call out Eric's name.

They hesitated.

And then they fled down the stairs when she began screaming.

## CHAPTER THIRTY-EIGHT

Carving a path in the evening sky, the plane soared over the Atlantic, hurtling towards New York and JFK.

Michael unbuckled his safety belt, reached for Leana's hand and squeezed it gently. She had been silent ever since they left Heathrow and he could sense her slowly withdrawing into that part of herself that no one could hurt. "I'll be right back," he said.

As he left his seat and walked towards the rear of the plane, the quiet rage that had been building within him since they left Monte Carlo finally struck. He knew his father was behind this, knew that it was he who had Celina Redman murdered. *He probably used Spocatti,* he thought. *Probably got that son of a bitch to do it for him...*

The stewardess smiled as he approached.

"Where are the phones?" Michael asked.

The woman motioned toward an area just outside the restrooms. "They're there, Mr. Archer."

He thanked the woman, moved in their direction and swayed slightly when the plane hit a pocket of turbulence. An older woman with a shock of blonde hair grabbed his arm as he passed her seat. "You're Michael Archer," she said.

Michael released his arm, aware that other passengers were now looking at him. Recognizing him. "No," he said. "I'm not. But it happens all the time. I'm flattered." And he moved on, ignoring the woman even as she said to the man seated beside her: "I could have sworn...."

He picked up one of the telephones, swiped his credit card and dialed. While he waited for the connection to go through, he thought back to earlier that evening: Leana picking up the phone, hearing the conversation with his father, and how he quickly severed the connection when Louis took a breath. Leana stepping into the bathroom, watching him while he showered.

At the time, Michael thought that if he ignored her, that if he just washed himself and acted as if nothing was out of the

301

ordinary, she would doubt what she heard on the phone and think perhaps the lines somehow got crossed in the storm. But what if she didn't think she heard someone else's conversation, not his? What if she recognized his father's voice and was just staying with him until she could safely escape? Since his life was at stake, the implications unnerved him.

Finally, the line was answered by a woman. "Manhattan Enterprises."

"Judy, it's Michael. Is my father in?"

"He's in a conference, Michael."

"Please tell him I'm on the line. I'm calling from a plane. It's urgent."

There was a sigh, a click and the abrupt sound of Muzak. Michael closed his eyes and felt the familiar knot tightening in his stomach. His life was out of control. Yesterday morning he shot and killed a man in his apartment after the man burned his manuscript. The police obviously were looking into that now, asking questions, following leads.

His father told him earlier that they found the charred bodies in his apartment and the Iranian cab driver dumped in an alley one block away. Although Michael rented the apartment under an assumed name, he knew that sooner or later the police would learn it was his apartment the bodies were found in.

He was famous. Although his apartment was surrounded by people whose reality was altered by drugs, certainly somebody had recognized him during the three weeks he'd lived there.

*But I can help you,* Louis said. *Kill Redman and the police will never know that apartment was yours.*

Although his father never said this, Michael knew the opposite also was true: *If you don't kill Redman, every cop in the world will be after your ass. As will Santiago.*

It was an endless cycle that offered no escape. Michael wasn't sure how much longer he could keep going, how much longer he could keep up with the facade.

His father answered the line. "What is it, Michael?"

"We need to talk."

"That isn't possible right now."

"Not good enough," Michael said. "We need to talk. Now."

"And I said it isn't possible."

"Who are you with?"

"That's none of your business."

"Fine," Michael said. "Then answer this for me and you can get back to your meeting--why did you have to kill her sister?"

"I'm not discussing this with you now. Call me when you arrive in New York."

Michael's hand tightened around the receiver. "Don't hang up on me."

The silence stretched.

"What is it?"

"I need to know if it's safe for me to come back."

"It's safe," Louis said.

"Are you sure?"

"I told you--it's safe."

But Michael could sense his father wasn't telling him something. He could sense that something was wrong. "If you're lying to me, Dad--"

"I'm not lying to you, Michael. You're going to have to trust me on this."

While Michael knew he had no choice but to trust his father, he couldn't help feeling that he was being pushed nearer to the edge of a cliff. "Where do you expect Leana and me to stay when we get back?" he asked.

"That's been taken care of."

"Taken care of?" Michael said. "When were you planning on telling me--next week? We'll be landing in another two hours. You've told me nothing--"

The line went dead.

\* \* \*

Leana watched the night pass by, only dimly aware of the jet's engines, the conversation of the couple seated in front of her, the diet-slim flight attendants as they whisked up and down the aisle.

She was still trying to understand and accept that her sister was dead and had been murdered only that morning. And she could still hear Harold's voice echoing like a cold whisper:

303

"Celina did love you, Leana. I can't tell you how many times she told me that she missed you."

At that moment, Leana ached with loss. She thought of all the times she and Celina could have been close and realized she never would have that opportunity now.

She was wondering who was responsible for Celina's death when Michael sat down beside her. He reached for her hand and Leana looked at him, remembering what had happened only hours before in their hotel suite. Whose voice had she heard when she lifted the receiver? It wasn't Michael's voice, she knew that. But she also knew that she'd heard that voice before--just as she knew that one day she would put a face to it.

"How are you doing?" he asked.

Leana shrugged.

"Isn't there anything I can do?"

"Not unless you can bring my sister back."

The silence hung in the air. Michael moved to speak, couldn't find the words and squeezed her hand harder. Leana squeezed back. "I'm sorry," she said. "That was uncalled for. I'm just not in a good place right now. It has nothing to do with you."

"It's all right," he said. "I understand."

She leaned back in her seat. "You know what I keep thinking?" she said. "I keep thinking how nice it's going to feel when I find the son of a bitch who's responsible for this."

Michael turned to her.

"And I will find him, Michael. I swear to God I will. He's not going to get away with this. He's not going to get away with killing my sister. I have you to help me and I have Mario. We will find who murdered her. We'll make him pay."

"Leana--"

Her throat suddenly thickened. "I did love her, Michael. I never thought I did, but I did."

He touched her hair. "We'll get through this. I promise." He leaned over and kissed her cheek. "I love you," he said.

Leana looked at him then, saw the pain on his face, the grief in his eyes and knew that he was telling her the truth. She felt guilty. How could she have mistrusted him earlier? He had never been anything but good to her. The telephone lines obviously got crossed in the storm.

Holding his hand in her own, she turned back to the window, where the world had disappeared into the darkness. For the first time in hours, she thought of Eric Parker, of the contract he had put out on her and wondered what would be waiting for her when she returned home.

## CHAPTER THIRTY-NINE

Anastassios Fondaras closed the final file Eric Parker stole on the takeover of WestTex Incorporated and tossed it onto Louis' desk.

Although the man said nothing now, his dark eyes gleamed with the sort of intensity that reminded Ryan of a tiger's eyes before the beast moved in for the kill.

Anastassios stood. "This deal Redman has with Iran," Fondaras said, as he moved to the far right wall of windows and looked out at the city, which was brilliant in the late afternoon light. "It's verbal, correct?"

"Yes," Louis said, remembering his conversation with Harold Baines. "It's verbal. Iran wouldn't agree to sign anything until Redman took over WestTex. They felt it was a waste of time to commit themselves otherwise."

"I see. But I assume that in the interim Redman has been in close contact with Iran," Fondaras said. "I assume the Iranians will keep their word."

"If circumstances were to remain the same, I'm sure they would," Louis said. "Under current circumstances, they actually need Redman. With the Middle East unstable, most major shipping and oil companies are reluctant to enter the Gulf--including your own. Iran needs to sell their oil in order to buy arms, but few are willing to take the risk--except George. Redman's advantage is that he knows the exact date the Navy moves into the Gulf. If Iran knew that date was as early as next week, they'd drop the deal, knowing that the Gulf would soon be secure again for trade and that they didn't need any private deal with an American company."

"If they knew the date," Fondaras said.

"Exactly."

Fondaras moved from the window and stepped to the bar. "I've known George Redman for nearly twenty years," he said. "And I have genuine respect for him. A part of me even likes him."

*But*, Louis thought. *But....*

"But this is business," Fondaras said, as he poured himself another tumbler of Scotch. "And business is about getting there first. It's about winning, regardless of the situation." Drink in hand, he turned to Ryan. "So, you have no interest in being part of this deal? You're simply going to give me this information for free?"

"Naturally, there will be a price--after all, Anastassios, as you yourself pointed out, this is business. But we'll discuss terms later. First, tell me your plans."

"My plans?" Fondaras said with a laugh. "It's textbook. Redman will be getting their oil cheap. Iran is desperate and he's played off their needs. I plan on doing the same--only I'm going to offer Iran more money for their oil. I've worked with them in the past and they'll work with me again. I plan on stealing this deal from George Redman." His eyes flashed. "But what's it going to cost me?"

Louis reached for his own glass of Scotch, came over to where Fondaras was standing and touched glasses with the man. "That, my friend, is the most beautiful part of all."

\* \* \*

Spocatti came only minutes after Fondaras left. "Eric Parker is dead," he said. "Diana Crane and Jack Douglas found him at the bottom of her staircase two hours ago. Her apartment is crawling with cops--and the cops are saying he fell. It isn't being considered a homicide."

Louis accepted the information with a nod. He was seated at his desk, facing the windows. As he stared at The Redman International Building, his eyes flickered with what might have been fear.

Spocatti was about to continue when he noticed the object of Ryan's attention through the great panes of glass. Would the man never learn?

He moved to Louis' desk, opened a side drawer and pressed a button--the curtains whispered shut. "One bullet, Louis," he said. "That's all it would take."

But Louis wasn't listening. He was thinking of the $90 million check he gave Eric Parker in exchange for the files he stole from Diana Crane, the very check that bore the name of Manhattan Enterprises' foreign branch, World Enterprises.

"The check," Louis said. "You're too smart to have come without it, so give it to me."

Spocatti sat in the chair behind him, kicked his feet up on Louis' desk. "There is no check, Louis."

"Of course, there is. I wrote it. You delivered it."

"Doesn't matter--the check's gone."

"Then where is it?"

"No idea. It wasn't on Eric Parker's body and it's nowhere in that apartment. I have contacts at the NYPD. One of them was there when they removed the body, which was searched before Parker was pulled out. There was no check, Louis."

"This contact," Louis said. "This friend of yours--he can be trusted?"

"Are you questioning me? Of course, he can. He's one of my best. While he was there, he also wired the apartment. You know as well as I do that Diana Crane will soon be missing those files. Now, we'll know when she misses them. Now, we'll be able to deal with matters more efficiently."

Louis rose from his seat. "That check didn't just disappear."

Spocatti watched the man pace, delighted by how all of this was affecting him. "Of course, it didn't disappear, but it's nowhere in that apartment. That I can assure you."

"Then where is it?"

"My guess is that whoever pushed Parker down those stairs is also holding that check."

Louis, a man rarely stunned by the events of life, looked at Spocatti, stunned. "Pushed Parker down the stairs? You said he fell."

"The police said he fell," Spocatti said. "There's a difference. And the police happen to be wrong. Eric Parker did not lose his footing and fall down the stairs like they said he did--Eric Parker was murdered. My contact and I are certain of it."

"Who killed him?"

Spocatti smiled a slow, knowing smile. "You tell me."

It was a moment before Louis responded. His mind filled with possibilities, made connections. And then he gradually realized that there was only one person who could have done it-- Mario De Cicco.

He sat heavily in his chair.

Spocatti watched the color drain from the man's face but felt no pity, no sympathy, only a slight annoyance at having been ignored. "I warned you, Louis."

"I know you did."

"Things aren't as simple as they once were. You're losing the game."

"The hell I am."

"But you are," Spocatti said. "I told you not to send a check. I told you to wire the money from one of your anonymous accounts into one of his anonymous accounts. It would have been clean but you chose not to listen. You got greedy. You wanted that information so badly, you caved into Parker's demands. That might turn out to be the biggest mistake of your life."

Spocatti stood and leaned over the desk. "Now, unless you listen to me, unless you do everything I say, you probably will pay with your life--and Redman will win after all."

Louis shook his head. "That's not going to happen."

"Good," Spocatti said. "So, you're going to listen to me? Do as I say?"

"That depends," Louis said warily. "What do you have in mind?"

Vincent told him.

## CHAPTER FORTY

The first thing Michael noticed when he and Leana cleared customs was Spocatti. He was moving in their direction, sifting through the crowds, eyes on Michael, tossing a cigarette into an ashtray as he passed it.

For a moment, Michael thought Santiago's men had somehow followed him here, but he looked around and saw nothing unusual. He turned back to Spocatti, who now was at a restroom entrance. He nodded at Michael and stepped inside.

Michael was tempted to keep walking, but couldn't. Spocatti once saved his life. If Santiago's men were here, he might repeat the favor.

"I need to use the restroom," he said to Leana. "Do you mind waiting a minute?"

The restroom was cool and quiet and painted deep blue. Spocatti was at the rear of the room, washing his hands at a sink. As Michael moved toward him, he noticed two other men standing at the urinals, both wearing business suits. Spocatti's men.

"What is it?" Michael asked.

Spocatti turned off the water and shook his hands over the sink. Michael noticed two long, red marks running horizontally on each palm. They looked like burns. Rope burns.

"I'm here to help you, Michael."

"Why? To make up for the life you took earlier?"

"I don't know what you're talking about."

Michael took a step toward him. "Why did you kill her sister?"

Spocatti raised an eyebrow. "Look at you--standing up so tall and brave."

"She didn't have to die."

"I just do as I'm told." He ripped a towel from a dispenser and began wiping his hands. "Actually, you're right," he said. "Of course, I killed her. And I enjoyed killing her. You should have seen the expression on her face when I cut the rope and tied it around her legs. Now we're talking fear--"

Michael lunged forward and pushed Spocatti against the wall. The two men at the urinals looked over their shoulders. One laughed. The other went to the door and blocked it so no one else could enter.

"Who's next?" Michael asked.

Spocatti didn't struggle. Instead, he looked bemused. "Everyone is next, Michael. Everyone will die. It's all going to be tragic. Blood will be everywhere."

His hands soared up. He shoved Michael against the opposite wall and withdrew the gun concealed beneath his black leather jacket.

Tried to withdraw his gun.

It caught on his shoulder holster and tumbled from his hand.

As if in slow motion, Michael watched the gun bounce off Spocatti's knee, drop to the blue tile floor and spin in his direction.

He lunged for it.

Tried to lunge for it.

The man at the row of urinals no longer was amused. Suddenly, he was standing in front of Michael, blocking his path to the gun.

Spocatti picked it up. He holstered it and said to Michael, "If you want to get through the next few days alive, and especially if you want to be rid of Santiago, I suggest you cut the bullshit, listen to me carefully and do as I say."

\* \* \*

Leana was nowhere in sight when Michael left the restroom.

He looked around the crowded corridor and found her standing across from him. She was on her cell phone, talking rapidly, gesticulating with her free hand. Michael wondered who she was talking to and if it concerned him and the conversation she overheard in Monte Carlo.

When she snapped the phone shut, he moved toward her, the knot hardening in his stomach--tightening. "Who was that?" he asked.

"Mario."

"Mario?" He couldn't keep the surprise from his voice. While they were in Monte Carlo, his father told him that De Cicco was running a check on them both. If the man somehow learned he was Louis' son, Michael knew that Mario would take him out.

"And?"

"Eric's dead," she said. "The contract's been canceled."

He searched her eyes, trying to see if there was something more she wasn't telling him.

"So, it's over," he said.

She looked incredulous. "Are you serious? Of course, it isn't over. First, the spotlights explode, then my sister is murdered. Someone is out to hurt my family. Are my parents next? Is it me? Nobody's been caught. Which one of us is next?"

Michael could say nothing.

Leana reached for the oversized handbag that was at her feet. "Look," she said. "I didn't mean to snap at you. I'm sorry for getting upset."

"You have every reason to be upset."

"It's just that I'm not sure how much more of this I can take." She started to leave. "Can we go home now? It's late and I'm tired. I want to get up early tomorrow morning and see my parents."


* * *


For Michael and Leana, home now was a new apartment located at the top of a Fifth Avenue high rise.

As their limousine neared the glittering tower, Michael thought back to the phone conversation he had in Monte Carlo with his father. The man thought of everything. Not only did he know his son would need a new place to live, but he also knew that that place would have to reflect the kind of wealth and power his new bride would be expecting.

He wondered if his father intentionally chose an apartment on Fifth Avenue. If Louis had, Michael wouldn't be surprised. Only yesterday morning, his manuscript by the same name had been burned.

The car hit a string of green lights, sailed up Madison and turned onto 59th Street, where it crossed over to Fifth. As it began moving down the avenue, Michael looked at the people on the sidewalk, at the illumined store windows and remembered what Spocatti told him in the restroom. *The doorman's name is Joseph. He's tall, dark hair, thick mustache. He's expecting you. When you see him, act as if you already know each other.*

The car pulled to the curb.

Michael looked out the window and saw a liveried doorman hurrying in their direction. For a moment, his heart seemed to stop. The man coming toward them was short and bald.

He looked past the man, toward the twin gilt doors, and saw one other doorman standing at the entrance--but he was young and blond.

His door swung open. "Mr. Archer," the man said. "It's a pleasure to have you back with us."

Michael had no choice but to go with it. He stepped out of the car.

"And you must be Mrs. Archer," the man said, looking past Michael. "It's a pleasure to meet you."

As Leana alighted from the limousine, the man flashed Michael an intimate, knowing smile. "She's every bit as beautiful as you said she would be, Mr. Archer."

Michael managed a smile of his own, hating Spocatti more now than he had before. "Where is Joseph?" he asked. "I thought he'd be working tonight."

"Flu," the man said. "We're hoping he'll be back tomorrow. Let me help you with your bags."

They took an elevator to the fiftieth floor. When Michael entered the apartment, he found it as sumptuous as Spocatti said it would be. It was filled with items similar to those that he lost to the bank only a few short weeks ago.

As he looked around, it came to him that the apartment somehow seemed lived in, even though Spocatti said it had been furnished only that morning.

313

Leana dropped her handbag onto a side table. She moved toward the center of the foyer and appraised the room with a sweeping glance. "So, this is where you live," she said.

Michael held out his hands. *I guess so,* he thought.

\* \* \*

When he joined Leana in bed that night, sleep wouldn't come. There were so many thoughts crowding Michael's head, he knew he would go mad if he gave into them.

Instead, he allowed his thoughts to drift to his mother. Sometimes, Michael thought if he could just see her again and talk to her, he could feel the rage his father had felt for years and go on with this, knowing that what his father swore was right.

But his mother had died when he was three. What few memories he had of her were only fragments tarnished by time.

Some things he did remember--the way she smiled, the toys she showered him with, the pretty cotton dresses she wore. He wished he could remember more, but he couldn't. It was his father who dominated his childhood memories.

Michael closed his eyes and let his mind slip into the dark.

He remembered....

He was a child and his father was moving toward him, loosening his belt, saying in his whiskey-stained voice that he wished Michael hadn't been born.

He remembered....

It was a late, snowy February evening and he could hear his father's drunken weeping in the next room, saying his wife's name over and over, almost as if it would bring her back.

He remembered....

He was eighteen years old and on a bus headed for Hollywood. Michael would never forget that day, the stale smoky air, the countless hours on the road. Every bit of it was better than the prison his father had confined him to. When the bus left Grand Central, he became Michael Archer and he swore to himself that his father would never again control his life.

He wondered now how he could have let that happen.

He imagined....

Leaving his father and New York, catching a plane with Leana, flying to some remote part of the world, starting over in a land where no one knew them.  But he knew he could do none of that. If he did, his father or Santiago would find them and kill them.

Michael's eyes opened.

Or would they?

# FIFTH AVENUE

## CHAPTER FORTY-ONE

On Sunday morning, George went through the rituals of death.

In his office at Redman International, he made phone calls. From the undertaker, he ordered an ornate mahogany casket with the initials CER engraved on each side. He phoned his daughter's favorite florist, ordered dozens of roses to fill the church and, later, the area surrounding her grave.

He phoned close friends and relatives, telling them the time and the place of the private wake and burial. And he spent time alone, still trying to accept the unacceptable. Not since his parents' death had George dealt with something so entirely personal. He felt numb, not vacant, but absent, as if he were standing outside himself, watching this hell happen to another man--even though he knew it was happening to himself.

Although the board was pushing to sign the final papers with WestTex and Iran on Tuesday, he shoved the takeover from his mind, not wanting or willing to deal with it until the day came and he had no other choice.

He left for her office.

When he stepped inside, it was like moving into a room where Celina still came to each morning. It was having her here that made him most proud. His office was next to hers. If a deal was going particularly well or sour, it wasn't unusual for them to communicate by yelling to each other through the wall. George's throat thickened at the thought.

He went to her desk.

Like himself, his daughter wasn't the neatest person. Her desk was cluttered with a litany of used Styrofoam cups and empty food containers. There were files pertaining to the takeover of WestTex and on the corner of the desk was a photo of them both framed in silver. They were standing in front of the new Redman International Building, father and daughter, smiling because this was their greatest moment. Together, they were invincible. Together, they had accomplished so much.

Who was he without her?

There was a knock at the office door. George turned to find Elizabeth standing in the doorway. She wore a simple black dress. Her mouth was a solemn line. She seemed like a ghost to him, as if this were still unreal, not happening.

Posture perfect, eyes dead, his wife lifted her head. "I'm ready," she said.

* * *

Walking into their daughter's apartment was perhaps the hardest thing George and Elizabeth had ever done. Looking around, it was as if she had just left for the weekend and would soon be returning. As they walked from room to room, each attaching a memory to objects Celina once held dear to her, they wondered how they would ever get through life without her.

They moved into her bedroom.

While Elizabeth stepped into a closet, George glanced around the room, noticing that the bed had been left unmade and that the shades were still drawn, shutting out an overcast sky. Behind him, he could hear the sharp clatter of wire hangers sliding rapidly across a metal bar.

"I think she should wear red," Elizabeth called. "Celina always loved red. It was her best color." Her voice was oddly light. It clashed against the sound of the clacking hangers.

George turned toward the closet, his brow furrowing as he said that he remembered.

"Or white," Elizabeth said. "I always liked her in white."

"Elizabeth...."

"I had no idea Celina had so many clothes," Elizabeth said. "She's not like me or her sister. I always thought she was a minimalist. But this? This rivals anything Leana or I have in our closets."

He stepped behind her.

"I thought it would take only a moment to find something appropriate, then we could leave." She pushed a rack of dresses aside--the metal scraped. "This is harder than I imagined it would be."

"Why don't you let me help?"

"That isn't necessary." She pushed more clothes aside, moving quickly, then stopped and lifted a white dress from the bar. She turned to him. "How's this?"

"It's fine, Elizabeth."

"Are you sure? I want her to look perfect."

An image of Celina as he'd last seen her forced its way into his mind. She had been stretched naked on a cold metal table in the basement of the M.E.'s office, her skin pale blue, her damp hair curling around a face that was strangely swollen. A part of George died in that moment, dissolving into something darker, uglier.

"She'll look perfect," he said.

Elizabeth raised the dress and inspected it quickly. Without looking at her husband, she said, "I won't come here again, George."

"You won't have to. I'll take care of everything."

With a last look around, they left the apartment, the door locking shut behind them.

\* \* \*

Elizabeth said nothing on the drive uptown.

Their daughter's dress folded like a barrier between them, her hands clasped neatly in her lap, she looked out the window beside her, oblivious to the two unmarked police cars following them, the sun occasionally glinting in her eyes, her breathing as quiet as the limousine's virtually soundproof interior.

She was fifty-four years old and she was beautiful, the fine lines around her mouth and beneath her eyes somehow enhancing, curiously enhancing. Watching her, George found himself thinking back to a time when they both were young and happy, the time when they first met and neither knew the storms that lay ahead.

He remembered their chance meeting at a mutual friend's dinner party and how he told her at the end of that evening that he was going to marry her. He remembered stealing a kiss with her on her father's doorstep and he remembered the way his heart used to quicken when she alighted from her home to greet him. Then, she was the most important thing in his life. But where were they now?

If someone had asked George that question two months ago, he would have had an answer. But now? Now, he was moving uptown to meet with the undertaker friends had suggested. Now, whoever murdered their daughter and caused the spotlights to explode was still out there, free. He had no answers for any of it. As the limousine stopped for a red light, George closed his eyes and began wondering who was behind everything that was happening to them.

He wasn't given the chance.

In the limousine, there was a disturbance in the air, a change in the silence.

Beside him, he sensed Elizabeth bristle.

George looked at his wife, saw her looking out the window beside her and followed her gaze with his own.

There, at the crowded street corner, was a newspaper stand. On the front page of the Post was a picture of Celina and Eric Parker, both standing outside Redman International's gilded entrance, arms intertwined. They were alive, in love and smiling.

The banner headline was huge. One simple word:

**COINCIDENCE?**

George reached for Elizabeth's hand.

As the light turned green and the car lurched forward, his gaze moved to the rack next to the Post. On the front page of the Daily News was another picture, this one of him, Elizabeth and Leana.

The banner headline screamed out at him.

**ARE THEY NEXT?**

319

## CHAPTER FORTY-TWO

When Leana left to meet her parents, the morning was warm and overcast. She stepped onto the sidewalk and into the waiting limousine. "Redman International," she said to the driver, and felt her stomach tighten as they pulled away from the curb.

She was dressed casually yet professionally. When she met them, she didn't want to appear as if she was trying too hard to make the statement that she had made it and moved on, even though she knew she was.

She had changed since the opening of her father's building. She'd moved out of their home, found an apartment of her own, landed a job with her father's rival, married Michael Archer.

She was independent. She had accomplished her goals and she'd done it without her their help. Never again would she need her parents to back her financially. Never again would she have to rely on them. There was freedom there, but a kind of sadness as well. Why did she feel that only she would recognize her accomplishments and not her parents, the very people she most wanted to recognize them?

The Redman International Building came into sight.

Leana saw a large group of reporters gathered outside its entrance. She hesitated, knowing that if she was going to see her parents, she would have to go through this pool of sharks and take the brunt of their questions. Resisting the thought of turning back, she asked the driver to pull as close to the entrance as possible. When the car stopped, she didn't wait for the driver. She opened the door, lowered her head and stepped out.

She pushed forward, ready for the assault.

But it didn't come. As she neared the crowd, a sleek black limousine, followed by two unmarked police cars, pulled to the curb.

Leana stepped back and watched in surprise as the doors to the two unmarked cars shot open and several men stepped out.

Holding the crowd of reporters at bay, creating a human shield around the limousine's rear passenger door, the men protected her mother and father as they left the car and began moving toward the entrance.

The crowd was relentless. Microphones raised, cameras flashing, voices rising above the increasing din, they pressed forward, shouting at her mother, screaming at her father, trying in vain to gain some insight into Celina's death, on the takeover of WestTex, on their reaction to Eric Parker's death.

The police were losing control. The place was erupting. In horror, Leana watched the crowd shift suddenly and knock her mother to the ground. George tried to help his wife to her feet, but the photographers knew a shot of her on the pavement was gold. They swarmed, making it virtually impossible for him to help her. Their cameras snapped, flashed and captured the moment for a world hungry for more.

Leana sprang forward, forcing her way through the crowd.

There was a moment when no one recognized her, when she was able to squeeze through and help her mother to her feet--and then, for an instant, everything went still as realization crossed the faces of seventy-five people. The outcast was here.

Elizabeth looked at her daughter in wide-eyed disbelief. A camera went off. George said Leana's name just as the situation blew.

The crowd started jumping, thrashing, taking photo after photo, knowing what an opportunity this was and refusing to miss it. The police pushed the crowd back, threatened them, determined to gain control.

When a path finally cleared, Leana grasped her mother's hand and they charged toward the entrance with George at their side, not stopping until they were safe inside and the doors were closed behind them.

For a moment, nothing was said.

Mother and father and daughter looked at one another, still shaken by what had just happened. Outside, the press were jammed against the windows, vying for position, recording everything that was happening inside.

"I thought you were hurt," Leana said to her mother. "I thought they were hurting you."

"I'm all right," Elizabeth said. "I'm fine."

"But they pushed you," Leana said.

Elizabeth glanced down at the tear in her black dress, at the scrape on her leg and then looked back at Leana. She seemed to hesitate, then she walked over and held her youngest daughter tightly.

Leana felt overwhelmed by her mother's embrace. She looked at her father, but sensed a cool distance. George was staring at her.

"I'm sorry," Leana said to her mother. "Michael and I came as soon as we received Harold's call."

Elizabeth pulled back, brushed a lock of hair from her daughter's forehead, but she didn't acknowledge Leana's marriage. Instead, she held Leana's face in her hands.

"Have they learned anything yet?"

Elizabeth shook her head. "Not yet," she said. "But they will."

"When I saw you fall, I didn't know what to think. First the spotlights, now Celina. I thought someone got to you." Her voice thickened. She looked over at her father. "I wouldn't let anyone hurt either of you."

George looked away.

The slight was like a slap to Leana's face. She tried to still the anger rising within her, but she couldn't. "Is there something you want to say to me, Dad?" she asked.

George looked at his daughter, moved to speak, but decided to let it pass. He began walking toward the family elevator, which was behind him.

And that's all it took. Leana went after him.

She moved past Elizabeth. Besides those members of security who had followed them inside, the lobby was otherwise empty.

Leana's voice--high and angry--echoed in the enormous space. "Don't walk away from me," she said. "If you've got something to say, just say it."

Her father stopped and turned. "All right," he said. "I want to know why you're going to work for Louis Ryan."

"Why?" Leana said. "Because you threw me out. Because I need work in order to eat and have a place to sleep. Because Uncle Harold suggested I contact him. Louis offered me a job and I took it."

"And so he did," George said. "And what exactly is that job, Leana?"

*As if you don't know.* "I'll be running his new hotel for him."

"You'll be running his new hotel for him," George said. "Well, well--that makes all the sense in the world. Here's a woman who has absolutely no experience managing anything other than her shoes and she's been asked to manage the largest hotel in Manhattan. Now I can understand why you got the job. You're obviously suited for it."

"George..."

"Stay out of this, Elizabeth."

"At least he's willing to take a chance on me," Leana said. "At least he's taken an interest in me, which you never have."

"You're so naive," George said. "Tell me, why is he taking such an interest in you? Certainly not because of your skills, so it must be to get at me. Can't you see that? Are you that blind? The man is using you. He'll probably end up hurting you."

While Leana sensed part of that was true, she wouldn't admit it to her father. "As if you'd give a damn. And besides, I don't believe that," she said. "He's done things for me that you've never done. He's treated me like the father you never were." She shot him a look. "And why is that, Dad? Why is it that you never brought me to Redman International when I was a kid? You brought Celina. You brought Celina every fucking day. You treated her like the son you never had."

George shoved a finger at her. "You leave Celina out of this," he said. "You're not going to drag her into this. Not this. Not now."

"Try and stop me," Leana said. "For years you gave her opportunities I never was given. For years you showered her with the love you refused to give me. You neglected me. You made me feel worthless, as if you wished I was never born. You pushed me from your life when I wanted to be close to you, you made me hate my own sister when I should have loved her. Jesus Christ, Dad--and people wonder why I got so screwed up on drugs. People wonder why I'm so goddamned angry now!"

"That's right," George said. "Blame your problems on me. Isn't that how you played it in rehab? Get the sympathy vote by taking your old man down?" He took a step toward her. "Let me tell you something, girl. You've had it good your entire life. You've had things millions of people will never have. You've been privileged and spoiled. So, please, don't give me any bullshit about how I neglected you, because that's hardly the case."

Leana shook her head sadly. "You just don't get it, do you? You really think you were a prize father. What a joke. You haven't heard a word I've said. The great George Redman does no wrong."

"I made mistakes," George said. "I admit it. I'm human. But you've been holding onto those mistakes for years. You've been carrying a grudge ever since you were a kid. Can you honestly say that you've given me a chance?"

"Yes," Leana said without hesitation. "Yes, I can say that."

"Then I guess you're a better person than I am," George said. "Congratulations."

He started to walk away again.

But Leana went after him.

"It's so easy for you," she said. "Build your buildings. Take over your corporations. Live your big life. Be that big dream. But what I see is a pathetic excuse of a man who has so lost control of himself and what matters in life that my sister is dead because of it."

That stopped him.

"It's true," she said. "Those spotlights exploded weeks ago. Why didn't you protect your family when someone obviously has it in for us. Someone *you* probably pissed off. You think they'll be coming after me and Mom because of something we did? Get real. When we're dead, it'll be because of something *you* did, not us. You've got blood on your hands now, and you'll have blood on your hands then."

"You don't know what you're talking about."

"Tell that to Celina."

"I've been in touch with the police daily about those spotlights."

"You should have been up their ass hourly. Tell that to Celina, too. You're partly responsible for all of this. You failed to keep your family safe. You suck as a father. You're not the man you think you are. You're just some schmuck who got lucky years ago, made his fortune, collected the rewards that came with it and the luck kept rolling until it stopped with my sister's death. You're the murderer here. You're a piece of shit and it's time someone told you so to your face."

"Get the fuck out of here," George said.

"If you think I'm leaving my mother alone with you, you're crazy. You're unstable. You get the fuck out."

George looked at Elizabeth, saw the pain on her face and the defeat in her eyes, and then he also noted something else--she was siding with Leana. He stepped alone into the elevator--only dimly aware of the press, who were still leaning against the windows--and pressed a button. The doors closed. He was gone.

\* \* \*

In his study, Michael Archer watched his mother move across the living room to pick up her son, watched her collapse with him on the damask sofa, watched her throw back her head and laugh when he tickled her ribs.

No sound came from her mouth. But her eyes were shining.

He picked up the remote, pointed it at the television, zoomed in and froze on her face. She looked happy. He held the shot for a few seconds, then pressed a button and faded into the next clip.

Michael leaned toward the television and tried to remember the lost scenes of his childhood as they unfolded before him.

Anne Ryan stood on tip-toe as she placed a large tinfoil star on top of a Christmas tree decorated with strings of popcorn, twinkling lights, frosted glass balls. When the star was in place, she stepped back and smiled at her handiwork. She turned toward the camera, curtsied, then made a face and pointed across the room.

The camera whirled and swept across a small apartment that was neat, festive and filled with people. His father was sitting in an antique rocking chair, cuddling an infant in the crook of his arm. Louis kissed the child on the forehead, brushed its cheek with the back of his hand.

Michael lifted the receiver to his ear. "How did you get these films onto DVD?" he asked his father, who had called moments before. Louis had asked Michael to go to his study and look in the drawer beneath the television. There, Michael found a DVD player and a stack of DVDs.

"I had them brought to a man on Third Avenue," Louis said. "He takes old home movie footage and puts it onto DVD." There was a beat of silence. "She's beautiful, isn't she?"

"Why isn't there any sound?"

"Your grandfather shot everything. He used his camera."

Michael watched his mother. She was now wearing a long, flowing white dress and holding a stuffed Easter bunny in front of her son. He watched himself giggle, watched himself grin.

"Why are you doing this to me?"

"I want you to remember your mother as she was. It's been a long time, Michael. You've forgotten."

"I haven't forgotten," Michael said. *I haven't.*

The line went dead.

When the phone rang thirty minutes later, Michael was viewing the final DVD. Feeling drained and exhausted, he paused the frame and reached for the telephone, thinking it was his father.

It wasn't.

For the next several moments, Michael listened quietly to the man who gave him the loan in Vegas. He listened to him threaten, he listened to him shout.

"I understand in a few days your father's going to ask a favor of you," the man said. "For your sake, you better do it, Michael. Because if you don't, if you decide not to kill Redman, your father won't give us the final payment--and then Mr. Santiago will be asking me to do a favor for him."

## CHAPTER FORTY-THREE

"How are you this morning?"

Diana turned from the window she was standing at and looked across the small living room at Jack Douglas. He was standing in the arched doorway, holding two cups of coffee and wearing a faded blue bathrobe that was spotted with purplish bleach stains and frayed at the sleeves.

Diana shrugged. "I'm all right," she said. "Considering."

Jack nodded--he knew.

His eyes puffy from lack of sleep, his hair tousled, he moved to the center of the room and sat at one end of a sofa. "I made coffee," he said. "Want a cup?"

Diana said she would love a cup. As she crossed the room, it occurred to her how strange it was that they were here together, comforting each another in his apartment. Yesterday, after the police left with Eric, Jack went upstairs to her bedroom, packed her an overnight bag and told her to come home with him.

Diana didn't want to be alone in her apartment. She was grateful for his kindness and agreed. Now, as she sat beside Jack, she wondered again how anyone involved in the takeover of WestTex Incorporated would get through these next few days without losing whatever sanity they somehow had managed to keep.

Jack handed her one of the steaming mugs. "That was Harold on the phone a few minutes ago," he said. "He and the board have been caucusing with WestTex, Frostman and Chase since last night. The paperwork's nearly finished. Chase has cut us a deal. Everything's a go."

"Then we leave tomorrow afternoon for Iran?"

Jack nodded, relieved that Celina's funeral was scheduled for early morning, hours before he, Diana and Harold would have to board Redman International's private Lear to London, then on to Iran.

"It's a long flight," he said. "By the time we arrive to sign the final papers, it'll be Tuesday morning in New York and the deal with WestTex will have just been completed. Harold seems to feel that everything will go smoothly from here on out."

Diana smiled wryly. She sipped her coffee.

"I see you're having a difficult time believing that, too," Jack said.

"Can you blame me?"

"Not at all. In fact, I'd be surprised if something doesn't go wrong. Too much has happened. My trust in this deal and in Redman International has dissolved. Someone is out to destroy George and his family."

"They still haven't found the man who murdered Celina, have they?"

Jack shook his head. All night long he had relived Celina's death, trying to convince himself that he'd done everything he could to save her, but nevertheless feeling that he hadn't done nearly enough. "Harold said they've found nothing. Not a thing."

"Are you going to be all right?"

"What's all right? I know that once this deal is complete, I'm out of here. I'm going to leave Redman International, disappear somewhere. Before I do anything else, I have to get my head on straight, Diana."

"You didn't sleep last night, did you?"

"Not a wink."

"Me either," she said. "And I'm dreading going back to my apartment. If I didn't have to go back, Jack, I wouldn't go."

"Then don't," he said. "You can stay with me until everything blows over. When you're ready to go back, you go back."

"I wish it were that easy," she said. "But there are a stack of files I have to collect before we leave for Iran--and much of them are in my office at home."

Jack finished the last of his coffee. "Let me go with you," he said. "To be honest, I'd be grateful for anything that can help take my mind off Celina."

\* \* \*

The air was still when they entered her apartment.

There was no commotion, no officers talking into their cell phones, no one there to kneel by her side and tell her that everything was going to be all right while she sat stunned as they wheeled Eric's body out of her apartment.

Instead, there was only quiet and it left her vacant. As Diana followed Jack inside, she kept thinking how unreal this still was. Just yesterday, she thought, as they moved into the living room and she saw the winding oak staircase, they had found Eric Parker dead at the bottom of it.

Jack must have sensed her uneasiness.

"Let's get this over with," he said. "Where's your office?"

Diana nodded toward the stairs, but she made no effort to climb them.

"Do you want me to get the files for you?"

She hesitated, but then said that she didn't. The files she needed were stored in her desk, packed away in a black crocodile briefcase. Not only would it be easier for her to get the files herself, but she also knew that Eric had been using her computer yesterday afternoon. She was still curious to see what he was so curious about. "But I'd like it if you came with me," she said.

When they reached the top of the stairs, Dana hesitated only briefly before she approached the closed office door. She turned the handle and gave it a push. The door swung open, coming gently to rest against the rubber doorstop, exposing a plain room filled with the muted light of an overcast sky.

She moved toward her desk and noticed the large, black smudges soiling the back of her computer. Jack noticed it, too. "Looks as if you've had some computer problems," he said. "What do you suppose he was up to?"

"No idea."

But she was determined to find out. She sat at her desk and turned on the computer. But when she flipped the switch, the machine did nothing. She checked and saw that it was unplugged. Plugging it back in awakened an odd buzzing sound, almost as if the computer's circuits were frying. The screen flickered--once, twice--and it then turned in on itself.

Jack reached over her shoulder and pulled the plug.

Diana stared at the screen. "He broke it," she said. "Why?"

"We could spend all day guessing about that."

She turned in her chair and looked around the room, still trying to figure out why Eric would use her computer and then break it. It didn't make sense. She wondered if he was after information of some sort, but even that didn't make sense. There was nothing Eric didn't know about all aspects of Redman International.

Like her, he had had top clearance to all files and he was well-versed in every one of them. And even if he had forgotten something in the two weeks that had passed since his termination--which, knowing him, she doubted--she had openly discussed several ongoing deals with him during the time they'd spent together. She had updated him on everything--including the takeover of WestTex Incorporated.

There was nothing he didn't know. And yet he used and broke her computer for a reason.

She looked over at the long line of metal file cabinets along the far left wall and wondered if he had found her key and gone through those.

She left her chair. As she moved past Jack, she thought of all the times Eric had used her, hurt her, taken advantage of her, and of all the times she swore to herself that he never again would he be given that chance.

Now, as she stopped in front of a white table that held one of her two printers, she couldn't help feeling that she'd been taken again by the son of a bitch.

She removed the table's only drawer and emptied its contents onto the floor--pens and pencils and scraps of paper fell at her feet. Taped to the back of the drawer would be the only other key to her file cabinets--the other key she carried with her at all times. But if this key was missing, if it was gone or put back improperly, she would know that he had been into her files.

She flipped the drawer over--and saw that the key was still there, still taped to the back, clearly unmoved. Eric hadn't broken into her files. And Diana felt foolish. It occurred to her that maybe he had just been bored sitting here alone and accessed her computer only to surf the Web.

Buy why break it?

Jack came over to where she was kneeling and began picking up the clutter at her feet. "It's probably nothing," he said, taking the drawer from her hand and inserting it back into the desk. "We might be blowing this out of proportion."

Diana wanted to agree with him, but she couldn't. "That computer didn't break on its own," she said. "It was only a few months old."

"There's a chance that we're reaching here. Maybe he didn't break it intentionally. Maybe it did break on its own."

She considered it, but it didn't feel right. Eric has lied to her too often to think that this was less than it seemed.

"What could he gain from going through your files and using your computer?"

Diana could come to only one conclusion--Eric needed money. She told Jack about the enormous hospital bills he had to pay when George terminated his insurance, about the pipes bursting in his apartment and how the water had seeped through to the apartment below, destroying Mrs. Aldrich's prized paintings and furniture.

"She was threatening to sue Eric and he was desperate," she said. "He was rapidly running out of money, he knew he wouldn't be able to afford a lawyer--certainly not a decent one--and I didn't offer to defend him. Before I left him alone yesterday morning, I asked how he was going to come up with the money he needed to cover those debts."

"What did he say?"

It was a moment before Diana could speak. As realization slowing threaded through her, the ramifications of what she was thinking chilled her. "He mentioned something about contacting Louis Ryan for a job."

"Louis Ryan?" Jack said. "But George hates that man. Celina told me that Ryan once accused George of killing his wife."

Diana didn't hear Jack. She wasn't aware of anything else except for the cold possibilities that were now in front of her. "All of those roses," she said to herself.

"What are you talking about?"

Diana moved to her desk. In the left-hand drawer would be the files she'd collected on the takeover of WestTex Incorporated--files Eric hadn't seen or read.

331

She opened the drawer, feeling only slightly relieved when she saw that the shiny black briefcase was still there, just as she had left it. She removed the briefcase and put it on her desk. Jack moved behind her. As Diana unsnapped the brass latches, she realized that if the files were disturbed, or if they were missing, she would have to tell George that Eric might have sold the information to Louis Ryan--or perhaps to some other competitor--and the deals with WestTex and Iran would need to fall through.

She opened the case.

Inside were several dark green folders--and every one of them was empty. Stunned, Diana fell into her seat. "There gone," she said. "He took them."

"Took what?" Jack asked.

"The files," Diana said impatiently. "The files on the takeover of WestTex. The files that outlines our entire deal with Iran. Eric took them." She slammed the briefcase shut, reached for one of the phones in front of her and dialed the front desk. Her heart was pounding.

While she waited for the line to be answered, she said to Jack: "While Eric was in the hospital, Louis Ryan sent him dozens of roses. At the time, I thought he was going to offer Eric a job." She nodded toward the briefcase. "Now I know what that job was."

A man answered the line.

"Billy," she said. "It's Diana Crane. I need you to answer a few questions for me."

"Of course, Ms. Crane."

"Yesterday morning, when I left, you were on duty, correct?"

"That's right."

"I need to know if Mr. Parker left the building while I was gone."

The man was silent for a moment. He cleared his throat and said, "He did."

Diana closed her eyes. Yesterday, when she returned from the market and found her apartment empty, she assumed Eric was in his own apartment, surveying the damage by himself. Sensing he wanted to be alone, Diana started lunch. And then came the call from George Redman, telling her the news about Celina's death and asking her if she could come to an emergency board meeting. In her haste to leave, she'd knocked over two bags of groceries.

At the time, Diana hadn't given a second's thought to Eric's absence. Now, she knew that he hadn't been in his apartment at all.

"Did he say where he was going?" she asked.

"He didn't," the man said. "But if it'll help, I can tell you that wherever he was going, he went by limousine."

The man added this information so smoothly, her instincts as a lawyer became acute. She knew he wanted her to know something she wouldn't know without his help. Glancing at Jack, she said, "Limousine? Did he order the car around himself?"

"Not to my knowledge."

"And I assume he returned by the same car?"

"He did," the man said. She could sense a mix of eagerness and caution in the man's voice. *He's holding back*, she thought. *Go easy.*

"Was Eric alone?" she asked.

"He was," the man said. "But he wasn't in your apartment long before he called the front desk, told me that he was expecting some friends and to just show them up when they arrived."

Diana looked at Jack. "Who were these friends, Billy? Did you recognize them?"

The silence that followed wavered like heat from a city street.

"I didn't recognize any of them," he said quietly.

In that moment, Diana knew he was lying

"Billy," she said carefully. "It's very important that I know who came to my apartment. It's very important that you tell me if you recognized anyone. Please tell me. There is no need to be frightened. Your name will never be mentioned. If you know anything, you've got to tell me."

Diana could almost feel the man making his decision, weighing whatever odds he felt needed to be weighed. And then he spoke. "I only recognized one of them," he said, his voice stronger than it was moments before. "And I'll be damned if he's going to intimidate me any longer."

Diana was riveted. She leaned forward in her seat. "What are you talking about, Billy? Who's trying to intimidate you?"

"Mario De Cicco," the man said. "The Mob boss. He and his friends came just after Mr. Parker's first guest left with all those folders. He told me that if anyone learned he was at Redman

333

Place, he'd make me and my family regret it for the rest of our lives."

\* \* \*

From his van on 59th Street, Spocatti waited for Diana Crane to hang up her telephone before he removed his headphones and sat in thought. He carefully dissected the possibilities he now was faced with, tossed around a few ideas and then made his decision.

He rose from his seat at the rear of the van and moved forward, toward the front of the van, where he reached for his cell phone and dialed Louis Ryan's private number.

While he waited for Ryan to answer to the line, he listened to the traffic rushing past him outside. It occurred to him that this assignment was drawing to an end. His time in Manhattan was growing short. For his own safety, for his own protection, he knew that he would soon have to implement a series of plans that would not only alter the future Louis Ryan planned for George Redman, his family and the Redman empire, but which also would assure himself of a safe departure.

While Redman and his family would indeed die after the fall of Redman International, it wouldn't be as Louis Ryan planned.

Ryan answered the line. Spocatti told him everything that had happened during the last twenty minutes in Diana Crane's apartment. He told him what had to be done. It was a moment before Louis responded. "And you're certain this will work," he said.

"Absolutely certain?" Spocatti said. He was delighted by the tension in Ryan's voice. "There are no certainties, Louis. But I can promise you this--if you want Redman International to crumble, if you want Redman to burn for what he did to your wife, then this is the way to go. There's no other choice."

## CHAPTER FORTY-FOUR

"Eric was murdered," Diana said. "I'm sure of it."

Jack sat at the edge of Diana's desk. As she told him the details of her conversation with Billy, the doorman, he couldn't help feeling that they were at the threshold of a series of revelations that ultimately would lead them to the person responsible for Celina's death.

"Where is Billy now?" he asked.

"In the lobby. He goes on break in fifteen minutes. I asked him to come here when he clocks out."

"You don't think he'll run, do you?"

"I doubt it," she said. "Now, more than ever, he needs help." She looked at him. "We're it."

Satisfied, Jack watched her reach inside her desk for a pen and pad of paper. She began to write. "What are you doing?" he asked.

"Before we call George, I want to have my facts straight, so give me a minute to write them down and we'll talk when I'm finished."

Jack left the desk and moved to the window across the room that overlooked Central Park. The sky was darkening, rain was threatening. The wind blew smartly through the trees, causing their leaves to turn upwards, exposing a paler shade of green.

Diana dropped the pen onto the desk.

"Why?" she said. "Why would Mario De Cicco want to kill Eric? It makes no sense."

Jack looked away from the window. The last time he heard mention of Mario De Cicco's name was the night Eric was beaten. He told Diana this.

"Celina and Leana were there? Why didn't they do something?"

"I assume it was because you were handling the situation."

"Handling the situation?" Diana said. "I'd just been beaten. I was no more handling the situation than they were." And then it occurred to her how odd it was that Leana was there. "Was Leana alone?" she asked.

"She was with two men."

"What did they look like?"

"That was a while ago, Diana."

She stared at him.

"I don't know," he said. "A couple of brutes. Black pants and black shirts."

Diana's mind flashed back to that evening. The two men who burst into Eric's bedroom were wearing black.

"When Celina called out her sister's name, they led Leana away," he said. "It was then that she said Mario De Cicco's name."

Diana leaned back in her chair. "Two years ego, Leana had an affair with De Cicco. She came to my office one afternoon and told me that she was in love with him. I've always liked Leana. And I've always hated how George treats her. I think she senses this. We aren't friends, but over the years she would ask for my advice, or she'd drop in to say hello. I don't know why she ever confided in me about her affair with De Cicco, but she did. Maybe she needed a sounding board. She doesn't have many friends."

"Was De Cicco in love with her?"

"No idea," Diana said. "I told her to stay away from him, but she wouldn't listen to me, as if that's a surprise. Leana doesn't listen to anybody."

"Do you think she's behind this?"

"I wouldn't rule it out," Diana said. "Yesterday, Eric told me that he and Leana almost slept with one another the night of Redman International's opening. He told me that someone must have tipped Celina off to them, because she walked into the room and caught them in bed together." She was quiet for a moment. "If Eric thought that person was Leana, there's no telling what he'd do to her--or what he did to her, for that matter."

"Like threatening her?"

"Maybe."

"If he did and she went to De Cicco for help, there's no telling what he'd do to Eric."

It sounded plausible, but Diana knew better than to work on whims. "It's a possibility," she said. "And that's all we've got--a

possibility. At the very least, George should know what we know."
She glanced at her watch. "Billy should be here in a few minutes.
Let's call George now."

She reached for the phone just as it rang. Diana answered it.
"It's Billy, Ms. Crane. A Mr. Timothy Parker is here to see you.
Shall I show him up?"

\* \* \*

Jack followed Diana out of the room and down the winding
staircase.

"You know Eric's younger brother?" he asked.

Diana nodded. "He's studying law at Yale. This summer he's
taking a course on constitutional law and I've been helping him
over the phone with his dissents. Eric's parents are in their 80s
and Tim probably came in their place to tend to Eric."

They moved toward the foyer.

"Why would he be coming to you?"

Diana shrugged. "Tim knows Eric and I were seeing each
other. I'm sure he knows what happened to Celina and thought
that here was the logical place to come before going to the
morgue." She sensed what Jack was thinking, and said: "Don't
worry--he won't stay long. The moment he leaves, we're calling
George."

There was a tap at the door. Diana wondered how she would
comfort Eric's younger brother when she herself hadn't dealt with
Eric's death. Deciding there was no best way, she turned the
handle--and stumbled back when the door was kicked open.

Diana tipped over a side table and went down like a ten pin.
Her head cracked against the slate floor. Her arm twisted
painfully behind her.

The man who stormed inside was not Timothy Parker. This
man was tall and dark, his features chiseled, black hair gleaming.

As Jack rushed forward to help Diana, the intruder shut the
door behind him and removed a gun from his inside jacket
pocket. He pressed it against Jack's forehead.

As cool steel met flesh, their eyes met.

337

# FIFTH AVENUE

Vincent Spocatti cocked the trigger.
Recognition flashed across Jack Douglas' face.
This man was Celina's murderer.

## CHAPTER FORTY-FIVE

The secretary tried, but couldn't stop Leana as she sailed past the woman's desk and stepped into Louis Ryan's office. Her hair and clothes were wet from the rain now beating the streets.

Startled, Ryan turned from the windows he was standing at, faced Leana and waved away the secretary as she rushed inside. "It's all right, Judy," he said. "Leana's always welcome."

The secretary looked with annoyance at Leana, then closed the door on her way out.

Louis began moving across the room, toward his private bath that was behind one of the doors to his left. "You're soaking wet"" he said. "Let me get you a towel so you can dry off."

Leana ran a hand through her hair as she watched him go. She was still trying to forget the argument she had with her father, but it was impossible. She had gone to see her parents with the best intentions and in spite of her mother's surprising embrace, she left with them shattered.

*We'll never be close*, she kept thinking. *He hates me.*

But that didn't mean she couldn't help find Celina's murderer.

She knew her father had exhausted his huge network of contacts, applied pressure to where it would be most effective, but he didn't have the kind of contacts she had. He didn't have access to the enormous underworld of power that was available to her. Her contacts were among the most powerful men in New York.

"I'm sorry for barging in like this," she called. "But I need to talk to you."

Ryan emerged from the bathroom with a thick, pale blue towel draped over his arm. With a sympathetic face, he came over to where she was standing and handed it to her. "I've been trying to reach you since I learned the news," he said. "There's been no answer at your apartment or on your cell. I'm sorry for what happened to your sister, Leana."

Leana patted her face with the towel. Later, she would tell him that he couldn't reach her because had been in Monte Carlo, marrying Michael Archer. Now, there was something more important she had to discuss with him.

"Celina is why I'm here," she said. "I want you to help me find the man who murdered her. You've got power, Louis. You've got contacts. Together, with my father, we'll find out who did this."

Ryan looked at her, but made no move to speak.

"I need you," Leana said. "Please help me."

Louis sighed. "You're asking me to help George Redman."

She expected resistance and was prepared for it. "In a way, I am," she said. "But I'm really asking you to help me and to help my sister. If you won't, Louis, then I'm afraid I can't work for you. I won't be at the opening of The Hotel Fifth."

She handed him the towel, which he tossed into the bathroom. He shut the door.

"We both know that's what you want," she said. "I'm not stupid. I understand the situation. You want my presence recorded by the press. You want to make my father a laughingstock. Right now, a part of me wants the same. If you still want this to happen, then I'm asking you to help me."

Louis' eyes softened. "Leana," he said, "regardless of how I feel toward your father, I would never have wanted this to happen to him or to you. What happened to your sister is a tragedy. Whoever's responsible should pay with his own life."

He was sincere. She could hear it in his voice, see it on his face and it surprised her. "Then you'll help me?" she said. "You'll do what you can?"

Ryan raised his head as if to study her. "Of course, I'll help you."

Leana thanked him and turned to leave.

"Before you leave, I'd like to talk to you about opening night. It's only two days from now and we haven't discussed it yet. I know this isn't a good time, but can you give me a minute?"

Leana hesitated. "Of course," she said.

"The invitations were sent out last week," Louis said. "And we've had a tremendous response. Everyone who matters in Manhattan and various parts of the world will be there--along with the press. They'll be expecting a speech of some sort."

Leana balked. "Louis, I'll be frank with you. I'll go to the opening party, as promised, and I'll mingle with the crowd as you want me to, but I really doubt I'll have the time or the concentration to write a speech--let alone the energy to deliver one. My sister is dead. Someone is out to destroy my family."

"The speech already is written," Louis said. "Zack Anderson wrote it. It's brief. It stays on point. People will sympathize with you. It strikes just the right tone. I've already approved it. Zack is preparing a final copy for your inspection."

Leana cringed at the idea of having to deal with her assistant, Zack Anderson. One of her first duties as manager would be to fire him. "And if I don't like it?" she asked.

"Then make whatever changes you want. You're the manager of this hotel, Leana. The floor is yours."

"All right," Leana said. "I'll do it. But one other thing. I'm going to need security. Can you provide me with that? There's no telling who will be in that crowd, or who might slip in. I want to be protected."

"I've already taken care of that," Louis said. "The building will be covered in surveillance. There will be men and women in evening wear who are there to trail you and protect you. You'll note guards around the room and at all entrances--and so will everyone else." He paused. "But beyond that, one of my best men has been assigned to you. He will be with you the entire night."

\* \* \*

When she left Ryan's office, she stood beneath a canopy on 47th Street, removed her cell phone from her handbag and punched numbers.

Curtains of rain were billowing down the avenue, lashing the cars and the crowds on the sidewalk, striking the buildings with peppered force. Finally, a man answered. "Mario's," the voice said.

"This is Leana Archer," she said. "I need to speak to Mario."

"Who is this?"

He didn't recognize her married name. "Leana Redman," she said, shouting above the howling wind. "I need to speak to Mario. Is he in?"

"Mario's out," the man said. "You missed him."

"This is important," Leana said. "Do you know where he went?"

But the man knew nothing.

* * *

As the limousine slowed in front of the brick warehouse, Harold Baines finished injecting the last bit of heroin into the exhausted flesh of his left forearm. He removed the needle from the scarred, swollen vein, and noticed that not one drop of blood leaked to stain his wax-like skin. Although the vein was plump, it was as though it had dried up, becoming nothing more than a purplish cord.

It was pouring, the rain literally beating against the roof of the car. As the drug gradually began turning his world into the illusion in which he found peace, Harold looked through the side window and up at the decrepit warehouse.

Glimmering in the rain, it seemed to beckon to him, this building with its rotting bricks and broken facade. Shining, it seemed to offer him some solace within its crumbling walls.

Along the street, several other limousines were parked, their engines idling. Harold checked his watch, squinted to see the time and reached for the briefcase on the seat beside him. He tapped a knuckle against the tinted glass that separated passenger from driver and the glass receded. "I'll be a while," he said. "But I want you to wait. I may leave early."

The driver nodded.

Bracing himself for the rain, Harold fled the car and began racing across the slick pavement. The water splashed at his feet. It drenched his shoes. By the time he reached the building's entrance, his clothes were soaked and he was out of breath, the nests of veins at his temples beating as rapidly as the wings of small birds.

The door he now stood before was parted slightly, revealing a darkness that was occasionally interrupted by flashes of blue light. Threading through the music that hammered down to him from the floors above, he could hear what sounded like crowds of people. Harold looked behind him, through the tumultuous rain, aware that Louis Ryan might have had him followed again, but not caring. No harm could befall him now. Harold was invincible.

Inside, his briefcase was accepted by a man in a gorilla suit, who then handed it to a naked woman sheathed in plastic wrap, who then placed it on the floor alongside several other briefcases. A man with a hose up his ass checked the contents and nodded at the gorilla.

Harold caught the nod, but he couldn't look away from the sizable penis jutting between the woman's legs. Smiling, the woman motioned to the stairs behind him. "There's a great crowd," she said, in a voice that was unnaturally deep. "One of the best I've seen."

Harold climbed the stairs as quickly as he could, wanting to put distance between them. He rarely spoke to anyone at these clubs. He usually just chose to watch, sometimes electing to perform. Although he felt sure some of the members recognized him from cocktail parties on Fifth or Park, it was better to assume they didn't--and remain one of the anonymous shadows that moved along the darkened walls.

Winded, he reached the main floor. As he stepped through an arched doorway and entered the cavernous room, his very essence breathing in the dim surroundings, he joined the line of people removing their clothes at the clothes check.

He listened. Executives from Wall Street were talking about which firms to avoid. Somebody was talking about the bargains available now in real estate. A woman in a Dior suit and thigh-high trucker boots was talking about her recent marriage and saying to a friend that her new husband knew nothing of this. "He has his sports, I have my water sports." They laughed.

Harold heard it all, but none of it really registered. He was removing his shirt when he spotted the young man.

Tall and dark, his body hardened by what must have been ruthless workouts, the man looked twice at Harold as he strolled past him. Harold caught his gaze, held it for an instant, and thought that he was beautiful.

The man leaned against a metal cage. Dark eyes gleaming, penis stiffening, he looked hard at Harold and enticed him with a half-smile. Watching him now and admiring his physique, Harold became painfully aware of his own body--so thin now, such a vague shadow of his former youth--as his clothes dropped from him like dead skin from an aged snake. He gave his clothes to the clothes check, held out the back of his hand, and the number "258" was promptly written on it in black Magic Marker.

"Now have some fun," the clothes check said, and she smiled a smile that had ceased being a smile. It was a smile that reflected desperation and loneliness. It was a smile life had eaten away.

Harold knew that smile and put his own face to it. He thought fleetingly of Celina then, knew that because of his own cowardice she was dead, and he was struck once again by a wave of self-hatred.

Shoving the thought to the back of his mind, determined not to deal with it because, in reality, it would kill his high, he approached the young man leaning against the metal cage. Music pounded through every pore of his body. The young man's smile broadened as Harold neared him.

And then Harold was being kissed by him. A tongue ran along the curve of his lips, and slipped between them. He felt a hand grasp his hand and lead it to the hardness between the man's legs. Harold opened his eyes and saw that the young man's eyes were closed. He could tell he was caught up in the moment and so he kissed him back. He squeezed the man's cock harder and was delighted by its size. Wrist thick and uncut. Harold dropped to his knees and put it in his mouth. The man moaned.

Harold worked on it. "Give it to me," he said. "Give me your load."

The man pressed down on Harold's head. He face fucked him, ignoring the choking sounds, and then he jammed all eleven inches down Harold's throat.

Harold pressed his hands on the man's things and shook his head. He couldn't breathe. The man began violently fucking his mouth. Harold pushed against the man's thighs, but the pounding became more intense. He was frightened and turned on at the same time. He was on the verge of passing out when the man stopped and lifted Harold to his feet.

His face was wet with saliva. The room spun.

"Why don't we get out of here?" the man said in Harold's ear. "Why don't we go to my place, where it's more private? I have a room full with toys this place hasn't even heard of yet."

* * *

The limousine hurtled through traffic.

As time passed and the city sped by, Harold's mind became clear. No longer were his senses cushioned by the heroin he injected earlier; no longer was his conscience quieted by the torrent of drugs.

Tomorrow morning, he would be expected to attend his best friend's daughter's funeral. Tomorrow afternoon, he would be expected to board a plane that would leave for Iran--a country that, because of him, held no future for Redman International.

How many other funerals would he have to attend in the coming weeks? How many other people would die because he had refused to speak up?

The need struck him then.

He opened the liquor cabinet, removed the black leather satchel and unzipped it, exposing the used syringe, the half-empty vial of heroin. He glanced at the young man seated beside him, looked briefly at that beautiful face and saw a world of promise shining in the liquid blue eyes. What was his name? Derrick?

"You want some of this?" he said. "You want--"

The man gripped his arm. "Don't do it," he said. "That shit killed a friend of mine. It'll fuck you up."

Harold couldn't help laughing. Did this boy know what he was saying? "I'm already fucked up," he said. "Now, let go of my arm."

But the man was prying the satchel out of Harold's hands. He lowered the window beside him and tossed it out.

Horrified, Harold watched it fade into the driving rain. "What the hell's wrong with you?" he shouted, more out of fear than anger. "What's wrong with you!"

The man bent to his knees and unzipped Harold's fly. "Let me give you a real high."

345

# FIFTH AVENUE

* * *

They arrived at a modest-looking brownstone on 12th Street.

As the car came to a stop at the curbside, Derrick lifted his head from Harold's lap and looked out a side window. "We're here," he said to Harold. "Come on. We'll be more comfortable inside."

Harold looked at the brownstone in surprise--it was beautiful. Although it was still raining, the sun had broken through the clouds and it now shined against the building's narrow brick facade. "You live here?" he said.

"That's right."

"What do you do for work?"

There was an uncomfortable silence. "Look," the man said. "I like to be discreet. You don't know me and I don't know you. We'll have a good time--that I can promise--but that's as far as it's ever going to go. Is that cool?"

Harold wanted him. He nodded.

They left the car.

Inside, the house was large and warm and smelled of roses in their prime. His interest piqued, Harold stepped further into the spacious foyer and saw vases filled with flowers, side tables by Chippendale, paintings tiling the walls.

He knew something was wrong even before Derrick locked the door behind them. This man could never afford such opulence, could never afford an original Matisse.

Turning, about to protest, Harold heard the sound of a door being shut behind him and footsteps clicking on parquet.

"Nice work, Derrick," he heard a man say. "Is he clean?"

"He's clean," Derrick said. "I tossed out the heroin myself."

"Excellent. See Nicky on your way out and he'll give you the money we agreed upon."

A chill enveloped Harold's heart. Knowing he had been set up, he looked quickly behind him and came face to face with Mario De Cicco.

## CHAPTER FORTY-SIX

Fragrant ribbons of steam curled from the silver coffeepot and lifted into the stale, smoky air. Lucia De Cicco crossed her legs and looked with annoyance at the uniformed maid as she bent over the table and poured the hot liquid into two porcelain cups.

She wanted to be alone with Mario's father. She wanted to speak to him in private. She willed this woman to go away.

"Will there be anything else, Mr. De Cicco?"

Antonio De Cicco gave the young lady such a surprisingly suggestive smile, that Lucia immediately became suspicious of their relationship.

"No, Gloria," he said. "That's all for now."

The woman left the room.

De Cicco leaned forward in his seat, chose one of the cups from the silver coffee service and lifted it to his lips. They were in the library of his Todt Hill mansion and the smoke from his ever-present cigar was beginning to make Lucia's eyes burn.

She looked at the man seated before her. He was amazing, really. Dressed immaculately in a gray suit, his face tanned from hours in the sun, the man was pushing seventy years old--and yet he looked fifty.

Ashamed of his meager beginnings in Sicily--and as vain as any person could be--Antonio De Cicco worked hard to look as professional and as educated as any man hustling on Wall Street. In repose, the illusion worked. But when he spoke, his fifth-grade education became embarrassingly apparent.

"You gonna have coffee?" he asked.

Lucia shook her head. She toyed with the diamond brooch fastened to the lapel of her white linen blazer and said, "We have to talk."

"I gathered that the other night when you called and said we needed to talk."

His humor was not lost on her. She smiled even though she was tense.

"I'm sorry we couldn't have talked then, but things have been pretty busy around here," he said. "So, what's the problem?"

Lucia gauged her words carefully. "It's Mario," she said. "He's sleeping with Leana Redman again. I'm sure of it."

De Cicco studied her. "Lucia," he said. "Lucia, where do you get these crazy ideas? Mario's no fool. He knows I'd kill the broad if he ever pulled that shit. We already talked."

"I don't care what he knows," she said. "It's the truth. When I called you Friday night, he'd just left to meet her at one of his damned shelters. He admitted it to me, Uncle Tony. He said that if I told you, if any harm came to him or Leana, he'd make me regret it for the rest of my life."

"Mario said this?"

Lucia nodded. "He frightened me."

"You got any proof he's fuckin' with her?"

"No. But I know he is. She calls all the time and he hasn't touched me in months. I go to bed alone and wake to find him in the guest bedroom. I'm fighting for my marriage and he seems determined to end it. Can't you do something?"

De Cicco drew on his cigar. He'd known this woman since she was a child. He loved her as if she were his own daughter. There was a threat against her life and yet she had left the safety of her home and come here to ask him for his help. Although he wasn't entirely convinced Mario was sleeping with Leana--hadn't the woman just married Michael Archer?--he would at least consider Lucia's request.

"What do you want me to do?" he asked.

Lucia's eyes darkened. "I want you to kill her," she said evenly. "I want you to kill her so Mario and I can start over."

De Cicco didn't blink. "And how would you want this done?"

"That I'll leave up to you," she said. "But I do know this--on Tuesday night, she'll be at the grand opening of The Hotel Fifth. I've been following the story in the Daily News, and she's almost sure to make a speech. She's the manager of the hotel."

De Cicco watched her intently.

"The world will be there," she said.

"So will security."

"You can handle security. It'll be one of her proudest moments." She knew that would get him. "Perhaps then...?"

# FIFTH AVENUE

* * *

The woman who strolled down 12th Street certainly looked like a mother.

Dressed casually in faded jeans and an oversized plaid shirt, her dark hair pulled away from an angular face, she pushed the pink carriage down the sidewalk and cooed to a baby that was non-existent. As she strolled, she carefully avoiding the bumps in the cement--knowing that any sudden, jarring movement could cause herself--and the area surrounding her--to explode into nothingness.

The rain had stopped and she was thankful for that. Spocatti didn't give her an alternative plan of action. If the sky hadn't cleared, she wasn't sure how she would have executed this plan-- and yet that was not entirely true. She was a highly trained operational agent and had complete confidence in that training. She would have found a way. Spocatti knew it.

She moved against the breeze, ducking beneath the sun-dappled trees. Her mind was sharp and focused. Her eyes were hidden behind dark glasses.

She could see them across the street, standing outside the attractive brownstone, guarding its entrance with their oversized bodies. There were two of them, just as she knew there would be, and both were young, handsome, their guns shielded by long, black raincoats.

They were idiots. They could not harm her. She would crush them.

Ahead was his car.

Parked at the curbside, the black Taurus seemed to call out to her, shining in the late-morning sun. The limousine idling beside it was an unexpected surprise that she welcomed. Its presence would help block their view when she ducked beside Mario's car, which now was less than twenty yards away.

As she neared it, the men on the steps glanced at one another, said something she couldn't hear and started watching. Cooing, humming softly to the explosives hidden in the carriage, she looked down the street and saw an elderly couple sitting on a

349

bench at the end of it. Besides herself, these men and the limousine's chauffeur, they were the only other people in sight.

She pushed forward--aware that the men had moved down the steps and were now watching her. Timing was everything.

As she approached the car, she reached into the carriage as if to adjust a blanket or a bottle, but instead tossed out one of the four stuffed animals that encompassed the pink satin interior, making it look as though a child had done it. The stuffed elephant hit the curb, bounced and rolled to a stop beside the Taurus' rear right wheel.

The woman stopped and looked crossly into the carriage. "Jillian," she said, her voice carrying across the street. "That's twice. If you keep throwing your toys out of the carriage, they're going to get ruined. Behave or we're going home."

One of the men laughed. The woman looked past the Taurus, over the limousine's shiny black roof and smiled at him. She was beautiful when she smiled.

"My kid is going to wear me out," she said.

The man mistook that as an invitation. He started across the street, leaving his friend at the base of the stairs. "I love 'em," he said. "How old is she?"

Her gun was within reaching distance, hidden beneath the mattress. As with every job she took, she came prepared to die. If she had to, she would fight him to the death--confident that if she lost, her own child, far away from here, would inherit the money Spocatti already had secured for her in a Swiss account.

"Eighteen months," she said, her smile unwavering. "And it looks as though she's got her father's strength." The man passed the limo and her hand went easily for the gun. If he came much closer, he would see there was no baby in the carriage.

His friend stepped onto the street. He raised his hands and his raincoat parted, exposing the gun nestled closely to his chest.

"Yo!" he said. "Come on, man. What the fuck you doin'? Get your ass over here and leave the lady alone. Mario will be pissed if he catches you over there."

The man stopped and looked hard at his friend.

"You know Mrs. De Cicco's gonna be home soon," his friend said. "You know she's paranoid about security. She'll bust your nuts if she sees you talkin' to that broad. Do yourself a favor and get the hell back over here."

She could feel the man weighing his decision--lose face and rejoin his friend, or say to hell with it and sneak a look at the kid. Their eyes met. And he shrugged.

"Sorry," he said. "Maybe some other time, okay?"

When she smiled at him, her smile was lit from within.

As he turned his back to her, she released the gun and gripped the small, magnetized black box from beneath the pink blanket.

It was over in a matter of seconds.

She bent to pick up the elephant, attached the box to the Taurus' gas tank and flipped the switch that activated it. When De Cicco started the car, the sudden vibration would trigger the explosives.

She stood and looked directly at the men. The elephant had landed in a puddle and was now swollen with dirty water. She held it up for them to see. "Can you believe this?" she called. "I bought it for her yesterday afternoon and now it's ruined. Kids!"

\* \* \*

In his study, Mario stood at the large casement window facing 12th Street, noted a woman moving down the street with a carriage and continued listening to Harold Baines, who was sitting behind him, his words coming in a rush.

Nothing Baines said was a surprise.

He knew that Louis Ryan was somehow behind what was happening to the Redman family. He knew it the moment Leana told him Ryan offered her a job thanks to Harold's help.

Earlier that morning, Mario learned that World Enterprises was the foreign subsidiary of Manhattan Enterprises. Earlier, he learned that thin scribble was actually Louis Ryan's name on that $90 million check made out to Eric Parker. The only thing Mario questioned was Ryan's intent. Why did he want to destroy George Redman and his family? What happened between the two men to spark such rage?

And then Baines told him.

# FIFTH AVENUE

Years ago, George took Louis to court and sued him over a bitter property dispute. Louis won--only to see his wife die two days later under suspicious circumstances. Ryan believed it was Redman who killed his wife, Anne. It was possible, Harold said, that Louis had waited all these years to get his own revenge so George would not suspect him.

Mario turned from the window and faced Baines. Although the man was pale, his body frightfully thin beneath his loose-fitting suit, he seemed somewhat relaxed, as if sharing the truth of what he knew was lifting a weight from him.

"Did George kill Louis' wife?"

"No," Harold said firmly. "George would never have killed Anne."

Mario cocked an eyebrow at him. "Why do you say it like that?" he asked. "Did she mean something to him?"

Harold said he wasn't sure. "For years, I've wondered the same thing, but I never knew Anne. George mentioned her in the past, but he's never elaborated on their relationship."

Legs unsteady, he stood. "Look," he said. "I'm tired and I've told you everything I know. I assume you'll see to it that Ryan pays for what he's done? That you'll protect Leana and her parents?"

Mario nodded. By the end of the day, Louis Ryan would be dead. "You have my word," he said.

Satisfied, Harold moved to the door--but then he stopped and turned. "One thing still troubles me," he said. "For years I did my best to hide who I am. I thought no one ever would find out--and yet you did this morning. How did you know?"

"You sure you want to know?"

"No," Harold said. "But tell me, anyway."

"Leana told me two years ago," he said. "Somebody photographed you at a club, gave Leana a call and approached her with the negatives. She sold a piece of jewelry, met the son of a bitch at a diner and paid a million bucks for them. I later had him quieted. We burned the negatives together. Leana got her money back, Harold. Because of her, you got to keep your secret."

Harold was barely breathing.

"She's known for years, Harold. And she's never stopped loving you. I want you to think about that. That's how special she is."

"I know how special she is."

There was a knock at the door. Startled, Harold stepped away from it just as Joseph Stewart, the Family's consigliere, walked through. "Got some real interesting news for you, Mario," he said. "It's about Leana." He glanced sideways at Harold. "Mind if he listens?"

Mario said that he didn't.

Stewart continued. "I've done some digging and I've learned quite a bit about Leana's new husband. Seems Michael Archer's just his pen name. His real name is Michael Ryan, and his father's name is Louis."

And there it was.

Mario drew a breath and his mind spun into motion. The blood drained from Harold's face. "We're going to have to move fast," Stewart said. "There's no telling what he has planned for her."

"Anyone else know about this?" Mario asked.

"No," Stewart said. "Just us."

Mario left his office and moved quickly down the long hallway. His face was leaden and set. He hesitated only briefly when he saw Lucia standing in the entryway, closing the door behind her with a firmness that suggested irritation. "Whose limo is parked out front?" she called to no one in particular. "It's blocking the street."

She hadn't seen him yet and Mario didn't answer. He had no time for his wife or for her questions. If there was another exit near him, he would have grabbed Stewart and taken off.

The carpet ended and their shoes now clicked on parquet as they entered the foyer. Lucia turned from the mirror she was standing at and she looked at him, her lips parting when she saw the cold determination in his eyes.

"Where are you going?" she asked.

Mario shoved a finger at her. "Stay out of this."

She took a step forward, blocked his path. "You don't intimidate me," she said. "Something's wrong. Tell me where you're going."

There was a moment of complete silence, a moment when neither moved or even blinked...and then Harold Baines was stepping past them.

Lucia looked at the man, her eyes widening as she recognized him. When it was announced that Leana Redman would be managing Louis Ryan's new hotel, the Daily News ran several pictures of her. In one of those pictures, her arm was around this man's shoulders.

She looked at Mario, her eyes like a light turned to his face. "It's Leana again, isn't it?" she said.

He walked past her. "We'll talk later," he said. "Not now."

He moved down the narrow brick steps, squinting in the harsh sunlight. He noticed that Harold Baines was gone. His limousine turned at the end of the street and sped onto Fifth. Reaching into his pants pocket, Mario removed his car keys and tossed them to Stewart, who was waiting on the sidewalk, looking behind Mario, toward the open door.

Lucia was standing there. "I've been with your father, Mario." Her voice was low and even and carried across the street. "He knows everything."

Mario's pace slowed.

"I told him you're fucking her," she said. "He said he'd kill her if you don't stop."

Mario looked at Stewart and saw the cool neutrality on his face. "Start the car, Joe," he said. "I'll be a minute."

Lucia came down the stairs. "No, you won't, Mario," she said. "Because neither of you is going anywhere. If Joe gets into that car, I'll see to it that he winds up in the Hudson. That's a promise. Now, come back inside."

Stewart's mouth tightened into a splinter of hate. He looked at Mario.

"You work for me now, Joe," Mario said. "Start the car."

Relishing the moment because he never liked this Lucia bitch, Stewart crossed the street, opened the Taurus' heavy black door and stepped inside.

And then Lucia was suddenly running toward him, sprinting across the street, plunging her hands through the open car window, grabbing hold of his arm with a fierceness that was surprising in its strength. Her long red fingernails dug into his flesh.

"Get out of the car!" she screamed. "Get out of fucking car or I'll kill you myself!"

Stewart jerked his arm free, the fabric of his gray blazer tearing. He looked across the street at Mario, who was running a hand through his hair. "Let it go, Lucia," Stewart said. "It's over."

He stuck the key into the ignition.

Lucia slapped at his face. She clawed at it and drew blood. He tried to push her off and heard Mario shout her name.

And then he started the car.

The explosion catapulted the Taurus twenty feet into the air, blowing off its doors and tires and fenders, causing it to flip in a violent somersault and destroy everything in its fiery path before it landed beside Mario, whose chest had been struck by the flying debris.

\* \* \*

At the subway terminal on West 4th Street, Harold waited for his limousine to fade from sight before he joined the crush of people hurrying down the terminal's seemingly endless steps.

He tried to keep up with them, clutching the handrail for support, but he nearly fell when a group of teenagers darted past him. It was difficult and it was exhausting, but it would be worth it.

By the time he reached the lower level, he was winded and perspiring, his heart beating dangerously fast. The train hadn't arrived. Groups of people were either leaning against the tiled columns or waiting impatiently along the cement precipice. It was insufferably hot. The air was unmoving. He hadn't taken the subway in years. He'd forgotten how ruthless it was in the summer.

He found an opening in the crowd, moved toward it and looked down at the grimy track. His stomach clenched when he saw a rat. Its tail flicking nervously, its ears quivering, the rat was eating the remains of a what appeared to be a dead cat.

Harold looked away. He wouldn't miss this city. He wouldn't miss this filth.

He closed his eyes and thought of Leana. She had known. All these years and she had known, her love for him never faltering. The idea that she had seen photographs of him made him want to cry in humiliation. How many times had she seen him and thought of those pictures? How many times had she held him and felt pity?

There was a sudden stir in the humid air. The cement floor vibrated and the people leaning against the columns became alert and moved forward.

Harold glanced down at the track and watched the rat disappear beneath a wooden tie, its grayish tail slipping from sight.

He thought of Louis Ryan then and wondered what would happen to the man once Mario De Cicco got hold of him. *I hope he cuts his throat*, Harold thought. *I hope he rips out his heart, crushes it in his hands....*

He trusted De Cicco in a way that surprised him.

Harold knew the Redmans would be safe in De Cicco's hands. He knew that Mario would protect them in a way that he hadn't. A part of him almost wished he would be here to witness tomorrow morning's headlines.

There was a rush of wind as the train charged into the tunnel. Looming into view, it bore down hard on the crowd.

Harold watched the train storm toward him and welcomed its presence with a certain bitterness. Three days ago he had tested positive for HIV. His heroin and cocaine addiction was out of control. He knew that even if Ryan died, the tape the man blackmailed him with would somehow resurface and fall into the hands of the press, thus embarrassing himself even further while destroying his family.

It was better this way. There was nothing left for him in this world.

The train was close.

He thought of Helen and his children, but mostly he thought of Leana. He loved her. He would miss her most. In his will, he had left her half of everything.

Just as the train was about to pass him, he welcomed its presence and jumped.

And in that moment before the train struck, Harold heard the stunned, primal cries of a society that had refused to let him be himself--a group of hypocrites taking a collective breath and then letting loose one monstrous scream.  The bastards wanted him to live!

Furious, Harold wanted to scream at them, tell them what an outrage it was that he had to live a life of lies, that he had never been given the chance they took for granted--that chance to be who he was without ridicule or fear, without pain or humiliation.

But when the train struck and rolled over him, severing him, his voice was crushed, silenced like so many before him, becoming nothing more than a wet, clotted gasp as his body was sliced into quarters.

## CHAPTER FORTY-SEVEN

Jack Douglas kept himself in check, but his anger was rising, becoming paramount, consuming him in waves.

He was on a sofa. Diana was at his side. He looked at the man seated opposite them. He had murdered Celina and now he would probably murder them. Jack wished, just wished that he could have the chance to show this son of a bitch what real fear was.

"It's remarkable, really," the man said. Earlier, he had introduced himself as Spocatti, merely Spocatti, and now he was sipping a drink he had Diana fix for him at the bar. In his other hand was a gun. It was pointed at Jack. "I mean, the way you pieced everything together." He cocked his head at Diana. "If I hadn't wired your apartment, I wouldn't have known what you two were up to today. Louis Ryan and I probably would be in jail."

He lifted his glass of Scotch. His eyes flashed. "To technology," he said, and drank.

Jack sensed the storm building within Diana. Although she hurt her head and arm when she fell, he saw no pain on her face, only a mixture of anger, hatred and disgust. He reached for her hand and squeezed it. "Don't."

Diana released her hand and glared at Spocatti. "Why are you here?"

The sun came from behind a cloud and Spocatti's face burst into brilliant bloom. He was still for a moment, the light refracting in his eyes, before he rose and went to the bar, where he put down his glass and turned to Jack. "Celina put up quite a struggle," he said, ignoring Diana's question. "She was hitting me so hard with her fists, I thought I'd never get that damned rope tied around her legs." He paused, as if in thought. "When I was swimming away, I heard her scream. Did you?"

The sound of Celina's muffled cry echoed hollowly in Jack's mind. He had a sudden image of her sightless eyes, her slack jaw

358

and realized once again that he had been only moments too late to save her.

"At the time," Spocatti said, "I thought how ridiculous that was--to scream and release all the air from her lungs." He shook his head, as if her actions had been inappropriate. "What she did was ridiculous. But, then, she never was as bright as the press led us to believe, was she, Mr. Douglas? Just another dumb blonde who happened to hit it big thanks to pappy."

Jack looked at the gun clutched in the man's hand and knew that if he made a sudden move, he would be shot and killed-- leaving him unable to help the Redmans and powerless to help Diana. He bit down hard on his anger and bided his time. Something would give. It had to.

Spocatti returned to his seat. "Your parents live in Florida, don't they, Jack? West Palm?"

Jack lifted his eyes to him.

"I've got a friend of my own in that area and gave him a call before I visited you. Nice place, West Palm. Your parents must have saved their nickels over the years and tucked away a little money for the future." He smiled. "If you've spent your life sweating at a Pittsburgh steel mill, like your father did, you don't move to West Palm unless you've been careful with your money."

His voice lowered a notch. "My friend paid them a visit, Jack. He says their home is beautiful--wide open and airy. He thought your mother was particularly nice. My friend was seeking directions and she was happy to help him. Gotta love the blue-collar elderly."

The anger Jack felt was like a pain in his chest. A thousand thoughts spun through his mind--but only one mattered and that was his parents' safety. "Have you hurt them?" he asked.

Spocatti looked affronted. "Hurt them?" he said. "That's the very last thing I want to do." He glanced at his watch, then at the phone that was on the table beside Jack. "Why don't you give them a call?" he said. "See for yourself if they're all right."

And in that moment, Jack knew they wouldn't be all right. He reached for the phone and dialed. The line rang several times before his mother answered. "Yes?" she said. Her voice was strained.

"Mom, it's Jack. Is everything all right?"

She burst into tears.

Jack closed his eyes and saw himself tearing Spocatti apart. "Listen to me, Mom. You're going to have to calm down. Do you hear me? Tell me what's wrong."

She spoke through sobs. "A man broke into our house."

"What man?"

"I don't know!" Her voice was shrill. "We thought you'd know. He's sitting beside your father. He has a gun. He said if you don't do what he wants, he'll kill us."

"That's not going to happen," Jack said. "You and Dad will be safe. Do you understand me? You'll be safe. I promise."

"He's hurt your father," she said. "He punched him in the face. He's going to kill us. You have to do whatever he wants." Before Jack could respond, he heard a sharp, frightened cry--and the line went dead.

He stared at the receiver. He felt helpless, inept. His parents were at the opposite end of the country. He could do nothing.

Diana took the phone from his hand and replaced it. They looked at Spocatti.

"This is what you're going to do," he said. "Both of you will attend Celina Redman's funeral tomorrow morning. Then, you'll board Redman's private Lear and fly to London, then on to Iran-- just as planned. You will tell no one--not Redman, not the police- -what you learned here today. You'll act as though nothing happened. If you don't, I'll kill your parents, Jack. That's a promise."

He looked at Diana and could sense a murderous rage rising from her like flames from a bonfire. "Your mother," he said. "She lives in Maine, right? Bangor, I believe. Why don't you give her a call and see if she's all right?"

* * *

A wild chorus of horns trumpeted behind the cab as it darted into the far right lane and jerked to a stop in front of The Hotel Fifth.

Stepping out, the sun hitting her hard in the face, Leana slipped between two parked cars and moved up the red-carpeted steps that led to the hotel's gilded entrance.

Almost immediately, she spotted Zack Anderson. Dressed immaculately in a slick navy blue silk suit, he was standing in the center of the busy lobby, his hands braced on either side of an intricately carved podium, the waterfall casting resilient waves of light through his thick, silvery gray hair.

He seemed oblivious to the steady stream of activity surrounding him. As workers prepared for the opening night party, Anderson's lips moved silently, almost as if he were rehearsing something.

Leana approached him, thinking this was not the first time he would see her looking her worst. After the rain that fell earlier, she knew she was a mess. "Zack," she said, smiling as he looked up. "Got a minute?"

He was startled to see her. "Leana," he said, shuffling a small stack of note cards. "I wasn't expecting you. Why didn't you call?"

"I didn't know I needed an appointment."

"Of course, you don't," he said. "It's just that I didn't expect to see you after what happened to your sister." His face softened. "I'm terribly sorry," he said, tucking the note cards into his jacket pocket. "You must be devastated."

Leana didn't answer. Instead, she looked around the cavernous lobby, surprised to see how much it had changed in the short time since she'd been here. There apparently was nothing left for her to do. Everything seemed to be up and running--the stores and the restaurants and bars all were ready to open. There was no doubt in her mind that Zack Anderson was responsible for this smooth transition and she supposed she owed him a debt of gratitude. Obviously, the man put in the long hours she herself should have put in.

Still, she was guarded. Hadn't he once told her that he wanted her job?

He unbuttoned his jacket and stepped away from the podium, appraising her with a sweeping glance. "Get caught in the rain?" he asked.

Leana gave him a cool, leveling look. She tapped a finger beneath her right eye. "Your mascara is smudged, Zack. I need you to check that before tonight's event."

His face flushed.

"Louis said you'd written me a speech for opening night. I'd like to see it." She nodded towards his jacket pocket. "Do you have it on you?"

"Just on note cards."

"So, I noted." She held out an open palm. "I'll want to make changes. Let me see the speech."

He removed the cards from his pocket and handed them to her. As Leana began reading through them, Anderson said, "I read about your wedding in this morning's paper. Congratulations. Michael Archer is quite a catch."

"So, am I. But you'll figure that out if you last long enough, Zack."

Her words had no affect on him. "This must be difficult for you," he said. "I can't imagine having to prepare for opening night when your sister's funeral will be the morning before."

He let a beat of silence pass. Leana could almost hear his mind working, could almost feel the precise movement of gears.

"I want you to know that if you're not up to it, that if things become too much, I'd be more than happy and willing to deliver this speech for you." He held out his hands. "I wasn't sure if you'd be here. I was practicing it when you came in."

Leana finished reading the speech, not surprised to find that it was eloquent and well written. She handed him the cards. "I did notice," she said. "But that won't be necessary."

"But the press will be here," he said. "They'll be expecting you to be at your best."

"And I will be," Leana said. "Don't concern yourself with it."

For an instant, the compassion in his eyes dissolved into something darker, and then they became carefully neutral. "With all due respect, I don't see how you could be at your best. You've gone through a terrible shock. The entire staff and Louis Ryan are concerned about you. I don't think it would be wise of you to face our guests and the press when I could do the job just as well."

Leana lifted her head. In him she saw a man who would cut his own mother if he thought it would get him this position. "Mr.

Anderson," she said, "I'm going to be frank with you.  I was hired by Louis Ryan to manage this hotel.  You were hired to be my assistant.   If you continue questioning my authority, if you continue lecturing me, you'll be looking elsewhere for work.  Is that understood?"

"I was just trying--"

"Shut up.  Please, just shut the fuck up."

Leana looked at her watch and wondered if Mario had returned to the restaurant.

"My office," she said.  "I assume I have one somewhere in this building.  Take me to it."

* * *

Her office was enormous.

It was located on the hotel's fortieth floor and it faced downtown, toward The Redman International Building.

As Leana stepped inside, she noted with interest the illumined Sisley paintings on the forest-green walls, the cream damask sofas and elegant red velvet chairs--each arranged in a way that suggested a designer's precision--before moving across the faded Persian carpet to her desk.

Anderson remained in the doorway.  "Does this suit?"

Leana sensed by the terse sound of his voice that his ideas, his tastes and his sweat went into the design of this office.  She had a sudden image of him standing in the center of this room, an artist using his mind as a palette, working tirelessly with a team of professionals until his vision was realized.

She knew, knew that he hoped this office would one day be his and she couldn't help feeling a little pissed off because of it.  "It's a bit much," she said.  "I mean, look at it--it's overkill.  It's unbalanced.  It lacks imagination.  It suggests that whoever did this is trying to impress instead of trying to get their work done.  Don't you agree?"

"I don't."

"That's understandable," Leana said.  "I grew up surrounded by this sort of shit.  My father's a billionaire, my mother likes to spend money. A lot of money. It's obvious you came from something more pedestrian than I did, so I get that being surrounded by all these little treasures might be meaningful to you. Still, for me? Boring."

"I'm sorry you feel that way."

"I'm sorry, too. But it doesn't work. It's kind of awful. It'll do for now, but only until I can get my own team of designers in here and gut the place."

She saw the steely hardness in his eyes, the slight change in the set of his jaw and sighed. "I mean, honestly," she said. "We're a hotel, not a museum. Whose idea was it to hang these fucking Sisley paintings?"

\* \* \*

When she was alone, she sat in the leather wingback behind her desk and found it nothing like the leather wingback of her childhood days, the comfortable leather chair that had been in her father's office and smelled so distinctively of his cologne.

She felt a sudden pang of regret and wished they hadn't argued earlier. She should call him now and apologize, she thought. She should swallow her pride and tell him that she was sorry, that she loved him and wanted his support and his friendship.

Still, when she reached for the phone, it was not her father she dialed. It was Mario's restaurant.

Oddly, there was no answer there and it was the lunch hour. As she leaned back in her chair and looked across at her father's building, it occurred to her that Tuesday would not only be her day, but her father's as WestTex became Redman International's. She wondered how that would feel, wondered if the realization of her dream would be as sweet as she always thought it would be.

Somehow, she thought, without her sister here and without her parents approval, it would be quite different. And she wondered again if she'd made a mistake by accepting this job.

It wasn't until later that evening, while at home and relaxing on the sofa with Michael, that she turned on the television to CNN and learned of the explosion that killed two members of the De Cicco crime Family.

## CHAPTER FORTY-EIGHT

Antonio De Cicco heard the bitch before he saw her.

In the intensive care unit at St. Vincent's Hospital, he was sitting at Mario's bedside, holding his hand, when he heard her voice coming from beyond the closed door. She was firm in her demands to see his son, reminding those doctors and nurses on duty that her father built a children's wing on this hospital and that if they didn't let her see Mario now, she would have their jobs by the end of the night.

Angrily, Antonio looked away from the network of tubes coursing through his son's body and knew that because of Leana Redman, he had lost his daughter-in-law, lost the Family's trusted lawyer, who was his cousin, and nearly lost his son.

The pain he felt earlier dissolved into fury and resolve. He would crush her, just as he promised Lucia he would.

And yet he couldn't--at least not here. If he made any scene, any threats in public, there would be witnesses--and the D.A., a man who for years had been waiting to lock his ass behind bars, would be on him the moment Leana Redman was murdered at the opening of The Hotel Fifth.

He sat in thought for several moments, now only dimly aware of the bitch's presence and her frequently raised voice, before making his decision and reaching for the call button at his son's side.

He pushed it and waited. When the nurse arrived, he caught a brief glimpse of Leana Redman before the door to his son's room closed. She was standing at the nurse's station, her back to him and she was gesticulating with her hands, arguing with one of the doctors.

"Yes, Mr. De Cicco?"

With an effort, Antonio stood and became aware of the trepidation in the young woman's eyes. "I hear a woman shouting about my son," he said calmly. "What's the problem?"

The nurse seemed perplexed. "It's Leana Redman, sir. She

366

wants to see him."

"And you won't let her. That why she's shouting?"

The woman nodded. "Only the immediate family is allowed to visit."

"Then throw her the fuck out."

The woman moved to speak, but then hesitated. "It's her father," she said. "He's done so much for the hospital. We're afraid that if we do--"

"She's disturbing the patients," De Cicco said evenly. "Don't tell me you're gonna allow that?" He saw that's exactly what they planned to do and felt a sharp pulse at his temples.

"Maybe I should speak to her myself," he said, coming around the bed and moving to the door. "Stay with my son. I'll be back."

\* \* \*

She was not the same person he remembered from two years ago.

As he stepped out of the room and moved into the corridor, Leana turned to him and he was struck at once by the change in her. Her skin was pale beneath the fluorescent lights, her features were sharpened by age, and there was a wise determination in her eyes that made him pause. She hadn't possessed that before.

As he neared her, Leana faced him with a defiance that was almost surprising in its strength. Resolve burned in her eyes. Her voice was firm when she spoke. "I'm not leaving until I see him, Antonio."

She was in love with his son. The woman had just gotten married and yet she was in love with his son. He could see it on her face, hear it in her voice and he was appalled at her nerve. Did she really believe she could tell him what to do? Order him around like he was one of her servants? He felt sick with his loathing of her--and yet his features remained impassive.

"Here's the deal, cunt. You're gonna be waiting awhile. You're not seeing my son." He looked at the doctor, an older man standing beside Leana. "She has no right to be here," he said. "If she enters that room, I'll sue. Is that understood?"

The doctor had no choice but to agree.

Antonio looked at Leana, saw the pain on her face, the hatred in her eyes and wondered if Lucia was right. He wondered if this Redman bitch was sleeping with Mario.

"You're not wanted here," he said to her. "Go home to your husband."

As he walked away, her death came to him.

He had an image of her standing in the center of a crowd, shining, immaculate, her eyes brilliant and glinting in the torrent of cameras flashing in her face, her voice clear and confident as she gave the speech he had been told about that morning.

And then he saw her lifting into the air, toward the chandeliers, her face crumpling as it rose into the halo of her own blood, the hail of bullets ripping from the rear of the room and mangling what had once been her head.

Behind him, her voice was high and thin: "Antonio--"

But De Cicco already was in his son's room. The door had swung shut behind him. He was through with her.

\* \* \*

Michael stared at the man standing in his entryway, stunned by the drastic change in his appearance, certain he couldn't have heard him right. "What did you just say?"

The man, who had flown from L.A. to see Michael, put a finger to his lips and motioned for Michael to follow him out of the apartment and into the hallway. "Hurry," he whispered. "My plane leaves in an hour and I'm not missing it for you. I'm tired of this bullshit. Your father's fucking crazy. I'm out of here."

Suddenly wary, Michael followed the man to the end of the hall, where there was an illumined wall of elevators, a window that overlooked Manhattan and a tall, potted plant that gleamed as though it had just been waxed.

The man went to the window, leaned against it and lit a cigarette. He drew deeply on it, the smoke lifting like a veil in front of his face. His name was Bill Jennings and he was Michael's business manager--a man Michael hadn't seen or heard from him since the banks foreclosed on him.

"What's going on, Bill?" he asked. "You're not exactly putting me at ease."

The man exhaled a cloud of smoke. "We can't talk in your apartment," he said. "The fucker probably has it bugged. If I hadn't shaved off my beard and dyed my hair blond, I wouldn't be standing here now."

Michael was losing his patience. "What are you talking about? And what's this about Santiago?"

The man couldn't look Michael in the eyes. "He doesn't exist" he said simply. "There is no Stephano Santiago. Your father made him up to scare you. For the past year, Louis has been making me skim money from your accounts so it would look as if you'd gone broke. He made me suggest that you try gambling at one of his casinos when the banks finally foreclosed. He knew you'd lose and he knew that you'd eventually go running to him once he made you believe the casino was Mafia-controlled."

There was a tension in the air, a disturbance in the silence. The man glanced at Michael, saw the disbelief on his face and screwed up his own. "Ah, shit, Michael. Santiago doesn't own the Aura--your father does, at least part of it. He arranged for you to be offered that loan, knowing you'd be scared shitless when you lost it all and had to pay back a man by the name of Stephano Santiago. He's been planning this from the start."

It wasn't possible.

Michael thought of the call he received only that morning, the call warning him to do as his father asked and kill George Redman. And then he thought of his dog. "But my dog," he said to Bill. "Santiago killed him. He left a note saying he'd do the same to me if I didn't come up with the money."

"Your father killed your dog, Michael. I'm telling you, Santiago doesn't exist."

Pieces of a puzzle he never knew existed began falling into place. Michael thought back to the men who chased him out of his apartment--men Santiago supposedly hired--and realized once again what a coincidence it was that Spocatti had been there to help him. But of course there were no coincidences. His father was behind it all.

"I hate myself for this, Michael," Jennings said. "More than you know. But your father said he'd kill me if I didn't go along with it. He promised he'd make me pay if I didn't make you believe. Now he's got people watching this building--that's why I changed my appearance. If they knew I was here, they'd kill us both."

Michael shot him a look. "Am I broke?"

Jennings removed an envelope from his jacket pocket and handed it to Michael. "Everything I skimmed was put into another account, under a different name. You have about three million dollars your father said you wouldn't be needing again." His last words lingered in the air. Their eyes met and he nodded toward the envelope, now clutched in Michael's hand. "Everything you need to know is in there."

He looked at his watch, saw that he had only an hour to get to La Guardia and swore beneath his breath. He dropped his cigarette into the silver ashtray beside him, pressed the elevator's down button and said, "I'm not going to the police. I'm leaving that to you. But if you need my help, you can count on it. After what your father's done, I want that son of a bitch behind bars."

The elevator doors slid open and he stepped inside. Michael was about to speak when he heard the faint ringing of a telephone coming from his apartment. The sound echoed hollowly in the empty hallway.

"Where are you going?" he said.

Jennings shrugged. In his eyes was a look of fear. "As far away from your father as a plane will take me," he said. The doors started to close. "I suggest you do the same. Leave New York. Take Leana with you. I don't know what your father is up to, I don't know why he's done this, but I do know he's dangerous. And I do know you're at risk."

\* \* \*

As Michael stood looking at himself in the division of the elevator's brushed steel doors, he thought he looked like an apparition, a ghost hovering between two separate realities, two worlds of lightness and darkness.

His father had been manipulating him from the start, playing on his fears and his love for his mother. Although Michael never fully trusted Louis in the weeks that had passed since their reunion, he was starting to do so and it was this that sparked his rage now.

How could he have allowed himself to be drawn in by the very man who once said he wished it was his son who died all those years ago, and not his wife, Anne?

Why had he believed in him? Had he been so hungry for the man's acceptance that he would believe and do anything? Marry a woman he barely knew? Agree to kill a man responsible for his mother's death? And what if that, too, was a lie?

The telephone rang again.

Michael considered ignoring it, but realized it might be his father and so he left for his apartment to answer it.

"Yes?" he said sharply.

"Mr. Archer?"

It was the front desk. Michael closed his eyes, willed himself to relax. "What is it, Jonathan?"

"You have a visitor, sir."

"Who is it?"

"It's George Redman. Shall I show him up?"

## CHAPTER FORTY-NINE

The knock came almost at once.

Michael stopped pacing and looked across the foyer to the door. It was in shadow, a narrow beam of interrupted light shining beneath it.

George Redman was beyond that door. The man accused of murdering his mother was about to enter his apartment. Michael wondered again why Redman was here and then realized it really didn't matter--he was glad he was here. Though they'd met only briefly at the opening of the Redman International Building, he now had the chance to stand face-to-face with the man. Alone.

As he went to the door, it occurred to him that if this apartment was indeed wired, his father would eventually hear every word about to be spoken. And that thrilled him.

He opened the door and the two men stared at each other.

Although Redman was well over six feet and had a broad, rugged build, he was somehow different from the man Michael remembered. He seemed smaller, less threatening. His resemblance to Leana was striking.

An awkward silence passed. Michael could hear one of his neighbors playing a piano. Then Redman extended his hand, which Michael shook. "Thanks for seeing me," George said.

Michael stepped aside and asked him to come in. George went to the center of the foyer and looked around.

"Is Leana here?" he asked.

"She's at the hospital."

"Then she knows?"

"We saw it on the news. I tried telling her there wasn't anything she could do, but she wouldn't listen and went to the hospital, anyway."

George looked disappointed. He wanted to break the news to Leana himself. "I'm not surprised," he said. "That man meant the world to Leana. She loved him fiercely."

While Michael knew that Leana once had an affair with Mario

De Cicco, she never elaborated just how deeply those feelings went and he was surprised now by the jealousy it sparked within him. Given De Cicco's notorious lifestyle, it also seemed odd that her father understood it.

"You wouldn't happen to have a drink, would you?" George asked. "I'm still a little shaken, myself."

Shaken about De Cicco?

They moved into the large room with its tall windows and red curtains, its paneled mahogany walls and illumined paintings and leather-bound books. Michael motioned toward the rosewood chairs arranged in the center of the room and asked George to have a seat. "What can I get you?"

"Scotch, if you have it," George said.

Michael stood at the unfamiliar bar, his gaze sweeping over rows of glinting bottles, deeply etched Faberge glasses, a shining, empty ice bucket. He had used this bar only once since he and Leana moved in and it was a moment before he found the appropriate bottle, which was half-full, its label scratched, as if it had been used. *You're a clever son of a bitch, aren't you, Dad?* As he poured, he wondered where in this room the microphones were hidden. Who was listening to them now? Spocatti? His father? Both?

Drinks in hand, he came across the room and noticed that Redman was watching him. His gaze was almost scrutinizing, as if he was looking at someone he hadn't seen in years.

Michael handed him his drink. "Is there something wrong?" he asked.

George shook his head. "No," he said. "I'm sorry. You just remind me of someone I knew some time ago."

Michael took the chair opposite him, his interest rising. "Who was that?"

"Her name was Anne," George said. "She looked a lot like you."

Michael tried to still his emotions. He couldn't believe this man had just mentioned his mother. All his life he had longed for information about her. He wanted to know things that only people close to her could know, but his father rarely spoke about her. He thought of the films he watched that morning and knew that while they offered a bridge to the past in fleeting scenes that

373

encouraged memories, they never could convey what a person's personal memories could. And so he pressed on.

"Were you friends?" he asked.

The sadness on George Redman's face was unmistakable. "Yes," he said. "I suppose Anne and I were friends. There was a time when we were even close. But things changed and I never saw her again. That was years ago."

Michael's heart was pounding. He was conflicted. If what his father said was true, George Redman murdered his mother. He'd taken a shotgun, blown out her tires and sent her over that bridge to her death. But he also knew that George couldn't understand the complexity of what was unfolding here. And since George might tell him more about his mother than his own father would, he decided to take this as far as he could, regardless of the repercussions.

"What was she like?"

"We don't need to talk about this."

"Leana could be hours," he said. "I'm interested."

"There are other subjects to discuss, like your marriage to my daughter."

"Leana and I agreed that we'd discuss that with you and Elizabeth together." He held out his hands. "What can I say?" he said. "You've made me curious about her."

George seemed to understand that and so he acquiesced. "She was beautiful," he said. "I didn't know her long and I only saw her on occasion, but there were times when I would have done anything for her."

"Were you two involved?"

The boldness of the question caught George off guard. He saw the rapt attention on Michael's face and finished his drink. "Anne was married when I met her and I respected that," he said. "I wanted to remain friends with her but her husband decided against that. We didn't get along." He lifted his empty glass. "Would you mind?"

Michael went to the bar and fixed him another drink. He replaced the bottle and listened to Redman shift in his seat. "Are they still married?"

"Anne's dead, Michael."

And there it was. Michael stood at the bar, a thousand questions tumbling through his mind, but he chose to ask only one because only one mattered--and Redman's reaction to it was almost as important as his answer.

He came across the room and handed George his drink. He saw the discomfort on his face and what might have been grief in his eyes.

"I'm sorry," he said. "How did she die?"

It was as if those words dropped an invisible veil. George straightened in his chair. He collected himself. Whatever world he had allowed himself to travel to was gone. "Let's talk about something else," he said. "Today has been difficult enough."

"Of course."

The phone rang.

"That might be Leana," George said.

Michael excused himself and left for the foyer, not wanting to talk in the library. He had a feeling it was his father calling and he was right.

"What are you doing, Michael?" Louis said. "Why are you with him?"

Michael looked back into the library and saw that Redman had left his seat. He now was standing in front of the Vermeer, in which a woman was holding a balance. And Michael thought, *Did you kill my mother?*

"Answer me, Michael. Why is he there?"

There was a sudden jangling of keys beyond the locked door and Michael turned as Leana stepped into the apartment. Their eyes met and Michael immediately sensed by the expression on her face that things had not gone well at the hospital. His father's voice was a sharp jolt on the phone. "Get him out of that apartment, Michael. Get him out now or I'll pay Santiago nothing."

With a firm hand, Michael replaced the receiver and walked over to where Leana stood. He put his arms around her and held her tightly. "Are you all right?"

Leana pressed her face into the warmth of his chest. She didn't answer.

Michael rested his chin on the top of her head. He could feel her trying to keep herself under control and his heart went out to her. "How is he?" he asked.

"Not good," she said. "It was awful. I fought with the doctor and Mario's father wouldn't let me see him."

"Is he going to be all right?"

"I don't know. Three of his ribs were crushed. He lost a lot of blood. The doctor says we have to wait."

Michael pulled back and touched her cheek with the back of his hand. He had fallen in love with her. He didn't know how or when it had happened, but the feeling was there and he realized that there was nothing he wouldn't do for her.

"We'll talk about it later," he said. "I promise. But right now you have to pull yourself together." He nodded toward the library. "Your father's here."

Leana's eyes widened. She looked behind her and came face to face with her father, who had stepped away from the painting and now was standing in the center of the library, near an ormolu writing table, his hands at his sides.

He smiled at her and it was one of the saddest smiles she had ever seen. "I wanted you to hear it from me," he said. "But I guess I was too late. Are you all right?"

Leana was confused. Her father hadn't come here to tell her about Mario--George hated the man. Years ago, he had forbidden that she see him. Something else was wrong. "What are we talking about?" she said, alarmed. "Is Mom all right?"

George was unmoving. "Your mother's fine." He looked at Michael. "I thought you said she knew?"

Michael was as bewildered as George. "She does know," he said. "She just came from the hospital. We saw what happened to De Cicco on the news." But Michael saw by the change in Redman's expression that his coming here had nothing to do with Mario De Cicco or with the explosion that nearly cost the man his life.

He looked at Leana, saw the cold fear on her face, the uncertainty in her eyes, and thought, *What has my father done now....*

The next few moments passed in a haze.

George came into the foyer, told Leana about the death of their best friend, a man he thought he had known but never truly had. He caught his daughter when her knees buckled and she began to cry in a shrill of grief. Over and over again, she asked why Harold had done it. George said he didn't know. He remained at her side, comforting her, his arms enveloping her in a way they hadn't since she was a child.

He pressed his face against hers as he saw, again, the haunting image of a train hurtling into a shadowy tunnel, bearing down toward an impatient crowd and then Harold inexplicably leaping from the platform and jumping to his death.

\* \* \*

The helicopter soared over the city and moved slowly down Fifth, its spotlight shining along the mirrored facades of tall buildings, illuminating their interiors with quick bursts of light.

In the dark silence of Louis Ryan's office, Spocatti watched the machine, watched it glide steadily toward them, its multi-colored lights blinking, steel blades flashing, chopping the heavy air with a smooth, measured fierceness.

Ryan was sitting opposite him, glass of Scotch in hand, a cigarette burning low between his fingers. He had not spoken since Michael severed the connection and, in a sense, blatantly told Louis to go to hell.

In an odd way, Spocatti was proud of Michael. Standing up to his father took guts. Perhaps Michael wasn't the man he assumed he was. Perhaps he was stronger.

The roar of the helicopter grew louder.

Ryan stamped out his cigarette. "Things have changed," he said. "I threatened Michael with Santiago and he hung up on me. I think he knows."

Spocatti could barely see the man's face. It was as if a net of shadows had been tossed over it. "I doubt that," he said. "If anyone told him, we would have heard."

"Not necessarily," Louis said. And then, his voice surprisingly bitter, "You're not perfect, Vincent. Neither are your men or the equipment you use. So do me a favor and stop pretending you're God."

377

The helicopter passed and Ryan's pale face was caught in the light as it wavered like water into the office.

Spocatti stared into that face--saw the stern line that was Ryan's mouth, the nightmare that was boiling in his liquid-brown eyes--before he watched it slide back into darkness. He wondered at exactly what point the man's mind had begun to turn. He wondered to what extent Ryan realized his carefully orchestrated plan was souring.

"I want you to keep an eye on Michael," Louis said. "I want you to increase security around him, record his every move. He'll be at the funeral tomorrow--I'm sure of that. Since there's no telling what he has planned after that, watch him. I have a feeling he's going to try something."

"I can take him out," Spocatti said.

"Not until I'm finished with him."

"And when will that be?"

Louis lit another cigarette and, for an instant, his face glowed in the fiery globe. "Tuesday," he said. "When we bury the rest of them."

**BOOK FOUR**

**CHAPTER FIFTY**

"It really is special," the Realtor said.  She was standing in the center of the large, empty foyer and her voice echoed off the stark white walls.  "As you know, apartments on Fifth are rare, especially in the 50s and 60s.  And this is a penthouse, which obviously amplifies its appeal further."  She let a silence go by.  "If you want to make a statement and live on Fifth Avenue, this is the place to do so.  Few in the city are better."

She allowed the man a moment to take in the space.

"Let's take a tour," she said.

The apartment was large and airy.  It comprised two floors and boasted sweeping views of the city.  It was completely white throughout--white walls, white carpets, white woodwork, white marble floors in the bathrooms, white fireplace in the library, everywhere white, white, white.

"From what I hear, the owners are arty, eccentric types," the Realtor said as they moved through the living room and stepped into the dining area.  "They're old money from Iceland and word has it that they missed their country so much that they surrounded themselves in white, in a sense giving them the illusion of being lost in a blizzard."

"You don't say?"

She caught the sarcasm and couldn't help a laugh.  "It's what we've been asked to say.  Whether it's true, I can't say.  But I can confirm that the apartment was featured this year in Architectural Digest."

The man walked down a bright hallway and stepped into the library.  She followed.  "This is my favorite room," she said.  "The windows sell it.  That's a true New York view.  You easily could fit two-hundred people in here for entertaining.  And at night, it's magnificent.  With that backdrop, you can imagine how beautiful

379

it is in here."

The man moved to the far set of windows. Hands clasped behind his back, he looked across 53rd Street to the city's newest hotel.

The woman stepped behind him. "And then you have that," she said. "The largest hotel in New York. Four thousand rooms, all of them booked for the weekend. Tonight is the opening night party. You've heard that Leana Redman is managing the hotel?"

"Didn't she just bury her sister yesterday?"

"She did."

"And now she opens that hotel tonight," he said. "That's a pretty quick recovery, wouldn't you say?"

The woman didn't say. "Do you like the view?"

"Very much," he said. "But I wonder if I might see it at night?"

"Of course," she said. "I could show it to you tomorrow evening."

"No," the man said. "I'm leaving the country tomorrow morning. I won't be back for weeks and you may have sold it by then." He turned away from the window and looked at her. "I'd like to see it tonight. And, if the view is as spectacular as you say it is, it's likely that I'll just write you a check for the full amount."

The woman kept her features neutral, but her mind was working. After calling in a number of favors, she had secured an invitation to the opening of The Hotel Fifth. She had spent a fortune on her dress and almost as much on having it tailored to her body. There was no way she could show this apartment tonight. The connections she could make tonight were invaluable.

And yet this apartment had been on the market for months. The asking price was $25 million. Because of the recession, here was the first person in weeks to show genuine interest in it. She couldn't lose this sale, for professional and personal reasons.

The man was watching her, waiting for a response. "If it's a problem," he said, "I can always look elsewhere. I really need to wrap this up today."

"No," the woman said. "That isn't necessary. It's just that I've been invited to that party tonight. Leana Redman and I are friends. She invited me herself. It's important that I attend and help her through what likely will be a difficult evening."

His gaze met hers levelly.  Unflinchingly.

The woman sensed he didn't believe her.

"Look," he said.  "If this party means so much to you, I wouldn't mind coming here alone tonight and checking out the view for myself.  Just give me a key and I'll return it to you tomorrow morning, before my plane leaves."

"That's actually against the law," the woman said.  "I'm not allowed to do that."

"It'll just be me."

"I could get into trouble," she said.  "I could lose my license."

"Or you could make a $2 million commission.  Who will know?"

"The doormen."

"Doormen can be dealt with," he said.  "A little charm, a lot of money--and their mouths become vaults."

She thought about this and made her decision.  "All right," she said.  "If it wouldn't be too much trouble.  And if this stays between us."

"Of course," the man said, gazing across at the hotel.  "Just between us."

* * *

They awoke in each other's arms to the abrupt sound of music.

Michael lifted his head from the pillow and glanced at the clock on the bedside table. He would have given anything to have awakened anywhere in the world but here.  He knew she had to get ready for the day and so he let the music play.  Leana moved closer to him.  She murmured something.

Michael put his arm around her and gently kissed the back of her neck.  Neither had slept well.  More than once in the night he turned to find her looking at him, her face pale and watchful in the moonlight, her eyes heavy and dead with memories of Harold and Celina.

Yesterday morning, at her sister's funeral, he stood alongside her and her parents at an elegant Connecticut cemetery.  He was a fraud grieving for a woman he hadn't known, yet easily could have saved.

Yesterday afternoon, while Leana tried to rest, Louis phoned, again threatening him with Santiago. Silently, bitterly, Michael listened, but what Louis didn't know is that Michael knew that Santiago didn't exist and that Michael no longer believed that George Redman killed his mother. Meeting the man and seeing how he spoke about his mother altered the landscape. He wanted to confront his father with his lies, but instead he spun some of his own, reassuring Louis that he also wanted Redman dead, that meeting the man had solidified his resolve.

His words still lingered in his mind. "I asked him, Dad. I asked him how Mom died, and you should have seen the look on his face. It was as though I had accused him of murder."

"And that surprised you?" Louis said.

"I'd be lying if I said it hadn't," Michael said. "I don't trust you. I never have and--after this experience--I never will. But this is now personal for me, too. When I saw the look on Redman's face, I knew he pulled that trigger and I want him dead for it. What you need to understand is this--once it's over, I never want to see you again. You'll pay off Santiago--just as you promised--and you will give me money to start over with. A lot of money. Those are my terms. Either you meet them or I'm out of here. Now, tell me what you want me to do and I'll do it."

There was a silence, almost as if Louis had been expecting something different from his son, perhaps another disappointment, certainly not this.

"All right," Louis said. "I'll call you tomorrow. We'll discuss everything in detail then."

Momentarily relieved, Michael hung up the phone, knowing that if his plan was going to work, if he was going to protect Leana and her family, he would have to assume the role of a lifetime and convince his father that his resolve was genuine.

Leana turned to him, her eyes warm and liquid in the bedroom's muted light. She was beautiful, he thought. If it cost him his own life, he would see to it that no further harm came to her or her family. He would see to it that his father was stopped. If Michael was wrong and George Redman had indeed killed his mother, then he would have to be brought to justice another way-

-not like this.

He brushed a lock of hair from her forehead. "Are you ready for this?"

Leana shrugged. "No. And I hope they're not expecting too much from me tonight," she said. "I'm not up to this at all."

And here was the opportunity he'd been waiting for.

Last night, while they were relaxing in bed, it came to Michael that if his father would murder Celina, then he almost certainly planned the same fate for Leana. Louis didn't want Leana to manage his hotel. He only gave her that job to publicly humiliate her father. And Louis wouldn't stop there. Before Redman was murdered, Michael knew his father meant for the man's family to die before him--so George would feel the pain Louis himself had felt for years.

On the clock radio, the music stopped and a segment on the morning news began. Last night, they'd intentionally turned up the volume so they wouldn't over sleep. Ordinarily, he would have shut off the machine. But this bedroom was wired, and if the radio's volume was loud enough, Spocatti wouldn't hear what he was about to say.

"Then don't do it," he said quietly. "Don't go."

Leana looked surprised. "What are you talking about?" she said. "I have to go."

"No, you don't. Call Ryan and quit. You told me last night you don't want this job. We can be back in Europe by the end of the day."

"I can't do that to Louis, Michael. He's done too much for me. It isn't right."

"Ryan's using you. You told me so yourself. Didn't you tell me that you only took this job to hurt your father?"

"That was only part of the reason."

"Maybe so, but the other night was a turning point. He cares about you. He came here because he wanted to tell you himself about Harold. Yesterday, I saw him reach for your hand at Celina's funeral. Last night, he called to see how you were. Don't mess with this, Leana. You finally have a chance to build a meaningful relationship with your father. Don't you see how precious this is? I would give anything to be in your place to have a father who cares for me the way yours is beginning to care for

383

you. Don't deny him another chance."

"I don't plan to," she said. "But I'm going through with tonight's opening. This isn't about my father anymore, Michael. This is about me--my abilities. All of New York will be there tonight. Those who matter will finally be watching me. I've waited too long for this. If I quit and go to work for my father-- assuming he'll hire me--there's no telling how long I'd have to wait for a moment like this."

She looked at him with such impatience, Michael was taken aback.

"Don't you see?" she said. "Ever since I was a kid I've watched my sister and him shine. Since I was a kid, I knew I could do everything they could do--but I wasn't given the chance." She stepped out of bed and moved naked to the bathroom.

"I don't want to discuss this," Leana said. "I'm opening that hotel tonight and I hope you'll be there to support me--"

She stopped suddenly and turned toward the radio, her eyes widening as it was announced that WestTex, the floundering shipping company George Redman reportedly paid $10 billion for, had become Redman International's earlier that morning.

"Watch Redman International's stock when the Dow opens this morning," the commentator said. "How this plays out will be critical for George Redman. If it falls any further, some critics say Redman will be a prime candidate for a takeover himself. In related news, the same isn't true for Anastassios Fondaras, the Greek shipping magnet who went public moments ago as Iran's new chief exporter of oil."

## CHAPTER FIFTY-ONE

Confident, magnificent, his heart full for the first time in years, Louis Ryan left his office, stepped smartly down the busy hallway to his boardroom and faced his directors, most of whom were spirited to New York only last evening--leaving behind previous engagements, summer vacations in progress, mistresses in foreign countries. The usual.

They were in groups of three or four, sipping steaming mugs of coffee or tea, unaware of his presence. As Louis stood in the doorway, only dimly aware of their quiet babble of conversation, his gaze swept the room for Peter Horrigan, the Wall Street lawyer who had been hired to advise the directors of their rights and duties, and saw with a smile that he wasn't there yet. If he had been, if these men and women even sensed what he was about to propose, Louis knew he would be entering pandemonium.

He closed the door behind him and the conversations stopped. They looked at him, their expressions ranging from minor annoyance to genuine concern. Why had he brought them here? What couldn't have waited until their scheduled August board meeting?

Louis moved into the room, an old friend greeting each director with a warmth that was almost beguiling. He asked after their wives, their husbands and their families, alleviating the tension with well-chosen jokes, a deep-throated laugh. He knew he had alarmed them with the suddenness of this meeting and if he was to garner their support, it was imperative that he make them feel comfortable now.

Never had he been more charming. His eyes shined with a light of mystery and sparkled with a sense of humor few had seen in him before.

And then, as he asked them to be seated, Peter Horrigan arrived.

To Louis, the crashing silence that followed was almost comical. As Horrigan moved into the room, smiling to those people he knew, nodding at the few he didn't, Louis looked at each of his directors and knew the time to act was now, while they were still too stunned to speak.

While the others sat, he remained standing and faced them all with a strength and purpose that was as compelling as they had come to expect from a man who had built from nothing a multi-billion dollar corporation.

"Welcome," he said to the group. "And again I want to thank you all for leaving your families and coming here on such short notice. I understand many of you were enjoying summer vacations and I promise you that your time in New York will be short. But since our last meeting, events have changed so dramatically with one of our competitors, I felt it was in the best interest of our shareholders to meet now and not only discuss the future of this great company, but also the fate of another-- Redman International."

He paused for effect, and noticed that all eyes turned briefly to Peter Horrigan, who was seated at Louis' right, before turning back to Louis himself.

Louis continued. "As I'm sure most of you are aware, this morning George Redman and his directors went against the odds and purchased WestTex Incorporated, the large shipping company based in Corpus Christi, Texas. In the first twenty minutes of today's Dow, Redman stock has fallen eleven points-- and it's still dropping.

"Before coming here, a source of mine at Redman International phoned to inform me that George Redman and his directors are in a state of panic. In order to make this deal with WestTex work, Redman was counting on a deal he made privately with Iran. It was a deal that not only would have made him Iran's chief exporter of oil, but one that also would have made him billions. In theory, it was a brilliant idea--but the agreement was only verbal. Redman chanced everything on a verbal commitment because Iran refused to sign anything until WestTex became Redman International's. They felt it was a waste of time to commit themselves otherwise, and they were correct."

He shook his head as though the risk Redman took was wildly inappropriate. "Unfortunately for George Redman, Anastassios Fondaras had a similar deal in the works with Iran--and his was finalized only minutes after Redman signed the final papers with WestTex, thus leaving him with $10 billion in added debt, and a shipping company that can't support itself."

Glances were exchanged while Louis sat. Then Charles Stout, a former chairman at American Express and a proverbial thorn in Louis' side, spoke. "So, what are you suggesting, Louis? That we take over the company?"

Louis smiled at Stout. "That's precisely what I'm suggesting, Charles. By taking over Redman International, we not only will become a world leader in steel and textiles, but we'll also acquire a commercial airline and some of the more attractive and profitable hotels and casinos in the world--not to mention the Redman International Building itself, which, if handled correctly, could be a veritable gold mine in rental opportunities. We owe this to our shareholders."

Stout was incredulous. "Owe this to our shareholders?" he said. "Are you implying that we owe it to our shareholders to take over a company that's just assumed $10 billion in debt? A shipping company that's been floundering for months? Our stock will plummet. We'll wind up where Redman is now."

Louis was absolutely calm. "Look at the big picture, Charles. We'll sell WestTex. We'll get rid of the debt."

"Who are we selling it to, Louis? Who in the world is going to buy that shipping company? We'd be lucky if we could give it away, let alone sell it to someone for $10 billion dollars."

For a long moment, no one spoke. Then Louis, who had shown no reaction to Stout's outburst, pulled his trump card and went in for the kill. "I already have a buyer, Charles. Before this meeting, I phoned Anastassios Fondaras in Iran and he's agreed to buy WestTex in the event that Redman International becomes ours. He needs a larger fleet with this new deal. And he's agreed to pay the full $10 billion."

Stout's eyes widened. He moved to speak, but now he was speechless.

Relishing the moment, Louis looked around the table, saw looks ranging from interest to mild surprise before his gaze stopped at Florence Holt, the civil rights leader and New York lawyer who was, without question, the savviest person on the board. She looked at him through narrowed eyes. "You're certain about this?" she said. "Fondaras is willing to put this promise of his into writing?"

Louis nodded. "If it's the board's decision to move on this, he told me himself that he'd immediately sign a contract." He paused. "I want you to understand one thing," he said to the board. "This decision is yours. If you're uncomfortable with it, just say the word and there will be no hard feelings. I won't push for it. But if you should decide to pursue this, I feel we could get ourselves a bargain--"

"Provided we aren't challenged," Stout interrupted. "What if there's a bidding war?"

Louis face remained impassive. "It's my opinion that there won't be. As you yourself have so eloquently pointed out, Charles, who would want to assume George Redman's $10 billion mistake? Privately, we've secured Fondaras, who is committed to the deal. We are the right company for this takeover. It's my belief that, if we move quickly, we'll also have management. Redman just lost his daughter. On Sunday, his best friend committed suicide. He is no longer emotionally fit to run that company and his board of directors know it. If we offer the board a number that is higher than the price their stock has ever traded for, if we agree to take care of their employees, then I'm certain we could work with them. We can get them out of this mess."

"I still disagree," Stout said. "If we go ahead with this, Redman International will be put into play. The stock will soar and we'll wind up paying billions more than we should." He leaned forward in his seat and looked at each board member. "Do I have to remind everyone in this room that Redman International is still one of the world's most powerful conglomerates? Yes, Redman made a mistake, but he's a brilliant man. In time, he'll rise above this. He'll make WestTex work-- regardless if he's just lost his daughter and best friend. And who's to say that he couldn't sell WestTex to Fondaras? If we go after the company, there's no question in my mind that Redman will try to take it private." He looked hard at Louis. "Especially if you go after it. No offense, Louis, but we all know that Redman would rather shit in his hat than let you run his company."

Louis looked at Stout, but said nothing. He pushed back his chair and stood.

"I'm leaving this in your hands," he said to the group. "But please consider what I've said. I know we can make this work. We have Fondaras. We have the means. I'm certain we can get management. And I know this could take Manhattan Enterprises to a new level of power and wealth. While I'm gone, think what a great team our two companies would make. Think of the absolute power we and our shareholders could rise to."

And he left the room, leaving the board to caucus.

* * *

They were not long in making their decision.

When Louis was summoned back to the boardroom, he looked not at the board, but at Peter Horrigan, who stood while Louis sat, his face coolly impassive, absolutely unreadable.

Suddenly, he was nervous. As Horrigan reclaimed his seat, Louis searched the younger man's eyes for some sign of triumph, some glimmer of victory, but found nothing. He looked down the length of the table and glanced at each grim face, hesitating when he saw what might have been a smile on Charles Stout's lips.

Could it be that they turned him down?

"Louis," Florence Holt said, "it's with regret that I inform you that it's the strong sense of the board that we're not prepared to let you go forward with the takeover of Redman International."

Thunderstruck, his heart stopped. *How could they...?*

Holt folded her hands on the desk. Her voice was firm when she spoke. "It's our belief that if we made a bid for Redman International, it would put the company into play regardless of George Redman's $10 billion error--and the stock would skyrocket, which ultimately would be detrimental to our shareholders should we end up paying top price. As you know, with Redman International at the forefront of the world's...."

Her voice became thinner and thinner until he heard nothing but his own blood, hot and searing, coursing through his system.

# FIFTH AVENUE

* * *

In his office, he moved toward his desk and the photograph of Anne that sat on top of it. After all these years, she still possessed him, still owned him, her grip as fierce as it had been when they first met on that windy afternoon in March, chasing a group of runaway dogs through downtown Cambridge. Looking at her now, longing for what could have been, he finished the last of his drink and closed his eyes, the years lifting like veils.

It was 1956 and he was stumbling blindly down a steep embankment, pushing past groups of horrified onlookers, slipping on the pockmarked snow, stopping just short of a river that no longer was choked with ice, but broken and splintered.

The air was cold and charged with worry and excitement. Snow blazed from the night sky. High above on the ruined bridge, police pointed beams of light down at the boiling water, exposing the large hole in the river's cracked surface and offering a brief glimpse of what might have been red paint.

From where he stood, only a few hundred yards from the bridge and the crater that lay beneath it, Louis could see his wife's fate, could see the glimmering fender of her car as it slowly dipped beneath the boiling surface.

Even then he had the idea that this was no accident.

Now, his mind clear again with resolve, he went to the wall safe that was behind his parents' tinted wedding picture and entered the code to access it. He opened the metal door to a flash of amber light.

Inside was Anne's journal, a thin, narrow composition book he found the year following her death. It was in an anonymous tin box she kept nestled behind an antique armoire in their attic. Could it be that their love had been so imperfect? Could it be that she really doubted his love for her?

The book was small and delicate. Its black-and-gray marbled cover was torn and faded with age, its binding was cracked, the pages were threatening to come loose.

Carefully, Louis brought the journal to his desk and opened it to Anne's final entry. Just seeing her handwriting again was like a pain in his chest.

The entry was dated just two days before her death. It was the day George Redman lost his last appeal in court. As Louis reread it, her damning words ignited like a fire in his gut, a dark rage overcame him, he saw what would be and he ripped the page free.

## CHAPTER FIFTY-TWO

Spocatti's cell phone rang as Leana alighted from the cab. She had a glittering black dress draped over her shoulder, a pair of black silk pumps dangling from her hand. It was early afternoon and the sun was as hot as she apparently planned on looking later this evening.

He looked at the phone, considered ignoring it but then reached for it and clicked it on. "What is it Louis?"

"It's Michael," he said. "He's not answering the phone and the doorman says he's not in his apartment. I told you to keep an eye on him. Where is he?"

Spocatti waited for Leana to enter the hotel before he pulled away from the curb and followed the cab down Fifth. "Everything's under control, Louis."

"Everything isn't under control. I told Michael yesterday not to leave his apartment until he heard from me. Now, he's gone and I want to know where he is."

Spocatti's jaw tightened--the man was losing it.

"Well?" Louis said. "Where is he?"

"He's in front of me."

"In front of you?" Louis said. "What do you mean he's in front of you? Are you with him?"

"No," Spocatti said in an agitated voice. "I'm following him. He just dropped Leana off at the hotel and now he's sitting in the back of a cab. Would you like to know what he's wearing, Louis? Would that ease your mind? Would you like to know what he had for breakfast, whether he showered, when he took his last shit? Jesus, you're beginning to annoy me."

"I gave you $15 million for this job. I'll annoy you all I want."

Something in the rearview mirror caught Spocatti's eye and he jerked the wheel to the left, pressed hard on the gas and nearly struck the Lincoln limousine that had been trying to pass him. He busted a red light and lurched into the center lane--but not before two other cars swerved in front of him, for an instant severing his view of Michael, who was now three cars ahead of him.

"All right," Louis said. "Just get his attention and pull him over. I want him here, in my office, before the party begins."

But the cab was picking up speed. It darted into the center lane, passed a stationary line of traffic and shot right, disappearing behind a bus that was lumbering into traffic.

Spocatti was incredulous. He was losing him.

"Shit!" he said aloud. He tossed the phone aside, squinted into the blinding sun, and ignored Louis' voice as it wavered angrily from the phone. For a moment, he couldn't tell which cab was Michael's--there were dozens of them.

Then, well ahead of him, he saw the cab, saw Michael looking out the rear window--and saw with cold disbelief the triumphant smile on the man's face.

He was rapidly approaching a yellow light. Michael's cab was sailing through a string of green. Betting against the odds, Vincent floored it, cut into the center lane and watched the light turn red.

Time seemed to stop.

He glanced at the halted lines of traffic on 48th, saw that they were being held up by a man crossing in a wheelchair. He pushed the van faster. He would make it.

The U.S. mail truck came out of nowhere.

He hit the brakes and spun the wheel sharply to the left. Spocatti watched the enormous rig loom toward him, its horn blaring, tires screaming. The city spun in the windows. He lost control of the wheel and felt the van tipping, tipping....

And then it righted itself.

He grasped the wheel, jerked it to the right and winced as the mail truck whizzed past him, horn still sounding as its huge, eighteen wheels rumbled across 48th Street. Faintly, he heard someone screaming--and then he realized it was himself. He closed his mouth, sat there grinning madly, his legs tingling, his white-knuckled hands still clutching the leather wheel.

He felt suddenly euphoric, his whole body surging with a vitality he hadn't felt in years.

He looked down the avenue, saw people rushing toward him.

But there was no sign of Michael. He was gone.

393

# FIFTH AVENUE

* * *

The cab zigzagged through traffic, hurtled down Fifth and twice nearly grazed the side of a car.

Michael continued looking out the rear window, not turning away until he was convinced they'd lost Spocatti. He looked at the cabbie, a young black woman who seemed perfectly at ease as she lit her third cigarette and busted her third red light. "You were incredible," he said, reaching into his back pocket and removing his wallet. "Absolutely incredible. Where'd you learn to drive like that?"

The woman looked over her shoulder at him, smoke jetting from her nose as her eyes widened. "Baby, are you kidding?" she said. "We're in New York City. Everybody drives like this."

Michael laughed. "Not quite," he said. "But I like your modesty. How much do I owe you for the favor?"

"How much you got?"

*Enough to get my ass out of this city*, Michael thought. *And start over someplace else with Leana.* "How about a hundred?" he said.

The woman drew on her cigarette, braked as another cab cut in front of her. "I know who you are," she said. "I've read your books, seen your movies. You were hot in that last one," she said, gazing at his chest. "You're probably worth millions. Hundreds of millions. Let's say you give me three bills and if anyone asks, I'll say I never saw your fine white ass."

Michael couldn't help a smile. "You got a deal," he said and handed her the money. He looked once more through the rear window, saw no sign of Spocatti's van in the torrent of traffic and felt peculiarly, unreasonably safe. "You can let me off here," he said. "I think we've lost him."

The woman pulled to the curb, where another fare was waiting to be picked up. Cars whooshed past in a rush of exhaust. "Oh, honey, I know we lost him," she said as Michael stepped out. "I was watching. Fool was almost hit by a mail truck. Trust me. If he's anywhere in the vicinity, I'll pull out my damn weave."

\* \* \*

He pulled out his cell phone and called Leana at her office.

"It's me," he said. "What do you say about a late dinner tonight, after the party? There's this small French restaurant in the Village that's open late. The food's great and so is the house wine. I know it's late notice, but a little romance might take your mind off things."

Leana was silent for a moment, thoughtful. Michael looked down the busy street, his gaze sweeping the crowds on the sidewalk, the traffic on Fifth. And then he saw Spocatti's van, black as the night, moving slowly down the avenue.

Absolutely unmoving, Michael watched the van until it faded from sight. Leana said, "Have I told you recently how terrific you are?"

"As a matter of fact, you haven't. But you can tonight. Should I take that as a 'yes'?"

"You can take that as a definite yes. Dinner sounds great. I'll see you later. It's a madhouse here."

\* \* \*

He took a cab to a travel agency on Third Avenue.

"I need two tickets to Madrid," he said to the agent. "Leaving tonight, on the red eye."

The agent, a middle-aged woman with dyed red hair and impossibly long eyelashes, started typing information into her computer. "It's going to be expensive," she said. "And tough to get seats. The airlines might be booked...."

"I don't care about the cost," Michael said. "And it doesn't have to be Madrid. It can be anywhere in Europe, but the flight must leave tonight--after midnight."

"After midnight," the woman repeated. "Right. Gimme a second...."

He looked through the agency's great expanse of windows, saw tourists and businessmen hurrying by on the sidewalk, well-dressed women carrying shopping bags, a homeless man pushing a rusty shopping cart. There was no sign of Spocatti.

"Madrid's out," the agent said. "So is London and Paris. Have you ever been to Milan?"

"Several times," Michael said. "And I love it there, especially in the summer. Why don't you give it a try?"

Her fingers danced over the keys. Michael looked back out the window--and this time saw a woman, standing at the curbside, leaning against a mailbox, flipping through a newspaper. She seemed familiar to him, as if he had seen her somewhere before. He couldn't remember where.

"Bingo," the agent said. "I can reserve two first-class seats for you to Milan." Michael's brow furrowed. He leaned forward in his seat and continued looking at the woman on the street. "Leaving when?" he asked.

"12:34 this morning."

Michael reached for his wallet. The woman on the street tossed her newspaper into a metal wastebasket and now was using her cell phone. She started punching numbers. She looked over at him. Their eyes met and she looked casually away.

Michael gave a start--he knew that face. Earlier, when he and Leana left their apartment to flag a cab, this woman had been walking toward them, a newspaper tucked beneath her arm. She had glanced at him as she passed.

At the time, Michael thought how striking she was, her dark good looks classically European. Now, he sensed with a cold needle of fear that she worked for Spocatti.

He looked at the agent, his heart pounding. "How much are the tickets?" he asked. "I'm in a hurry."

The woman told him. "I'll need your name," she said. "Along with the name of the person you're traveling with."

"I'm traveling with my wife," Michael said, handing her the cash. "Mr. and Mrs. Michael Ryan." He looked back out the window and saw with a start that the woman was gone. He left his seat, went to the windows and searched the crowds on the street.

But there was no sign of her.  It was as if she had disappeared.
"Is something wrong, sir?"

Michael felt heavy with dread.  He turned away from the windows, faced the puzzled agent and saw that she had placed a receipt for their E-tickets in an envelope.

"As a matter of fact, something is wrong," he said.  He crossed to her desk, pocketed the tickets and removed his wallet, handing her a hundred dollar bill.

"If there's another way out of here," he said, "that's yours."

## CHAPTER FIFTY-THREE

Leana moved swiftly across the busy lobby, checking each table as she passed it, Zack Anderson at her side. "It's getting late," she said. "Why haven't the flowers been delivered?"

"Good question," Anderson said. "I called the florist an hour ago, gave them hell and was told that they're on their way."

"On their way?" Leana said. "Where is this florist located?"

"On Third and Forty-fifth."

Leana shook her head. "That's a ten-minute drive from here. Give them a call and tell them if they want our account, they'll have those flowers here within those ten minutes. No excuses."

"Right."

"What about security?" she asked. "Shouldn't they be here by now?"

"They are here," he said. "They arrived shortly after you."

Leana looked around the lobby. At first she noticed only the staff of decorators who had been there for days, fussing over details she herself would never have considered. The lobby now held three hundred tables for six, four ornate bars flown in from Hong Kong, a sophisticated sound system that would amplify her voice to hundreds of people.

And then, to her right, she noted a tall, rugged man in a black dinner jacket. He was speaking into his lapel as he stepped behind the waterfall. High above on the third level, she noticed another man inspecting one of the alarm systems. And behind her, the wait staff was listening closely to a group of five identically dressed men.

"How many are they?"

"Thirty," Zack said.

"Not enough. Talk to whoever's in charge and tell them I want at least twenty more brought in. In a few hours, this place is going to be filled with some of the most influential people in the world. I want them safe."

Anderson nodded and as Leana watched him walk away, she wondered if their scene the other day had worked. He was a different person now--not judgmental, willing to take direction, polite. Without his help, she knew none of this would be going so smoothly.

With a last look around, she took an elevator to her office and phoned Louis Ryan at Manhattan Enterprises.

"It's Leana," she said. "I hope I'm not disturbing you."

"Of course you're not disturbing me," he said. "I was just about to call you. Did you receive my flowers?"

Leana admired the enormous spray of roses on her desk. "Of course, I did," she said. "How could I miss them? They're take up the room--and they're beautiful. Thank you."

A thought occurred to her and she laughed. "You know," she said. "I might have to use them in the lobby."

"Having trouble with the florist?"

"You could say that."

"Don't worry about it," he said. "Something always goes wrong at the last minute and then it rights itself. The florist will show and things will be fine. Are you having trouble with anything else?"

"No," she said. "Everything is going smoothly."

"Then what can I do for you? Need a Xanax?"

Leana smiled. "Actually, I'm not nervous at all. I was calling to ask if you've made any progress in finding the man who murdered my sister."

"That's one of the reasons I was about to call you."

Leana was suddenly alert. "Have you found him?"

"No," Louis said. "But I've hired a man who will. His name is Vincent Spocatti, he's one of the world's best private investigators and he's certain he can find the man who killed Celina. Tonight, after the party, I want you to meet him."

She thought fleetingly of her dinner date with Michael. He'd understand. This was important.

"Of course, I will," she said. "And thank you, Louis. This means a lot to me--more than you know."

She replaced the receiver and went to the windows behind her--she would bring Michael to the meeting and they could have dinner later. She had a sudden impulse to call Harold, to tell him the good news, but then she realized--once again--that he was gone. *Why?* she wondered. *You could have come to me. Didn't you trust me enough to know that I wouldn't care if you were gay or straight, fat or thin?*

It occurred to her that maybe he hadn't known and that maybe she should have approached him about what she knew. The idea that he might be alive now if she had intervened was too overwhelming for her to consider.

She reached for the note cards on her desk. Neatly typed on them was the speech she'd rewritten and memorized that morning. As Leana flipped through them, reading aloud as she paced before the windows, she noticed a tiny pinpoint of red light dart across her sleeve and spiral across her hand before slipping from sight.

She stopped before the windows.

She looked across 53rd Street to the neighboring building, saw nothing unusual, then heard the faint sound of an engine and looked up at the helicopter that was soaring above the city. Sunlight struck its glinting blades and cast rainbows of light across her face and body. She winced from the sudden light and lifted a hand to shield her eyes.

The helicopter seemed to be circling the hotel. Its door was open and she saw someone leaning out--there was a video camera on his shoulder. Obviously, the news was going to cover the event by air. Leana wondered about that pinpoint of red light, looked at the helicopter and decided it must have been the source.

She stepped away from the windows and returned to her notes.

* * *

The afternoon sun slid through the canted blinds and striped the narrow hospital bed where Mario De Cicco lay. His body was sheathed in perspiration.

Antonio looked away from the monitors that surrounded the bed and turned to face his two youngest sons, Miko and Tony. "Tonight," he said, "while she's on camera, we take her for the world to see."

The two brothers came to the bed.

"I did some callin' around," Antonio said. "Sal's boy, Rubio, knows a couple guys tending bar at the opening. As a favor to me, he said he could get you two into that party, promised it wouldn't be a problem."

One of the monitors beeped and Antonio swung around to look at Mario, who was lying pale and motionless in the bed. His breathing was deep and measured. Antonio looked at the monitor, then down again at his son, hoping to see some flicker of life in his face. There was none and Antonio wondered if Mario would never wake.

He turned back to Miko and Tony, for the first time looking every one of his sixty-nine years. "All you have to do is clean a few glasses and wait for her to take the stage," he said. "When she's in the middle of her speech, while everyone's watching her, that's when you make your move and blow her to hell. If you move fast and if you stay near the rear doors, you shouldn't have a problem getting out of there."

"What about security?" Miko said. "That place will be crawling with cops--not to mention the press. Some might recognize us. What's the back-up plan?"

Antonio leveled his son with a look. "Since when do you give a shit about security?" he said. "Or about the press? If somebody gets in your way, blow their fuckin' head off. Once you fire that first shot, there's going to be so much goddamned commotion, nobody is going to get in your way. Then you seek out Leana Redman, snuff her and get out of there."

He nodded toward Nicky Corrao, who was sitting across the room in the blue vinyl chair, listening to their plans. "Nicky's driving," he said. "He'll be at the 53rd Street entrance, ready to bolt when you two come out."

He looked over at Mario. "I want her out of his life," he said. "When he wakes, I want her obituary to be the first thing he sees. If it isn't, if any of you let me down, I'll never forget it. Is that understood?"

Perfectly.

"Then I suggest you get moving," Antonio said. "Call Rubio now and find out what he wants you to wear and where he wants you to meet him. Nicky, you stay here. When Pauly comes, tell him to keep an eye on Mario. If he wakes, I want to know about it."

"Yes, sir."

"And Nicky," Antonio said, a slight edge to his voice. "You make sure you're parked at that entrance tonight. If you're not, if Miko and Tony don't get out safe, you'll wind up as cold as Leana Redman."

Nicky watched the men step out of the room. He was thinking what a bastard De Cicco could be when one of the monitors beeped again.

He looked at Mario, then up at the monitor--a green jagged line was racing across the screen. Curious, he stepped to Mario's side and looked down with naked wonderment at the web of tubes and wires that netted his body.

He had always respected Mario--the man was fair, had class. When Nicky earned his bones, it was Mario who was first to congratulate him, Mario who took him out that night and got them both drunk. Nicky wanted him to live. He squeezed Mario's shoulder, and was about to say his name when Mario's eyes snapped open.

They stared at one another. Mario's eyes crinkled and he managed a tentative smile. "Are they gone?" he asked.

Nicky's lips parted. He looked quickly toward the door and was about to speak when Mario grasped his hand. "No," he said. "I don't want to talk to them. I only want to talk to you. Now, come here. Come closer. And just listen to me, Nicky. I'm about to make you a very wealthy man."

\* \* \*

Spocatti pushed through the revolving brass doors of The Manhattan Enterprises Building and left the searing heat of midtown behind.

He moved quickly across the crowded lobby, took the last hit off his cigarette and tossed it still burning onto the floor. He stopped at a bank of elevators, pressed the already glowing button and smiled at the woman who had moved beside him. She was beautiful, her long, dark hair tumbling down her back in thick waves.

The doors slid open.

The woman stepped inside and Spocatti followed. Again he looked at her. She was wearing dark sunglasses, faded jeans and a white T-shirt. Her lips were full and painted deep red. He nodded at her, smiled when she nodded back.

The door closed and they were alone. Spocatti pressed a button and the car lurched into motion. The woman continued staring straight ahead.

He glanced sideways at her. "Have you found him?" he asked.

"Of course. We nailed him at a travel agency on 40th Street. He's now at your apartment."

If Spocatti was relieved, it didn't show on his face. He looked up at the elevator's lighted dial and watched the floors tick by. "And where was our friend hoping to go?"

The woman opened her black leather handbag and removed the receipt for the airline tickets. She handed it to Spocatti. "He bought two first-class tickets to Milan. The flight leaves this evening from JFK. My guess is that he was planning to take Leana on a trip."

Spocatti pocketed the envelope and studied her reflection in the elevator's brass doors. She was stunning in her arrogance. Her name was Amparo Gragera, she weighed less than 110 pounds--and he had once seen her kill a man twice her size with her bare hands. She was an important member of his organization, had complete weapons training, a solid knowledge of computers and once had been the love of his life. He knew she could be just as deadly as he.

"Is everything set for tonight?" he asked.

"Terry took care of everything this morning."

"And you know what's expected of you?"

"Have I ever let you down?"

"Just personally," he said. "But no, not professionally."

"What a relief."

"This is our last night in New York. How about dinner once the job is done?"

The elevator stopped. The doors slid open and several people began stepping inside, reaching in front of them and pressing buttons on the elevator's control panel. Spocatti left the elevator and turned back for a response.

"I don't think so," she said. "I'm fucking somebody else now. She's actually more your style than mine--her ass is as hard as stone--but she does give good head. When I'm through with her, I'll give her your number. I think she does men, too."

Spocatti couldn't help a smile. The elevator doors slid shut.

\* \* \*

Louis tossed the airline tickets onto his desk. "Where is Michael now?"

Spocatti was at the bar. He dropped ice into two glasses. He reached for a bottle and poured. "He's at my apartment, being watched by one of my men."

"What about Jack Douglas and Diana Crane? You've been following them. Where are they?"

Spocatti came across the room and handed Louis his drink. He thought the man looked older. Cheeks a bit hollow. Eyes set deeper into his face. "They should be arriving at Heathrow within the next few minutes. They'll refuel and fly back to New York."

"And they've telephoned no one?"

Spocatti sipped his drink. "They've phoned their parents from the plane," he said. "But no one else. They're won't try anything, Louis. They know what's at risk. They know the plane is wired. They know somebody will be at Heathrow watching to make sure they don't get off. By the time they reach New York, it'll be over."

"Don't be so sure," Louis said. "We're cutting it close. What are your plans when they arrive?"

Spocatti raised an eyebrow. "What do you think my plans are? They know too much. When they arrive at JFK, they'll be assassinated. So will their parents."

Satisfied, Louis stepped to the windows and looked out over the city. It was still hours before the sun would set, but anticipation was building. He listened to the quiet. The only sound was the clicking of ice against glass as he lifted the drink to his mouth.

Spocatti watched him tap the glass against the side of his thigh and sensed a disturbance in the air. He wondered again what kind of woman Anne Ryan had been.

"So, this is it," Louis said. "The envelope's on my desk. See to it that Redman gets it by nine o'clock tonight."

Spocatti lifted the envelope, tucked it in his jacket pocket. "You're sure he'll meet me?"

Louis turned away from the windows. "He'll meet you. Once he reads that journal entry and realizes what I've done to his daughter, he'll be there. You can count on it."

"What about the police? He might call them."

"No, he won't," Louis said. "Redman is a lot of things, but he's no fool. He won't call the police--not if he wants his wife to live. Just bring Michael and him to Leana's office. Don't let anyone see you. Use one of the side entrances. Make sure they're both there by ten. Leana and I will meet you as planned."

* * *

The Learjet glided through darkness and clouds and rain. It trembled in the turbulence and then dropped through the sky as it hurtled toward the lights of London and Heathrow Airport. The captain's voice came over the speakers: "Should be about ten minutes, folks," he said to Diana and Jack. "Sorry about the bumps, but it's pretty wild out there. If you'd keep your safety belts fastened, we'll land, refuel and begin the trip to New York."

Diana looked across the desk at Jack. He was writing on a yellow legal pad, stopping from time to time to glance out the windows, his face set, determined.

She was frightened. What they were proposing could backfire--yet they had no choice. If they didn't act, the consequences would be equally severe.

The plane banked right, slipped below the cloud line and London burst into sudden, glowing bloom. Diana looked down at the brilliant, intricate web of lights shining beneath them and thought of Louis Ryan. He murdered Celina. He may have destroyed Redman International. In a matter of hours, Leana would open his new hotel. Was she next on his list? Was it George? Elizabeth?

Jack finished writing and slid the legal pad across the desk. Diana picked up the pad of paper. Twice she read what he'd written before laying the pad back onto the table. Her heart was racing when she closed her eyes. *This won't work*, she thought. *It's too risky. If he's caught, my mother dies--and so do his parents. Who are we to jeopardize their lives?*

Jack must have sensed what she was thinking, because he reached across the desk and took her hand in his. He looked hard at her and if this compartment wasn't wired, he would have said what his eyes already conveyed: *We have no choice. You know that. Pull yourself together. I need you.*

She released her hand and nodded briskly. She had been put in difficult situations before and she would handle this. She turned back to the window and watched the rain beat against the glass. Outside, it seemed as though the world was melting.

The plane was about to land.

Diana gripped the sides of her seat and braced herself, wincing as the wheels struck the wet tarmac. The engines and the brakes screamed. Jack was out of his seat the moment they stopped beside Terminal Four.

The captain alighted from the cockpit, his smile fading when he saw Jack standing in the middle of the aisle, a finger to his lips, legal pad in hand. The man looked past Jack and toward Diana, who also was standing, her face as pale and as watchful as a ghost. "What's the matter?" he asked, unsure how to read the situation. "Was the trip that bad?"

Jack's face darkened.

"No," he said. "The trip was fine--it was the weather that was a little scary. At one point, I think Diana wasn't going to make it."

Before the man could speak, Jack approached him, handed him the legal pad and motioned for him to read it. The man's brow furrowed, he moved to speak, but Jack shook his head firmly and pointed to the pad of paper.

The captain read. When he was finished, he lifted his eyes to Jack's. On his face was a look of cold understanding. "We'll be on the ground for about thirty minutes," he said. "Meantime, if either of you wants to go inside the terminal and browse around, there's plenty of time."

"No," Diana said. "We'll stay here. Thank for getting us here in one piece."

The man managed what might have been a smile under different circumstances and removed his cap. He tossed it to Jack. "No problem," he said. "But if you two would excuse me, I have to go inside. I promised my daughter a souvenir from the trip."

And he started to remove his flight uniform.

\* \* \*

Five minutes later, Jack Douglas was wearing the pilot's charcoal-gray uniform and his oversized trench coat. He left the plane and hurried down the Lear's slick, narrow steps, his head bowed as he moved through the wind and the driving rain.

Diana sat at a window and watched him go, not looking away until he had reached the glowing terminal and slipped behind one of its lighted doors. She knew they were being watched, could sense it just as she had sensed Jack's fear before he left. Whether they were being watched by a member of the ground crew or by someone looking down at them from Terminal Four's great expanse of windows, she couldn't be sure.

She turned away from the window.

The pilot had removed his carry-on bag from a small closet and was quickly changing into a pare of khaki pants, a white cotton shirt and a blue baseball cap. He didn't look at Diana as he dressed, but instead looked past her and watched his co-pilot, the young man who was standing at the Lear's open door, squinting in the damp breeze, motioning to a member of the ground crew.

The man bounded up the wet steps, his bright yellow slicker shining, his face flushed and wet and smiling. "What's up, mate?" he asked, shaking the co-pilot's hand. "Damn good to see you. How's your wife--still cheating on you?"

The co-pilot laughed and led the man inside, moving him away from the open door and handing him the yellow legal pad. Diana watched him read. The co-pilot said, "You sorry bastard, it's your wife who cheats. When are you going to stop lying to yourself and admit it?"

The man finished reading. The humor left his face and he looked down the aisle toward the pilot, who had closed his suitcase and was waiting at the rear of the plane, where there were no windows.

"I've got the happiest lass in London," he said. "She'd never cheat on me."

And he removed his yellow slicker.

\* \* \*

The rain was beating against the Lear when the pilot left Diana and his crew behind. He hurried down the steps and crossed the tarmac, the baseball cap shielding his lowered face, the rain and the wind pressing hard against his bright raincoat.

He had an impulse to glance up the terminal's glowing windows, but stilled it and instead entered the building. He darted up a flight of stairs, opened a door and turned right, cutting through the streams of people hurrying to make their connections. He checked for inconsistencies in the crowd. If he was being followed, they were doing a damn good job of concealing it.

He went to the men's room he and Jack agreed upon.

"Hurry," Jack said, when the man stepped inside. "I've got twenty minutes to get my ass on that plane. Move!"

The washroom was large and clean and empty. They entered the last two stalls and started undressing.

"Did anyone follow you?" Jack asked.

The pilot tossed his clothes over the stall partition. "No," he said. "No one followed me." He paused to grasp the uniform Jack slipped under the gray metal wall and said, "Before you get on that plane, you should call Redman."

"Can't," Jack said. "His phone might be bugged."

"Then call ahead to the police. You won't be there for another seven hours. Ryan might have done something by then."

Jack left the stall and went to the full-length mirror. The clothes were loose, but not too loose. The baseball cap concealed his sandy hair.

"Forget it," he said. "Louis Ryan probably owns the police."

The pilot stepped out of the stall and stood beside Jack. Their eyes met. "Besides," Jack said, "by the time we arrive, Ryan will be at the opening of his new hotel. The event will just be getting underway. We know he's planned something significant, but it won't happen at that party."

"I disagree. That's exactly when he'd plan it."

"I don't think so," Jack said. "I've got a hunch."

He moved toward the door, but stopped to shoot the pilot a look. "Buy your daughter a gift. They'll be watching."

FIFTH AVENUE

## CHAPTER FIFTY-FOUR

As soon as Elizabeth laid eyes on him, she knew that something else was wrong, knew it had to do with the envelope he just received by messenger. It was not a familiar look, that brief glimpse of horror she saw in his eyes, but she recognized it just the same.

She closed the door behind her and stood there, not far from him or his desk, watching his features slowly return to normal as he folded the letter in half and tucked it in his jacket pocket. For a moment, he was unmoving, his gaze fixed on the photo of Leana that was on his desk. Then he took a breath and looked up at his wife. The years he had never shown were suddenly there on his face.

Elizabeth took a step forward, out of the shadows and into the light. "What is it?" she asked. "Is it about Celina?"

George didn't answer. With an effort, he rose from his seat and crossed to the bar. He chose a gold-rimmed highball glass and poured himself a glass of Scotch. He drank.

Watching George, sensing his fear almost as surely as she sensed this sudden tension, Elizabeth felt inept, unable to help him.

She stepped beside him.

George put the empty glass down onto the bar and poured himself another drink. It seemed that forever passed before he finally spoke. "No," he said. "This isn't about Celina."

"Then what's it about?"

"I can't tell you," he said. "At least not now. So, please don't push me on this. I have to leave."

Elizabeth watched him walk away from her.

Across the room, through the long stretches of darkness and silence, was the dim glass of an enormous, 18th-century beveled mirror. George hesitated before it and his back stiffened. Framed in gold and heavy with age, his pale face loomed in the night, glowing like some odd, faraway moon. He stared at himself, and there was the sense that he didn't recognize the person staring back.

Elizabeth went to him.

She put her arms around him and held him. She was eager to know where he was going, but she trusted him enough not to ask and instead stood there, holding him, feeling his body relax slightly against hers.

"I have to go," he said.

"I know."

"I want you to stay here."

"I can't."

He turned and kissed her on the lips. They looked at one another for a long moment and then George broke the embrace. He made and effort and smiled at her. "I might be a while," he said. "Don't wait up for me. Okay?"

Elizabeth suddenly felt sick. She took a step back and watched him look around his office. It was as though he was seeing it for the first time, maybe the last.

Reluctantly, she watched him move toward the twin mahogany doors and step into the hall.

She went after him.

"I'm really not that tired," she called. "I can't imagine falling asleep."

The hallway was long and in shadow, so dim it seemed almost gaslit. Isadora, the family cat, left the library and now was trotting after George, her tail high and full. Above them, their shadows joined on the ceiling in a delicate sort of embrace.

"Well talk when you get back," Elizabeth said. "All right?"

"I love you," she said.

George lifted a hand in response. He turned the corner and was gone.

\* \* \*

Ten minutes later, when he pushed through Redman International's revolving glass doors, George hesitated only a moment before he walked the few steps to the black Mercedes

411

limousine that was waiting for him at curbside.

Vincent Spocatti was leaning against the driver's side door. "Mr. Redman," he said, with a slight bow of his head. "Glad you could make it."

George looked at the man, committed his face to memory, but said nothing. He stepped inside the limousine and came face to face with a woman.

She was striking. She was dressed completely in black, her long, dark hair pulled away from her face. Her mouth tightened slightly when he sat down next to her.

And there was someone else in the car. He was sitting next to the woman, his own face a frozen mask. It was Michael Archer.

The two men stared at each other. Ropes of silence spun out between them.

George was about to speak when the woman started frisking him. Her hands were quick and thorough. She looked at Spocatti when he leaned inside the open door. "He's clean." she said.

Spocatti glanced at Michael and George. "Jesus," he said. "Would you look at yourselves? You'd think we were going to a morgue and not a party. Lighten the hell up."

## CHAPTER FIFTY-FIVE

Music swelled, there was a sharp burst of applause and Leana continued moving through the crowd, smiling to people she didn't know, nodding to those who suddenly knew her, wondering where Michael was.

She had no escort. She was surrounded by hundreds of smiling, laughing people, yet never had she felt more alone. Where was he? She specifically asked him to be here by eight, so they could join the party together at eight-thirty. Yet now it was pushing ten and he was nowhere in sight.

Neither was Louis.

Alone, she had just finished greeting, by name, the better part of eighteen hundred guests, including the French ambassador, the British ambassador, Countess Castellani and her blind husband, Count Luftwick, and the mayor and governor of New York. Alone, she had given interviews to select members of the press--an exhausting task that hadn't gone well. Everyone wanted to know why she took this position given the public feud that existed between her father and Louis Ryan. And everyone wanted to know if there was any information on Celina.

Leana had handled them, cleverly skirting their questions and instead concentrating on the hotel and its future. But she was tired and not having a good time. She looked around the crowded space. At least the flowers had been delivered.

She panned the room for Michael. She saw men her father had once cut deals with, powerful women Celina once charmed, couples her mother once invited to dinner. She saw old money and new money, wealthy widows and wealthier divorcees. But there was no sign of Michael. He hadn't arrived.

There was a hand on her arm. Leana turned and saw Louis Ryan.

"Dance?" he asked.

Leana looked crossly at him. He was wearing a black silk dinner jacket and a maroon-and-gold striped bow tie. His crown

413

of hair gleamed in the lobby's warm glow. "Where have you been?" she asked. "People have been asking where you are, I had to greet the guests myself and you said you'd be here hours ago. Where were you?"

Louis lifted a finger to his lips. "I know I'm late and I apologize. But I do have an excellent excuse." He paused, then said in a quieter voice, "I've found the person who murdered your sister."

Stunned, Leana could only look at him. "You've found him?"

"That's right," Louis said. "Spocatti came through. I told you he is the best."

"Who is he? Where is he?"

"I won't talk about it here--not in this crowd--too many people are listening." He motioned toward the dance floor, where society was whirling. "Come," he said. "Dance with me. I'll whisper what I know in your ear."

She followed him to the dance floor, hesitating only briefly when a photographer stepped in their path to take their picture. A light flashed, the photographer moved aside and as Leana walked passed him, she saw on his face the hunger and desperation her sister must have seen when she was in this very position.

Louis led her to the center of the dance floor, put his arm around her waist and they started to dance. "It's amazing," he said, looking around the jammed lobby. "For years these people, these members of New York society, have ignored me. Like the Baron and Baroness over there. Do you know how many times I've been invited to one of their famous dinner parties, Leana? Zero. Zero times. They've had that fucking penthouse on Fifth for twenty-five years and I've never stepped foot in it. But when I hire you to manage the hotel, the whole world comes running. Life's funny that way, isn't it?"

"Either that or you made the right decision in hiring me. Tell me what you know."

It was as though the question went unheard.

Louis held her slightly closer and turned her so they were dancing in front of the orchestra. "I'm sorry to hear what happened to your father today," he said. He saw the disbelief in her eyes and said, "I mean that. Believe it or not--despite my feelings for the man, I do respect him. And I do admire the balls it took for him to buy WestTex. If it had worked out for him, if Iran only waited a while longer, your father would have made history. Now, I'm afraid he'll lose everything."

"Louis--"

"What do you think he would have thought of this, Leana? Do you think he would have liked the hotel?"

"I really don't care."

"But I do."

"Then we'll discuss it later."

"No," Louis said. "Let's discuss it now. I don't think your father would like any of this. Years ago, when we worked together, he didn't respect my ideas. It was George's way or no way." He shrugged. "But maybe I'm wrong. It's tough to trump what I've just built. At the very least, if he was here, he'd be jealous and wish it was his own."

Leana tried to step away from him, but his grip was so firm, she knew she would create a scene if she did so. She glared at him. "What's the matter with you?" she said. "Let go of me. People are watching."

"Then stop struggling." He held her closer and said softly in her ear, "I thought you wanted me to tell you about the man who murdered your sister?"

His mouth was now so close to her face, she could smell the alcohol on his breath. He had been drinking. Incredulous, Leana said, "What I want is for you to stop playing games." It came to her that they were barely moving, that people at the surrounding tables were watching them, wondering what they were talking about.

"All right," Louis sighed. "This is what I know. It seems that your father made an enemy years ago. I don't know the man's name--Spocatti will tell you that later--but I do know that your father destroyed the man. First through business and then it became personal."

People were dancing around them, smiling that faintly secretive smile so many people of wealth assumed.

"The man is out for revenge," Louis said. "He wants Redman to see what it feels like to lose the most important things in his life--including his business, his daughter and who knows what

415

else, maybe you and your mother."

Louis nodded at a woman as she breezed past them and touched his arm.

"Tell me who he is."

Louis was about to speak when a ripple of excitement went through the crowd, followed by the distinct sound of glass shattering. There was the sound of men shouting somewhere in the distance.

Louis said, "What the hell...?" But Leana was already gone, moving toward the bar that was near the east entrance.

The head of security, a former marine lieutenant, saw her and intercepted. "No need to be alarmed, Ms. Redman. Everything's taken care of."

Leana looked past the man and saw several members of security muscling two members of her bar staff from the lobby.

"What happened?"

The man glanced at the crowd, then took Leana gently by the arm. "Let's talk where it's more private."

Leana followed him through a set of doors that led to the outer lobby, where the barmen were being handcuffed. She studied them for a moment and thought they looked vaguely familiar, as if she'd met them somewhere before.

"What have they done?" she asked.

Before the lieutenant could respond, a door swung open and Louis Ryan stepped into the room. His face was flushed. His forehead was shiny. He glanced over at the two barmen, then looked with confusion at Leana. "What's going on?" he asked.

Leana refused to look at him. "Obviously there's been a problem," she said.

Louis turned to the lieutenant. "What kind of problem?"

The lieutenant nodded at the two barmen, who were now leaning against a marble wall, waiting in angry silence. "We received an anonymous call asking us to check the bar staff. I gathered a few of my men, we came upon these two, saw they were armed and brought them here. Unfortunately, they decided to put up a struggle. Otherwise, no one in that lobby would have known that these gentlemen existed at all."

"Who are they?" Louis asked.

The lieutenant shrugged. "We don't know. But something tells me these boys have been through this before. We'll find out who they are once the police bring them downtown. We'll print them, we'll run a check and we'll find out who they are."

He must have noted the guarded look on Louis' face, because he said, "Don't worry, Mr. Ryan. We'll wait until after the party to contact the police. These boys aren't in a hurry and neither am I. There's no need to cause a commotion on a night like this."

Louis nodded his thanks.

The lieutenant turned to Leana. "But I am going to have to insist that you forgo your speech, Ms. Redman. I know what happened to your sister. I understand her death might be connected with the bombs that exploded on top of your father's building. If that's the case then you are not safe and I can't take the risk of having you at that podium tonight."

He glanced over at the two barmen, then with disappointment at the three men watching them. "I thought security was tight tonight," he said, more to the three men than to Louis and Leana. "We took every conceivable precaution against this very thing happening and I'm embarrassed to say that these men somehow slipped through. While I think they're an exception, I can't be sure there aren't others. I need you to forget the speech and allow me to shadow you for the rest of the evening."

Leana couldn't conceal her disappointment. All her life she had waited for this moment and now it was being taken from her. A wave of stubbornness rose in her. "I have to give that speech," she said. "People are expecting it."

"I'm sorry," the lieutenant said. "But as long as I'm in charge of security, I won't allow it." He studied her for a moment. "Is this speech really so important to you? Think about what you're saying. We've just proved that mistakes have been made. There's no telling who else is in that crowd."

He was right. There was no telling what could happen if she stood at that podium. The presence of these barmen suggested there could be others.

Her anger dissolved into frustration and sadness. Once again, another opportunity had passed her by. Once again, it wouldn't be her front and center. "Well," she said, more to herself than to anyone else, "I came close, didn't I?"

The lieutenant didn't know what she was talking about, but Louis did and when Leana looked at him, hoping to find sympathy and a hint of understanding in his eyes, she saw nothing but a controlled look of rage that was becoming difficult for him to suppress.

He addressed the lieutenant. "Would you please excuse us? I'd like a moment alone with her."

The lieutenant nodded and started moving in the direction of the two barmen.

"No," Louis said. "You've got three men watching them already. I want you in the lobby, where there could be others. Find Zack Anderson and tell him to inform the crowd that for personal reasons, Leana Redman will not be delivering tonight's speech." He saw the hesitation on the man's face and said, "Let's not forget that you work for me."

The man left the room.

"I know how much that speech meant to you," Louis said to Leana. "I'm sorry things didn't work out."

Leana lifted her head. *I'll bet you're sorry*, she thought. She knew that having that speech delivered by her meant more to him than the opening of this hotel. But she had more important things to address. "I need you to tell me what you know. Who murdered my sister?"

He led her across the empty lobby, toward an illumined bank of elevators. "I'll do better than just tell you," he said. "I'll take you to him."

"Take me to him?" she said.

"Spocatti has him upstairs. Right now, the man you've been looking for is waiting in your office. I suggest we confront the son of a bitch and end this now."

\* \* \*

Jack Douglas heard the clicking of Elizabeth Redman's heels and saw her shadow stretching along the far north wall before he actually saw her.

He stopped pacing in the rose-colored foyer and turned to watch her round the comer at the end of the long hallway. She was wearing a cream silk suit that was so delicate, it might have been transparent had it not been for the paleness of her own skin. As she came toward him, Jack saw nothing in her demeanor that suggested she was annoyed or surprised by his unexpected presence.

Yet he knew she wouldn't be pleased to see him. She had made it well known that she held him personally responsible for Celina's death.

Jack started walking toward her, thinking that if she didn't cooperate with him, she might be facing the reality of another dead daughter. "I'm sorry for intruding," he said. "But I have to speak to George. Do you know where he is?"

At the mention of her husband's name, there was the slightest hesitation in Elizabeth Redman's stride. Then she stopped in the center of the hallway and said coolly, "My husband isn't here, Mr. Douglas."

And without another word, she stepped into the sitting room.

Jack stood there a moment, weighing his options and then he went after her. He found her across the room, facing a window that looked uptown, toward the swirling lights of The Hotel Fifth. If she knew he was there, she didn't let it show.

There was no time for games. "I know who murdered Celina," he said. "I know who rigged those spotlights with explosives. If you want me to catch the man and put a stop to this, then I suggest you cut the bullshit, Mrs. Redman, and help me."

Stunned by the tone of his voice and what he'd just said to her, Elizabeth turned.

"Where is George?" he said again. "You must know where he is."

"You know who killed Celina?"

"I do," he said. "But I need to speak to George."

She stepped away from the window and sat in a white chintz chair. She seemed very tired when she said, "I don't know where he is. He left an hour ago. He didn't tell me where he was going."

"Is that unusual?"

"Of course, it's unusual."

"And you have no idea where he could have gone?"

419

"None," Elizabeth said. "He received that letter by messenger and then he left. He wouldn't tell me where he was going."

Jack's mind was racing. "What letter?" he said. "Who sent it?"

"I don't know."

"Did you read it?"

"He wouldn't let me."

"And he left after receiving it?"

"Yes. Whatever was in that letter disturbed him very much."

"Disturbed him how?"

"It was a look I haven't seen in him before. George looked frightened. I could see it on his face when he put the letter in his jacket pocket. It was clear that he was scared, but there was something else, some other emotion I couldn't define. At least not then."

"But you can now?"

Elizabeth was silent a moment, but then she nodded. "Yes. I've seen that look before. I saw it quite a bit in Leana when she was growing up." She took a breath. "George looked incredibly sad, as if he had been cheated out of something he always wanted. That's what I saw in his face--beneath the fear."

"What could it be?"

"I don't know. But I might have a better idea if you tell me who murdered my daughter

"It was Louis Ryan."

She had little reaction to this and while Jack was surprised by that, he supposed that perhaps a part of her always had known it was Ryan, but that she never assumed he would go this far after so many years.

For a moment, she was still, then she rose and stepped again to the windows that looked uptown. "And now he has Leana."

Jack picked up the phone on the table beside him.

"Who are you calling?" Elizabeth said.

"The police."

"That letter was from Louis Ryan," she said. "You do know that, don't you?"

"I know that now. I think your husband is with him."

"He thinks George killed his wife, Anne. He's always thought that. But I suppose you know that, too."

A dispatcher came on the line. While he spoke to the man, briefly telling him what he knew, Elizabeth started talking. "But George didn't kill her," she said. "How could he? Anne Ryan was his first love."

Jack looked sideways at her. The mood in the room was changing. "Forget it," he said to the dispatcher. "A lot of people are involved in this--including my parents. Tell Lieutenant Greenfield that I will meet him at the hotel. And get a crew out at JFK. Diana Crane's plane will be landing there at midnight. I want to make certain nothing happens to her or her mother."

He hung up the phone. Elizabeth was far away in thought. "I have to go," he said.

But Elizabeth was in another place, another time. She looked at Jack and said, "What would you have done, Mr. Douglas, had you been in my shoes? He didn't think I knew, but I did. I followed them one night to a hotel in Hartford. While I sat in my car, no more than a hundred yards away, I watched them go inside."

He was about to say this was none of his business, that he needed to go, when he realized what was unfolding here.

"You can't imagine how much that hurt," she said. "Seeing them like that, laughing, holding hands. But I loved George. We were engaged and I was willing to do anything to keep him. As far as I was concerned, Anne Ryan was poison. And so I killed her. I took one of George's shotguns, drove out to her home and saw that her car was gone."

She looked up at the ceiling. "It was late," she said. "I knew she would be coming back sooner or later, and so I parked my car a mile down the road and hid in the woods near her house. The weather was awful that night. We were having a blizzard. I must have stayed in those woods for hours before I saw her car coming down the road and skidding in the snow as she approached the bridge. When I pulled the trigger, I remember being perfectly calm, like I am now. Even the sound of gunfire didn't startle me. And when her car toppled over the bridge, I felt nothing but relief. She was out of our lives. Problem solved. I hurried back to my car and left before the police could arrive."

Jack couldn't believe she was confessing this to him. "You killed Anne Ryan?" he said.

Elizabeth smiled. "You're a sharp man, Mr. Douglas. Brighter than I imagined. Yes, I killed her. I was desperate and so I killed her. It was the best and worst thing I've ever done in my life. While I may have gotten Anne Ryan out of our lives, my daughter is now dead because of what I did, and now my husband and my other daughter are at risk."

Jack stood there, dumbstruck. "You could have stopped this."

If she heard him, it wasn't apparent.

"I've never told George," Elizabeth said. "But I think he's always known. He's just never had the heart to ask." She looked at Jack. "But you'll change all that, won't you, Mr. Douglas? You'll tell George. And you'll tell the police."

"I have no choice."

"Of course you don't," she said. "You're an honest man."

It was getting late. He had to meet Greenfield at the hotel before he and his men went inside. He was walking past Elizabeth when she said, "I love my family, Mr. Douglas. I've told you this for their benefit, not mine. I understand the repercussions--I'll go to prison. But the trade-off is worth it if you get there in time and don't let Louis Ryan hurt either of them."

## CHAPTER FIFTY-SIX

"Have I ever told you that you remind me of my wife?"

They were standing in one of the exterior glass elevators. Beyond the tinted windows that overlooked Manhattan's Upper East Side, glittering Fifth Avenue skyscrapers rushed past them. Leana looked at Louis, who seemed to be leaning against the city, his hands resting along the chrome rail, a faintly nostalgic look on his face. While the subject had never been discussed between them, Leana knew that he once accused her father of murdering Anne Ryan.

She didn't know why he mentioned this and she certainly wasn't about to ask--Leana had other things on her mind. She looked up at the elevator's lighted dial and said, "We're almost there, Louis."

But Louis ignored her dismissive tone. "I think Anne would have enjoyed tonight," he said. "She always liked parties. She was the perfect hostess--beautiful, smart, witty, sophisticated. Anne could make friends as easily as I seem to make enemies." He smiled at the memory of her. "If she were alive today, you can bet your ass that the Baron and Baroness would have invited us to one of their dinner parties. They would have fallen in love with her just as I did. Everyone liked her."

Leana knew that she should respond to this, but she didn't want to encourage him. The man who murdered her sister was in her office. It was this she wanted to focus on, not Louis Ryan's wife. Willing the elevator to move faster, she said, "She sounds wonderful, Louis. You must miss her very much."

"Oh, I do," Louis said. "We were perfect together, Leana. You can't imagine how much I miss her."

He looked away and she saw something in his expression change, as if a switch had been shut off, a curtain dropped. "I suppose that's why your father murdered her."

He leaned forward and pressed the button that stopped the elevator. Beyond the windows, the city froze.

Fear crept into Leana's heart. She couldn't have heard him right.

"She died thirty-one years ago," Louis said, his finger still on the button. "Victim of a freak car accident." He cocked an eyebrow at her. "At least that's what the police said. But I know differently. I've always known differently. Your father murdered my wife. Have I ever told you what happened, Leana?"

She didn't answer him. She checked the dial and saw that they were between the twentieth and twenty-first floors.

"I see that I haven't. But I do think you should know what your father did. I think it's time that you and the whole world knew exactly what happened."

Leana's heart was beating in her throat. She remembered how strangely he acted on the dance floor, how preoccupied he had been with her father and she had a sudden premonition of danger.

"The weather was terrible that night," Louis said. "Anne and I had an argument and she left the house in the middle of a blizzard. I tried to stop her, but she wouldn't listen to me. Instead, she got into her car and left. I couldn't go after her. We had only one car back then and I remember how worried I was for her. Anne never drove in the snow. Hours passed and nothing, not a word. So I started calling around to friends, family--but nobody had seen her. Nobody knew where she was."

He seemed to slip further into the past, sinking straight into a time and a place in which she sensed he wasn't comfortable. He closed his eyes. "And then the police called," he said. "They told me that Anne's car went off the road and over the bridge that was down the road from our house."

He removed his finger from the glowing button and the elevator lurched into motion. Leana watched him pull his hand away. All of this was a set-up. She'd played right into it. She looked at the elevator doors and wondered what would be beyond them when they opened.

"It was awful," Louis said. "Leaving the house, running through the snow to the bridge, seeing her car like that in the river, knowing there was no way she could have survived that fall, knowing that my Anne was dead." Anger shot into his voice. "Do you know what that did to me? Do you know how long I've waited for this moment?"

*What moment?*

Leana stepped back to the elevator doors and her bare back pressed against them. Somewhere, far in the dark corners of her mind, she knew where this was leading, knew what he was saying, but she refused to believe it, because it couldn't be true.

Louis closed the distance between them, the rage suddenly there on his face, heated and alive. It was as dark as her fear, as black as her dress and it filled the elevator to capacity. In a low voice, he said, "Even before I learned her tires were flattened by a shotgun, I knew this was no accident. Your father and I had been battling in court for years. When I won that final appeal, he got his revenge two days later by killing one of the few people who mattered to me." His eyes became hard stones of hate. "And now I'm taking everything away from him."

She shrank away from him, her eyes growing wide with disbelief. She felt her knees start to give as realization washed over her. Her world began to blur as all of the pieces of the past several weeks clicked into place. "You!" she gasped.

Louis reached out and grabbed her by the arm. "That's right," he said. "Me."

The elevator stopped.

The shiny chrome doors slid open, revealing a long, elegantly appointed corridor that stretched before them in varying degrees of light and darkness.

Leana's office was at the end of the hall. Louis pushed her so hard through the doors that she hit the wall opposite the elevator. A table was there. She reached out to grasp it in an effort to stop the momentum, but she missed. She fell on the table and went down with it.

"Get up."

But the table wasn't bare. On it was a lamp, which now was at her side. Leana clutched it and turned to throw it at him, but Louis was there. He grabbed the lamp as she swung it at his face and flung across the room, where it smashed on the floor.

"You'll need to be quicker than that," he said. "Get up."

She did what he said. He took her by the arm and they started walking toward her office, their footsteps echoing like drum taps on the polished marble floor.

Leana was numb. Louis Ryan's words beat in her head. He killed her sister. It was him all along. "You won't get away with this," she said. "Everyone knows I'm here."

"That's right," Louis said. "Everyone knows you're here. But what you're forgetting is this, Leana. Everybody also knows what happened to your sister. The whole world knows that somebody is out to harm your family. If you're found shot dead tonight, no one's going to be surprised by it." He thought of the two barmen that had been found in the lobby. "Security already has been breached."

Leana looked furiously at him. "You planted those men at the bar."

"Actually, I didn't," he said. "As a matter of fact, I don't know who they are or why they were here. But I am glad they came. Their presence just made things a lot easier for me."

They were nearing the end of the hall. Leana could faintly hear voices coming from her office. She turned and looked back down the length of the corridor, toward the elevator. She had to escape. She had to get help. But how? She could feel Louis looking at her.

"I know what you're thinking," he said. "And I have to tell you that you'd be wasting your time. This entire floor has been sealed off. Every door is locked, every exit is barred. Your only way out is through that elevator and in a moment, Vincent Spocatti is going to take care of that. You run and I promise you'll get shot in the back."

They were at her office. He opened the door and said, "By the way--your husband's last name isn't Archer. That's just a pen name he used to escape from me. His legal name is Michael Ryan."

Leana looked at him in disgust. She knew he was lying. "Bullshit," she said.

"Hardly." He pushed the door open and they came face to face with her father and Michael.

Time and space drew in on themselves.

They were seated across the room in matching red velvet chairs. The city blazed behind them. Pale as ghosts, they looked up at her when she walked inside. Seeing them here, realizing just how carefully Louis Ryan had orchestrated this, Leana could no longer still the panic rising up in her. *He's going to kill us.*

"Stand up, Michael," Louis said.

Michael did as he was told.

"Michael isn't my son, Leana," Louis said in an oddly detached voice. "There was a time when I thought he was, a time when he meant the world to me, but when I found Anne's journal and read that final entry, I knew what George Redman did to her. I knew how he manipulated my wife."

He looked across the room at George, who was unmoving. "Michael's not my son," he said. "He's your father's son. You married your brother."

\* \* \*

Forty floors below, The Hotel Fifth was quietly being surrounded by members of the New York City Police Department, while inside, a special task force led by Lieutenant Vic Greenfield was rapidly combing each room on each floor.

Jack Douglas already had been debriefed by Greenfield, but for security reasons, he wasn't allowed inside the building. He stood across the street on the sidewalk, watching yet another trio of police cars turn onto 53rd Street and drive without lights to the hotel's east entrance.

All eighteen hundred guests had been evacuated. Crowds of people were along the sidewalks. The press was there, recording it for the world. Jack heard a faint chopping sound and turned to see a sleek police helicopter moving up Fifth Avenue, toward the swirling lights of The Hotel Fifth.

He felt his stomach tense and his head pound in time with the rapid beating of his heart. It was happening, he thought, but was it happening fast enough?

\* \* \*

In Leana's office, the silence expanded like a balloon.

Spocatti stood at the rear of the room, watching the color drain from Leana Redman's face. George Redman didn't deny Ryan's claim. Neither did Michael. Spocatti watched her lips part and felt a kind of thrill.

George stepped forward. Spocatti gripped his gun and longed to use it.

"This is between you and me, Louis. Nobody else. Why don't you be a man and let them go?"

Louis pushed Leana forward. He shut the door behind them and started moving across the room, toward Spocatti. "Be a man?" he said. "Is that what you were when you fucked my wife? Is that what you were when you got her pregnant? Were you a man when you loaded that shotgun and killed her?"

"I never touched your wife."

Louis stopped mid-stride. He was incredulous. "Never touched her?" He shoved a finger at Michael. "Then explain him. Explain your goddamn son. You read the portion of Anne's journal I sent to you. In her own words, she wrote about how you got her pregnant only weeks after I terminated our partnership and bought Pine Gardens on my own." He looked at Leana. "He was fucking her while he was engaged to your mother."

Spocatti glanced at his watch. He wanted to be out of there in five. He looked across the room at Amparo Gragera, who was standing beneath one of the illumined Sisley paintings, watching it all go down with interest. He told her to take care of the elevator. He waited for her to leave the room before coming around Leana Redman's desk and moving in front of the windows that overlooked 53rd Street.

He gazed across to the neighboring building he'd visited with the Realtor earlier that day, raised a hand and then looked down at his chest as a swarm of tiny pinpoints of red light spiraled over his heart.

He nodded at men he could not see and the red lasers winked off.

Spocatti knew the risks he'd taken by meeting here tonight. He knew the hotel was crawling with security. But he also never finished any deal without having secured a safety net. The one he had tonight was airtight.

He turned away from the window and waited for someone to speak. If things didn't happen soon, he would take matters into his own hands.

"So, this is it, Ryan?" George said. "You're going to kill us with a lobby full of people? Is that the plan?"

Louis shot him a fierce, warning look. He went to Leana's desk, opened a side drawer and removed the gun he placed there earlier. He pointed it at George. "Yes," he said. "That's the plan."

"And what do you suppose that will solve?"

"Everything," Louis said. "You ruined my life. You murdered Anne. Did you really think I'd let you get away with it forever? I've waited years for this."

"Anne's death was an accident," George said levelly. "You know that as well as I do. I did nothing to Anne. I loved her more than you ever did. Your problem is that you've never been able to accept the fact that Anne fell out of love with you and in love with me."

The words were like a blow to Louis. For an instant, the gun wavered in his hand.

"If you want someone to pay, then I suggest you shoot me and let Leana and Michael go," George said. "This has nothing to do with them. This is between you and me."

Louis moved to speak, but then turned and pointed the gun at Leana. Alarmed, she took a step back.

"I want you to see how it feels, George," he said, and he fired the gun.

The sound echoed hollowly in the room. Thunderstruck, George watched Leana stagger back, her eyes wide with horror and surprise. There was a tiny hole in her dress, just to the left of her navel. Leana looked down at the hole and covered it with her hands as blood leaked between her fingers and spilled onto the floor. She looked at her father, then at Louis and Michael, and crumpled to her knees. A rush of air escaped her lips.

Michael ran to her side. He knelt beside her, put his hands around her waist and applied pressure to the wound.

Outside, in the hall, Amparo Gragera was suddenly shouting. There was a rapid exchange of gunfire and she screamed.

Spocatti removed his gun and hurried across the office. He closed the office door, locked it and became aware that his cell phone was ringing. He snatched it from his belt, listened to the frenetic shouting on the other end and turned in disbelief to the windows. For a moment, he saw nothing. Then the police helicopter descended into sight, its blinding spotlights flooding the office.

Spocatti looked into the light and for a moment, he couldn't see. "Why didn't you warn me?" he said into the phone.

The machine was hovering just beyond the office windows. Furious, Louis turned to look at Spocatti, but instead came face to face with George Redman as he lunged for the gun in Louis' hands. George tried to wrench it free, but couldn't. And so he tackled Louis so hard, the gun slipped from the man's hands and spun across the floor. With everything he had in him, George kept moving, kept pushing Ryan back until he was mashed against the great panes of glass.

The police were pounding on the office door.

Nerves wired, heart pounding, Spocatti backed away from it. He looked briefly at Leana and Michael, then across the room at George and Louis, who were struggling against the glass, the gun somewhere between them.

He had an impulse to shoot them both, to finish this once and for all, but there was no time. He darted to an area of the office where there were no windows and ripped the cover off a heating duct. He threw it aside and was about to jump into it when he heard Ryan's gun ring out.

Spocatti watched George Redman slump to the carpet, his face caught for an instant in the brilliant glare of the helicopter's spotlight. Louis shot him in the chest. George fell on his side and lay there, his eyes opened and unseeing.

Ryan pointed the gun at the man's head. He said something Spocatti didn't hear and was about to fire when the office door crashed open and the police burst into the room. Their guns were drawn.

"Put the gun down!"

In that split second, Louis made his decision. He fired the gun--and saw the bullet go into the floor beside George Redman's head. He missed! *Missed!*

He was about to shoot again when the police peppered his stomach and chest with a flurry of bullets.

430

Louis' mouth gaped open.

The gun jerked from his hand and fell to the floor.

He took another bullet in the chest and stumbled back against the trembling windows--just beyond them the helicopter roared. One of its doors was open and two men with sniper rifles were tethered to a rail and leaning out. Their guns were pointed at Louis. As he turned to them, they let loose a hail of bullets, which splintered the glass and sent Louis stumbling backward. Spocatti watched him fall, wondering how many times he'd asked Louis to keep the blinds closed.

Louis sank to his knees, his crown of silvery gray hair caught by the helicopter's sharp beams of light. He was on the cold rails of death. He was leaving himself. There was no pain, only a dull, spreading warmth in his chest and stomach. He knew he was dying and he didn't care. He looked across at Michael and saw Anne staring back at him in horror. His body was nearing weightlessness. He was wondering if this was all an illusion when his brain flickered out, he fell forward and his face struck the floor.

Spocatti shrank into the shadows. He was standing at the opposite end of the office, watching the police watch Louis Ryan die before their eyes. He said something into his cell phone and then listened to his men in the neighboring building empty rounds of bullets into the helicopter's gas tank.

Spocatti leapt into the heating duct and began the rapid plunge.

In spite of all the noise, there was a moment when it seemed that everything went quiet, when the helicopter's glinting blades hesitated, and then the machine sank, it ignited and exploded into the building.

# FIFTH AVENUE

## SIX MONTHS LATER

## EPILOGUE

Diana Crane, Chief Attorney
Redman International
49th Street & Fifth Avenue
New York, NY 10017
(212) 555-2620

Dear Jack:

So, here we are again. Will you receive this letter? Will you answer it this time? I have sent you dozens of letters over the past few months, only to have them returned unopened. Where are you? I send the letters to your parents and they tell me they forward them to you. Are they? They only tell me that you're well. Are you traveling? Has it gotten easier?

I don't know if you're connected to the world or if you unplugged yourself from it. Knowing you, I'll assume the latter and hope for the former.

Wherever you are, do you get the news? Are you aware that the stock market crashed? We survived it. That Monday, while Wall Street was crumbling, we were signing a deal with Anastassios Fondaras for $8 billion. Iran insisted he buy more ships to keep up with demand and we were happy to offer up WestTex. After a massive round of layoffs and restructuring, Redman International's stock is now trading in the high fifties. Not where it used to be, but better.

If you've been reading any of these letters, then you know that George made a full recovery. But do you know that Elizabeth was indicted last week? Ten years. I think she'll do five. Maybe three, if she's lucky. I did my best.

Also, I've written this before but the status hasn't changed. Leana is still missing. No one has seen her since she left New York Hospital last August. She disappeared, though we know she's alright. At a benefit last Saturday, Helen Baines told me that Leana has called her, but she refuses to tell anyone where she is. I'm thinking she's with Mario De Cicco. I checked and he's no longer in New York.

I'll leave you with this. Three weeks ago, I was on Wall Street when I saw Vincent Spocatti in the crowds on the street. I know it was him, just as he knew it was me. We looked at one another and then he lifted his head and smiled before turning the other way. I reported it to the police, but there's little they can do and Spocatti knows it.

There's nothing more to tell you, really, only that I miss you and wish you were here in your office at Redman International. Nothing is the same anymore. Everything's changed. I don't live at Redman Place. I sold my apartment and moved to the West Side. Now, I have a different view of Central Park, a cat and...what else? Nothing, really. Thank God for work. As my father used to say, our work saves us.

If you receive this, please write. You've had time. I need to know that you're all right and that at least one of us is moving forward.

With love,
Diana

P.S. I still think about him, you know? Given all that he did, it's ridiculous. But after all this time, Eric is still part of me. Do you still think of Celina? Sometimes, it's as if they never died, isn't it?

\* \* \*

Jack Douglas folded the letter in half and returned it to its envelope, which he'd carefully opened with a knife. Like all the

433

letters Diana sent, he would return this one to his parents and they would forward it back to her. He sealed each letter in such a way that suggested he'd never opened it or read its contents. Jack wasn't ready to renew their friendship. He would contact her again, but he would wait a while longer before doing so.

Just now, he was sitting in the back of a dusty white Jeep, his skin brown from months in the sun, the top of his sandy hair bleached with streaks of blond. He was leaner than he had been in years, his body hard and toned from hiking through the jungles of Venezuela. Above him, he could hear the faint but familiar shrieking of macaws and cockatoos. Below him was the sound of rushing water. He was three thousand miles away from New York City and he loved it.

He thought of Diana's letter. Of course, he still thought of Celina. A day didn't go by that he didn't think of her and all that could have been. He loved her. With Elizabeth Redman now going to prison, he wondered if he ever would see the Redman family again.

He wondered if he cared?

He left the jeep and walked to the center of the long, rickety bridge that stretched before him. A woman had just jumped from its rotting planks and now was screaming as she plummeted to the roiling river below.

Jack moved to the wooden rail and leaned forward. He watched her bounce thanks the bungee cord strapped to her ankles and her long dark hair cracked like a whip in the humid air. Watching her and listening to her jubilant cries, he felt strangely at peace and knew what he was doing was right. This was part of his own healing.

Beside him, a young Venezuelan woman began pulling the frayed bungee cord back to the bridge. She was tall and slim, her arms and shoulders taut with muscle. Her bare feet dug into the gray wooden planks as she continued to hoist up the heavy cord. Once the cord was retrieved, she turned to him.

"Listo?" she asked.

Jack nodded. "Listo."

"You do this before, yes?"

"I've done this before," he said.

From his pocket, he removed the blindfold he promised to wear when Celina jumped all those months ago. He showed it to the woman, who shrugged. She helped him over the wooden rail, attached the bungee to his ankles, pulled hard on the nylon strap and checked the buckles.

Jack put the blindfold into place.

With the sudden darkness, his senses became acute. The river was louder, the sun somehow stronger. He could feel the thrum of nature and then his heart beating in his chest.

The woman touched his arm. "Jump," she said. "Fly."

Poised at the edge of the bridge, Jack took a breath, nodded and let go of the wooden rail. For a moment, he just stood there, perfectly balanced with his arms held out at his sides. His hair stirred in the breeze. His palms faced a brilliant, cloudless sky he couldn't see. He was aware of everything and nothing. The faint, exotic smells of the jungle enveloped him, consumed him and for the first time in months, he smiled.

He thought of Celina then and when he jumped, he jumped hard, rising gracefully into the air and into the sun. For an instant, he was free.

\* \* \*

Michael Archer remained in New York. In the six months that had passed since his annulment from Leana, he had left their apartment on Fifth and moved into a large, airy loft in the Village that overlooked the Hudson.

His life was quieter. He rarely went out and he saw only close friends. He refused prime roles in movies and on Broadway, and he refused to be interviewed. Although his agent was hounding him to write another book, he hadn't written a word in months. His dreams were bad. He supposed he was now something of a recluse.

It was in late September, two months after the incident at The Hotel Fifth, that he received a letter from one of George Redman's attorneys, suggesting that he join George for a blood test. Michael refused. He didn't need a blood test to confirm that he was George Redman's son. His mother's journal confirmed it.

In her own hand, Anne described--in detail--her affair with George and how she knew that Michael was George's son. If Redman couldn't accept that, then Michael decided it was best that he wasn't part of the man's life.

Leana came to him in dreams.

He would be walking up Fifth Avenue and she would suddenly appear in the crowd, wearing the very dress she wore that night at The Hotel Fifth, her skin pale and lucent, a tiny pinpoint of bright light wavering from the hole in her stomach. In the dream, she held out her arms to him, called out his name in a voice that wasn't her own but one that strongly resembled his mother's. And then she disappeared. When Michael ran after her, it was Louis Ryan's face he saw, not Leana's.

He heard from Leana only once since they annulled their marriage. When she called, she was somewhere in Europe with Mario De Cicco, though she wouldn't say where. In spite of all that had transpired between them--and the truth that they were half brother and sister--he admired her for keeping the conversation as light as she could.

"I'm an expat," she said. "Imagine that. And I'm happy. For the time being, we're travelling Europe. We'll visit other parts of the world and then we'll choose a place to settle and raise a family. I'll call you when that happens. Could be several months or several years, but I'll call."

"I'm sorry for everything, Leana."

"I know you are," she said. "But it's not your fault--we both were used by him. Just hear me on this--if we don't let go of all of it, if we don't move forward, it will color the rest of our lives until we do. And if that happens, he wins, which we can't let happen. I'm moving on with my life. I want the same for you. We deserve to have our lives back."

"You're right."

"Take care of yourself."

"Call me when you've settled."

"You'll hear from me again," Leana said, and she was gone.

It wasn't until January that he was ready to sit at his desk and look seriously at his typewriter, the one his agent sent him months ago as a gift.

He knew he couldn't go on like this.  By withdrawing from the world, by hanging onto the past, he was killing himself and everything he'd worked so hard for.  His agent had given him a number of story ideas, but only one mattered to Michael, only one was paramount, and if he wanted to move on, if he really wanted to deal with the past, the only way to do so would be to write about it.

He looked at the typewriter.  He never wrote on a computer and his agent knew it.  He liked the sound of a typewriter.  He liked the feeling of removing a piece of paper when he was finished creating something on it.  He liked the rhythm of the words as they were pounded out.

He put a blank sheet of paper into the typewriter and closed his eyes.  That title, that opening sentence and the first few paragraphs came to him at once.  They had been lingering in his mind since the original manuscript was burned.

But could he do it?  Could he really write the story that had changed so many lives? And if he did write about it, if he did tell the truth even if he did change the names, would he be ready for all the controversy that would ensue?  Michael wasn't sure.  Novel or not, people would know the story he'd written was based on fact.

Maybe he'd change the names later.  Maybe he wouldn't.  What mattered now was getting it all on paper.

And then he remembered what the man Cain said to him that day in his apartment.  Just moments after he read the first chapter and destroyed the manuscript, Cain asked how Michael could use these events, these places.  Michael's answer was immediate--perhaps he would use a pseudonym.

He rested his hands on the typewriter and was relieved to find that it no longer seemed as threatening.  He thought of Leana then, thought of all the Redmans, chose a generic pseudonym and after a moment, he began to type:

FIFTH AVENUE

A novel by Christopher Smith

BOOK ONE

FIRST WEEK

CHAPTER ONE

July
New York City

The bombs, placed high above Fifth Avenue on the roof of The Redman International Building, would explode in five minutes.

Now, with its mirrored walls of glass reflecting Fifth Avenue's thick, late-morning traffic, the building itself seemed alive with movement.

On scaffolding at the building's middle, men and women were hanging the enormous red velvet ribbon that would soon cover sixteen of Redman International's seventy-nine stories.  High above on the roof, a lighting crew was moving ten spotlights into position.  And inside, fifty skilled decorators were turning the lobby into a festive ballroom.

Celina Redman, who was in charge of the confusion, stood before the building with her arms crossed.  Streams of people were brushing past her on the sidewalk, some glancing up at the red ribbon, others stopping to glance in surprise at her.  She tried to ignore them, tried to focus on her work and become one with the crowd, but it was difficult.  Just that morning, her face and this building had been on the cover of every major paper in New York.

She admired the building before her.

Located on the corner of Fifth and 49th Street, the building was the product of thirty-one years of her father's life. Founded when George Redman was twenty-six, Redman International was among the world's leading conglomerates. It included a commercial airline, office and condominium complexes, textile and steel mills and, soon, WestTex Incorporated--one of the country's largest shipping corporations. With this building on Fifth Avenue, all that stood in George Redman's way was the future. And by all appearances, it was as bright as the diamonds Celina had chosen to wear later that evening.

####

# FIFTH AVENUE

Thank you for purchasing and reading "Fifth Avenue." I hope you enjoyed it.

Please contact me at **FifthAvenueNovel@gmail.com** for any comments or suggestions. Agents, I'm seeking representation, so please contact if you're interested.

Follow me on Twitter at **@WeekinRewind**.

Visit my entertainment blog at **WeekinRewind**.

Please join my fan page on Facebook **here**.

**Below is a sneak peak at my next book, a Wall Street thriller entitled "Running of the Bulls." Look for it in 2011.**

Thank you again.

Christopher

## RUNNING OF THE BULLS

### A novel by:

### Christopher Smith

### BOOK ONE

### PREFACE

New York City

The bright bedroom was swimming, the walls rippling in peach-colored waterfalls.

With an effort, Kenneth Cole turned his head, tried to focus, couldn't and closed his eyes. Blackness enveloped him. He took a breath and felt his body lift, felt his soul soar. Everything was enhanced. He could hear voices in the charged silence, could taste the dried blood on his bruised lips, could feel a great weight pressing down on him, suffocating him, squeezing the air from his lungs. The drug they'd given him last night hadn't worn off. He still felt as though he were shifting through separate realities, moving through different realms of consciousness.

Maybe he was dreaming. Maybe none of this was real. Maybe he hadn't gone through with any of it last night. Maybe he'd run like hell, as Hayes had.

He brought a hand to his chest and felt the bandage they'd wrapped around him. This was no dream. He'd done everything they'd told him to last night. This was real.

But where was he now? Was this his bedroom? His home? He didn't know. He didn't care. He drifted off.

He was awakened by a loud metallic clanging. This time it was he who moved, not the bedroom. He sat up in bed and looked around. His head ached and he was exhausted, his body drained, as though he had been ordered to run a marathon, forced to win.

Clang, clang, clang--coming from downstairs.

He swung his legs around and put his bare feet on the cool hardwood floor--perhaps too quickly, because he became dizzy, disoriented. He licked his tingling lips and fought the urge to lie back down. He wore no clothing. Bandages covered his chest in a bloody patchwork quilt. He was a rich man who had enjoyed a life of excess and greed, and he weighed over 300 pounds. His stomach--hairless and pale and dimpled with fat--rested in his lap like a great ivory-colored balloon, taut and ready to burst.

Clang, clang, clang!

Cole stood, tentatively at first, and shaded his eyes from the resilient sun. Every window was open, every shade was up. It was the middle of winter and the bedroom was freezing. He could see his breath forming before him in little white clouds, could feel his skin shrinking against the cold. He was a man used to comfort and this was ridiculous.

Clang, clang, clang!

"Bebe!" he shouted. "What the hell is that noise?"

Clang, clang, clang!

"Bebe!"

Silence.

"Jesus."

He had to pee. He looked across the room to the closed bathroom door and thought he'd never make it. But he was stubborn. Resolved, he set off toward the bathroom, but one leg seemed shorter than the other and he stumbled. What had they given him last night? Meth? He couldn't remember. He hadn't wanted any drugs. He wanted to experience everything with a clear mind. Had they given Bebe that opportunity? He couldn't remember that either....

Almost there, almost to the bathroom, his feet shuffling like sandpaper along the cold floor. He reached out a hand to push

442

the bathroom door open but missed it and bumped into the wall.

"Christ," he said to himself.

He groped his way inside, found the toilet, lifted the seat, lifted his stomach and relieved himself. The house was quiet. All he could hear was his own sigh and the urine shooting into the toilet's dark blue well of water. He was exhausted. His eyelids were heavy. In the moment he closed them, he heard the urine hit the rim, splash onto the tile floor. *Fuck it*, he thought. *Let Angel clean it up.*

He shook himself dry, flushed and reached behind him for the white terry cloth bathrobe hanging on the door. He pulled it around his enormous frame, tied it tight around a stomach that had been flat in youth and shut out the cold. He wanted to brush his teeth, wash his face. He wanted to get rid of every trace of what they'd done to him last night. But when he stepped in front of the marble vanity and looked at himself in the spotless mirror, all Cole could do was stare.

His face was swollen and bloodied and bruised, as though they had beaten him. But all Cole could remember were the hands and the smiles and the screams and the joy and the eyes shining like quicksilver through the darkness. He couldn't recall being beaten, couldn't recall any pain.

Tentatively, he brought a hand to his face, touched his numb, bloated right cheek and recoiled when his fingertips met the tender edge of bone. How would he ever explain this? Eventually the media would find out. Eventually all of New York would know that something had happened to Kenneth Cole, the first of twelve who years ago had sold out to the SEC and sent Maximilian Wolfhagen to prison. The press would be all over this. There was a time when his testimony had helped destroy the greatest insider trading ring in financial history.

Clang, clang, clang!

He turned away from the mirror. "Bebe?"

Silence.

Was she drunk? He left the bathroom and stepped into the cold hallway, heard nothing, gently stroked his cheek. In front of him, a winding staircase swung down to the sunny foyer. "Bebe!" he called.

Clang, clang, clang!

Clutching the handrail for support, he descended, already knowing that if he found her sprawled beneath van Gogh's White Roses--as he had so many times before--he would finally have to get professional help for her.

The library was enormous, paneled in dark oak, so dim in the curtain-drawn light that it seemed almost gas lit.

Cole stood in the doorway and took it all in. It was here that he and Babe used to entertain. It was here, as one of Wall Street's golden boys, that he first supplied Wolfhagen with privileged information on impending takeovers. Now, as Cole looked across the room to the illumined van Gogh, the famous painting Wolfhagen made him buy anonymously at auction, promising Cole that its $40-million price tag would help seal his place in society--which, for a time, it had--he realized once more that Wolfhagen never had been his friend. He had only used him to make himself a billionaire.

The silence was heavy. The room was too dark. Moving tentatively across the Aubusson rug, wondering where his wife could be, Cole turned on a lamp.

He saw his wife first.

Strapped to a Queen Anne chair in the center of the room, her carefully dyed blonde hair tousled and hanging in her face, Bebe was surrounded by video cameras. She was naked, shivering and gagged. Her eyes were wide with horror. There was a scrape on her forehead. She moaned.

Alarmed, Cole took a step back.

Bebe shook her head, tried to spit out the gag, but couldn't. She struggled to release herself from the heavy rope that bound her hands and legs to the antique chair, but it was impossible. She writhed in frustration and looked wildly to her left.

Cole followed her look.

Sitting in the shadows in a matching Queen Anne chair, dressed entirely in black, was a stranger. The man rose from his seat, lifted his eyebrows at Kenneth and started smashing the priceless Tibetan funeral doll in his left hand against an Egyptian brass urn--clang, clang, clang!

He tossed the ruined doll to the floor and stepped beside Bebe, who followed his every move with her terror-filled eyes. "Well," he said to Cole. "It's about time you woke up. We've been

444

waiting hours for you." He kissed the top of Bebe's head. "Haven't we, dear?"

Bebe jerked away from him. She thrashed in her chair and looked at Cole for help.

Amused, the man leaned forward and removed the gag from Bebe's lipstick-smeared mouth. He reached behind his back, withdrew a gun and pressed it against her temple. Bebe gasped. Her shoulders drew in and she looked imploringly at her husband, whose own mouth had parted in shock. The gun, Kenneth saw, had a silencer. He looked at the four video cameras surrounding Bebe and could hear them humming.

Cole forced himself to think, willed himself to act. Behind him, in the top drawer of Bebe's writing table, would be a loaded gun. He took a step back toward the table, his eyes level with Bebe's, his hand reaching out. But the man was having none of it. He shook his head at Cole and pressed the gun harder against Bebe's temple, pulling the trigger just as she uttered her last words: "Wolfhagen!" she gasped. "He's hired--"

The shot was flat, muffled, the sound of steel striking bone. Bebe's eyes grew huge with sorrow and disbelief, her body jerked from the sudden impact and she slumped slightly forward in the chair, dead.

Kenneth's knees sagged. Bile rose in his mouth and he gagged.

Suddenly a hand was on his arm, strong and firm. Kenneth turned and saw the woman just as she jammed the gun into the small of his back and urged him forward, toward his bleeding wife, the man in black, the humming cameras. "Fight me and I promise you won't die as quickly as your wife."

He was pulled across the library by a hand far steadier than his own. The man had dragged Bebe off to one side and now was placing a matching chair where she had sat. Here the floor was polished oak and it gleamed darkly with his wife's spilled blood. Cole was led to the middle of it, his bare feet resting in the warm pool that had kept her alive.

Now, the cameras surrounded him.

They'd murdered his wife. They'd do the same to him.

He looked at the woman. Tall and attractive, thick brown hair framing an oval face of cool intelligence, her eyes the color of chestnuts and just as hard. She wore black leggings and a black shirt, no jewelry.

The man moved behind her, his face partly concealed behind the video camera now poised on his right shoulder. "Open his robe," he said to the woman.

She opened his robe.

"Now get rid of the bandages."

She ripped them from Cole, who stared straight into the camera's opaque lens and saw his own bruised, bloated face floating up at him from the dark, rounded glass. The equipment was small and sophisticated and digital. He knew the contents would probably be put on a DVD, and Wolfhagen would view them.

But would he view the other DVD? The one being recorded by the camera hidden in the wall above the fireplace? The one his insurance company demanded he install in the event that someone tried to steal the van Gogh? Would he see that?

The woman took a step back. She looked with revulsion at Cole's bloody chest and then looked at him. Cole held her gaze and willed himself to remain calm. It wasn't too late for him. Everyone had a price, everyone could be bought. Hadn't Wolfhagen taught him that much?

"I have a lot of money," he said to them both. "Millions. I'll triple whatever Wolfhagen's paying you. Both of you can walk out of here right now and never have to do this again. You'll be set for life. Just let me live."

The woman's lips, rouged red, broke into a half-smile.

"Millions," Cole said.

She lifted the gun.


\* \* \*


**Six Months Later**

**Pamplona, Spain**


446

# FIFTH AVENUE

Ever since he was a child, Mark Andrews wanted to run with the bulls.

As a boy in Boston, he would sit on his grandfather's lap and listen to the old man's stories of his days in Spain, when he was still young and single, and had traveled the world on the trust fund his father gave him upon graduating from Yale.

Mark would marvel at the man's retelling of La Fiesta de San Fermin, the week-long orgy of bull worship that honored Pamplona's patron saint San Fermin, who was martyred when bulls dragged his body through the city's narrow, dusty streets. Mark's grandfather had run with the bulls. He had stood among the thousands of men in white shirts and red sashes impatiently waiting for the first rocket--and then the second rocket--to signal their release.

Even then, some thirty years ago, in his parents' home, Mark could hear the thunderous clacking of hooves as the twelve beasts came crashing down Calle Santo Domingo, through Plaza Consistorial and Calle Mercaderes, their horns sharp and deadly, their murderous rage focused on those foolish young men running blindly before them.

Now, at thirty-nine, Mark Andrews himself stood among fools in white shirts and red sashes, the early morning sun beating down on his face, the delicious anticipation of the impending event flooding his system.

Pamplona was a city gone mad.

All week long, fifty thousand people from around the world had participated in La Fiesta de San Fermin--known to the locals as Los Sanfermines. They paraded drunkenly through the streets with towering, colorful *gigantes*, went to the afternoon bullfights, drank gallons of wine, made love in alleyways, and rose each morning from brief catnaps to watch the spectacular running of the bulls.

Earlier in the week, the mayor had kicked off the festivities at noon by lighting one of many rockets from the Ayuntamiento's balcony. And now, as Mark waited along with nearly a thousand other men for the rocket that would signal the beginning of *el encierro*, he watched and listened to the cheering crowd that looked down at him from open windows, wrought-iron balconies, the Santo Domingo stairs and from inside the Plaza de Toros

447

itself.

Never had he felt more alive. He would run as his grandfather had.

A hand was laid on his arm. Mark turned and faced a stranger.

"Do you have the time?" the man asked. "I left my watch at the hotel. They should be firing the first rocket any minute now."

Mark smiled, delighted to be in the company of a fellow American. He checked his watch and said, "In a few minutes, we'll be running like hell from twelve very pissed off bulls." He extended a hand, which the man shook. "I'm Mark Andrews," he said. "From Manhattan."

The man's grip was firm, his teeth bright white when he smiled back. "Vincent Spocatti," he said. "L.A. What brings you here?"

"My grandfather," Mark said. "You?"

The man looked surprised. "Hemingway," he said, in a tone that implied there could be no other reason why he had traveled three thousand miles to be at this event. "I even brought Lady Brett with me." He pointed down the barricaded street, toward a building where a young woman stood at a second-story balcony, her dark hair and white dress stirring in the breeze. "That's my wife, there," he said. "The one with the video camera."

Mark looked up and caught a glimpse of the woman just as the first rocket tore into the sky to signal that the gates of the corral had been opened.

He felt a rush. The sea of young Spaniards lurched forward. A cheer went through the crowd and rippled down the narrow streets, reverberating off the stone walls, finally blooming in the Plaza de Toros itself. Moments later, a second rocket sounded, warning the crowd that the six bulls and six steers had been released.

The chase--which usually lasted only two minutes--had begun.

Mark ran. He heard galloping behind him, felt the earth trembling beneath his feet, and ran, knowing that if he stumbled, if he fell in the street, he would first be trampled by the men running behind him, and then by the 1,500-pound beasts themselves.

He moved quickly and easily, suddenly euphoric as he shot past the Calle La Estafeta and the Calle de Javier. He thought fleetingly of his grandfather and wished he could have been here to see this.

The crowd of spectators was screaming. Shouting. The terrific pounding of hooves filled the morning air with the intensity of a million small explosions. Mark shot a glance over his shoulder, saw his American friend, saw the crush of young men behind him--and saw the first bull rapidly closing the distance between them all.

He was delirious. He was beyond happy. He knew that not even the day he testified against Maximilian Wolfhagen could compare to the rush he experienced now.

He was nearing the Plaza de Toros when Spocatti, fan of Hemingway's lost generation, reached out and gripped his arm. Startled, his pace slowing for an instant, Mark looked at the man. He was now running alongside him, his face flushed and shiny, his eyes a shade darker than he remembered. Mark was about to speak when Spocatti shouted, "Got a message for you, Andrews. Maximilian Wolfhagen sends his best. Said he wants to thank you for ruining his life."

And before Mark could speak, before he could even react, Vincent Spocatti plunged a small knife into his left side. And then he did it again. And then again, sinking the knife close to his heart.

Stunned, the pain excruciating, Mark stopped running. He looked down at the knife jutting from his bloody chest and fell to his knees, watching in dazed silence as Spocatti leaped over one of the barricades and disappeared into the jumping, thrashing crowd.

Mark had fallen in the middle of the street. Hundreds of men were darting past him, jumping over him, screaming as the animals drew near. Knowing this was it, knowing this is how he would die, Mark pulled the knife from his chest, turned and faced the first bull as it loomed into sight and sank its lowered horns into his right thigh.

He was thrown effortlessly into the air, a rag doll tossed into the halo of his own blood, his right leg shattered, the bone jutting from the torn flesh.

He landed heavily on his side, so stunned that he was only dimly aware that he was being trampled. A seemingly never-ending series of hooves dug into his face and arms and stomach.

The men rushing past him tried to move him out of the way, tried to grasp his shirt and pull him to safety, but it was impossible. The beasts were upon them. There was nothing anyone could do but watch in horror as twelve angry bulls and steers ripped apart an innocent man.

When it was over, Mark Andrews lay in the street--his body bruised and broken beyond recognition, his breathing a slow, clotted gasp. He looked up at the narrow slit of blue sky that shined between the buildings on either side of him.

In the instant before his mind winked out, his failing eyesight focused on Lady Brett Ashley herself. She was standing just above him on one of the building's wrought-iron balconies, smiling as she filmed his death with the video camera held in an outstretched hand.

####

2476966R00239

Made in the USA
San Bernardino, CA
27 April 2013